Sandcastles by
The Jupiter Hotel

Sandcastles by The Jupiter Hotel

An Alba White Mystery

Martin Hurcomb

Copyright © 2023 Martin Hurcomb

The moral right of the author has been asserted.

Apart from any fair dealing for the purposes of research or private study, or criticism or review, as permitted under the Copyright, Designs and Patents Act 1988, this publication may only be reproduced, stored or transmitted, in any form or by any means, with the prior permission in writing of the publishers, or in the case of reprographic reproduction in accordance with the terms of licences issued by the Copyright Licensing Agency. Enquiries concerning reproduction outside those terms should be sent to the publishers.

This is a work of fiction. Names, characters, businesses, places, events and incidents are either the products of the author's imagination or used in a fictitious manner. Any resemblance to actual persons, living or dead, or actual events is purely coincidental.

Matador
Unit E2 Airfield Business Park,
Harrison Road, Market Harborough,
Leicestershire. LE16 7UL
Tel: 0116 2792299
Email: books@troubador.co.uk
Web: www.troubador.co.uk/matador
Twitter: @matadorbooks

ISBN 978 1803136 868

British Library Cataloguing in Publication Data.
A catalogue record for this book is available from the British Library.

Printed and bound in the UK by TJ Books Limited, Padstow, Cornwall
Typeset in 11pt Adobe Garamond Pro by Troubador Publishing Ltd, Leicester, UK

Matador is an imprint of Troubador Publishing Ltd

To my mother
And in loving memory of my father

You taught me so much
including cribbage

'The Jupiter Hotel'

Staff

Manager	Cliff
Chef	Alan
Bar Steward	Jed
Receptionists/Waitresses	Lizzie, Robyn

Guests

Room 1	Annabel Lloyd-Kent
Room 2	Nicholas Goodwill
Room 3	Emily Hibbert
Room 4	Daniel Jones
Room 5	The Detz family
Room 6	Geoffrey and Cecilia Constance
Room 7	Joshua and Stella Mallory
Room 8	
Room 9	Alba White
Room 10	Martha Peacock

Contents

Chapter 1	Back	1
Chapter 2	Hundreds and two mice	18
Chapter 3	Friday: breakfast	30
Chapter 4	Restormel Castle	49
Chapter 5	Thursday: Twelve noon	65
Chapter 6	Full Circle	77
Chapter 7	Jackstraws	91
Chapter 8	King John's Crown	110
Chapter 9	Drops, corners and doors	124
Chapter 10	Déjà vu	137
Chapter 11	Three enter	152
Chapter 12	"Take the sleeper"	158
Chapter 13	Just like Captain Briggs	165
Chapter 14	Rod of Asclepius	178
Chapter 15	Trelyn House	198
Chapter 16	A grand Tudor kitchen?	208
Chapter 17	Stannum	229
Chapter 18	Eve	250

Chapter 19	Mission call	269
Chapter 20	'Haslam's Faithful'	281
Chapter 21	Sandcastles by 'The Jupiter Hotel'	294
Chapter 22	Cecilia is caught out on the rocks	312
Chapter 23	'Two for his heels'	330
Chapter 24	Monday morning	340
Chapter 25	Alba shows her hand	350
Chapter 26	With the turn of a card	368
Epilogue		374
Acknowledgements		377
Also by the same author		381

CHAPTER 1

Back

'It was good to be back' thought Alba to herself. 'No, that didn't quite express it. It was *really* good to be back', she decided. She closed her eyes, moved her head to rest against the high back of the aged green leather chair she was sitting in, and allowed her other external senses to attune themselves to where she was.

She would have obviously preferred it if Andrew had been able to make it too but that was not possible, not in the circumstances, and she completely understood the priorities which kept him away. So, here she sat alone.

Nonetheless, for the thought played itself out in her mind once more, 'it was really good to be back'. For there are places in the world where one feels completely at ease, completely safe. Not wrapped in cotton wool safe, rather secure as one could be safe – as in a well-built boat in a storm-tossed sea. Completely at one with one's surroundings, where one can truly sense 'is', truly experience 'being', where one has no inclination to look at one's watch, for time becomes meaningless, where there was no desire to be anywhere else. She was here.

Alba had three such places in the world that created this sensation within her but, of the three, this was the purest. It did not quite have to be this chair or even this room, the snug which adjoined the restaurant, for she had felt it earlier in the day when she had entered her bedroom, she had felt it before that, when she had first walked into reception, and before that still, in fact before she had even got to 'The Jupiter Hotel', as she had left the main road and taken the lane which brought the traveller here. Well, it brought them here or took them on further to the headland where the road ended – as it had to, for the land ceased and one was left with just the cliffs that took one down, literally down, to the majestic, foam-covered sea.

Here she felt a connection to the place. Over the years she had never quite worked out why, given she was not from Cornwall. Further, the long journey home, at the end of each stay, always sapped her spirits and the last time she had been here, with her now former fiancé, had not been a good time. Yet none of that mattered. She loved the place, the views, the cove that was below the hotel, the wild farmland that lay behind the hotel and the hotel itself, nestled as it was in the hillside. She also loved the plants and wildlife – even the windswept hawthorn trees with their branches growing at strange angles, due to the prevailing westerly winds – and the randomness of the other hotel guests, who collectively always seemed to bring everyday life and their passions into this remote corner of the country. She felt connected to here, somehow, and, as she continued to sit with her eyes shut, she was wholly at one with her surroundings. Connected, she imagined, as walkers might feel about 'The Old Man of Coniston' as they ascended that Cumbrian Fell or connected as someone watching a village cricket match, on a Saturday lunchtime by the boundary rope, would feel to the game taking place before them.

Inevitably, in that moment, she thought of Vaughan.

She opened her eyes, for she needed to drive the image of finding him dead from her mind. As she did so, she saw the waitress approach her.

"Your starter is ready, Alba, if you'd like to move to your table."

"Thank you, Lizzie."

"My pleasure. And may I say it's lovely to see you again – it's good to have you both back with us. I assume he'll be down in a minute for mains."

"Actually," replied Alba. "It's just me. Things didn't work out between us. I won't bore you with the details."

"I'm sorry to hear that. I thought you two were well suited," offered back Lizzie.

"It seemed he felt more suited to someone else. Not that he admitted it at first. Oh well, you live and learn but it broke my heart at the time – but that's just between you and me. Don't go and tell Jed." Alba did not feel the barman needed or would want to know about her personal heartbreak.

"Of course not," replied Lizzie. "Although the diary did say to set your table for two people, so I naturally assumed you were both back with us."

"Naturally. However, I was hoping a friend of mine, Andrew, was going to be joining me this week but his grandfather has been taken poorly and he needs to be with him. So, it's just me you've got for the week."

"Well, if I may say so again, it's lovely to have you back here – even if you're alone. But you're not really alone, not here, not you, you're almost part of the furniture! Oh, don't take that the wrong way – I'm not saying you're old and leathery or covered in sand!"

"No, it's fine. I know what you mean and I was just thinking something not dissimilar."

"That's alright then. But I've set the table for two, so would you like me to clear the extra setting?" volunteered Lizzie as Alba stood up and started to follow her into the restaurant area.

"No, it's not an issue."

As Alba moved away from where she had been sitting, she glanced once more at the empty chairs and tiny cylindrical tables that were further back in the snug. Her eyes once more fixed upon the full pint glass on one table and the envelope propped up against the glass, which carried the single word 'Dad'.

Alba stopped and stared at the envelope, which, despite the overwhelming simplicity of it and the solitary handwritten word on it, entranced her. Lizzie, sensing a lack of movement behind her, turned and, seeing what Alba was looking at, said:

"You'll have realised by now, Alba, given you've been sitting here in the snug a while, that there's no one else using those chairs."

"I had," replied Alba. "Which is why it is puzzling and odd. Neither you nor Jed would have left someone's drink there and no one else has left it there as he or she made their way to the toilets. I'm intrigued. I'd say – "

"Yes?" said Lizzie, as she wondered how close Alba would get to the truth.

"I'd say it's definitely been placed there intentionally. Furthermore, the envelope, which is of the size of your average birthday or greetings card, has also been deliberately placed there. Given the envelope says 'Dad', the logical inference is that it's been placed on that little table by someone's son or daughter. But what puzzles me is…"

"Is," interjected Lizzie, "that no person has appeared to claim either the drink or the card in the whole time you've been sitting there."

"Exactly," concurred Alba. "Even when I had my eyes shut, I'd have heard someone move so close by. No one's coming for it, are they?" offered up Alba, whose instinct had told her the pint glass had been there a while – since there was no condensation on the glass. "How long has it been there, since you or Jed served it and, I assume, placed the card against it? Yesterday evening?"

"Cor, blow me. You should be a detective, Alba!"

"This friend Andrew once said the same thing to me. But enough about that. So, was I right – was it yesterday?"

"Yep, spot on and it was Jed but the form you're on, you'd have guessed that too, somehow."

"I don't think so – I'm not that good!" said Alba in a genuinely self-depreciating tone. "And, without reading the card, I can't deduce why."

"It would have been Jed's father's birthday yesterday. Jed 'served' him a pint of what was his favourite beer and left it and a birthday card at the table you're still staring at."

"Would have been?" repeated a puzzled Alba. She then added, having realised the significance of the use of the past tense, simply "Oh."

"Yes," said Lizzie, confirming what Alba had just grasped.

After a pause, Lizzie continued. "Getting on for six months now since Jed's father passed away. Jed will clear the glass this evening I reckon but, if not, I'll do it tomorrow morning as I'll be first in – I'm on early shifts for the next few days, you see. Jed will be OK with that."

"I didn't know. I had a Christmas card from Cliff, your manager, but he didn't say – I guess it wasn't for him to tell me. Oh, I am sorry for Jed. He and his dad were very close, weren't they?"

"Absolutely. Jed was still living with him, caring for his ageing father and looking after the cottage they shared. The rest of the staff here could see his dad was growing frailer, when he did make it along for his Sunday afternoon pint each week, but I don't think Jed wanted to see it himself. Hit Jed hard when his dad did finally collapse. Yes, it hit Jed hard emotionally and practically, too."

"Practically? How so?" enquired Alba.

"Not for me to say," replied Lizzie in neutral tones. "Best you catch up with Jed." With that Lizzie fell silent and started to move once more towards Alba's table.

It was one of the many things that Alba found so refreshing and endearing about 'The Jupiter Hotel', that the staff were so loyal to one another. They were kind of a quasi-family, like her own gardening family back at Hillstone Hall, she thought. Perhaps it was one of the reasons that made this hotel what it was, the fact the staff themselves were as much a feature of the place as the grandfather clock in reception or the mighty ship's wheel which adorned one wall of the dining area. They worked here year after year, growing and ageing whilst 'their' hotel remained unchanged.

"I'll speak with him," concurred Alba, keen to stress she had taken Lizzie's hint, as she reached the table the other woman had stopped at.

"Pineapple juice, as usual?" checked Lizzie as Alba sat herself down.

"Please."

"I'll bring it over with your starter. Good choice the goat's cheese and caramelised onion tartlet."

As Lizzie headed off, first to the bar to get Alba's drink and then to the kitchen to collect her starter, Alba glanced down at her place setting and, as she instinctively turned the pudding spoon round, thought once more to herself how good it was to be back.

*

Sitting with her back to the wall, Alba looked into the dining area. Of the dozen or so tables, most were taken. To the left of Alba were two middle-aged women, who had already finished their main courses. They were talking about the state of the coastal path and, in a completely disconnected way, how one of them would go for the gammon again tomorrow night even though they were staying for only two nights and despite the fact the rest of the menu looked equally enticing. However, to Alba's right were Geoffrey and Cecilia Constance.

"Evening, Miss White," said Geoffrey somewhat formally, as he nodded ever so fractionally, to acknowledge Alba's arrival.

"Hello, Mr Constance," replied Alba. Alba then turned to his wife and added, "Mrs Constance, an equally warm 'hello'. Good to see you both again – keeping well?"

"For goodness' sake," offered back Cecilia. "Call him Geoffrey, it won't kill him. And dear," now directing her words to the gentleman in his mid-sixties sitting opposite her, "she has a first name. It's Alba, remember? We've seen her enough times here to call her that."

"Naturally I remember," retorted Geoffrey. "My memory is as good as ever." Then, turning once more to Alba, he added, "Miss White, I have been instructed to call you by your first name. My apologies for the informality. You have every reason to move to a different table if you so desire."

"Geoffrey," said an exasperated wife, "you're being a clot. Just say 'hello' and let her enjoy her starter which Lizzie has just brought her."

In an effort to stem a conversation that she feared might go on all mealtime and, in part, because she did want to make headway on her food, Alba held out her hand to Geoffrey and simply said, "Evening Geoffrey."

Geoffrey Constance reciprocated and took Alba's hand. He squeezed it ever so gently and smiled, adding:

"Alba. Good evening. Hope you will be here a while. It will be lovely to catch up with you. From what I hear, you've had quite an exciting time of late."

"Have I? How so?" enquired Alba.

"Ah, I have my ways." He paused but, not wishing to string his young friend along needlessly, quickly continued. "A friend of mine, who lives in Betchworth in Surrey, in a delightful little white cottage near the church, not that that bit is important, sent me a clipping from her local newspaper about some goings on at a certain Hillstone Hall. Very interesting, very interesting indeed. My friend was amazed when I called her and told her I knew you, the star of the show – she just thought I'd be interested in the article as it centred around a country house."

"Likes his large houses, does Geoffrey," said Cecilia.

"I do," agreed her husband. "Just not enough of them down here changing hands to have given me enough work over the years. It's just my luck, too, that Trelyn House will come on the market just after I retire – blooming typical!"

"Trelyn?" queried Alba.

"Yes. That would have been a fascinating sale to be involved with but that will be too late for me. But never mind that," continued Geoffrey, "from what I read, you did well and it would be lovely to hear about it from you, Alba."

"Well, I'm staying a week but there's not a lot to say. I just did what I could but I'm surprised a local paper all the way over in Betchworth picked up the story."

"Justice, Miss White, justice. You brought justice to a situation. That deserves to be reported. I wish more people had the courage to get involved and ensure the guilty get punished. If I had my way – "

"Dear!" pleaded Cecilia. "Let the poor girl eat. There'll be plenty of opportunity to talk over the next few days, no doubt, given we're staying here too at the moment. I'm sure one day she'll walk us down to the cove or something and you can talk then but, for now, let her eat. Plus, she'll be tired no doubt if she's journeyed here today." Turning once more to Alba, Cecilia added, "Just ignore him from now on; ignore him, I say. You have my permission."

To ensure Alba had a moment's peace, Cecilia instructed her husband to go and get her a second glass of wine from the bar, even though all three of them knew full well Lizzie would have happily brought one over.

Once he had departed, Cecilia spoke once more:

"Since he's retired, retired that is apart from this one matter for Jed he promised to see through to completion, he does like chatting to people. He misses speaking to both the other solicitors he worked with, as well as the clients. Plus, nothing ever happens down here, nothing. All he now has is me – well, me and the plants in the garden and I'm beginning to realise we're not enough for him. He needs something, anything, to fill the void. Hopefully, for this evening at least, someone else will be at the bar he can chat to for a few minutes.

If not, hopefully Jed will be serving as it's Thursday and they can talk for a few minutes. It will be useful if it is Jed, for Geoffrey will be needing to speak to him formally in the next few days, meaning, if nothing else, they can arrange a time to meet. But I'm talking too much myself now, sorry. I'll leave you in peace."

With that, Cecilia consciously lapsed into silence until Alba had finished her starter.

*

Once Lizzie had taken Alba's plate and moved away, Alba turned once more to Cecilia:

"You said you were staying here. How come, since your beautiful Georgian house is only a few miles away? You haven't moved from it, have you? Last time I was here Geoffrey said he'd show me the garden next time I was down; he's told me so much about it over the years as you and he have come in for many an evening meal here. I hope you haven't moved."

"No, don't fear. We're still very much at 'The Grey House' and the garden remains Geoffrey's pride and joy – he was working in our garden all afternoon. So, you won't be surprised to hear, even though I was with him to begin with, I was still able to go out to meet someone and be back before he'd even noticed I'd gone. So, if he's promised to show you around, he won't have forgotten even after all this time since your last visit. He never forgets anything. As for why we're staying here, well, we're having some work done on the house and we just decided it would be much easier to be out of the workmen's way for a week or so. That said, we can't go and have a proper holiday as we need to be close by to be available – for only when they start to lift floorboards, re-instate two windows and strip back to the original brickwork will we fully know what needs to be or can be done and plans may need to be changed."

"Oh, that's a relief," replied Alba. "But that sounds a lot of work for what is, at least from what you can see of it from the road, a beautiful Georgian house already."

"Oh, it is beautiful, in one sense, but whilst you keep describing it as Georgian it's not truly that any more. Successive owners over the years have altered it or 'enhanced' it but, in so doing, as the trained eye will tell you, lost or, perhaps more accurately, tarnished the property's true heritage. A coarser way of putting it is that it has had a succession of poor face-lifts which Geoffrey has decided have to be addressed."

"Clearly, I have an untrained eye! Best not tell Geoffrey that I think it's lovely as it is," replied Alba.

"Yes, it's lovely, don't get me wrong. For Geoffrey though, it became an issue – I guess what with him having been a property solicitor all these years, that's probably why."

"Well, thank goodness you haven't moved," said a relieved Alba. "I was so hoping to get to see your garden this time I was down. This county is famous for its gardens – I'm hoping to get over to Trengwainton whilst I'm here to see the magnolias – and yours will be beautiful too I expect."

"Of course, dear, but it doesn't compete with Trengwainton. Nonetheless, it'll be lovely to show you around. You might have to step over the odd bag of cement, weave around a skip or two and pirouette around scaffolding poles but, that aside, simply let us know a day that would suit. Even if Geoffrey is meeting Jed that day, he'd make the time for you as well."

"That's very kind of you both."

As Lizzie brought over Alba's main course, Cecilia, having asked Alba to mind her handbag, excused herself, in order that she could retrieve her drink, even if not her husband, from the bar.

*

Her trio of fish, fish almost certainly landed at Newlyn that morning, was Alba's 'first evening ritual' whenever she came back to 'The

Jupiter Hotel'. The chef, Alan, knew that would be her order tonight – it always was. As she sated her culinary desire, a desire which had bizarrely seemed most intense on her drive here, as she passed the 'BP' petrol station on the A303 just after the Tintinhull turning, Alba studied the remaining diners around her.

There was a woman of a similar age to herself, wearing a full-length gypsy-style dress. A tasteful dress, thought Alba, slightly retro and definitely more gypsy than Spanish and the fine brown tassels at the cuffs and across the chest were an enchanting touch.

Next there was a family of three – or more specifically a father and two children. With no fourth place setting nor a woman's jacket slung over the back of the fourth chair, Alba sensed she was looking at the family as it now existed. The father, in his jeans and navy sweater, had an unfortunate monotone look about him. The two boys, aged about ten and twelve, were still young enough to be happy, as they were, in their matching grey hoodies. They were playing a 'Top Trumps' game and Alba, momentarily, honed in on their conversation –

"Goals, twenty-six."

"Twelve."

"Nineteen – you win Ben."

"Next card," said Ben. "Major trophies, five."

"None."

"Six. I win!"

"Six," said two boys in unison. "Lucky dad."

"Yeah, lucky that go," replied Gerry, the boys' father. "Right, one more round then I want you both to finish your vegetables – and boys put your hoods down, I've told you once already this mealtime. Hoods down now, please."

"But dad," griped back Gregory, "mum would have let us keep them up."

"Yeah, mum would've," agreed Ben.

"Well, mum's not here, I'm afraid. So, hoods down otherwise

I won't take you to the castle tomorrow and I mean it. So, hoods down."

As Alba watched two pre-teenage boys act as if they were both going on seventeen, as they slowly and begrudgingly lowered their hoods, she felt she had listened in long enough to their conversation – particularly as they were clearly playing a football 'Top Trumps' game. 'Why couldn't the makers do a 'Georgian and Victorian Plant Hunters' version, with categories like 'countries travelled to', 'plants brought back' and 'invasive species that should never have been brought back', with three or four more categories besides' thought Alba to herself.

"Yes, the Romans have a lot to answer for in bringing their ground elder over with them," said Alba quietly to herself. She then admonished herself, for the Romans considerably pre-dated both the Georgians and the Victorians.

Next, there was a solitary man, early fifties and slightly stocky, who had an appearance of someone down on business but dressing casually yet without pulling off a genuine holiday look – the shoes were a bit too clean and the trousers, casual as they were, were just too pristine for this isolated part of Cornwall.

Then another man, younger and slimmer than the person Alba was just studying, entered the dining area and took his seat at one of the empty tables and was effectively facing Alba and the two women to her left. He'd brought in his small suitcase, with its collapsible handle and two wheels, and tucked it under his table, indicating he had just arrived but hungry enough to eat first and then book in. Alba heard the man's opening comment to Lizzie:

"Just arrived and famished so hope it's alright to eat first and then book in. No starter, just the vegetarian lasagne, some garlic bread and a glass of water, thanks."

After a nod from Lizzie, who then moved away, the man took out some papers from his shoulder bag and started reading them.

Of the empty tables in the room, the one to Alba's right was still awaiting Geoffrey and Cecilia's return and another had an engraved wooden 'reserved' sign on it; Alba guessed for Stella and Joshua. She had met them earlier as she, Alba, had arrived at the hotel at lunchtime. Sipping at her pineapple juice, Alba considered what a small world it really was – to bump into Stella after all these years and, more than that in fact, to be staying at the same hotel as each other. However, as Alba touched her Fabergé egg pendant necklace to her lips, she hoped the other had forgiven her after all these years.

As for the remaining empty tables, for a Thursday evening this early in the season, given the remoteness of the hotel, it was very unlikely they would get taken. A relatively quiet night would hopefully allow Alba to chat some more with Lizzie and even Alan might take the opportunity to slip out of the kitchen and say 'hello' to her.

*

"I'm tired," said one of the two women to Alba's left. "Do you mind if I forgo a coffee and just head up to my room? I'll read for half an hour or so but then just go to sleep. It was a tough, long walk today, as I've said. There were lots of occasions where the coast path drops all the way down into the coves themselves, and then up again – as you'll discover for yourself the day after tomorrow."

"No, that's fine, Martha. You head up," replied Annabel.

"Thanks, see you for breakfast," said Martha as she got up. Putting on her fleece and, as people do when they have had their back to a room for a period of time, she glanced around the room as she did so, noting the other diners. One or two looked back, due to that strange human sixth-sense of knowing when someone is watching you, before Martha turned once more to her companion and said 'Goodnight'.

Alba, feeling suddenly puzzled by something and having watched the woman head out through the side door, between the dining area and the snug, turned and spoke to the remaining woman:

"Staying long?"

"No," replied Annabel. "Just tonight and tomorrow night, as we're having a rest day tomorrow, and then we're off."

"Rest day?" queried Alba.

"Yes. We're walking the South West coastal path and we've built in the occasional rest day to give our boots a bit of an airing and our legs a bit of a rest."

"I've done small chunks of the path – a few miles here, a bit there – but never anything grander or more organised; nothing like what the pair of you are doing. It must be quite tough in sections but at least you have a walking companion to get you through."

"Well, kind of – " but her voice tailed off.

Alba was unsure whether the other was simply trying to spare her some technical details or was not in the mood to talk. Alba, trying to be friendly, decided to persevere:

"Kind of? That sounds intriguing. I'm Alba by the way. I've stayed here lots of times and have got to know one or two locals over the years, who come in for the occasional evening meal, like the couple to the other side of me, Geoffrey and Cecilia."

"I'm Annabel and my walking companion, if you can call her that, is Martha – who was very taken with the gammon steak she had tonight – as you probably heard her say more than once! I've never been here before but don't think I'll be back. The food is good but the hotel doesn't really cut it for me. Anyway, to explain properly, we're walking the coast path, staying at the same hotels, but walking it in opposite directions."

"Opposite directions," repeated Alba but Cecilia's return prevented a fuller comment.

"Jed's not around which is odd as he always works Thursday evenings. Still, Geoffrey is quite happy sitting at one of the window seats looking out; it's a beautiful sky tonight. Sorry, I think you ladies were chatting – you go ahead, don't mind me," said Cecilia.

Accepting the prompt, Annabel explained her peculiar walking arrangements to Alba:

"You see, we learnt the first time we did a long distance walk together, that despite being good friends, we are not suited as walking companions – really not suited. We were doing the 'Coast-to-Coast' walk, which is St Bees Head in Cumbria to Robin Hood's Bay in North Yorkshire in case you didn't know. We weren't even out of the Lake District, I think we hadn't even reached Haweswater, before we both realised we drove each other mad as walking companions: one wanted to stop for a drink and the other wanted to swig from a bottle as they walked, one wanted to stop to take the perfect picture – even if that meant waiting for the clouds to move out of shot or a duck to swim into the scene before taking it – the other was content to take a quick snap and move on, one wanted to send a postcard seemingly from every village we walked through – "

"I sense that was Martha," interjected Alba.

"Absolutely," replied Annabel. "Why her aunt or neighbour needed postcards from particular villages heaven only knows. I sent two the whole trip and both were written and posted the day before we'd even started. How we didn't murder one another that walk I will never know. But we both like walking, discussing possible routes and the planning that comes with it. So, we came up with the idea of breaking future long-distance walks down into chunks that involved two walkers starting off at opposing ends of each chunk. Then we'd plan – plan where we'd meet for each section, how we'd leave one car at that meeting point, then drive together in the other car to the other end of the section. There one of us would get out, leaving the other to drive back to where the first car was left. Then we'd start our walk, meet at a hotel at the mid-way point, ensure car keys were handed over, enjoy one another's company but – "

"But not murder each other along the way!" offered up an understanding Alba.

"Exactly. Takes a bit more planning and there's a bit more dead time as you have to wait for one of us to do the extra drive but, once we're walking, we can walk at our own pace, stop when we want and send as many postcards or not as we desire along the way. We've walked Hadrian's Wall that way and the Eleanor Crosses and it worked so much better. So, we're doing it again – this time with the South West Coast Path."

"And that's why," said Alba, "Martha was telling you what to expect in your day's walking the day after tomorrow. It didn't seem to make sense to me, at the time, but it does now, given you weren't walking with her."

"That's right," replied Annabel. "I think I've got the tougher day's walking when we start again on Saturday, from what she's been saying," she added but in slightly louder tones as a female's agitated voice carried through to the dining area from reception. "But if you'll excuse me, I'm quite tired too, so I'll head up to my room. I'll try and get through reception before whatever is going on escalates any further and I find myself getting stuck down here."

"Of course. Sorry, I didn't mean to delay you," said Alba, almost apologising and somewhat taken aback by the other's sudden abruptness and lack of sympathy, never mind compassion, for whoever it was that had just entered the hotel's reception area. As Alba watched Annabel walk surprisingly quickly for someone so recently claiming weariness, Alba suddenly wondered whether Martha was as happy with the arrangements as Annabel was – for it suddenly felt as if Annabel had created a format for a holiday that perhaps suited her irrespective of what Martha really thought about it all.

"I wonder what's going on out there?" commented Cecilia, rocking her now empty wine glass between her fingers as she spoke.

"Not sure," contributed Alba somewhat weakly, "but I sense whatever it is, it won't trouble the woman who was the other side of me until a moment ago."

"No? I wonder – no, hold on, I think I can hear my Geoffrey's voice now. Sounds like he's got involved."

Despite Alba and Cecilia hearing repeated requests, now by both male and female voices, to 'speak slower', 'tell us again' and 'have some water', the woman, whoever she was, was getting more agitated by the moment.

Alba and Cecilia then heard Geoffrey's voice clearly say to at least one further person out of view:

"You stay here with her; I'll just go in there and get some help."

Whereupon Geoffrey entered the dining room and, as discretely as he could, walked over to Cecilia – which was an entirely pointless attempt at discretion, for everyone in the restaurant had stopped their meals or their card games and watched him as he approached his wife's table and could hear him say:

"Cecilia, I need you in reception."

He then turned to Alba:

"I think you should come as well – I have a hunch you will be able to help."

CHAPTER 2

Hundreds and two mice

Some claimed the reception area of 'The Jupiter Hotel' was a bit too overwhelming, a bit too dark, a bit too all encasing – and definitely a bit too wooden. Others, Alba included, just loved the floor-to-ceiling oak panelling. They felt warmed by it, enjoyed running their fingers along its grain and would marvel at the craftmanship as they, perhaps, sat and waited for someone before heading off together to nowhere in particular.

To be fair, to those who did not take to the room, the about shoulder height dado rail, coupled with the narrower rectangular panelling above the rail, compared to the sections below, and somewhat gothic carvings, did rather hint at the impression that one had stepped into a monastery or cathedral's Chapter House, rather than the reception area of a coastal hotel. However, for anyone entering the hotel, any hint of monastic peace within the space was all too quickly shattered. This was due to the noise and activity around the reception desk which one came to at the far end of the reception area. The requisite desk bell, telephone – either ringing itself out or being answered by Robyn or Lizzie – and the out of sight fax machine, beavering away, drove any sense of calm or reflective soul-searching, far, far away.

As if there were not enough wood, there was also an aged

grandfather clock. However, its noise was never truly heard, not because it was silent, rather because its continual mechanical ticking, as the hands acknowledged the passing of every second, minute and hour, was a constant sound. The single golden orb, which sat atop the clock's casing, offered just a hint of the fine mechanism that was contained therein.

A selection of leather armchairs – deemed too large for the 'Snug' and too expensive for the bar – a couple of grey high-backed but surprisingly comfortable chairs, a low table, with newspapers from the last few days, and, pushed back against one wall, one standard size table made up the furniture of the room. Upon that last table, in addition to the local bus timetable, the little booklet of tide times and a couple of flyers, placed there by locals, offering boats for hire to either go sea-fishing or to look for wildlife, be it seals, dolphins or a whole array of sea birds, aboard '*Callisto II*' or '*Wandering Star*', there was the inevitable cardboard display box, provided by the local Tourist Information Office, full of leaflets on local and not so local visitor attractions.

The stone fireplace, entirely serviceable, had a fire made up but, for those who reflected on such things, made up a tad too perfectly. The well-placed logs, all end on, the intricately woven-in kindling and the precisely placed fir cones, cumulatively announced that this was a fire made up for purely decorative purposes and that it would be like that until well into the autumn. Whereas, had Jed or Lizzie made a fire up, one Friday morning in November, to be lit later that day to warm the weekend's arrivals, it would not have been nearly so organised; you would have had no trouble in seeing the scrunched-up newspaper – the unread supplements from the previous weekend's newspapers, be they the motoring supplement, the one reviewing independent schools or yet another one promoting cruising for the over-50's – underneath a handful of randomly placed kindling and a few unevenly split logs slung on top; combustibility, rather than presentation, was what mattered in November.

It was not a November day in Cornwall, however. The spring warmth guaranteed the fire was definitely made up ornamentally. The main front doors were held open by a pair of little wooden wedges, with their beautifully carved mice adorning them – unnoticed and unappreciated to all but those whose veins ran with just a little Yorkshire blood – allowing the warm salt-ladened air to waft into reception and through to each subsequent room.

The other main feature of the reception area was the large, framed, early nineteenth century map of the county, divided into 'Hundreds', those administrative areas from an earlier time, and with an inset drawing, in the space to the right of the Lizard Peninsula, of a grand country house. It was grand then, when the artist captured it. Now, though, in the early years of the twenty-first century, it did not look quite so good, being semi-derelict as it was.

*

Cornwall, as an English county, Alba would think to herself whenever looking at that map, was a unique, spell-binding and yet somehow illogical county. It drew the traveller down or across – though never up, given it contains the country's most southerly point – and somehow forced them to ignore the beauty of South Somerset, the cathedral city of Exeter and the lush Devon countryside. Forcing them ever westwards until over the River Tamar and into Cornwall itself.

For Alba at least, Kent by comparison, Cornwall's opposite county on a map, bottom right as opposed to bottom left, did not quite hold the same allure. Yes Kent, the 'Garden of England' and a neighbouring county to where she lived, was beautiful and, like Cornwall, has its share of historic castles – such as Rochester and Dover – but, whereas those castles spoke 'power', 'domination' and 'presence', Cornwall's castles of Tintagel and Restormel spoke 'romance', 'beauty' and 'enchantment'; in Alba's mind, the Angevin

Kings Henry II or John would always lose out to the unfulfilled potential of Edward of Woodstock – the 'Black Prince' and the first Duke of Cornwall – or the mythical King Arthur.

Or, Alba would further reflect, whereas Kent boasts a fine cricket ground at Canterbury, for the lover of sports, Cornwall offers gig racing out at sea. Further, thought Alba, whilst Kent offers some of England's finest gardens in Sissinghurst, Chartwell and Emmetts, Cornwall could more than match those with Trengwainton, Glendurgan and its new 'jewel in the crown' of Eden.

Not that Alba disliked Kent. She had had many a fine day exploring Canterbury, often drawn to the spot where Becket was slain. She immersed herself in Rochester's Dickens festival and she always enjoyed walking in the deer park at Knole. However, for her, Cornwall trumped the other; just but it did. Maybe she lived a bit too close to Kent to really appreciate it but, whatever the reason, Cornwall had the allure, the romance and, as she was about to discover, the intrigue.

For Alba was not thinking of holidays in the West Country, long ago Kings and Queens or fine English gardens as she entered the reception area. Nor did she see the pair of doorstops, the golden orbed grandfather clock, the map of the Cornish 'hundreds' or anything else the reception area could offer up – she had seen them when she had first arrived, around lunchtime, this Thursday and treasured each of them in their own small way but not now, not this evening, for other things were happening. For all Alba's thoughts and attention were, as she followed both Geoffrey and Cecilia in, given to the source of the noise of the distress – an agitated, distraught woman, with panicked eyes, Stella.

Stella – a person who, fifteen or so years ago, Alba had sat next to during every school registration period for their five years at secondary school. They had been best of friends then but Alba had subsequently and overwhelmingly let Stella down and abandoned her when they had been in their early twenties. Stella had, consequently, not spoken to Alba for almost ten years out of hurt and yet who was now right before Alba in a state of panic and fear.

*

As Alba, with Mr and Mrs Constance, entered, the commotion, muffled noises and confusion of the situation – as she had experienced from where she had been sitting in the dining area – cleared, in a way not dissimilar to someone regaining their senses of sight and sound as they step out of a shower and the water clears from their eyes and ears. Revealed was a woman, beside herself with worry, at the reception desk, pleading with Robyn, who was behind the hotel's reception desk, to help. Alba listened to the conversation that was ongoing.

"...so that's why. Please call the police!" pleaded Stella.

"We have," replied Robyn as calmly as she could.

"I mean call them again – they must come and help," insisted Stella, at a loss as to why no one else seemed to grasp that something horrible was unfolding.

"We've already called them several times and explained the situation. I really don't think calling again will make any difference," offered back Robyn.

"Well, why aren't they coming?"

"As I've already said – they've got a major incident going on up in Camborne. From what I've heard on the local radio, a school bus, returning pupils from an after-school swimming gala, has been involved in an accident with a car and, more significantly, a lorry transporting livestock. Thank God, so it seems, no child has been killed but several are in hospital with serious injuries. Consequently, the police have a lot to do – accident investigation, liaison work and community reassurance. Plus, if that wasn't enough, there's been a robbery at the Post Office over in Breage; for a rural force like ours, they've got a lot on." Robyn, in a further attempt to calm the woman opposite her, added "The person who I spoke to said he'd noted everything we've said and will be in touch."

Inevitably, Stella could not process the logic of what Robyn just relayed. Yet any chance of Stella gaining that level of calm that is always needed – but hardest to obtain – in stressful and emotional moments was completely shattered by a further comment by Robyn – well-meant but regretted by Robyn before she was even half-way through saying it:

"Plus, he's only been gone a couple of hours."

"But he's gone! He's gone; did you tell them that?" Stella spouted, as her eyes filled with tears of dread once more.

"Yes, she did, we all heard her." This time it was Cliff who spoke, the hotel's manager, as he sought to support his member of staff. "Robyn told them he's been missing but, as you've told us yourself, for two hours – two hours, no longer."

"Two hours, yes! But, well, I mean, what's obvious is, no, what I mean to say is, no help, I mean, oh, I can't believe this is happening," Stella replied now almost hysterically. Thankfully, both for herself and her audience, she then constructed a whole meaningful sentence:

"Two hours, two days, that's not the point, Joshua's gone. He wouldn't just walk off, he wouldn't just disappear, he wouldn't just forget the time. He's missing. Missing I tell you – and he's in danger or had an accident or been kidnapped. Something's happened to him."

"But – " Cliff said in response. However, he was cut across by Stella.

Her words, though, were lost to Alba's ears as Geoffrey summarised the situation to both Alba and Cecilia, as he quietly pulled the door to the dining area shut behind them:

"She came down from her room about half an hour ago. She's staying here with her husband. She says her husband hasn't returned. As you can see, she's rather distressed and agitated…"

"Rather? I'd say 'very'," interjected Cecilia – which got a nod of agreement from Alba.

"OK, very distressed," conceded Geoffrey. "Apparently, they'd gone out together earlier in the afternoon but then he went off to some meeting."

"A meeting. What sort of 'meeting'?" quizzed Alba.

"Don't know. She hasn't explained – unless she said something when I came and got you both just now. Anyway, the husband hasn't returned from wherever he went. She's very worried, saying he wouldn't just not come back. However, the police are busy, they've logged the call and will pass it through to their 'Missing Person Unit' but" at which point Geoffrey dropped his voice even further, "I'm not sure they'd come even if they weren't busy, at least not yet. The bloke's probably gone for a wander and lost track of time – it's a lovely evening after all – or got on the wrong bus or car broken down and the nearest phone box has been vandalised. He'll be back before she knows it. But," and Alba could tell Geoffrey was speaking from experience now, "before I get told off later, obviously I'm not minimising her distress but the police can't instantly respond every time a husband goes for a walk longer than his wife would like. She's agitated, though, that's clear for all to see. Or they've had a holiday row – you know how it goes, you're tired from the journey down, still stressed about all the work you've left on your desk back at the office, worried whether colleagues will pick up any crisis coming out of your workload and you're feeling guilty because you're not 'enjoying' your time away in the way that all the marketing brochures and TV adverts would have you believe everyone else does. They've probably had a quarrel; he's gone off in a strop and staying away long enough to make a point."

"They seemed fine at breakfast this morning and dinner last night," reflected Cecilia.

"Yes," concurred Geoffrey. "So, as I say, just a holiday coming together, 'venting some steam' and all that. Not nice at the time but it'll blow over the moment he returns. Give it half an hour, maybe forty-five minutes and he'll be back. Still, until then, I think she needs a little bit more female handling than Cliff and I can offer her – plus Robyn needs to be freed up so she can do her job."

This final comment by Geoffrey was highlighted by the fact that two other women now came into reception – local farmers' wives who had been trying to escape for an hour or so from the relentless workload and worry of their trade. They had come through from the bar because of a lack of service. Seeing the commotion, they promptly excused themselves and left – heading back to the lambing barns, letters from the supermarkets they supplied to and, somewhere within all that, to motivating teenage children to get to bed.

With the context explained, Alba listened once more to what Stella was saying. It was instantly evident to Alba that Stella was by now repeating what she had already said several times.

"No, surely the police will come if only we explain it once more to them. They must come – a man's life is in danger. Hours! He's been gone several hours, that's a long time."

Stella, sensing she was not getting anywhere, buried her face in her hands and slumped over the reception desk, sobbing.

No one said anything. Robyn looked to Cliff, who returned her unsure look and Mr and Mrs Constance seemed unable to decide quite what to do. Alba, however, had a simple idea.

*

Alba purposefully, and making sure she worked the handle as noisily as she could, simply opened the door behind her.

With her head buried in her arms and somewhat spread-eagled across the reception desk, Stella had no way of knowing whether someone had gone out, come in or, as in fact had been the case, simply opened a door and not moved. Inevitably Stella, driven by hope, assumed that someone had just arrived. Not just anyone, though, someone; someone special, someone she was currently shedding tears for. She lifted herself up, cleared her eyes of tears as best she could and turned to where Alba, Geoffrey and Cecilia were standing with an open door behind them, calling out instinctively as she did so:

"Joshua?"

"Sorry, Stella," answered Alba, keen to help but in a way that would not involve going round in circles as the hotel staff had experienced. "Just me, I'm afraid. He's not back yet but let me help."

With that and not really waiting for an answer, Alba took Stella's hands and led her towards the now empty bar, speaking to her as she did so:

"Robyn has done all that she can at present. Best we leave her in peace so when the police call back, she's able to take the call and speak to them on your behalf; I think that would be best as you're not in a fit state to take much in just now."

A passive non-response from Stella was taken by everyone as agreement from Stella.

"I'll organise some tea for you," offered Cliff.

"Decaffeinated, please," replied Alba without turning to look. "It's late. Plus, a bowl of soup and a roll for Stella. She hasn't eaten this evening and she will need something. Charge it to my room; the hotel shouldn't have to lose out. It's the least I can do for my dear friend." Alba added, this time just to the woman on her arm, "Let's sit in here for a bit and you can tell me what's happened."

"Alba, oh Alba. Please help me, you've got to help. Joshua's gone," said Stella in response as they sat down at a random table. "Joshua's gone," she repeated.

*

A couple of hours later Alba approached the table where Geoffrey and Cecilia were sitting, in the otherwise now empty dining area. The remaining tables, empty of plates, glasses and condiment racks, glistened from having been recently wiped down by Lizzie and were now ready to be re-set by her for the next day's breakfast. Geoffrey and Cecilia, content in their own space, as if they were in their own dining room at 'The Grey House', were playing cribbage and Cecilia was in the act of laying her hand down.

"Fifteen two, fifteen four, two's six," said Cecilia to Alba's understanding – having been taught the game by the couple on an earlier holiday.

Geoffrey then spoke, as he in turn played his hand:

"Two pairs," he said as he moved his rear peg four ahead of his other. "You're still well ahead, dear. Let's hope I've a good box."

As he laid down a four of clubs, a three of spades and the two red nines, with the ace of spades already sitting on the top of the deck, the disappointment in his voice was evident from what the cards in his box offered him:

"A pair – that's all," and he moved himself a meagre two notches on his wooden rectangular board, drilled, as it was with four rows of little holes, laid out in blocks of five at a time.

"That's a shame," said Cecilia unconvincingly. "It feels that that hand should give you more than just two points but it doesn't, does it."

"You're right – it doesn't. Oh well, your deal."

As his wife shuffled the now gathered cards, he looked up, having heard the approach of Alba.

"Well?" he enquired as his wife dealt their new hands but then, she too, looked to Alba.

"She's settled," replied a drained Alba.

"Well done you," Cecilia said warmly. "She was quite agitated, wasn't she?"

"I'd say. It was a good idea of yours to call me through," Alba replied, though directing most of the comment to Geoffrey for obvious reasons. "I'm not sure I'd have involved myself, otherwise, for the travelling had caught up with me on top of the fine food."

"But you could have declined to involve yourself, you could have said something along the lines of 'I think there's enough people involved already' or some such weak comment to 'justify' doing nothing or you could have given up before really doing anything – just stood on the side lines and then decided to leave it to someone else, like those two women who left as you started to take charge," offered back Cecilia, keen to praise her young friend, who she could sense was now 'running on empty'. "You did involve yourself, though," reiterated Cecilia to Alba. "Any news on this woman Stella's missing husband?"

"No. She last saw him late afternoon when he went off for his business meeting – he's an architect and had a site visit arranged. Stella said they were having this mini-break built around this meeting he had to come down for," replied Alba.

"Right," stated Geoffrey.

"And he hasn't returned," continued Alba. "If they've had a row – if they have, she hasn't let on to me – but if they have rowed, he'll either wander in when the pubs have closed or he'll appear in the morning, having stayed in some other hotel or B&B in Marazion probably in his hurt, anger or spite. The police aren't interested at the moment, given he's not in a vulnerable category, but said they'll call tomorrow evening which obviously will be the twenty-four hour mark. Stella has finally accepted that. I've said to Stella I'll now be more use to her in the morning and we've agreed to chat over an early breakfast. I mean, what else can I do tonight?"

"Nothing, my dear," said Geoffrey. "You've done all and more than anyone could have asked. I don't think anyone else could have calmed her down as you did. Best you get yourself up to your room, crash out and, as you say, pick things up in the morning. It's a waiting game now."

"Exactly," agreed Cecilia. "We can't have you walking the cliff path looking for him at this time of night or heading all the way back to Marazion now. It's dark and late. If this bloke – "

"Joshua," interjected Alba.

"That's right, Joshua. Well," continued Cecilia "if he has collapsed on the roadside or at the property he was at on business, someone would have called an ambulance at least. So, he's probably fine but, understandably, his wife is worried sick."

"Understandably," concurred Geoffrey. "I'd be beside myself if something happened to Cecilia."

CHAPTER 3

Friday: breakfast

Although worried for her friend's situation, tiredness, the sea air and being in her favourite room of 'The Jupiter Hotel', meant Alba had a surprisingly good night's sleep. Thus, it was with renewed energy that she found herself sitting in what last night was the dining area but now the breakfast room.

She stirred her pot of tea, which Lizzie had already brought her, and wondered whether her thin jersey top, with its angular block design, in black, burgundy and white and with its off-centre angled neckline, was quite her. She had picked it up from the now not-so-newly-opened community café-come-charity shop in her village but, as she continued to stir her tea, wondered, whilst it didn't clash with her navy three-quarter-length trousers, whether some other top would have been the safer option.

She looked around the empty room. She was at a different table to last night and as she looked across to where she had eaten the previous evening, a nagging undefined thought re-surfaced, an unspecified something, tugged at her brain. But tug it did – something did not 'fit'. She admonished herself for missing something, whatever that something was, last night but she had been tired, had been hungry and had been distracted – enjoying, as she had, catching up with Mr and Mrs Constance. As she sipped her tea this Friday morning, she 'trawled' her brain for whatever it was but without success.

She watched a seagull land on one of the outside windowsills, walk the length of it a couple of times and then, having preened itself under one wing, take to the air once more. She sipped from her cup again as she waited for Stella to join her.

*

"Morning Alba, nice top" said a red-eyed and drawn looking Stella, several minutes later. "Sleep well?" Stella added but, understandably, without any real energy in her question.

"Not too bad," replied Alba, not wishing to ignore the half-hearted question but keen to move on to vastly more important matters.

It was evident to Alba, from her friend's disposition and solitary entry into the breakfast area, that Joshua had neither returned nor even made contact with the hotel to reassure his wife that, whatever else was going on, he was safe. Nonetheless, Alba asked the obvious, the only question that she or anyone would ask:

"Any news?"

As she sat opposite Alba, Stella closed her eyes and, unable to confront having to say the word out loud, simply and slowly shook her head a couple of times.

"I sensed that was the case having just watched you come in." Then, somewhat abstractedly, Alba added, "Unimportantly, Lizzie says she'll bring you some coffee, a bowl of fresh fruit and some muesli – she says she didn't know whether you'd want anything but equally didn't want to hover over you as you ordered. She did add that she'll bring you whatever else you want. We can't have you not eating anything, especially as you left most of your soup and rolls last night; the rolls, apparently, are now destined for the lake over at Helston for Lizzie's children to feed to the ducks later."

"I don't know what I want to eat but you're right, I need to eat something, I guess. Just hope they don't put banana in the bowl of fruit."

"Oh, that's right," commented Alba. "You never could stand bananas when we were at school together. I remember that time –"

A look from Stella, however, cut Alba off from what she was about to say.

"Sorry, not important," continued a chastised Alba. "Reminiscing about our time at Greensands Comprehensive can wait for another day." Then, putting her cup down, which she had been cradling, Alba simply said – as much to bring herself back to the matter in hand, as Stella:

"So, nothing?"

"Nothing," repeated Stella. "He didn't return to the hotel last night, he hasn't walked in this morning and no message from him or from anyone."

"Surely the police –" prompted Alba.

"No, nothing. Nothing at all. Maybe, just maybe, this morning I can now understand perhaps them not rushing over last night to search for Joshua; I could, in the cold light of this morning, as I lay awake, accept that they had other priorities last night. Of course, as I lay there, I was hoping to hear the door go or a knock at my door, as someone brought a message of good news or even of a sighting of him at least. Yet, as I say, nothing. But, going back to the police, we're now twelve hours on from when he was reported missing, longer from when I last saw him, so you'd have thought someone from the Devon and Cornwall Constabulary would have at least called me or the hotel at some stage to ask after my welfare if nothing else. What I'm going through is horrible, just horrible; it's like my heart has been ripped out and hidden somewhere. My head is spinning and I just don't know what to do. So, you'd think they would at least be in the practice of calling to see whether I'm coping – which I'm not, I might add, and only just about got myself together to come down to breakfast."

FRIDAY: BREAKFAST

As Lizzie brought over the coffee, cereal and a bowl of fruit salad, Alba replied, as she removed the fruit from in front of her friend:

"But you have made it down. We need to see if there's anything else you can remember from yesterday that might help you or the police. And you need to eat something so you can think clearly and be ready for his return." Then, to the disappearing Lizzie, in a way that Alba would never have done had other people been down for breakfast, called out, "Sorry to be a pain, Lizzie, could Stella have another bowl of fruit but without banana. I should have said but, after all these years, I'd forgotten that she can't stand them – I mean, really can't stand them. We'll tell you why in a less serious moment."

"OK," replied a slightly puzzled waitress, resigned to yet another fussy and pedantic hotel guest, this time one who, whatever state she was in, was clearly unable to move three or four slices of banana to the side of her dish.

"I won't waste it," Alba felt compelled to add having seen Lizzie's expression. "And could we trouble you for some toast for both of us and a fresh pot of tea for me?"

"Of course," answered Lizzie.

With breakfast ordered, Alba closed her eyes for a moment, focussed on her breathing and then, as she took up her tea cup to cradle it once more, said:

"OK, Stella. I saw you and Joshua in reception here, as I checked-in yesterday lunchtime, so he disappeared sometime after that. Best you take me over what happened yesterday afternoon."

With that, Alba waited on her friend to take her through the hours which preceded Joshua's failure to return to the hotel at dinner time.

*

Stella drew herself up and looked directly at Alba sitting opposite her. Yet the moment was clearly too much for Stella and she slumped down into her original position, with her elbows being the only things stopping her from slumping even lower still. With head down, she spoke to her cereal bowl.

"There's not a lot to say. After we'd seen you here at lunchtime, we headed off to Marazion to visit St Michael's Mount. We had a nice time on the island, did the castle, walked back off the island and then he went off for his site visit which he hasn't returned from. Annoyingly, as I said last night to you, I don't have the address of where he went."

"I assume you've searched his suitcase or any papers he's left in your room for the address," prompted Alba.

"Of course, multiple times. Nothing."

"Pity. Shame he didn't tell you."

"You're telling me!" With that, Stella shut her eyes and shook her head in frustration at herself. With eyes open once more, she added, in an attempt to forgive herself:

"Why would I ask? I have complete trust in him and it probably just slipped his mind – we had a busy day after all. Why would I ask?" Stella repeated. "I mean nothing was going to happen to him, was it? Why would it? We're down here on holiday for a few days, he had a simple site visit and getting a taxi back here was straight forward enough. So, there was no reason for me to even think of asking after the address – I don't any other week of the year."

"But you've phoned the office this morning to get the address, surely," stated a puzzled Alba, who felt something was awry.

"Sort of."

"Sort of? What do you mean by sort of?" asked Alba.

"I've phoned but no one answered – which was what I expected. Yes, I know it's Friday and not the weekend but the other partners were all due out on visits today, the two office staff are on annual leave and the receptionist had a funeral to go to. Rather than try to summon one of the office staff in, the senior partner said closing the office for the day was acceptable as a one-off so long as the receptionist was willing to go in tomorrow morning for a few hours, which she'd be allowed to take back another time, to sort the post and process the phone messages – which she was happy to agree to. So, I can't get the address because the office is shut as no one is there."

"A good time to go missing then," mused Alba.

"As I keep saying, he hasn't gone missing. Something has happened. We had had a nice day. On balance, I preferred our morning boat trip rather than the castle but there was nothing untoward about either. That's it really; there's not a lot more for me to say. Have you been, by the way, to the castle? Do you know where I'm talking about?" asked Stella.

"I've been a few times to the island but it's the gardens I really go for. You don't really see their magnificence as you walk up the steep cobbled path and even from the top you can't fully take in their beauty – in my opinion that is. I think you have to be in the gardens themselves, studying the amazing variety of plants they have there, to grasp what the gardeners are doing in that micro-climate."

"If you say so," answered Stella. "Not really our thing. Joshua much prefers the architecture of the castle and how they built it there and, almost more impressively, how they are able to maintain it. He was pointing out to me, as we were there yesterday afternoon, marks on the rocks and the external walls where he reckons scaffolding had been recently. He was just amazed with the mechanics of how they sometimes have to encase part of the walls with scaffolding to do repair work."

"Any scaffolding up this spring?" enquired Alba.

"No."

"Oh, that'll be nice. It's been a few years since I saw it without any metal cladding at all. But I didn't think architecture was your thing. Perhaps your interests have changed; it has been too many years after all but, besides always getting the leading role in the school productions, fashion and design were always your passion I seem to remember."

"No, you're right, I much prefer the inside," concurred Stella. "The softer side of buildings is my way of putting it and my career is very much in interior designs. Some of my work comes through Joshua's firm – they do the structural stuff and then my company comes in and turns a building into a home. Obviously, we're guided by what the client's brief is but often we can introduce themes, colours, textures that they'd never have considered themselves but suddenly find they can't be without once they see how we can utilise them. Of course, it's not always an entire new build, maybe just an extension that we're asked to work with or sometimes just a single room that we're tasked with turning into an exciting and dramatic 'space'. Just to be clear, though, only some of my work comes from Joshua, for it is important my business isn't built on his coat tails; I'm out there promoting myself and generating my own customers."

Alba mouthed a silent 'thank you' to Lizzie, as she brought their order, but then to Stella said:

"The castle's 'Blue Drawing Room' is my favourite room. Such an enchanting colour of blue and such a well-proportioned room. It must be your favourite too?"

"No," answered Stella to Alba's surprise – and Alba's look prompted her friend to explain:

"I mean, I can see why it would be a favourite room for many visitors and it is definitely in contrast to the other medieval or Edwardian rooms."

"You must have a favourite room though?" challenged Alba.

"Not really, no. I guess the 'Blue Drawing Room', by being so different, shows that you can introduce something different, something original, without ruining the remainder. But, if truth be told, I'd really like to be given a free rein and redo most of the interior."

An unmissable look of sadness on Alba's face, reflecting her love of that most distinct of island castles, which was connected to the mainland by a tidal causeway, and her almost childlike desire that nothing about it should ever be changed, forced Stella to be a little bit more positive, well what she thought was positive, for she added:

"Well, the church itself that's there within the castle, I'd probably leave that pretty much alone. The exposed stone work, the wooden beams and the light cascading in through the vaulted windows, would make it a fine living space or an absolutely grand dining room – truly grand. So, yes, wouldn't need to do a lot to that room, just clear the clutter away."

"But it's a church!" replied a shocked Alba. "I'm sure you can still go over for a service on a Sunday – well, I think you can but I'd have to ask Cliff to be certain. You can't just take away the wooden chairs, rip out the organ and throw away the pulpit-thing; that would be sacrilege."

"Oh, Alba, really! Just listen to yourself. You've either gone soft or you've gone all religious on me. Please don't tell me you have gone and found God! Alba White surely hasn't gone and got a pair of angel wings since we last met, has she?"

With that, Stella laughed but the laugh put Alba on the defensive.

"No, don't worry yourself on that score."

Yet, somehow Alba felt driven to add:

"That said, a friend of mine, Helen, would be most upset to hear of another church building being sold off. She thinks…"

However, Stella, perhaps because talk of interior design, a friend's company or perhaps some breakfast inside of her, allowed her to keep her mind off Joshua for a moment longer, cut Alba off:

"And anyway, none of it really makes sense, does it? I mean why, if this Jesus bloke was meant to be God, did he get arrested so very easily? He hardly put up a fight. Where was his resolve? He caved in to the Romans pretty quickly in the end. And as for the group of men he chose to follow him around, well, what a pitiful group of men they turned out to be when it mattered."

Alba, not knowing whether she agreed with her friend, nor how to answer if she wished to defend the church of her parents, was spared working out how, if at all, to answer, as the heavy metal handle on the door to the hotel car park – the one straddling where the dining area and snug merged – was worked and someone walked in. The bright morning sunlight made it impossible to make his features out but Stella, hope resurfacing, responded to the possibility that Joshua may have returned.

"Is that you?" she called. She stood as she did so, palms on the table with fingers spread-eagled as she leant in the direction she was talking to, expectantly waiting for an affirmative answer.

"Depends who you want," replied Gerry. "I'm definitely me," he added, as he made his way through the room and towards the internal door to the reception area. Being preoccupied with his task in hand, he spoke without looking across or having given a thought about the person to whom he might be speaking. He then stopped, mid-stride, put his right hand to his chin and pondered for the briefest of moments. Sensing his *faux pas*, he turned and headed over to where Stella and Alba were sitting – the still only occupied table.

"Not back?" he said.

Stella dejectedly sat herself back down and unwilling to speak to a man who was not her husband, took a mouthful of muesli and left Alba to converse.

"No," Alba confirmed.

"Sorry," added Gerry. "I'd heard a guest had gone missing last night but, from my understanding, as it wasn't being spoken of as a cliff fall or being stranded on a stretch of coast somewhere by an incoming tide, I assumed he'd have come back."

"No," repeated Alba on her friend's behalf.

"As I say, sorry. Insensitive of me and all that. I was rushing, trying to get the car sorted out before bringing the lads down for breakfast. At least one of them is meant to have got in the shower before I get back to the room; here's hoping. We're off exploring again after we've eaten."

"I had been thinking of heading over to Restormel Castle myself today," replied Alba.

"Small world," said Gerry. "That's where I was thinking of taking the boys today."

"Small world, indeed," agreed Alba. Then, somewhat abstractedly, she added, "I learnt recently that modern prison design is nothing like the circular nature of Restormel's keep."

"What do you know about prisons?" asked Gerry.

Alba was surprised by the sudden nervousness in Gerry's question and she wondered why her comment had unsettled him; she sought to reassure him:

"Oh, nothing really. Just that I visited a friend not so long ago who was being held on remand. Charges against him got dropped thankfully. I just remember noticing, as I was walking up to the prison that first time I visited, how modern prisons are not built within perfectly circular outer walls."

"Oh, right, oh OK," said Gerry with more than a hint of relief in his voice.

Then, sensing Stella's frustration as to where the conversation was going, given the way Stella dropped her spoon into her now empty bowl, Alba asked Gerry:

"Clearly you haven't just seen Stella's husband out in the car park. But, given that, I don't suppose you noticed anything odd, anything missing or, perhaps, anything that was there but shouldn't be?"

"No, should there be? You're being a bit inquisitorial, if I may say. I hope you're not a plain clothes police officer – you should have cautioned me before questioning me if you were and probably not in front of the missing man's wife. Plus, your questioning style is quite leading in nature and a good defence barrister would be on to that in a flash."

He had been trying to sound 'jokey' but his nervousness had unmistakably resurfaced.

As the solitary female diner from last night, quickly followed by

Geoffrey and Cecilia, entered the breakfast area, Gerry caught Alba and Stella completely off guard as he added:

"Sorry, I sense I'm not coming across at my best this morning and any half-awake person should be able to detect my edginess but I've had my fill of police officers of late. Had my fill of being questioned and of having the local press outside my house as I try to get the boys off to school. I was really hoping this time away would enable me to switch off from it all for a bit. So, I'll trust you're neither a police officer in plain clothes nor a reporter following me. If you're not, I'll try to calm down."

"Promise you I'm not," replied Alba. "Meaning you can be calm – well, calm until you get back to the room and discover both your boys still in bed."

With that, Gerry smiled back at Alba, nodded and then said:

"I wouldn't be surprised. I'll give you a rasher of bacon off my plate if even one of them has ventured so much as a leg out from under the duvet." As he shook his head, he added "I thought saying we were off for a day at a castle would have motivated them to get up and be ready before me today. Can they be too old for castles and adventure already?"

It was said as a rhetorical question but, worried in case either person he was talking to felt compelled to answer, he added:

"I'm Gerry by the way."

"Alba," responded Alba, adding, as she gestured to her friend, "And this is Stella."

"Morning, nice to meet you but obviously not quite in your circumstances. My boys are Gregory and Ben. As for your missing man, and I accept this may sound hollow, try not to worry. Give it a couple more hours. If he hasn't had an accident, which seems unlikely for no hospital seems to have got in touch with the hotel, he probably went off in a strop over something so insignificant that you never even noticed it at the time. He'll have found some place to stay, will be forcing himself to have a protracted breakfast there or in a café and then walk in here and hope you'll be so relieved to see him he won't have to apologise for what he's putting you through."

"Why is everyone saying we've had a row!" retorted Stella, finally looking up and with defiance in her eyes. "We were having a lovely day, we didn't row, there was no 'slight', no falling out and no misunderstanding. We parted as agreed and I haven't seen him since. Something has happened," and turning to Alba, Stella added but now almost pleading, "Will someone hear what I'm saying, someone, anyone, surely you, Alba? Something has happened to Joshua and I've got to do something about it. I'm done with this breakfast, especially as the toast is now cold. I'm heading up to my room to get my coat and then driving over to the police station in Helston – well, I assume there's one there, guess I'll find out soon enough – and finding out what they're going to do about it. Joshua wouldn't just go off."

"That's not a bad idea, Stella," responded Alba. "But give me five more minutes here."

"Yeah, sorry," interrupted Gerry. "I don't think I've really helped at all. Speaking to the police direct is probably no bad thing. If I can help, please ask but best now I go and rouse two boys and drag them down for breakfast."

With that Gerry moved away but as he reached the inner door to reception, he turned back and called to Alba:

"Come with us, if you'd like."

"Pardon."

"Come with us. Seems silly taking two cars – the roads in this part of Cornwall are busy enough as it is. If you were planning on going then you'd be very welcome to tag along with us. You don't have to do the children's quiz with us, not that either lad will get beyond question three before they give up or have turned the sheet into a paper aeroplane, but we could at least take you there, meet up for a drink and a sandwich and then bring you back when we're all done."

"That's kind of you," replied Alba in unsure tones.

"I accept," said Gerry as he walked a couple of steps back towards Alba and Stella, "we hadn't spoken until five minutes ago and you don't know me from Adam but, my view is, if we were on one of the campsites up the road and on adjacent pitches there, we'd have been mucking in together by now no doubt – one of us would have helped the other to erect their tent, one would have said 'I'm off to the camp shop, can I get you anything?', my lads would have sniffed around to see if you had any biscuits and hoping you weren't a teacher, fearing you'd turn their week's camping into a week-long field trip. I accept this is a good hotel and we're not camping but my philosophy is the same, in that we can still offer to help or muck in together where it makes sense; the barriers between us are really only as thick as that imaginary tent fly-sheet."

"Well, err, I'm not sure, I – "

"You don't have to decide right now. Doesn't bother me either way. I mean, your decision won't put me out whatever you choose and we'll probably bump into each other there if you are going. As you know, we're still to have breakfast, so no rush. Let me know, that's all, if you fancy catching a lift."

"OK," offered back Alba. She was unable to disagree with the logic but his offer had definitely caught her off guard. "I'll let you know," she added.

"Room five if you miss me down here."

With that, Gerry headed up to his room, leaving a still nonplussed Alba exchanging looks with Stella.

"Blow me! My husband has gone missing but meanwhile men are still falling at the feet of Miss White. Just like the olden days – well, save for my husband going missing."

"It was never so," said Alba.

"It was so," insisted Stella. "You always got the boy, my boy on one occasion I seem to remember."

"Oh, please don't bring that up. It was never what you made it out to be at the time and it was a long time ago."

"Dear Alba, don't fret yourself. I'm not about to bring it up again."

Alba bit her tongue to stop herself from saying 'but you just did'.

"Right," said Stella as she stood up. "As I was saying before you got asked out, I'm going to head off to the police station. I've got to do something; might as well find out if the police are minded to do something too. Thanks for having breakfast with me."

"That's alright. But look, before you head off, sit yourself down a moment longer and let's quickly go over what happened yesterday. Delaying five minutes won't do any harm and it might just jog something in your memory, something that will prove useful later on. Come on, sit yourself down and let's go through things properly, once."

Stella, reluctant to be inactive any longer, frustratingly sat down once more.

"Five minutes but then I must *do* something," stated Stella. "If I were missing, I doubt Joshua would be sitting around having a leisurely breakfast."

"I'm sure he wouldn't," replied Alba. Yet, she was keen to learn what, however insignificant, had unfolded yesterday afternoon. Alba therefore added, "but talking me through yesterday afternoon might save you a lot of time later on."

"Look, there's nothing to say. We parted in the car park in Marazion, the one where you park on the grass near the playground, I drove back here and he was heading off for his meeting. And, as I've said, he was due back here for dinner. That's it."

As Lizzie cleared their breakfast dishes, having taken Cecilia her boiled eggs and brown toast and Geoffrey his full English with extra tomatoes, Stella repeated her final comment:

"That's it, I assure you. Nothing else happened."

"But look, Stella – " However, Alba cut herself short, sensing she was about to go round in circles once more. She changed tack:

"Does Joshua have a history of going off by himself?"

"No, of course not."

"Does he have any friends down here he may have gone and visited and lost track of time?"

"No, at least not that I know of."

"And excuse the bluntness of this question, any suspicion of him having a girlfriend or boyfriend living down here or who may have come down to meet him here?" Seeing the anger in her friend's eyes, Alba added, "Sorry but I might as well ask. After all, it's almost certainly the first question any half-decent police officer should ask. So?"

"No," answered Stella, conveying all the emotion that she could muster in that single incredibly short word. "No," she repeated. "No, he did not," Stella stated a third time.

"Good. Sorry for asking. But look, if Joshua hasn't had an accident, gone drinking with old rugby mates or met up with someone you've tried to be 'blind' to, then you're right – something or someone has purposefully done something to him, possibly knowing that last night and today he was somewhat isolated from his colleagues. So, let's go over yesterday afternoon properly; what happened yesterday after I saw you in the hotel reception area?"

Stella nodded her agreement and, as she twisted her wedding and engagement rings round, and as Annabel entered for breakfast, Stella began.

*

"We'd done a boat ride in the morning, which Joshua wanted to do even though he can't swim. He said he had to overcome his fear of the sea – he had his lifejacket on pretty securely though." With that Stella smiled a sad brief smile. "Then we came back here for a simple bite to eat – which we had in our room. But you know that bit, since you were checking into the hotel as we got back from the boat trip, and we said 'hello' to you. Then, once Joshua and I had eaten –

what do you reckon, about forty-five minutes later? Yes, about three quarters of an hour, we headed off to St Michael's Mount – seeing you in reception again as we headed out."

"That's right. I hadn't even made it to my room during that time! I was catching up with Robyn and then, once she'd called through to the kitchen about who had just arrived – as in me – Alan brought me out a pot of tea."

"Alan?" queried Stella.

"The chef here. Absolutely charming and a brilliant chef – you really must try his fish dishes, if you haven't already. They are so delicate but, I guess, the Cornish fishermen must take a lot of the credit for the quality of the food Alan is working with. And as for his pan-fried salmon, it's hard to believe you can get it that sweet, almost caramelised, and succulent, yet he does. So, yes, I was in reception when you left. I did head up to my room almost as soon as you'd gone."

"If you say so. Right, we left the hotel via the front door – see, I'm trying to be precise about this given, as you say, the police will want me to be accurate if ever they decide to take me seriously. So, we exited via the front door. Guess we could have gone out via the side door between the dining area and the snug but if I'm paying to stay somewhere I'm going to use the front door; none of this going in and out of what, even in my short time staying here, seems to effectively be the staff door. As we got round to the hotel car park, we passed a woman, getting out of a taxi. I've never seen a woman look so nervous as she did. She kept looking around – like a child expecting her mother to catch her with her hand in the biscuit jar – burdened with a rucksack and walking poles but, as I say, getting out of a taxi."

"Maybe she'd twisted an ankle?" offered up Alba benevolently.

"Perhaps and yet I don't recall her walking funny but we were walking to our car and obviously not focussing on her, so maybe she was pained; guess I couldn't say for certain for I only glanced back at her once. We got into our car and headed off to Marazion."

"Then?" prompted Alba.

"Then, well, not a lot really," and Stella's willingness to go along with her friend's inquisitive style ebbed. "I mean, I feel we've already covered it this breakfast time; we walked over to the island, didn't go into the gardens, rather a quick look in one of the gift shops and then up to the castle past the Dairy. Never having been before it was nice to see but I've told you what I thought of the inside. Thereafter, we walked back down from the castle, across the causeway and parted at the car park; that was probably about five o'clock. I drove back here and he headed off for his site visit."

"Headed off – how?" queried Alba.

"Walked. The property he was visiting was somewhere in Marazion I believe, so Joshua said he wanted to walk the half mile or so to get a better feel for the town. Apparently, a property that hasn't come on the market before – ever – so it's a rare opportunity. It will need lots of work doing, almost a rebuild according to Joshua, but an exciting chance for him to modernise, especially to get a lot more natural light into the rooms so he was saying to me the other day. Oh, and turning the little garden into an outdoor living space. He said it belonged to an elderly man who has died and whose grown-up children are now selling; my recollection is that the eldest child, who lives in Winchester, so not local to here at all, is the Executor but acting on behalf of them all. That bit isn't important. What is important, is that Joshua was due back here by taxi for dinner but he didn't arrive."

"Not good enough, again," stated Alba.

"Pardon," replied a puzzled Stella. "What do you mean?"

"Again. Go over it again. I mean, go over it again, *please*. Look, there may be more."

"More? But I've told you everything – more than once it now feels."

"Well, yes and no. See, you've told me what the pair of you did, what you thought of where you were and how you travelled. But

FRIDAY: BREAKFAST

you haven't told me about anyone else – not quite as blatant as was there someone following you who was wearing a long fawn raincoat and dark glasses or some supposed room steward in the castle with a surprising Russian accent. Rather, did anyone talk to you? Equally, and a bit like you just heard me quiz that bloke Gerry, was there anyone loitering around the Marazion car park who somehow caught your eye, some vehicle in the car park that seemed 'wrong', someone in one of the island shops but neither buying something nor browsing. You know, that kind of thing or did someone slip Joshua a note or make a comment that you ignored but Joshua was meant to hear as a threat or some coded message. Did something, anything, anyone just feel odd? So, again."

"Alba, I know you're trying to help but this all seems a little bit naïve – as I keep saying nothing strange happened in the afternoon. Whatever has happened will require the police to go through his office back in Salisbury, speaking to the receptionist tomorrow morning and contacting his bank. I wonder whether it has got something to do with a former employee who was done for fraud a while back – not, I'm afraid, to consider whether the person in the ticket booth to the castle was right to refuse entry to someone trying to get in, on what he said was, his wife's ticket."

"Alright," conceded Alba. "I thought it might help but you're probably right. I'll stop interfering. But you definitely don't want me driving us to Marazion and having a look around ourselves."

"Alba, you're kind but, as I keep saying, I don't have the address on me and, even if we do go and wander round the town, it would be somewhat aimless – even you have to accept that. I think it's better if I go to the police this morning. But no, you weren't interfering and I needed a friend to be with me this morning, so thank you. Now though," Stella said as she stood up, "I'll get my coat and go and see what the police say."

"Then?"

"Then I'll come back here and wait, try and eat a sandwich at least for lunch but don't feel you have to be here to sit with me. You're on holiday after all. You should go and do whatever you were planning or whatever you fancy; no point us both sitting here simply waiting. I'll be fine."

"Really?"

"No, of course I won't," replied Stella. "But I'll manage. It can't be any worse than last night, lying there alone, fearing the worst, desperately lonely and – oh, never mind, all I'm saying is, I'll cope, just."

"If you say so," replied Alba.

With that, and having finished her breakfast too, Alba also stood and the two friends walked up to their rooms. They reached Stella's room first but a further quizzical look from Alba prompted Stella to say:

"Look, we parked and followed the constant trickle of visitors across the beach. Then we walked over the causeway. After that we got stuck behind some bloke at the ticket office – something to do with trying to get himself and his children in on a woman's ticket. Inside the castle, Joshua spoke to the room steward in the library about whether the books were real or just mock-ups and if they were real were they valuable. I don't recall speaking to anyone else on our walk back from the island and I don't recall either of us losing anything or finding anything." Stella paused, as she searched her memory a final time, before adding, "And I don't recall anyone being suspicious or out of place. There was a four-by-four off-road car next to us in the Marazion car park with lowered suspension and sport tyres but that's not suspicious, just stupid."

"Cars aren't really my thing," commented Alba.

"Trust me," insisted Stella. "What with its tinted rear windows as well, just plain stupid."

CHAPTER 4

Restormel Castle

Having been thanked once again by Stella for her company over breakfast, Alba realised she had left her room key on her breakfast table and so headed back down.

Annabel remained, Mr and Mrs Constance had left and the other lone female, who Alba took to be the artist, whom Stella had referred to as staying at the hotel, had also finished eating but was in conversation with Lizzie, asking whether it was possible for the chef to make her up a picnic supper as she wanted to be out painting that evening around Kynance Cove. Lizzie assured her it would be fine, for a slight charge, and was about to ask her what she might like when Alba's reappearance caught her eye.

"You're back. Everything alright?" queried Lizzie.

"Yes, fine thanks, just left my room key down here, that's all," said Alba.

"Oh, OK. By the way, this is Emily," said Lizzie, referring to the woman she had been talking to. "One evening I should sit you at adjacent tables as I think the pair of you would get on." Then, turning to Emily, Lizzie did the introductions the other way round:

"This is Alba. She's also from Suffolk."

"Actually, I'm not but never mind," corrected Alba.

"Aren't you? Oh, I do get confused with anywhere beyond Exeter," admitted Lizzie.

"Don't worry. The counties are easily confused." Then, to spare Lizzie any further embarrassment, Alba spoke to Emily:

"Nice to meet you. Suffolk is a lovely part of the country. I gather you are an artist."

"Likewise. Well, I dabble, sometimes it's not too bad but it's a passion that torments me. Hoping to be out painting this evening in fact; it's meant to be a stormy night so I thought if I could be over at Kynance, capturing the dying daylight as the storm clouds come in, well, that could make for a very dramatic skyline."

"Wish I could paint but on the occasions I've tried I find myself trying to paint every leaf, every window, every single little detail and I get frustrated and give up. The intention, each time I've tried, is to create an impression of what I'm seeing but it ends up as some juvenile attempt where I've crammed too much into the picture, where the proportions are wrong and as for identifying the light source and all that, well, the less said the better."

"Persevere if you think you'd enjoy it, that's what I say," replied Emily encouragingly. "And try and hold onto that desire of painting an impression of what you are seeing. That's very much my approach – reminds me of that, possibly apocryphal, tale about Turner; you must have heard it."

"No, don't think so," said Alba.

"No? Well, apparently someone was looking over his shoulder as he painted and commented that they could not see the colours in the sky that he had put on his canvas, to which Turner is supposed to have replied 'but don't you wish you could?'. So, approach it with that philosophy – of painting what you would like the scene to be."

"I'd never thought of it that way before; that's really interesting. Still, I'd better not keep you and Lizzie and I'd better go and pick up my key before I forget a second time. Maybe we can chat over dinner one evening, if you'd like."

"Perhaps but it depends on where my painting takes me and how well a session is going. I do rather want to have a go at the Godrevy Lighthouse as well this week."

"Of course. Well, nice to meet you."

With that, Alba left Lizzie to suggest what Alan could include in a picnic. Having retrieved her key, and picked up a little plastic peg which she suspected belonged to Geoffrey's cribbage board, Alba decided to go to her car and collect her flask, so she could refill it for the day ahead even though she was still unsure whether to take Gerry up on his offer.

*

Walking round to the car park, Alba saw Martha before she'd got to her, Alba's, car. Martha was sitting on the second to lowest step of the metal staircase which was on this side of the hotel. It was one of the hotel's fire escapes but it served as an access to the staff accommodation, where Cliff lived, and as an alternative access for those guests who were at the furthest end of the corridor on this side of the hotel – as Martha's room was. None of the hotel staff would necessarily encourage the guests to use it, especially not Cliff, who enjoyed his privacy, but those guests, especially those in room ten, who were canny enough to realise that using the door at the top of the stairs never set off any fire alarms, used it as a quicker route to their cars, the restaurant or, as Martha was clearly doing, simply to have a cigarette.

"It's Martha, isn't it?" Alba said. "You alright?"

As Martha tapped her cigarette against the metal railings to her right, her pensiveness and anxiety were evident for Alba to see.

"I shouldn't really be smoking," said Martha, confessing in a way Alba would have expected a fifteen-year-old schoolgirl might have, had she been caught by the Head of Geography beyond the sports hall amongst an overgrown privet hedge. Indeed, to Alba, Martha definitely had a look of a bewildered youngster out of her depth and floundering.

"Not really," Martha added.

"No? Why's that?" replied Alba.

"Well, what with being on a walking holiday and all that. I'll probably get told off for having the odd 'ciggie' too, knowing my luck."

"Told off? By whom?"

"Never mind. Not important," replied Martha as she took a further, satisfying, draw on her cigarette. "Forget I said it."

"If you say so. I'm Alba by the way – you sure you're alright?"

"Yeah, guess so, well, will be once I've finished this. You were on the next table to us last night, weren't you?"

"That's right," answered Alba.

Alba watched as Martha looked intently at the smouldering end of her cigarette, held between her first two fingers of her right hand. Martha studied it a moment longer, then tapped it once more against the railings before taking a further draw. Alba wondered whether the other, in that fleeting, transient moment, had found the peace and escape that she, Martha, was so clearly desperate to find.

As she looked once more at Alba, Martha asked:

"Is she still in there? Annabel, I mean? Having breakfast?"

"Err, yes," replied Alba. "Well, she was until I came out the front a few moments ago? Do you want me to go and get her – she's been down a good while; she's probably almost finished."

"No, please don't. I was just wondering, that's all. Think I'll finish this first before I head in."

"Are you sure you're alright?" Alba said.

Alba sensed Martha was tempted to open up about something but any inclination passed as quickly as it came for, as Martha momentarily squeezed her eyes tightly shut and winced to herself, it was as if the shutters came down or the barricades went up.

"Yes, thank you," Martha resolutely said.

"I could bring you a coffee out," offered up Alba.

"No, I'm fine. I'll go in in a moment."

"OK," said an unconvinced Alba. "I'm just looking for a couple of things in my car."

With that, wishing to give the other woman, a woman in her mid-fifties, slim and gaunt looking, as opposed to petite, and attired in trekking trousers and a sleeveless pink shirt, some space, Alba headed to her car. On Alba's return, flask in hand, Martha had gone.

*

As she passed through reception for a further time this morning, Gerry, or more accurately his two boys, Gregory and Ben, came bounding down the stairs and, not looking where they were going, almost collided with Alba. They were past her before they had even noticed her, leaving Gerry to apologise.

"Sorry about that."

"Well, they're up I see," responded Alba.

"Finally – but I'm afraid I don't owe you any bacon for they were still very much in bed when I got back to the room. So, made your mind up yet? But with the two of them almost bowling you over just then, you probably are angling for a safer day than coming out with us, such as swimming to the Wolf Rock lighthouse, trying to hang glide to the Scilly Isles or jumping the Carrick Roads!"

Curious as to why the local press had been at his door, why Gerry was nervous when police and prisons had been mentioned over breakfast and having had her fill of driving after the long journey down yesterday, Alba was tempted to take Gerry up on his offer. Then a further comment from him swung it for her.

"Look, it's daft taking two cars if you're still going but I understand it's a bit awkward. So, tell the waitress we're heading off together and that I promise to have us all back by mid-afternoon and remind her of where we're going and what my car registration is. Can't protect you much more than that. Also," he added having made sure Stella wasn't within earshot "if you're worried that I'm going round bumping off the hotel guests one by one, there must be more discrete ways than pushing you off some castle battlements with my two boys watching."

"Alright. We'll give it a go. It's a bit of a drive after all but you must let me buy your boys an ice-cream or something in the gift shop whilst we're there in return."

"Deal," responded Gerry. "Plus, I haven't got a grudge against you, so you'll be fine."

"That's nice to know," said Alba. Yet, she was left wondering whether inadvertently he had let slip that he did have a grudge against someone else staying at the hotel. "I'll let Lizzie know," Alba made a point of adding.

"We'll be ready in thirty," confirmed Gerry.

*

It was not one of those properties that took all day to visit. The bailey part of the castle was devoid of structures, save for the little ticket office and shop – a building which was definitely not fourteenth century – and the shell keep, which sat on a natural mound as opposed to a man-made motte, as Gerry had tried to explain to his boys on more than one occasion, was not on the scale that necessitated a lengthy exploration.

It was the type of property that was lovely to go round but somehow lovelier to sit and simply look at; to immerse yourself in the atmosphere, to try and imagine how it would have looked limewashed centuries ago and to appreciate the surrounding countryside. So, what would normally have been a late-morning tea break, before tackling the next section of a castle such as Dover, Bamburgh or Kenilworth, became an early lunch as Alba and Gerry sat on one of the wooden benches having seen everything they wanted to see.

Alba read the little metal plaque fixed to the back-rest of the bench:

In memory of Herbert Thompson 01/08/20 – 17/11/87
Who loved this place.

To the Reverend Matthew Quinn's encouragement, she studied the dash, that little line between the dates, and wondered what joys, unfulfilled dreams and sorrows lay behind that single simple horizontal line. Her mind's eye showed her once more a picture, a picture Matthew had shown her of his late wife but it was gone in an instant as Gerry said:

"Do you want coffee? I've got plenty."

"No, I'm alright with what I've got, thank you," replied Alba, as she poured some hot water onto a tea bag that she had placed in the cup lid of the flask. As it brewed, she commented:

"Some impressive oak trees to look upon but shame there aren't a few more in the surrounding farmland."

"Suppose so," concurred Gerry. "People like driving in straight lines, farmers included, I guess. The boys have enjoyed it here more than I thought they would – oh, and thank you for what you've bought them in the shop. You really didn't have to."

"I said I would get them something. You sure they're alright off by themselves?"

"Yes," replied Gerry. "They're good lads, it's been rough for them this past year. They can wander round it again or just find their own place to sit and chat, even if it's just to talk about whether West Ham can survive in the League this season. They won't do anything daft. Even if they walk round the top of the walls again, they'll behave themselves. It was a nice idea of yours to get them to buy a postcard each to send to their grandparents; had I said it, they might not have been so keen. You even got them to buy them out of their own pocket money – I am impressed."

"It's nothing, just a little life lesson someone taught me a long time ago," replied Alba.

"Thank you for coming today, it's nice to have some adult conversation for a change, nice to be able to have a coffee and my sandwich without also having to play 'Top Trumps' with them and nice not to be barraged with lots of random questions, which they seem to pick up from their Scout Master or youth club leader."

"Such as?" queried Alba, curious as to what they might be.

"Let me think," replied Gerry. As he did, Alba took a bite of her scone, which she had filled with butter and jam in her room before she had left the hotel, and added some milk to her tea.

"OK, this one definitely came from their Scout Master on one of their many hikes. It concerns 'trig points', you know those concrete pyramids that the Ordnance Survey set on numerous high points around the country, so they could do a triangulation of the country in the 1930s. It was upon the pyramids that the OS would set their theodolites and measure angles and distances between that trig point and two others on surrounding high points. So, bearing in mind the importance of there always being three points and the geometric shape of the triangle, the Scout Master's question was 'Why do trig points have four sides and not three?'"

"No idea," Alba said after a pause.

"OK. Try this one – this one came from their youth club leader when she got them making Easter nests, probably out of shredded wheat and melted chocolate, a few weeks back. Actually, a bit early for Easter but never mind that. She asked them to name a food that you can only eat fresh; never frozen, tinned, cooked, pickled or dried, only fresh. I mean, does anyone care? But, of course, the boys come straight home and rather than research it, come and ask me; how on earth am I meant to know?"

Alba offered up oyster and avocado but Gerry rejected both. She opted to finish her scone instead of guessing again.

"Last one then, before you decide to walk all the way back to the hotel rather than listen to these oddities any longer."

"Promise?" challenged Alba.

"Promise and you can probably blame Gregory's history teacher for this one; if a Duke is married to a Duchess, a Marquess is married to a Marchioness and you have Viscount and Viscountess, why is the wife of an Earl a Countess rather than an 'Earl-ess'? So, you can see what I'm up against and why I'm quite happy to let the boys have a bit of freedom at times; gives me a break."

"That's probably something to do with having been conquered by the Normans. It's the same type of inconsistency around having both shires, as in Devonshire, and counties, as in the county of Devon; one's old English and one is Norman French. These are all," Alba said, but now more philosophically, "quirky observations on life and society, aren't they? They remind me of the ones that my favourite university tutor would throw out from time to time. Nothing to do with our subject and often right in the middle of a lecture or tutorial just to keep us on our toes. For example, why, given a toaster toasts, a frying pan fries and a grill grills, do we have the word kettle? A kettle doesn't 'kettle' and no one, as far as I know, says 'I'm going to kettle some water'. It was always about encouraging us to think abstractly, to never assume and to always question why things are the way they are – and to get us students talking amongst ourselves."

With that, Alba smiled to herself and nodded ever so fractionally and unnoticed by Gerry, in appreciation of her former tutor, Dr John Sunday. "Thinking about it," Alba said, "I should write to him again and put your boys' questions to him, especially the one about trig points."

As his boys walked past, discussing who should be dropped from the West Ham United team for the weekend game, Gerry called to them that they had about ten more minutes before heading back to the car.

"As we've finished here much earlier than I expected, I'll have time to take them down to the beach before dinner once we're back at the hotel, which the boys will enjoy."

"Another day you should take them to Glendurgan Gardens, they're over by Falmouth. Very impressive and managed by the National Trust now."

"Look, I can get them to come to a castle and have them spend a few moments thinking about the history of the place but you kind of witnessed the battle I had with them this morning trying to get them up for this outing – I can't even imagine the challenge I'd have if they knew they were going to some gardens!"

"Yes, I realise that," replied Alba. "But there's an impressive maze there and the gardens drop down to the most idyllic cove at the bottom – almost heavenly apart from the fact that the toilets are all the way back up by the ticket office. Think your boys would enjoy it, so long as you 'sold it to them' as losing themselves in a maze and discovering a lost cove. Given you've got English Heritage membership, have you got National Trust membership as well? Oh, and thank you again for paying for my ticket here, I must pay you back before I forget."

"Sort of. And, as for paying me back, please don't worry. It was nice to hear you chatting to the lads about the Black Prince whilst I sorted out tickets and it didn't cost me anything."

"Didn't it? But it must have," said Alba.

"No, really, but if anyone asks whilst we're here, you're officially my wife – you came in on our family ticket."

"You're married?" said a surprised Alba.

"Yes, just about. You are a better version if I may say so whilst the boys are out of earshot. It's been nice to not have been told off by my 'wife' so far today, be it for my driving, how I interact with the boys or quibbling over money in the shop. Still, I am married. Our birthday presents to each other, each year, are English Heritage membership, which she gives me, and National Trust membership which I give her. So, I should be able to take the boys to, where did you say?"

"Glendurgan Gardens."

"To Glendurgan but I might have a problem getting in, since the membership department made a mistake this year and rather than send her a family National Trust ticket, they sent her an 'Adult and one'. Only noticed it yesterday when I tried to use it at another of their properties and had a bit of a 'to do' with the offish ticket office attendant. I kept saying the surname was correct and the boys were very much her children but they wouldn't have it as she wasn't with me; I had to go and buy tickets to get in. Really annoying; just hope I can reclaim the money, once I'm back from holiday and can write to the membership department. Would probably have the same problem at these gardens near Falmouth which you are recommending."

"So, where were you yesterday?" asked Alba.

However, the return of his two boys prevented any response from Gerry.

"We're bored now. Can we go?" said Ben, Gerry's younger son.

"Yeah, we can eat in the car going back and you've had your lunch already," stated Gregory.

"Where did you get taken yesterday, lads?" asked Alba as casually as she could.

However, both children blanked her as they persisted in pressurizing their father.

"Can we go? Please!" pleaded one.

"Please," echoed the other.

"Alright," said Gerry. "Well, hold on, let me just check with our guest." Turning to Alba, he asked:

"Is that OK with you – are you done here?"

Alba, had she been here by herself would have happily walked around the castle grounds once more, challenging herself to identify as many wild flowers as she could and photographing the ones she could not, to research once she was home and had had the pictures developed. Feeling outnumbered and recognising that the boys were now bored, she acquiesced – well, almost.

"Yes, that's fine. I'll just put my stuff away." As she took the last mouthful of tea from her flask lid and then shook it dry, she added, as she gestured with a wave of her left arm, "Can we walk round that way back to the car? I think I saw something earlier that I'd like to show to you two boys."

"Sounds good to me," said Gerry.

"What?" said the boys in unison. "What have you found?" added Ben.

"Some soldiers!" proclaimed Alba to the bewilderment of the two boys.

"No, no you haven't," insisted Gregory. "We've been wandering round for ages, whilst you two have been sitting here doing nothing."

"Yeah, ages," agreed Ben.

"And there are definitely no soldiers anywhere in this castle," continued Gregory.

"Oh, but there are – and sailors, too!" replied Alba.

"No, there aren't, you're just being daft," insisted Ben.

"Yeah, mucking us around – what do you reckon dad?" asked Gregory.

"Well, if Alba has seen something we've all missed, best she shows us but she's probably teasing you both."

"I'm not – promise you," stated Alba.

"Come on then," called out Ben, as he made off in the direction Alba had indicated. "Come on Gregory."

"You owe us an ice-cream if you're playing a trick on us," said Gregory.

"Another one?" replied Alba but her comment went unheard by Gregory as he too ran off, trying to overtake his brother.

"Trick or not, they seem happy again. Good to go?" asked Gerry.

"Yes, thank you."

"Lettuce, before I forget," said Gerry.

"Pardon?"

"Lettuce – the food you can't tin, cook, freeze, whatever but can only eat fresh. Lettuce," confirmed Gerry.

"Oh, yes," concurred Alba, making a note to herself to ask her friends back at Hillstone Hall that one.

*

As the four of them approached another oak tree on their way back to Gerry's car, Alba announced:

"There, under that oak."

"Where? I don't see nothing," threw back Ben.

"Anything, I don't see *anything*, not nothing, Ben" corrected his dad.

"OK," Ben replied but he was more focussed on whatever trick or lie his dad's new found friend was playing on himself and his brother. "But there's no one there," he added.

"Yes, there is," repeated Alba. "You have to look carefully, mind you. Can you see? There nesting in the shade of the tree – some soldiers and some sailors, too. They're quite small, so don't tread on them."

And there in the shade of the tree, just as Alba had said there would be, were some little blue and pink flowers belonging to *Pulmonaria officinalis*.

"What, I don't see any soldiers, just some silly flowers," said a disappointed Gregory.

Alba, though, bent down to the flowers and cradled one stem in her hand. She spoke ever so softly, almost reverently, and for some inexplicable reason, and to Gerry's amazement, the two young boys crouched down beside Alba to look as well.

"Soldiers and sailors – see. Told you there'd be some. Red and blue flowers coming off the same plant; don't you think that's amazing? I do," said Alba.

"Cool!" said Ben.

"They're called that as the red is the colour of the jackets soldiers used to wear before it all became khaki; you know that dull browny-yellow colour."

"Red, like we would have worn at Waterloo," offered up Gregory.

"That's right – where General Blücher saved the day," but Gerry's comment was not picked up on by the boys, who were still down at ground level with Alba.

"And the blue, by means of elimination, represents the uniforms of sailors," added Alba.

"Cool!" repeated Ben. "Come on Gregory, let's go and see if we can find some more soldiers and sailors, come on, bet I can find more than you." As Ben stood up, he turned to his father and said, "Can we have five more minutes dad, just five, I want to see if there are any more?"

A nod of consent from Gerry was all that was needed before both boys were off, rushing this way and that.

"I'm speechless," admitted Gerry.

"*Pulmonaria officinalis*, 'soldiers and sailors', such beautiful spring flowers. Common name Lungwort."

"Lungwort?" repeated Gerry in uncertain terms.

"Yes – lungwort. So called as the speckled green and white oval leaves are meant to symbolise lungs. Hence the first part of the name – 'lung'. And the fancy name, *Pulmonaria officinalis*, well that derives from the Latin, *pulmo* for lung. In centuries past, doctors, or perhaps more accurately herbalists, would use this plant to treat infections of the lung. There was a belief back then that plants with medicinal qualities, took on characteristics of that part of the body that they were meant to treat. The leaves look like a cross-section of a diseased lung."

"Really?" said an unbelieving Gerry.

"Yes," insisted Alba. "I mean, I wouldn't start eating it now but somewhere within that folklore will be some truth – and enough of my horticultural books mention it, so there's something to it."

"Well, I'll be – " but Gerry was drowned out by a shout from beyond the castle's chapel of "Found another one, that's three more than you."

As Gerry and Alba slowly walked the remainder of the distance to his car, Alba, worried how far the boys would go off in their new found enthusiasm for plant hunting, asked:

"They're not going to get lost, are they?"

"No, they'll be fine."

"Good," said Alba. "Wouldn't want more people going missing from the hotel, one's enough."

Gerry stopped, turned to Alba and then spoke.

"You don't really think he's missing do you? Surely, he's simply left her, taken the car, rushed back to their home in wherever to collect what he wants and will have moved in with his new love before wifey realises what's going on. He's not missing."

"But he didn't take the car," responded Alba. "Stella drove back to the hotel and Joshua, her husband, was meant to return by taxi."

"OK, so he didn't drive off. He probably got a taxi himself, I guess to Penzance station, and was on a train before she was even missing him."

"Perhaps," Alba said. "And yet –"

"And yet what?" queried Gerry.

"And yet, I know her. Stella's an old school friend, you see."

"Is she?"

"Yes, sat next to her every registration period for five years. Having been with her yesterday evening, comforting her, and again with her over breakfast this morning, there was nothing, absolutely nothing from her to even suggest there was anything untoward going on between the pair of them."

"Well, if you say so but I've never spoken to the husband."

"Nor had I, until yesterday," admitted Alba.

"Hadn't you? Oh, I'd got the impression just then that you were good friends – surely you'd have gone to her wedding, stayed in touch and so on, if you'd been friends for so many years?" queried Gerry.

"Well, I guess. We were but – " with that, though, Alba fell silent.

Gerry, not sure whether he had 'unscrewed a bottle' he should not have, but having learnt from his wife not to pursue something she did not want to talk about, opted for a more positive comment:

"Well, maybe he'll be back by the time we've driven back. Wonder what he's like; I saw him across the breakfast area yesterday but I wonder what he is like as a person."

"As I say, I only saw him briefly yesterday," said Alba.

"Did you? When?"

"Yesterday lunchtime, just as I'd arrived at the hotel. In reception."

"What was he like?" asked an intrigued Gerry.

"Hard to say. I'd just walked into the hotel's reception and the clock was striking twelve."

CHAPTER 5

Thursday: Twelve noon

And so, Alba recalled to Gerry the events of her arrival at 'The Jupiter Hotel' the previous lunchtime. Her recollections described it thus –

*

The aged grandfather clock was striking the hour as Alba walked into reception of 'The Jupiter Hotel'.

"Ah, it is good to be back," she announced even though there was no one to hear her but herself.

She placed her two bags down, one a purple 'Trespass' rucksack, which she had been carrying by the grab handle, and the other a medium-sized black canvass holdall, so she could look at her watch. Her watch was a couple of minutes fast, or at least faster than the clock that was currently chiming, but accurate enough to inform her that the final two chimes were the eleventh and twelfth of the sequence. The clock then once again resumed its relative silence.

"Twelve noon, I've made it in good time," Alba said to Robyn, who had now appeared at the reception desk having heard the front doors go – Robyn making a mental note to herself to wedge the doors open, with the wooden doorstops, to ease the passage of entry for any other similarly encumbered traveller.

Alba repositioned her sunglasses, with their tortoiseshell effect rims, on her head and, as casually as she could as she tried to contain her joy at being back, said:

"Afternoon Robyn."

Robyn had noted Alba's name in the diary earlier in the week, as being due to arrive today, but the usual busyness of the hotel, plus having offered to cover for Lizzie this Thursday lunchtime, had pushed it from Robyn's mind – so, it was only with Alba's personal address did Robyn actually recognise who had just walked in, bag in each hand and with sunglasses on the cusp of slipping down her head.

"Alba! So sorry, didn't recognise you, well, I sort of did but didn't process, actually was thinking of something else and, oh, never mind, it's lovely to see you." With that, Robyn extracted herself from behind the desk and warmly embraced Alba. "It is really good to see you again," said the member of staff.

"Keeping well, I trust," said Alba and with that the two women lost themselves to a world of catching up, the traffic on the A30 once past Bodmin Moor and Robyn's dogs – with Robyn suggesting that perhaps the two of them could take her dogs for a walk together one afternoon. Robyn, who was in her late twenties, so a few years younger than Alba, returned to the 'business side' of the reception desk and called through to Alan about Alba's arrival.

As the two women continued to chat, the front doors opened once again and, in addition to Robyn's, Alba could hear new voices from the people who had just entered:

"Didn't think we'd make such good time – reckon if we have a quick bite to eat as we change, we might make St. Michael's Mount as well today after all; would be good to get there as well as we're here for such a short time. That boat ride was lovely – excellent idea of yours dear," said a male voice.

"Yes, it was, wasn't it! You go up – shower if you need to since you got wetter than I did. I'll order some lunch to eat in the room; I just hope they'll have time to bring it up," replied a female.

"I'm sure they will. We've had food in the room on previous days – I don't see it being a problem for them now."

"OK," conceded the female. "What do you fancy by way of food?"

"Cheese sandwiches, actually maybe a roll and some Cornish Blue. Egg, at a pinch. Anything vegetarian as you well know. Thanks love."

With that he bounded up the stairs, calling out as he went "I'll leave the door wedged with my sandal so you can get in if I'm showering."

"Alright. I'll be up as soon as I've ordered," replied the female.

Alba took a step to the side, to allow the other woman the 'floor' and to indicate to Robyn that she could deal with this other guest first. Robyn followed Alba's prompt and spoke to the newly returned guest:

"May I help?"

"Good afternoon, yes, sorry, unless you were dealing with this other person already," replied Stella.

"No, it's fine," contributed Alba, not looking up as she studied the opening times for Restormel Castle in her guidebook, which she had retrieved from her rucksack.

"Thanks," said Stella. Then to Robyn, she continued, "Would it be possible to have some lunch brought up to our room?"

"I'd have thought so but I should check with our chef first," answered Robyn.

"Oh, OK. But it's been alright the last couple of days when we've asked."

"I didn't know," replied Robyn. "I don't normally do lunchtimes but Lizzie wanted the time off. If the hotel has done it for you on previous days, then that's OK; I'll just take your order through to Alan and I'll bring it up when he's done it. What would you like?"

"Cheese sandwiches, maybe rolls, perhaps with Cornish Blue or some similar cheese, otherwise some egg sandwiches," said Alba out loud, in a way that Diane Chambers would have been proud of in that very first episode of the American TV sit-com 'Cheers'.

"As for anything else, well, I can only guess," continued Alba, her cheekiness emboldened by her recent arrival and sense of feeling that she had come 'home'. "Perhaps some grapes, a pot of chutney, I can't decide whether to go for butter or margarine, probably no crisps given the swiftness of your husband as he headed up the stairs, too unhealthy for him I guess, and so, instead, a couple of apples. Definitely no cold meats."

With that Alba lifted her eyes from her guidebook and turned to the woman to her right, adding as she did so, "Sorry, couldn't help overhearing your conversation as the pair of you came in. As for drinks, mineral water perhaps? Maybe fruit juice? As for something sweet – "

Yet Alba did not finish what would have been her suggestion of a slice of carrot cake with two forks so it could be shared, for a stunned bewilderment fell upon Alba as she studied the woman she had just been addressing. Stella stared back – as she tried to match the other's voice to someone she once knew. A stunned silence fell across both of them as they each processed who the other was.

*

"Oh my word!" said Alba first. "Stella! It's you. I don't believe it."

"Alba, Alba White! It can't be!"

"Stella Winterman! My dear Stella – gosh, how many years has it been? Five, six?"

Yet Stella, still stunned by the other's presence did not answer. Instead, as she got over her shock, or perhaps so she could process who it was that was standing next to her, she turned to Robyn and said, "Yes, that'll be fine for our lunch if we can have one bottle of sparkling mineral water and one of apple juice, please. And taken up to our room please, we're in a bit of a rush."

Only then did Stella return her attention to Alba:

"It is you, isn't it? I can't believe it. What the blazes are you doing here?"

"Just got here on holiday; I – "

"You're staying here?" interrupted Stella.

"Well, I will be once I finally stop boring Robyn with my news and actually let her book me in."

"She's not boring me, not at all," said Robyn to Stella. "It's good to have her back with us and it's been lovely to catch up. She's like one of the family – she always stays with us when she comes to Cornwall. Well, that's what she tells me!"

With that, Robyn gave Alba a wink before continuing, having taken something off the board from behind herself:

"Alba, here's your room key; room nine, as always. I can formally book you in later when you're not here. But I'll leave you two chatting, guess you are old friends. I'll take the food order through to the kitchen."

"Less of the old," replied Stella. "But yes – we were at secondary school together. We were good friends."

"Greensands Comprehensive," added Alba but Stella's use of the past tense, when describing their friendship was not lost on Alba, even if it went undetected by Robyn. "Same form. Sat next to each other every registration period morning and afternoon for five years. Had to sit in alphabetical order, you see. Could have been a dull five years but Alba White and Stella Winterman got on riotously."

"Winterman?" said a puzzled Robyn, not recognising the name.

"My maiden name," Stella clarified. "Here, obviously, I'm signed in as Mrs Mallory."

"Oh, right," said a comprehending Robyn. "I'll get your food sorted. You still want me to bring it up or have your plans suddenly changed now you've bumped into Alba?"

"No. If Joshua and I could have it in our room, that would be good."

"OK," replied Robyn. "Oh, I'll also bring up a phone number or two for taxi firms which you were asking after last night."

"Thanks, that would be useful since he'll be needing one later."

With that, the person behind the desk headed into the kitchen, leaving Stella to explain why her plans were not about to change. Alba would have loved it if Stella and her husband did change their plans, if only so she, Alba, could offer some kind of face-to-face apology to the others – not that Alba, even after the passing of a few years, could even formulate into words why she had let Stella down. In one sense she still did not know herself but Alba hoped that if she just could say 'sorry', even if she still could not explain why, then that at least might start the healing process. 'If only Stella would change her plans' thought Alba but she knew she could not press it.

"We're due off home tomorrow," stated Stella. "Joshua is keen to see St Michael's Mount before we go. That's why we've rushed back from our boat trip this morning, which was something I wanted to do, and we are going to try and fit the island in before Joshua has to be at a property he's going to be working on. He's an architect, in case you'd forgotten."

"No, I remembered," insisted Alba, keen to stress she had not erased Mr and Mrs Mallory from her mind. "So, is most of his work based down here now?" Alba added.

"No, it's just a one-off," stated Stella. "Someone from Winchester is selling his late father's property down here; selling it to a friend, or a friend of a friend, something like that. Then, knowing the buyer would want to modernise it and knowing about the firm Joshua works for, the person selling recommended the firm to the person buying it. The architects' firm Joshua works for is still in Salisbury, as we are, too. He's not a partner yet but he will be one day soon – they're very happy with him and the senior partner, in particular, likes his approach to sustainability within the plans Joshua comes up with."

"Salisbury is lovely. A friend – "

Yet Stella cut across what Alba was about to say:

THURSDAY: TWELVE NOON

"Lovely, yes, just so long as you don't have to be anywhere at eight thirty in the morning. The ring-road, if you can call it that, is just awful and as for the Southampton Road, just don't get me started. But I really must head up to the room, we were tight for time already and I've been down here far longer than I expected to be."

"Sorry," said Alba. "I didn't want to detain you but it is nice to see you. A surprise for sure."

"I'll say," agreed Stella.

"But really nice to see you. It has been too long. Sorry I haven't written more recently."

"It's fine," stated Stella matter-of-factly. "Look, I must head up, wash my face and change – these jeans have absorbed so much salt, they're beginning to feel like an exoskeleton."

"Sorry," repeated Alba.

"Look. Joshua will wonder what's going on down here and he wants to see the Mount. As I say, we're due off tomorrow morning but maybe though we can catch up this evening. It is nice to see you."

With that, Stella placed her right hand on Alba's upper left arm, offered a smile and then moved to head up the stairs. She turned, just before she went out of sight and added:

"You're looking well. Slim as ever – see you after dinner perhaps."

With that, Stella was gone from view, leaving Alba to listen to the creaks of the wooden staircase, as Stella took them two at a time.

*

Key in hand, Alba was about to pick up her two bags and head up herself when Robyn's reappearance with a lunch tray, prompted the former to stay still and let the other get by and up the stairs to deliver some warmed rolls, a small cheese board and a couple of bottles of drink. As she went past, Robyn spoke:

"Actually, Alba, don't disappear. I need you to confirm your car registration. I'll only be a moment."

"That's fine. You get them their lunch as they're in a hurry. I'll be here – I'll see if there are any interesting leaflets in the box on the table whilst I wait."

"Don't get your hopes up – they're the standard ones! They're the same year after year," Robyn called down, though now out of sight herself from Alba, and said out of several years of having to stare at that same box from the reception desk and the almost daily ritual of having to tidy them up; to undo all the mess young children would make, whenever they passed, as they took a glut of leaflets to show their parents and duly being forced to return almost all of them. On being so instructed, they would simply dump them in the slot with the most space or simply leave them strewn across the table, if they made the table at all – the child somehow thinking that if the leaflet was on, or even under, the same piece of furniture as the box it came from was on, that counted as 'putting it back'.

*

"Don't tell me you've found a new one!" exclaimed Robyn on her return a few minutes later – having noticed Alba holding a leaflet, though now studying the aged map of the county on the wall.

"Probably not but it's one of the tin mines I haven't got to yet. It's over in the Penwith District so I might not make it this week but we'll see."

"Any definite plans whilst you're with us?" asked Robyn.

"Hopefully Restormel Castle tomorrow but, as for the rest of today, falling asleep on the bed, listening to the gulls as I drift off, given I set off really early this morning."

"Oh, I'm walking the dogs this afternoon. As I was suggesting earlier, you'd be very welcome to come with us."

"It's kind of you but I think I'll just crash out in the room this afternoon. Another afternoon would be lovely but I promised myself, as I stood in the queue at 'Stapleton's', our little village store

THURSDAY: TWELVE NOON

back home, as I waited to cancel my newspaper delivery whilst I was away, that once I'd got here today, I wouldn't rush off and try and do anything else. I would simply enjoy being here – call me boring, call me simple, call me unadventurous but, at this moment in time, I just want to be here. OK, I might, just might, walk down to the cove later this afternoon, with a flask of tea and a hand towel and dip my toes in the water, but nothing more than that."

"Ah, bless you. Lizzie always says you're like part of the family down here and wishes you came a bit more often. So, I hear you – but promise you'll come out another day with me."

"Promise," replied Alba.

"Good, it will be nice to have someone to walk with. I mean, I'll enjoy this afternoon's stroll but some girlie chat wouldn't go amiss!"

"Another afternoon, I promise."

At that moment Alan brought out a pot of tea and two slices of Victoria sponge.

"I could hear you two still chatting so I thought I'd bring you something out. Lovely to see you Alba. Staying long?"

"A week. Good to see you too. This is kind of you – how much do I owe you?"

"On the house. They're the last two slices and might be a bit too dry for anyone coming in later this afternoon. I'll make another one for people coming in tomorrow but someone has to eat these soonest. Can't stop just at the moment but I'll catch up with you. Enjoy!" With that, Alan returned to his kitchen.

"Blow, I'm never going to get up to my room at this rate."

"Nor me get to walk the dogs!" added Robyn. Nonetheless they both tucked in.

"You'll need to give the dogs a good walk to burn off this cake," joked Alba. "It's delicious – definitely not as dry as Alan was claiming. These would have been fine to have served to any walker or the like calling in for tea and cake this afternoon. Alan's too kind."

Once again, the two women were lost to a world of catching up and random conversation, though this time accompanied by the pot of tea and what remained of their slices of cake.

*

Over half an hour later, they were still chatting but Robyn had at least, somewhere within that time, formally booked Alba in to room nine of 'The Jupiter Hotel'. Voices from the stairs, announcing the presence of other guests, drew their conversations to a close.

"I really must head up and let you get on," concluded Alba. However, she was somewhat drowned out by a male voice who was down the last few stairs and at, and then past, Alba's right shoulder before she had looked round.

"You hand the room key in, Stella dear, and book a table for tonight. The dining area was pretty full last night and I don't want to go having to look for somewhere else to eat tonight once I'm back from my site visit. I'll see you at the car." Then noting Alba's continued presence in reception, he added, in slightly sarcastic tones, "And Stella, dear, please try to be quicker than when you ordered us our lunch – we're going to be pushed for time as it is now."

With that he was out the front doors and heading round to the hotel's car park, jangling his bunch of keys as loudly as he could as he did so as if to make his point once more.

"Yes Joshua," replied Stella, as she in turn came down the stairs. She, though, stopped at the reception desk to do the other's bidding.

"Ah, you're still here, Alba. Sorry to butt in but may I?"

"Don't worry," answered Alba. "You're in a rush; I'm not."

"We are, rather." Then directing her comments to Robyn, Stella continued:

"Just returning the room key – don't want to lose it on the beach or the island. And the key fob is so cumbersome."

"Intentionally so," replied the woman behind the desk. "They do somewhat encourage residents to leave them with us when they go out for the day. Definitely fewer get lost over the season as a result."

"Clever," commented Alba.

"And may we have a table booked for this evening; by a window would be nice as it's our last evening here," said Stella.

"Well, the best two have already been booked but we'll find you the next best one, if that's OK? Time?"

"That's fine. Seven, seven-thirty perhaps?"

"I'll book you in for seven-fifteen."

"Perfect, thanks." With that, Stella literally ran out to catch her man up – and prompting Robyn to once again think she needed to utilise the two wooden, mice adorned, doorstops to wedge the hotel's front doors open.

Robyn then spoke to Alba:

"With regards to table bookings for tonight, Alba, don't worry, we've already given you one of the best two tables; you're virtually family, after all."

"You're kind. Right, this time I really am heading up to my room," and with that, and room key in hand, she picked up her luggage and headed up the wooden staircase.

"See you this evening," called up Robyn.

Robyn, who heard an 'OK' in reply, picked up her shoulder bag and car keys and was about to head out herself but a commotion at the front doors prevented her speedy departure. This was because a different, a new, woman got herself caught up, or more precisely got her rucksack straps caught up, on the handles to those front doors and then duly dropped one of her walking poles, which virtually tripped her as it fell between her legs.

As Robyn went to assist, Alba, who had not made it into her bedroom and so heard the doors go and voices down in reception, rushed back down the stairs, in the hope that Stella and her husband had had a change of heart and now wanted to include Alba in their afternoon plans after all.

However, as she descended and made the final turn of the staircase, she could see at the opposite end of reception another woman – but clearly not Stella – still untangling herself and her baggage from the front doors. Seeing Robyn was already helping, by wedging one of the doors out of the woman's way, Alba ventured down no further and instead headed back to bedroom number nine. Room nine was *her* room. It was not, on paper, the best room the hotel had to offer but it was her favourite.

*

Once she had helped to extricate the new arrival from her entanglement, Robyn booked the woman in as quickly as politeness would allow, fearing her dogs would never get walked otherwise.

Paperwork completed and room directions given, Robyn returned Stella and Joshua's room key to the relevant hook on the wall behind her. As Robyn departed, it slowly rocked itself motionless until it too was as still as the two wooden mice in their new locations, which were now very firmly each wedging one of the hotel's front doors wide open.

CHAPTER 6

Full Circle

With her finally having got to *her* bedroom and telling herself that it was 'good to be back', Alba's account of her arrival on Thursday lunchtime drew to a close.

*

"…So, with all of that, by the time I headed up from reception, with Robyn saying she was also heading over to Marazion, the clock was nearer to striking one than to twelve, as it had been doing as I arrived," continued Alba to Gerry. By now, they were back at his car having 'done' Restormel Castle. "On reflection," she added, "it was more Stella I spoke to than Joshua. He was in a rush."

"No wonder," contributed Gerry. "If I had had a meeting to be at by five o'clock yesterday afternoon, I'd have been rushing the boys as much as he was rushing his wife to get to the island; if anything, I'm surprised he wasn't more agitated than you've just described in your recounting of your arrival at the hotel yesterday."

"Fair point." Alba then fell silent as she looked back to the castle over the roof of Gerry's grey Audi car.

Having put rucksacks and boys' coats in the boot, Gerry finally broke into Alba's silence:

"Sure you're finished here? I mean, I hope so – don't really think the boys fancy doing it a second time in one day."

"Sorry, I was just thinking."

"Something from the gift shop you're regretting not buying? That bottle of strawberry wine that you sampled?" teased Gerry. "Though the ginger wine was better, if you want my opinion."

"If you say so. But look – " and, with that, Alba looked straight at Gerry and said:

"Do you think he got to his meeting?"

"You still think he's missing?"

"Yes, I do," answered Alba.

"I think," replied Gerry as he moved around to the front of the car and gently sat against the bonnet – inviting Alba to do the same – "you're confusing 'missing due to foul play' with 'missing because he's done a runner'. You've already said he was in a rush, so much so he hardly spoke to you, but perhaps he was in a rush as he didn't want to keep his lover waiting. Maybe she was parked up somewhere waiting to collect him. Or, perhaps, he had to be at Penzance station for a particular train or the helipad near Gulval to fly over to the Isles of Scilly and hide there for a few days. So, yes, he's missing but I think you need to consider from whom he's missing."

As Gerry twirled his car key around one finger, he continued:

"Look, my instinct is he's done a runner to hook up with his new love, maybe with an old love or maybe with a lover he's always had but somehow a marriage to someone else, this Stella woman, got in the way. Maybe, even, his lover isn't meeting him, well not yet, but he's gone to get things ready for when she can join him – when she, too, can 'flee' wherever she currently is. So, in order to put his half of their plan into action, he's found the quietest, remotest, most reserved of hotels and has gone missing himself. Probably it was a sham meeting he set up for five o'clock, or at least one he definitely had no intention of keeping and so gained himself a few extra hours 'flight' time."

"I guess – and yet, I feel I should help."

"Why? I mean, I get she's an old friend but you've been a bit cagey on that, if I may be so blunt. Where does this compulsion to get involved in a former friend's failing marriage come from? It will, as seems to be beginning to happen, ruin your holiday. I don't get it – better, surely, to leave it all to the police."

An elderly couple parked next to them. As the new arrivals got out of their car, the man, under his cloth cap, clinked his two metal walking sticks together, as he retrieved them from behind his driver's seat. As he did so, his grey-haired wife pulled herself up out of her seat by holding, with a vice-like grip that was very much out of keeping with her age, onto the open car door on her side. As they emerged, Alba spoke softly to Gerry:

"It's complicated."

Gerry turned and looked at Alba, perched as she was next to him on the car bonnet. Turning back to admire the view, he simply, quietly said:

"Try me."

Alba sighed.

The sigh prompted Gerry to speak again:

"I won't judge – we've all got skeletons in our closets."

Alba sighed again. However, just as Gerry was about to give up on her, stand up and make for the driver's seat, Alba spoke:

"I let her down."

"OK," acknowledged Gerry. "But haven't we all let friends down over the years? Life gets busy and promises, plans, offers to help hastily agreed over the telephone, as you chat on a random evening, with a glass of wine in your hand."

"Or cup of tea," suggested Alba.

"Or some other drink," conceded Gerry, "but promises which are then regretted in the cold light of the following morning as you realise you've over-committed yourself: what seemed like a good idea the night before, you suddenly see as ruining a quiet weekend that you'd set aside for yourself. Never phone friends after eight o'clock in the evening that's my advice!"

"I don't know about that but I let both of them down. Both of them, Stella and Joshua."

"How so? You've made out so far today you hardly knew him."

"I didn't go to their wedding."

As the elderly lady, from the adjacent car returned to collect her coat, she spoke to the 'couple' perched on the Audi's bonnet:

"Weather's on the turn, so I think I'll take this with me after all. And my Frank says a proper storm is coming in this evening as well, don't you know," she said as she jiggled her quilted 'Bonmarché' jacket in their direction. "Your boys are behaving themselves nicely, if I may say, as the two of you sit there chatting."

"Oh, errr, thanks," responded Gerry. "Packs of 'Top Trumps' are worth their weight in gold sometimes. Enjoy your visit."

"Thank you – we come every week."

With that the elderly lady headed back to her husband, so they could go and sit on the same wooden bench that they sat on every Friday to have their lunch, the same lunch they always had – a pork pie, cut into eight pieces, lettuce, tomatoes, some pickled onions, for him, one slice of buttered brown bread each and one small packet of crisps between them. This week, it was his choice of flavour and to his wife's annoyance he had selected cheese and onion – still, she would get her own back on him next week when she would choose ready salted.

*

"Sorry," said Gerry to Alba, once the lady was out of earshot. "Thought it was simpler to let her think they're our boys. If we'd started to explain that you and I only met this morning, that my actual wife is somewhere else and we're talking about a missing person, we might have given her too much to take in."

"Good call and, if she goes off thinking we're a happy family, is that so wrong?"

"No, I don't think it is."

"Sometimes beauty is better than the truth," declared Alba.

"Very poetic," offered back Gerry.

"It's sort of CS Lewis – a friend, our local vicar in fact, has lent me some of Lewis's books which I've been reading," explained Alba.

"That's nice of him. But going back to what you were saying – not going to your friend's wedding hardly warrants you placing yourself in purgatory for ever and a day. There was a friend's wedding we never got to; it happens."

"I only told her on the morning of her wedding."

"Unfortunate but not the end of the world," offered back Gerry supportively.

"I was her sole bridesmaid – well, was meant to be."

"Oh!"

"Oh, indeed," observed Alba.

"Ah," said Gerry – offering a different sound but still expressing the same shock.

"Yes," stated Alba to the questions and thoughts that were only just beginning to form in Gerry's mind. "Yes," repeated Alba, "I was meant to be Stella's solitary bridesmaid – she had only ever wanted one, she said, and when she asked me, she added 'she wouldn't need more than me if I was there for her'. So, 'Oh!' probably doesn't quite capture it. Mind you, 'Oh!' is definitely 'cleaner' than what Stella said to me on the phone that morning once I'd called her."

"At least you called. That's something, I guess," offered Gerry clutching at the only straw going.

"You're clutching at the solitary straw," replied Alba. "I clutched at it for a while but it didn't get me anywhere; didn't repair my friendship with Stella, didn't take my guilt away, didn't explain it, didn't –"

"Why?" Gerry asked, unable to restrain himself any longer. He turned to study her as he waited for an answer – though he was not convinced one would be forthcoming.

As he did so, however, something caught his eye just beyond Alba. It was not that the thing which had caught his eye had just moved, for it had not. Rather it was perhaps a dip in Alba's shoulder as she sunk into herself a fraction more as she sought for an answer to his question; an answer, that in some real sense, she had been searching for for several years. Or perhaps it was the gust of wind that caught her hair and his eyes followed the line of movement until they rested on what he had just seen. Or maybe he felt just a little bit of guilt in looking at her in the way he knew he was when he was already married.

"They've left their car window down," observed Gerry as he verbalised what had just caught his eye.

"Have they?" replied Alba, grateful to be drawn out of her memories and guilt.

"Yeah – and enough for the rain to get in, if it does start coming down, or for someone to get their hand in and reach the handle."

"We ought to go and tell them," stated Alba. "Can't drive back to our hotel, pretending we haven't noticed."

"Tell you what. I'll ask the boys to run and tell them."

"Think they will?" challenged Alba.

"Yeah, I think so. They're good lads and, once I explain why I want them to help, I'm sure they will."

"We'll have to promise to leave as soon as they return: they've been sitting in the car a good while already."

"Yes," agreed Gerry.

*

As the boys headed off, after their initial grumble, Gerry turned once more to Alba and he tried not to gaze at her in the way he knew he just had been doing.

"So?" he resumed. "And look," he added encouragingly, "as I said we've all got skeletons in our closets."

"So you say. And yours is?" she said almost petulantly and she immediately hated herself for how she had just spoken to her companion for the day. "I'm so sorry," she instantly said. "That came out all wrong and it wasn't a challenge. Please try and forget what I just said." With that she placed both her hands, palms down, with fingers interlocked, on top of her head, arched her head and neck backwards and thought to herself what an insensitive fool she could still sometimes be.

"As I say, please forget I just said anything," she repeated.

"Think I should have got you running to find the elderly couple and not my boys," replied Gerry, keen to lift the burden from Alba's shoulders. "That way, that comment would never have been said."

"I'll say," replied Alba, relieved the other had opted to lighten the mood.

"But since you asked, I might as well tell you."

"No, I wasn't asking, really I wasn't," and this time it was Alba who turned and was speaking directly to the other.

Gerry, though, chose to tell her anyway:

"My wife, Tania, is in prison. Unlike the friend, who you mentioned earlier at breakfast, my wife is a sentenced prisoner. She's serving two years and four months; I've yet to understand why it's such a seemingly random length – part of me wants to say make it two and a half years and be done with it, stop all the silliness with this third of a year, but of course that's me thinking in the abstract for this is my wife I'm talking about and I wouldn't wish her to be in there any longer than she already has to be, for the boys' sake if no one else's."

Gerry pulled at one of his ear lobes and then crossed and uncrossed his arms before adding:

"For the boys' sake. For me, I'm embarrassed to admit, life seems just a little bit simpler without her around. Well, maybe not simpler, what with her ongoing appeal and the reporters at the door."

"Yes, you mentioned them in the breakfast room earlier – along with police officers," contributed Alba.

"Did I? Oh, yes, I did, didn't I?"

Alba nodded.

"Not simpler," continued Gerry, "but definitely less intense. I'm getting used to not being told off and these past few months I've felt I've been able to breathe; I'd forgotten what that was like."

He paused before adding, as if he had to convince himself of the fact:

"But she'll be home soon, sooner if her appeal is successful. She'll have served half her time but will be released subject to licence for a few months thereafter – meaning she'll be answerable to the probation service. Well, that's how it's been explained to me. But the appeal could change all that."

"She's innocent, then?" queried Alba optimistically.

Yet to Alba's intrigue, Gerry simply stated that the appeal was ongoing before he added:

"However, Alba, err; you know what? I don't actually know your surname – mine's Detz, by the way, Gerald Detz."

"White," volunteered Alba in return, "I'm Alba White."

"That's an elegant name," said Gerry. "But where was I? Yes, I know. However, enough of my travails, for now at least. Perhaps another day, perhaps not, I'm just saying we all have skeletons in our – "

"Closets, yes, I get it and I'm sorry, I really wasn't prying," insisted Alba.

"Look, it's fine. I'd been feeling bad when we were having lunch that I hadn't mentioned it but it's not the easiest thing to bring into a conversation – especially as I was having, am having, such a nice time. Still, I've mentioned it now. So, Miss White, before the boys get back, for I think I can hear them again, so they must be heading back, do you want to say why you let Stella down?"

Alba glanced at the sky, closed her eyes for a moment, took a series of deep breaths and then spoke:

"I don't know, not really, not even after five or so years. To be clear, though, it wasn't that I was jealous of her, for I was thrilled to be asked, I really was. Nor was it out of spite or that I have some wicked, dark side to me, although I guess I did that morning. I just froze that morning. There I was, in a luxurious hotel bedroom, with the dress laid out on the bed. It was a lovely dress – high neck, fitted bodice, sleeveless and with a slight flare down at the feet. I can still see it in my mind's eye, with its thin satin banding around the waist and with fine, such fine, shoulder straps going half-way down my back. In one sense it was understated for a bridesmaid's dress and definitely not the first one we considered when choosing it but it was one that complimented Stella's dress perfectly and, originally, I thought it looked good on me. The morning of Stella's big day, as I stood there in the hotel room, this panic attack came over me, driven by a feeling that I didn't look good enough."

"That you didn't think you looked good enough?" stated Gerry. "But you're…"

Alba, though, did not listen to what he said, lost as she was in her recollections. She simply continued once Gerry had fallen silent:

"Not that I'm vain or highly manicured, I mean, blow, you should see me when I'm out in the garden in my scruffy gingham shirt, threadbare jeans and sturdy boots – I look a right scruff-ball then, with dirt under my nails or perhaps with a forearm shredded after a climbing rose cane has whipped itself across me as I try to re-tie it to the wire support. Rather, I guess, it was that I felt I couldn't look good enough for Stella. You've seen her yourself and she's as stunning now as she was then. So, this panic attack came over me, driven by a sense of inadequacy and that I was about to let my friend down. Somehow my brain then told me that I'd let her down less if I didn't show up at all. I think her mother stood in and took my place. That's by-the-by and none of it makes any sense now but, back then, when I was a silly little young woman, it just overwhelmed me; I literally fled."

Alba paused before concluding:

"I still have the wedding invite in a box on my dressing table and I take it out, too often perhaps, and study it and I just sit and feel an overwhelming sense of guilt and a whole heap of embarrassment. I wrote of course, weeks later, to try and explain but I couldn't explain really, could I? She never wrote back. I never expected her to and, in a way, I was pleased she didn't, after all I let her down. That was the end of it; well, it was until – "

"Until, until what?" asked Gerry.

"Until she appeared next to me at the reception desk yesterday lunchtime. So, you see, that is why I have to help her, for she is my friend. No, was my friend, oh, I don't know."

With that, Alba paused, thought for a moment and then spoke again, as much to herself as to Gerry, and there was passion in her voice:

"No, she is my friend, damn it! How she regards me is a different matter and, actually, not important; she was friendly to me yesterday lunchtime, which was nice and definitely a relief. But what matters is that she is my friend and I have to help her. Something has happened to Joshua – they were well suited and no one from the hotel has given any hint that they were arguing or that there were tensions between them – not you, not Geoffrey nor Cecilia, not Robyn or Lizzie, no one. So, something is wrong and I should help however I can. Not to buy myself back into her friendship but because I care. He hasn't just 'wandered off', met up with some golfing chums or chosen to sulk in some nearby second-rate hotel because they've had a row. Something has happened to him or, perhaps, someone has done something to him."

"That's a fine and endearing quality you have about you but what can you actually do about it?" asked Gerry, as he stood up and moved to face Alba. With his elbows at his side, he put his hands out to Alba, palms upturned. His gesture was somewhere between 'I have nothing for you', 'I can offer you nothing' and 'I am at a complete loss as to what your next step should be'. Then, to reinforce the visible gesture, Gerry said:

"Even if something has befallen him – though have you considered that perhaps whatever that something is, might be deserved? Is he someone we should be saving? After all, is he really a nice man? What are his relationships with his colleagues? Does he only engage in ethical business practices? Is he all he seems?"

"Well, I haven't considered any of that, not really," conceded Alba. "But if Stella wants him back, then that is good enough for me. Plus, no one here at the hotel knows him, for Stella and Joshua have never stayed here before – so, surely someone from afar has followed him here."

"Alright," said Gerry, not wishing to press his personal view that bad things happening to bad people was not always a bad thing.

"Alright," he repeated, "but the trail is cold."

"Cold?" responded Alba.

"Cold. For one, no one knows where he went after he left Stella at the car park, do they?"

"No," agreed Alba. "Apart from he went on foot to a dead man's house. Stella said it was half a mile or so. So, that does give us, roughly, a semi-circle with a half mile radius from the car park. Could be worse," she stated, trying to sound optimistic.

Gerry smiled as he fractionally shook his head. He then said:

"It is worse – your search area is bigger than you think. You're overlooking something."

"What? How can the search area be any bigger than what I've just described: a half circle with a half mile radius – any point up to half a mile from the car park where they separated."

"Exactly – *any* point," said Gerry, with particular emphasis on the 'any'.

"What?" repeated Alba.

"Why are you ruling out a search area of a full circle from the starting point? If it was me…"

"Because, you dimwit, they parted at a beach car park. So, unless he was abducted by someone on a motor-powered surf board, we have my search area of a half circle."

Gerry nodded his understanding but persevered:

"If it was me, I would consider where that car park was."

"At the seaside – sea one side, land the other."

"Yes," acknowledged Gerry. "And no. Remind me, if you would be so kind, where they had just been – where had Joshua and Stella just spent a rushed afternoon."

"St. Michael's Mount."

"Which is where?" queried Gerry, hoping Alba would cotton on.

"On an island."

"And where do you find most islands?"

"In the sea."

"Exactly."

"Oh," said Alba.

Gerry said nothing.

"Oh, I get you," continued Alba, with understanding at last in her voice. "Joshua could have headed back to the island – to one of the fishermen's cottages on the island – couldn't he?"

"Of course, he could. In your haste, Alba, don't, figuratively speaking, forget to look both ways. All you know is he went to view a property that's being sold; sold, so you've been told because the owner or tenant has died. Joshua parted from the last person to see him alive at a coastal car park but here, on the Cornish coast, as opposed to, I reckon, the Sussex or the Lincolnshire coast, that doesn't mean he had to head inland – there's often an island out there, leading people, kind of, back 'out to sea'."

"That's a good point and I feel silly for missing something so obvious. And yet – " but Alba paused, running what she was about to say through her head first, in case she had missed something else obvious. She was certain she had not, allowing her to continue:

"But why not separate on the island? Why hide the location from her?"

"Being chivalrous? Wanting to know she'd got back to the car safely before he focussed on his work?" offered back Gerry.

"That's very magnanimous of you, especially so given that a moment ago you were rubbishing him as unethical and not a nice man. Equally, I would suggest you're about forty, perhaps fifty, years out of date with that comment."

"Maybe. And, as for being magnanimous, was I? I was just trying to help you see the scale of your search area, that's all. But, if you would rather, I said, that he was deliberately keeping the address secret because he was buying the property for himself and his mistress, soon to be the next Mrs Mallory, I could say that instead; I could happily say that. Either way, if you are keen to help your friend, you may find yourself heading over to the island yourself, whatever the 'backstory' is. And," but with the 'and' Gerry's tone changed – it was heavier, more sombre and he spoke directly into Alba's eyes:

"If you're going to help Stella, you realise you might be putting yourself at risk; if your hypothesis proves to be correct, someone might not stop at harming just one person if they suddenly find you poking your nose into things. You're OK with that, are you?"

The woman still perched on his car bonnet starred back. She studied him, and as Gregory and Ben came bounding into view, Alba said:

"I must help my friend."

"They said 'thanks'," called out Ben.

"They said they'd finish their lunch and be along shortly; they said there was nothing of value in the car, so we didn't have to hang around to wait for them. We said we were hoping to go to a beach for the rest of the afternoon and that you'd promised to build sandcastles with us," added Gregory.

"A sand-fort!" declared Ben.

"Best we head off then," announced Gerry to Alba and the boys.

Then, directing his words to Alba, as the boys got in the back seats, he added:

"You need to head back. You're not going to learn anything here. If I get you back, you can see if there have been any developments but, if you do get involved, please take care. But I'll be amazed if we find Stella and Joshua sitting down and having afternoon tea together in the bar area upon our return."

"I will and I fear you're right about Joshua's probable return. But best we head back," agreed Alba. "We did promise your boys, after all."

"Yes, you did," insisted both boys from the back of the car, demonstrating that universal quality which children have, of being able to hear perfectly well whenever an adult says anything in their favour.

Once they were all strapped in and as Gerry started off down the lane that would take them back to Lostwithiel, and ultimately onto the main road, Gregory said:

"She gave us a packet of crisps to share in the car as a little 'thank you'."

"We said we didn't want anything," pleaded Ben, fearing his dad would turn the car round and make them return them and so forcing them to visit the castle for a third time in one day. "We didn't ask for them," he stressed.

"Really, we didn't," agreed Gregory, who shared his brother's fear. "She gave them to us and smiled as she did so."

"Don't worry lads, I won't make you take them back," said Gerry.

Following loud and long-lasting 'Phews' coming from the rear seats, Alba asked:

"What flavour?"

"Cheese and onion – wasn't that nice of her," announced Ben.

CHAPTER 7

Jackstraws

Upon their return to 'The Jupiter Hotel', as Gerry, with Gregory to help him, collected their day bags from the car boot, Alba and Ben walked round the front of the hotel. As they stood by the entrance doors, waiting for the others to catch up, they watched the waves reach the shoreline of the cove beneath them. Alba commented on the car Ben's dad had, using all of the motoring knowledge that she possessed at once:

"Nice car your dad has – comfortable seats."

"Yeah," answered Ben. "But it's mum's car and it'll be going soon, probably next week."

"Going? Are you getting a new one? The one you have looks pretty new to me."

"Dunno," said Ben. "I hope we get another one. I like mum's car – it has buttons to make the windows go up or down. How cool is that? Dad says the judge has confetti-ed mum's car. I think that's why dad has taken us out of school for a few days, so we can make use of mum's car one last time. It puzzles me."

"What does?" queried Alba.

"Just, you know, like, well, I would have thought judges would be rich enough to buy their own. Do you know that everyone has to bow to them? Also, that they come out of their own special room into the courtroom? Well, that's how it is on TV. So, surely they're mega-rich already. Dunno why this one has to take mummy's car. I'm told she's been a bit naughty but don't see that allows him to be naughty in return. Maybe it's because he's locked her up so knows she is not around to stop him and so can be naughty back. But I dunno why dad doesn't hide the car key from this judge man to stop him from confetti-ing it."

"Confiscating it," said Alba but her correction was lost on the child at her side.

"Dad is taking us to see her on Saturday."

"Tomorrow?"

"No," said Ben, "we're here tomorrow, guess it's the following Saturday, the first weekend when we're home. Dad says we'll be travelling by train so, even if the judge man has taken mum's car by then, we'll still be able to visit. It'll be nice to see her – she was always working so hard before, staying late at work and working away at weekends, me and Gregory didn't see that much of her."

"Gregory and I," corrected Alba – pointlessly, so it transpired.

"Yeah, me and Gregory didn't see that much of her. Then, even though she was working so hard, the judge man said she'd done something wrong and sent her to a girls' prison for ages and ages."

"That must have been so tough for you two boys," suggested Alba sympathetically.

"Yeah, it's a bit easier now, as the weeks and months have passed, but sometimes I'll still go and sit on Gregory's bed and we'll talk about her. I really missed her at Christmas. So, it'll be nice to see her on Saturday; no not tomorrow, you know which one I mean," said Ben, as he hoped his dad's new friend wouldn't get him further confused as to when he was actually going to visit his mother.

"Yes," agreed Alba reassuringly. "The Saturday when you're home. Do you know which one she's in? What the prison is called?"

"Think so," said Ben confidently and he stood as tall as his ten years would allow. "'The Queen's Prison Faraway', think that's what dad said it was called."

'Close enough' thought Alba to herself, guessing correctly, so it would prove several days later, that Ben had conveyed to her that his mum, and Gerry's wife, was a serving prisoner in Her Majesty's Prison Holloway – a women's only prison in north London.

"I hope you have a lot of time with her," said Alba supportively but Ben's mind was back in the here and now –

"Cor, that was a big one that just hit the beach. Did you see that one break?" he said.

"Yes. You do get a good view of the cove from up here, don't you?" replied Alba, relieved the child next to her could compartmentalise his mother's incarceration so easily from his current holiday with his father.

"Yeah but I prefer being down there. Dad has said he'll take us down before tea time."

"Well, I'm sure he will. You might get wet though as the clouds are building and I reckon, as did the lady you helped at the castle just now, some bad weather is coming in."

"Whatever, I just want to get down and build something on the beach," said Ben.

"I reckon," said Alba realising it can only take so long to sort out some walking boots and a rucksack or two, "your dad and brother went in by the hotel's side door. What do you reckon? Shall we wait here a bit longer or go and find them inside?"

"Oh no!" said Ben in exasperation. "They'll already be in the room and Gregory will have chosen the TV channel! Rats!"

"I thought you wanted to go down to the beach," said Alba to the disappearing child as he ran in to reception. She then added, more positively, "Thanks for a nice day – see you at mealtime perhaps."

Alba then turned back to lose herself in the view once more as the storm clouds built.

*

As Alba stood there, a woman emerged from the stepped path which, depending on the direction you were heading, led down to, or up from, the cove.

Once the woman had crossed the lane that ran in front of the hotel and was part way up the hotel's drive, Alba called out to her:

"Stella. Any news?"

"No," replied Stella without breaking her stride, determined as she was – though as her physique evidently allowed – to make it all the way up from the cove without stopping.

Only once she was up and at Alba's side – standing where Ben had been just a moment ago – did she continue, not that she added to what she had just conveyed:

"Nothing."

"Oh, you poor thing," responded Alba as she instinctively gave her friend a warm hug. For doing so, however, Alba made her jersey top damp, drawing as it did moisture from the other woman's wet one-piece swimsuit, which lay beneath Stella's loose fitting striped beach dress.

The climb had kept Stella's body temperature up but Alba was keen not to delay her friend from going in, getting dried off and getting more appropriately attired for a warm enough but nonetheless spring day – particularly this spring day as the sun's warmth was now lost behind the approaching sombre clouds. Nonetheless, Alba could not keep herself from echoing Stella's answer:

"Nothing?"

"No," confirmed Stella. "But walk up to my room with me and I'll expand but the bottom line is still nothing; Joshua hasn't returned and no one has offered up any sightings of him."

As they headed into the hotel, Stella continued:

"As I said I would, I headed over to the police station in Helston. Once I proved who I was, they confirmed they could see details of me reporting him as missing, as of yesterday evening, on their computer system. They added the Force's Missing Person Unit was based in Penzance and would be contacting me in due course."

"Right," said Alba.

"I was told by the Front Counter staff," continued Stella "to come back to the hotel and wait. Thankfully the hotel manager is letting me stay a few extra days. Obviously, he, as I am, is hoping this nightmare of mine will be over very soon. The police said there was nothing I should be doing, other than informing them the moment I got any news. They strongly advised me against trying to undertake any kind of search myself and definitely warned me about the risk of getting caught out by the tides if I were tempted to go looking along the base of any nearby cliffs or down in little, tucked away, frequently deserted coves. They also advised I shouldn't trek along any coastal paths nor venture out on to any headlands and, by so doing, get myself lost or trapped in some old mine workings."

"Sensible advice but hard to heed when it's your own husband," noted Alba.

"Exactly," concurred Stella. "Fine words by the police, when said in the abstract, but so painful to abide by when it's my Joshua who's missing. If he did go for a walk or opted to jog back because the taxi firm let him down – he does do the odd five or ten kilometre runs, you know – and fell and is lying somewhere with a broken leg or became entangled in some long forgotten about piece of farming machinery as he jumped a wall, he'd want me out looking for him, surely?"

"Yes but also no – he wouldn't want you putting yourself at risk, would he?"

"I guess not," acknowledged Stella. "Yet the hanging around was driving me insane and…"

"And so, you've been down and had a swim? Not a bad idea and you timed it well, given the weather is on the turn. And," added Alba, "I'm pleased Cliff has allowed you to stay in your room. If not,

I hope you know you could have slept on my floor, no, sorry, in my bed. I'd have insisted on taking the cushions on the floor – for I don't think you would be in a fit state to drive yourself home even if that's what the police had advised."

Having nodded in agreement to that final point by Alba, Stella added:

"Thanks, that would have been kind of you. And yes, a swim has helped – not proper sea swimming but at least I got in, did a few breaststrokes one way and then the other but never went out of my depth."

"Sensible," agreed Alba. "But what if you'd been needed on the phone?"

"The manager said he'd go into my room and hang a big towel out of our bedroom window. Not instant communication, I know, but I just couldn't sit in my room, the bar or the lounge any longer. It was sheer torture and I just had to occupy myself at least until five o'clock; that's when the police said they'd contact me here. Worryingly, no towel was hung from my bedroom window but I've come up to shower and ready myself for the call."

"If there's anything, just anything, I can do, please just ask," insisted Alba as they reached Stella's bedroom door. "Drive you to the police station, take you back to Marazion, sit with you as you take the call or whatever."

"No, it's fine but thank you. I'll come and find you later this evening if there are any developments but I'm not getting my hopes up. Something nasty has happened, I've come to accept that today, I just hope, if this doesn't sound too wicked, he's in a hospital bed unconscious, having been knocked over by a car or robbed and knocked out – a traumatic event either way but at least meaning he's alive. I just can't countenance the thought of him having fallen off a cliff path or down some disused mine workings. I just hope he's in a hospital somewhere and the nurses are unable to find out his name or where he's staying."

"Oh, poor Stella, you poor poor thing. If I may say, you're being so brave and, even if you don't feel like you are, you seem to be coping remarkably well. You are sure you don't want me or someone being with you when the police call?"

"No, really, I'll be fine, kind of. I'm not expecting good news and, given the police haven't called so far, I'm expecting the five o'clock call to be a routine one but this time from the Missing Person Unit. They'll give me a point of contact within that team and simply confirm the details I've already given. Tomorrow morning, though, that's the critical time."

"When they can call through to his office and find out where this meeting was meant to be happening?" suggested Alba.

"Exactly. Look," offered Stella, "it's a routine call I'll be getting shortly from the police and no news will be good news, kind of. Then I'll have a simple meal in my room – I really can't face the other hotel guests staring at me, which they'll do, no doubt."

"Perhaps but not maliciously, it's just human nature," offered up Alba in defence of the guests that she knew.

"Even so, I'd rather eat in my room. Then mental exhaustion will finally catch up with me and I'll sleep." As she opened her bedroom door, Stella added, "But you can do breakfast tomorrow with me, can't you?"

"Of course."

"Good. We can take stock then; I'll tell you what the police had to say and what further advice they've given me. If we meet the same time as this morning, the breakfast area should be pretty quiet. We'll see what the new day brings."

"Hopefully something positive. Unless you come and find me tonight, I'll see you for breakfast in the morning – nice and early."

"Nice and early and thanks again for being here for me Alba," said Stella.

As Stella took herself into her room, Alba found herself speechless, having never expected her friend to say those words to her ever again.

*

Thinking she too would benefit from an early-ish night, in order that she was ready to offer her friend whatever advice and help she might be seeking in the morning, Alba headed promptly down for her evening meal. However, she did first head back to her own car, to collect her little sewing kit that she always kept in the glove compartment of her car. This was due to the fact that she had torn one of the straps from the bodice of her camisole that morning, having caught her nightwear between her feet when she had been drying herself after her shower.

As she clutched her sewing bag, still convinced she had left her cami-top on the corner of the bed rather than the floor, as she showered, she saw Martha once more – sitting exactly where she had been that morning.

"Evening Martha. I know you haven't been sitting there all day, since you weren't there when Gerry brought me back from Restormel Castle, but you'll wear those metal stairs out if you're not careful," Alba said jokingly.

"Hi, Alba. I haven't been there myself and definitely too far inland to detour to this trip; worth a visit another time, you reckon?"

"Oh, absolutely," replied Alba.

"I'll bear it in mind. And, yes, here I am again. I was just thinking if only my room had a balcony – my own little bit of privacy in the fresh air, to have the odd cigarette or just to sit and think."

"Or both?" suggested Alba.

"Yes, probably both, you're right."

"You are giving the impression of someone wanting their own peace and quiet; I should leave you," said Alba.

However, as Alba was about to move away, Martha continued:

"No, it's fine. I'm OK chatting to you. You are very easy to talk to, which is kind of odd, since I don't even know you, but you seem sympathetic. I just need my space from other people."

There was something about Martha's tone, which was somewhere between resignation and weariness but coupled with a craving for genuine companionship, that captured Alba's curiosity. It prompted her to sit down next to Martha.

"I'll sit with you for a few minutes then," said Alba. "Would it help to talk?" she added.

"No, not really," answered Martha.

"I don't smoke, I'm afraid – meaning I can't offer you a cigarette."

"It's fine. My pack is in my room and I only smoke occasionally. Just when things really get to me or I'm worrying over something."

"Like this morning?" reflected Alba.

"Like this morning," agreed the woman to her side. She then fell silent for several minutes.

As Alba sat, listening to the distant sound of the waves down beneath the hotel and the sound of a distant dog yapping away at something, a puzzle, an unsolved puzzle resurfaced in Alba's mind – something that had crept in yesterday evening. She trawled her brain, again without success, but Alba felt it just had to involve Martha, the person she was now sitting beside.

Martha then spoke again:

"It's only the occasional cigarette but it still makes me feel like a fraud."

"A fraud; how so?" queried Alba.

"Oh, just that I'm on this strenuous walking holiday, pushing myself to the limits each day and people back where I used to work being all impressed with what Annabel and myself have set ourselves to do and yet I seem to find greatest happiness when sitting somewhere alone having a nicotine fix. So, I'm a bit of a fraud – which is ironic really, given I'm here with the 'Empress'."

"The Empress?"

"Yes, the Empress." With that Martha shut her eyes, smiled painfully to herself and shook her head slightly as she did so. "You've met *the Empress* – my walking partner, Annabel Lloyd-Kent."

With that, though, Martha turned to Alba and stressed:

"That's between you and me, mind you. Don't go and tell her that's what I call her when she's out of earshot. You can't, just can't!"

Surprised by the tension in the other's voice, Alba sought to reassure Martha:

"No, promise you, I won't. Just our little secret."

"Thanks," said a relieved Martha. "I must have my little secrets from her."

This time, it was Alba's turn to fall silent for a moment. She played with the clasp on her sewing bag, straightened her legs out in front of her, to stretch her calf muscles, and then glanced once more at the woman next to her. Then it clicked in Alba's mind, the thing that had been there since yesterday dinner time – the thing she had been trawling for.

Alba spoke quietly to Martha:

"I know another of your little secrets."

"Pardon?" said Martha, anxiety manifesting itself all over her face.

"Another of your secrets that you are keeping from the 'Empress'."

"Do you? But I don't have any others," pleaded Martha. Yet the weakness in her voice spoke volumes and Alba knew that she, Alba, was right.

"But you do, don't you? After all, you've just said 'secrets' in the plural," continued Alba. "Don't worry – I won't tell and, if you're getting away with it, I think it's rather clever on your part."

Yet Martha remained cautious, not willing to reveal whatever it was to Alba voluntarily. Realising the other was 'forcing her hand', Alba continued:

"I saw you arrive at the hotel."

Yet Martha still did not engage, necessitating Alba to speak once more:

"Yesterday, to be clear. Yesterday I saw you arrive at the hotel."

"But you couldn't have," insisted a shocked Martha. "There was no one in reception, just the receptionist. There wasn't anyone else there – I swear. Meaning, you weren't there; you're guessing."

"And yet I was – well, almost. I was out of sight part way up the stairs. I was hoping you were someone else: someone who'd decided to change her plans after all, in order that we could catch up. However, even from the distance and the angle I was looking from, and though I saw you only briefly, you clearly weren't her, so I didn't linger and headed back up to my room. It was definitely you, though, who I saw arrive."

"What if you did? Obviously, I turned up at the hotel yesterday – I'm staying here after all. What is your point?"

Martha's response was neither vindictive nor outwardly hostile but it was evident still she was unwilling to concede anything to Alba that Alba had not earned.

"You arrived at lunchtime, didn't you?" stated Alba.

"So you claim."

"And yet, over dinner last night, having enjoyed your gammon steak, you were relaying to your walking companion, or non-companion, well whatever she is, to Annabel, what a hard day's walking you had had and how long and tough she, Annabel would find it when her turn to do that stretch came."

"Well, it was long and tough."

"But you did it in pretty quick time – if you got here by lunchtime," stated Alba.

"I'm a fast walker," claimed Martha weakly.

"Perhaps but faster still if you do it in a taxi."

"You didn't see!" exclaimed Martha. "You just said yourself you were halfway up the stairs and then went up to your room – you didn't see how I arrived!"

"No, I agree," said Alba. "I didn't. And, please, I'm not judging, for as I've already said, I think it's a rather clever little scheme you've got going on."

"You didn't see!" repeated Martha. "You couldn't have!"

"No, you're right, I didn't. However, Stella did."

"Stella?"

"The person whose husband has gone missing. She saw you – she told me over breakfast this morning. As she was recounting to me her and her husband's movements yesterday, she said to me that, as they left the hotel yesterday lunchtime and walked to their car here, in this hotel's car park, the car park that we're looking across right now, they saw you get out of a taxi. Stella said you were burdened with your rucksack and trekking poles – as you were a moment after that, as I saw you come in to reception – but that you were very much getting out of a taxi. Not injured, not hobbling, simply burdened with a lot of walking equipment for someone having a car ride."

"Oh," said Martha, as she bit her lip and looked forlornly at Alba. "Oh," Martha repeated.

"Rather clever," said Alba, keen to lift the other's anxiety. "As I say, what was your little secret is simply ours. I won't tell – really, I won't. The 'Empress' Annabel will never know; at least, not from me. But, as I say, rather clever – doing no one any harm at all and admirably sneaky."

"You really won't tell?"

"Of course not. I've promised, haven't I?"

"Well, yes but – "

"No 'buts'," interrupted Alba. "I've promised. End of. But I am curious to know whether you did any of Thursday's walk or not."

"Some," answered Martha. "You really won't tell?"

"No," said Alba simply. With that she tapped her right foot against Martha's left foot – as if they were two glasses 'chinking' – to underwrite her promise and, with that, Alba could sense the tension easing from Martha's shoulders.

Martha turned to Alba as she spoke:

"Some. I walked some of it yesterday; I do like walking, after all. Just no longer on the industrial scale that Annabel demands of me, as she plans these holidays for us. I reckon I did about two-fifths maybe half of yesterday's planned walk. You see, I've got to always do some to have something to describe over dinner with the 'Empress'. Equally, I have to stop soon enough and have a taxi arranged, so I get to where we're staying early enough to make sure Annabel can never have arrived before me and so catch me out. Yesterday's pick-up was at another little cove, miles further back along the coastal path but somewhere I could, by arrangement, have a taxi standing by – this time from a Truro based taxi firm, nice friendly driver I had, an elderly chap, Jack I think his name was."

Martha paused before offering a completely different take on her 'arrangements':

"You know, I almost feel like a spy, who's forgotten or, perhaps even, no longer cares, who she is spying for or against, because they have come to the realisation that they simply enjoy the thrill of it all – deception can be quite an addictive game to play."

A further pause followed before she added:

"Thank you for not challenging me about it over dinner last night, in front of Annabel."

"No need to thank me for that – I hadn't worked it out then. I was tired from my drive and thrilled to bump into Mr and Mrs Constance; they were the couple sitting the other side of me, by the way. I mean, I heard what you said about a tiring day's walking and I knew, on another level, that you'd been around the hotel all afternoon but I just didn't see then the contradiction – not then. Even when Stella told me this morning, about you coming by taxi here, I still didn't see."

"Ah, this woman Stella and the man she was with – "

"Joshua," offered up Alba.

"If that's his name," continued Martha. "Yes, they saw me get out of the taxi. I said 'hello again' to him as I thought saying something would be less conspicuous than blanking the pair of them. Thankfully they seemed in a rush."

"They were," corroborated Alba. "They were trying to get to

Marazion and the island before he then had to head off for a meeting he had arranged somewhere nearby – he's an architect and had a site visit for a possible conversion project his firm was hoping to get."

"But he's returned by now, surely?" queried Martha.

"No, he hasn't," replied Alba.

"That's a worry," said Martha. She paused before adding, "For the wife, I mean – a worry for her."

"Yes," agreed Alba, at which point a car powerfully brought itself up the hotel's steep drive and turned out of sight, behind the part of the hotel where Cliff, the hotel's manager, lived.

"Well, I guess Joshua will reappear in due course. Anyway, to conclude my little confession, I rushed in, tangling myself up in the doorway as I did so – turned myself into a right set of jackstraws – and then, once safely in my room, took out my hip flask and had my, now ritualistic, drink of brandy to acknowledge another 'mission complete'. Yes," and there was now defiance, resolve and something approaching joy in Martha's voice, as she added, "I toasted myself upon another successful fraud which I had pulled off at the Empress's expense. Yes, I toasted my fraud – I was proud of myself."

Yet, in her own personal moment of triumph, and as 'alive' as Alba had seen the other woman to be, Martha's fragility, timid countenance and fear of her holiday companion resurfaced all too quickly, as she concluded:

"Which is odd, when I say it like that, given Annabel is really the fraud."

*

"How so?" prompted Alba, immediately curious as to what Martha had just inferred.

Martha allowed herself a half-smile but said nothing until Mrs Constance, who had been dropped off when Mr. Constance was turning the car, had walked past and exchanged pleasantries with

Alba – Alba assuring her that she would be in for dinner in a few moments and would speak then.

"Ah, yes, the fraud that is the 'Empress Annabel', there in her *bijou*, incredibly expensive, London flat. You know, I could never work out how she could have ever afforded it – I mean, simply renting it would have been prohibitive – so how she ever came into the funds to buy it was a mystery to me."

"Was but isn't now?" suggested Alba.

"No, not now," concurred Martha. "But I shouldn't really say," whereupon Martha fell silent.

"Probably not," agreed Alba.

Yet Martha, unused to having someone of Alba's calming presence to talk to, did not stay silent for long:

"We both worked for the same London gallery, you see. She still does, as their curator; I used to work on the events side, you know, organising special exhibitions – where we'd get works of art loaned to us – or the renting out of the gallery for evening functions, be they private or corporate events. A whole range of things. Didn't have to know too much about the artwork itself just how to plan, bring people on board, organise and host different types of events; Annabel, on the other hand, is the art whizz. But I was very good at my job too, mind you."

Martha turned to look at Alba for reassurance – which she found, allowing her to continue:

"Putting on fund-raising exhibitions were my favourite, especially for wildlife or children's charities; they were always worthwhile, so much better than doing something for some big city bank, private equity firm or insurance company, and, because charities were involved, it made it so much easier to source original works of art, frequently from private collectors, to put on display in the gallery. They would lend us pictures, often ones that had never been out of their private collections since the day they purchased them direct from the artist, entrust them to us and we'd raise lots of money for the said charity and duly return their pictures afterwards. All very prestigious and worthwhile and everyone was happy – the charities did well, not only in raising funds but in simply keeping their name out there, as the press and entertainment reviewers would cover our exhibitions. Equally, we, the gallery, did well and it kept us apart from similar sized ones that were more nervous about handling other people's works of art. Finally, the private collectors always felt they'd done well out of it, especially as we kept stressing how it was only due to their lending us their precious works that the charities could do so well – so the owners felt they'd put something back into the community."

"An important feeling to be left with, if you're a wealthy private art collector," said Alba, sounding every bit as sarcastic as she meant her comment to be.

"Oh yes," agreed Martha. "Some would go away even more puffed up with themselves than they were when I first approached them. They were always so desperate to be seen to be doing something for 'good causes' and yet, what lay beneath really, was a desperation to be known as the owners of those pictures. Which is also ironic, really."

"How so?" pressed Alba.

"Because they ended up not being the owners of those pictures. Well, perhaps, more accurately, they remained the owners but they definitely stopped being in possession of them; works were switched, you see."

"Really," exclaimed Alba. "Can you name some – some works or some artists?"

"I could but I'd better not, not yet. It's why I left, you see."

"Left?"

"The gallery. I worked out what was going on – the 'Empress' working late on evenings that she shouldn't have been, her giving private tours to artist friends of hers, her insistence on where pictures, in a given exhibition, should be displayed, particularly the ones to be, so I noticed after a while, nearest to fire escapes or out of security camera shot. But I never had anything concrete, just suspicions. That was until I called by her flat once, when she wasn't expecting me to. I needed something signed or agreed to, something that needed an answer that evening, and I caught her out, so to speak. Significantly, she didn't see what happened as I was taking my coat off in her hall – you see, as I was there, hanging my coat up, her cat pushed at the door to her spare bedroom and there, against the bed, was the exact same picture as one we currently had loaned to us, for whatever exhibition we had on at the time. A beautiful picture of a young woman, sitting at a window, in a worn but evidently once fine dress, sadness in her eyes – a sadness captured by the artist so well, it's as if the woman is peering out to you, the observer of the picture, in the pitiful hope that you will be able to do something to help her in her distress. A beautiful but tragic picture. Then the door swung back closed, once the cat had got in, and it was lost from my sight. Thankfully Annabel didn't see, so she never knew I knew."

"The same picture you say?" quizzed Alba.

"Oh, absolutely. Whether I had seen the original or the forgery I don't know but I am sure that the picture of the girl, which I handed back to the owner, was the forgery. Plus, the one I saw was stacked against another frame but I couldn't see that picture – so, whether that was another picture from the same exhibition or a previous exhibition, I don't know. However, as I say, the door closed itself as quickly as the cat had opened it and there was no way I was going to risk being caught in that room having a poke around."

"Oh, my," exclaimed Alba.

"So, I got the papers signed or some decision agreed to and left her flat as quickly as I could. Then I resigned – I wasn't going to be part of her enterprise, even if unwittingly. With hindsight, I handed my notice in a bit too soon after my visit to her *suave* London apartment. I can guess now how she could afford it and, also, some of the artworks that hung in her hall and living room – works that she, so to speak, had to allow me to see but which perhaps she'd have taken down and hidden if she'd expected my calling. Not works taken directly from the gallery but works that neither her salary nor even any sizeable inheritance would have paid for but, it would seem, that she could somehow afford."

A spectrum of questions scrolled through Alba's mind but she opted, having glanced around her to ensure Martha's walking companion was not in earshot, for one that considered the here and now:

"Why holiday with her then? If she's a fraud – and I have no reason to doubt your story – why stay friends or, at least, maintain this façade of friendship?"

"As I say, I regretted leaving the job so quickly after that visit to her home, in case she linked the two events. To cut all social ties with her as well, would be even more risky I felt. She's a controlling personality but at least I don't have to spend time walking with her, nor find myself being told off for walking too slowly or taking too many pictures – why not take lots of pictures I say, if you're walking through our beautiful countryside? Thankfully she's not interested in photography, meaning she hasn't yet noticed I only ever now have photos from the first half of any walk she has planned for me! Anyway, I tolerate her over breakfast and dinner and, by so doing, hopefully keep her suspicions of me at bay."

"Keep your friends close but your enemies closer," mused Alba.

"Exactly. Plus, I do like walking holidays, even if half day walks seem to suit me better these days! And, it's sad to admit," whereupon Martha grimaced, "I don't have that many friends and definitely none that like walking."

"Come down to Sussex," offered back Alba, spontaneously. "There are lovely walks around where I live – several around Hillstone Hall and many seem to end up either at the tea shop at the Hall itself or at the little community café come charity shop come advice centre that we have in our village. And to mark your escape from this Annabel lady, the first time you come down and visit, I'll ask my friend Mrs Rowan to bake us some millionaire's shortbread for our inaugural walk."

"You really mean I could come and visit? That would be lovely but I hardly know you; I really couldn't put you out like that."

"Well, obviously we don't really know each other yet," agreed Alba, "but I didn't know Gerry until this morning and I've just spent the day with him and his boys and that was OK. Maybe don't come and stay for a week the first time, perhaps just a night to start with and see if we get on."

"That's incredibly kind of you and it would be an escape, really, it would."

"No smoking in the house, mind you!" insisted Alba.

"Promise," agreed Martha. "We'll exchange phone numbers later but best I go in for dinner now – I don't really want Annabel coming out looking for me. This is my little sanctuary out here and I don't want her cornering me on 'my' staircase. I'll enjoy the gammon steak again tonight, more so, I think, having spoken with you, especially if you still really mean I could come and see you at your home sometime soon."

"I do and Sussex and Surrey are lovely counties to go walking in – some really lovely walks locally, as I say, and, if it works out, on another visit I'll take you over to Mole Valley. Look, you go in now and enjoy Alan's excellent cooking; I'll go round the front of the hotel and take this sewing kit of mine up to my room and kill a bit of time up there. Only then will I come down for my meal. Let's not allow the 'Empress' to think we've been in cahoots – you and she are moving on tomorrow, as you resume your coastal walk, so she need never know you've been telling me about her."

CHAPTER 8

King John's Crown

Having delayed, as she promised she would to Martha, Alba, in time, entered the dining area. Dressed as she now was in a rich deep brown coloured blouse and black jeans, Alba nodded to Gerry and said 'hello' to Gregory and Ben as she passed their table and then forced herself not to search out where Martha was sitting with Annabel.

As Alba sat at her designated table, she was grateful to once more have Mr Constance one side of her – with his assurance that his wife would be down shortly. On the other side, to her left, there was a lone male; he was the solitary man, who had been in the dining area the previous evening prior to Alba taking her table. Last night Alba had felt he had not quite pulled off the holiday look – he had looked too 'tidy' despite his attempt at casual dressing. Tonight, that feeling was less evident to Alba but she remained curious as to what had brought him to this part of Cornwall.

In front of Alba, the two farmers' wives had returned to the hotel. This time they were enjoying a leisurely meal as opposed to a rushed drink in the bar. For, because it was a Friday night, they had no children to get up at some unearthly hour in the morning, to be taken to a remote bus stop in some nondescript country lane, to get them to a school that they did not want to go to. A school that was trying to teach them how glacial valleys formed, what Venn diagrams were and to consider the writing of Anton Chekhov within his 'Three Sisters' play – none of which, to the children at least, seemed particularly relevant to farming life.

Each time Alba lifted her eyes from studying the menu, looking through those two women, she saw Gerry glancing back at her. Her top, with its colourful heavy, though nonetheless vibrant, floral pattern, set against the deep brown was definitely eye-catching – as if William Morris had progressed from nineteenth century wallpaper and embroideries to ladies' clothing.

As she listened to the rain start, and with pudding spoon turned, she toyed with the slender silver bar, which hung from her necklace, until Jed approached her table.

"Evening, Miss White," he said, in his deep west country voice. "Pineapple juice?" he proffered.

"Alba, please and thank you – you know me too well."

He nodded in agreement, for he had served her too many times over the years to know what she would have to drink. On her final evening, prior to her departure on the morrow, she would have a post-dinner liqueur, normally a 'Baileys' Irish cream, though she would occasionally catch him out and have Amaretto or a Tia Maria instead, meaning he could never pour her that drink in advance, but with her evening meals it was always – always – pineapple juice.

"Staying long?" he enquired as he placed the drink down and proceeded to fill her tumbler, which was already on the table, with water.

"A week. Got here yesterday."

"I know," Jed replied. After a hesitant pause, he added, "I just wasn't sure how long you were staying. A week is just long enough."

"Just," concurred Alba, "but every time I head home at the end of my stay, I always tell myself that I'll book for eight days next time. Yet, I never quite manage to find the time – there's always so much to do in my garden at this time of year, with everything bursting into life, plus what I do up at the Hall."

"Still volunteering there, are you?" enquired Jed. "Surely, they've taken you on to the payroll by now?"

"They sort of offered to, a while back, whilst the deputy head gardener was away for a bit but I declined – said they should offer it to Sally, another volunteer gardener, instead. I love working in the Hall's gardens but I crave my freedom a bit too much to go onto the payroll. Sally did a brilliant job until Tom returned. Anyway, there'll be plenty to do in both gardens after my week here."

"In dad's garden, too," replied Jed. "There were a couple of things dad wanted to ask your advice on."

With that, though, Jed Peters fell silent and the gruff, weathered Cornishman, Alba had erstwhile been speaking to, suddenly looked close to tears.

Alba, deeply flattered that Jed's father would have sought her horticultural advice, spoke softly back:

"Lizzie told me. Plus, yesterday I saw the card you left him in the snug; I'm sorry. I always enjoyed chatting to him during my stays down here and, from all you've told me about him over the years, I know just how much you thought of him."

"Oh, absolutely," agreed Jed. "Thought the world of him. And he was never any trouble to care for. If anything, in his final years, despite his failing health, we were the closest we'd been."

"That's comforting and must help somewhat," suggested Alba. "Never could see the likeness between you, though."

"You're not the first to say that," replied Jed. "Bit more of my mum in me, I guess. But, yes, his frailty did mean we spoke a lot more, even down to plans for his small garden that he had with the cottage; what vegetables had done well, what we'd grow next, whether he could fit in an extra blackcurrant bush, that kind of unimportant thing, you know. Actually, once I'd mentioned to him you were booked in once again, he was going to ask you about why some of the buds on his fruit bushes seemed somewhat swollen. We had a few like that last year but there are more swollen ones this year. The blackcurrants still cropped fairly well but, whilst I can't see any creepy-crawlies, I suspect there's a sinister reason behind some buds being larger than they should be and so, probably not something I want. Any ideas? Though, I really should take your food order – things are a bit hectic here tonight, given Robyn should be waitressing but has evidently been held up. I wasn't even meant to be working today but Cliff called me an hour ago and asked me to come over to help out even though I was meant to be having a few days off. I've only been in about twenty minutes. Thankfully, as far as the bar is concerned, we're quiet – I reckon people are staying away due to the predicted weather that's coming in later."

"Later? Sounds like the rain's already here."

"It's going to get much heavier compared to what you can hear now. But I must get on."

"Oh, OK. We'll chat plants and stuff later but it sounds like 'big bud': the buds swell due to microscopic mites living inside and sucking the sap from the embryonic leaves. As you've said it's not too excessive, my best advice would be to remove and burn the infected stems and then continue to monitor."

"Right. Thanks for that and it shows you're a proper gardener as you didn't advocate simply spraying everything with some multi-action all-purpose spray."

"Goodness me, no," replied Alba. "Spraying just means you kill all the good, beneficial, insects as well as the few bad – for the spray can't differentiate – and then you are also poisoning the birds as they eat the poisoned insects. Why can't the chemical companies see that for themselves?"

"As I say, you're a serious gardener, as dad was. You know, dad used to joke that one of the first things he'd do when he got to heaven would be to kneel down so he could marvel at the quality of the soil."

"Very good," agreed Alba, as she watched the tears swell in the barman's eyes once more.

"Anyway," said Jed, as he sought to gather his emotions. Yet further words failed him as he fought to keep his composure and he simply tapped at his little notebook with his stubby yellow pencil.

Alba, aware she needed to change the subject of conversation to help Jed, for now at least, take a small step away from his raw emotions, opted to address the matter in hand, specifically her menu choice:

"As for food, the fish pie please, with vegetables."

With that and with an agreement to catch up later, followed by a detour to clear some of the plates from the table where Martha and Annabel were sitting, at one of the two tables in the large bay window that looked out to the front of the hotel, Jed departed.

*

It would have been easier to turn to her right and start chatting to Geoffrey and, when she appeared, Cecilia Constance, as she waited for her food, but Alba, still intrigued by the man to her left, turned that way and spoke:

"Good evening. I must apologise but I saw what you were eating and decided to go for the same – even down to opting for the vegetables over the salad."

"That's alright," the gentleman replied. "This fish pie is excellent, with proper chunks of fish and some king prawns, too. Plus, perfect texture to the mash on top. And, as for me, even after all these years since I was last living in India, it will always be vegetables over salad."

"India?"

"Yes, India. There I had it instilled in me as a child to always try and eat cooked food. You see, salads might look fresh but, out there, they'll have been washed in water of questionable quality. It's still a hard habit to break, despite the good water quality in this country, and I find myself having ordered veg before I've even considered whether I might rather fancy some lettuce, tomatoes, slithers of red onion and peppers."

"That's a far more exotic reason for choosing the veg than I had," conceded Alba. "I simply took the view that it is still a bit too early in the season for salad, even here in Cornwall and even with all their polytunnels which they have to bring their season forward, meaning the salad's probably been shipped in. In comparison, the vegetables will probably be the more locally sourced option – less 'food miles' and all that."

"Very admirable of you. I think you will enjoy your choice," he said.

"I'm Alba, Alba White. I'm staying a week – got here yesterday."

"I must confess, I watched you relaxing in the snug before dinner last night," he replied. "Plus, it was you, wasn't it, who was one of the people called out to help that distressed lady in reception last night?"

"Yes," confirmed Alba.

"Thought so. Her husband hadn't returned, so I hear."

"Still hasn't," added Alba.

"Oh," the man said. "That's a surprise. I'd have thought their row, not that I heard anything myself, would have blown over by now. Guess he travelled further away in his mood than we all probably first assumed. Did you, like me, assume he'd gone and had a sulk in a Penzance or St Ives hotel? Maybe he got as far as Exeter before he realised how late it was and looked for somewhere to stay – but I'd have thought he could have got back from even there, though, by now. But my money was on Penzance or St. Ives originally. Yours?"

"I don't know, really. In helping her, Stella, I mean, her name is Stella, yesterday evening, I didn't quite have time to come up with my own 'theory' then, if you can call it that. Stella insists they hadn't rowed. He was due back here after a meeting he had in Marazion. Stella is hoping, as odd as it sounds, he has had an accident and it's a case of waiting for the hospital to make contact."

"I guess that's possible."

"Possible but with each passing hour, less likely I'd say," mused Alba. "I fear, as dramatic as this sounds and I wouldn't necessarily say this to Stella this evening, that Joshua – that's the person who's missing – is being held against his will. Whatever this meeting was that he went to clearly did not work out as planned and something went wrong, very wrong."

"That would make the not hearing from him or from anyone, such as a hospital administrator, more understandable. But why no ransom note or manifesto statement or some such thing?"

"I've wondered that, too. Best I can come up with is he, she or they are deliberately staying quiet for a day or two to up the 'ante' and to make sure people are listening when they do make contact," said Alba.

"Yes, I can see that as a theory. Or perhaps he's withheld where she's staying, from his captors, fearing they'll snatch her next. An admirable quality, if that's the case. I have always found missing people very interesting but this one is clearly a bit different to my normal type of case."

"Normal type of case," reflected back Alba. "Does mystery and intrigue follow you around quite a bit, then? I guess it must – after all, you haven't even given me your name yet."

"Haven't I? Oh, please don't read anything into that. Sorry, no secrets there. I'm Daniel, Daniel Jones. Pleased to meet you," said Daniel. Whereupon he held his hand out to Alba.

As she lightly shook it, her surprised look was not lost on him.

"I know, I know," he said. "Daniel Jones does not reflect my Indian heritage; my English father somewhat dominated my Indian mother in the matter of naming me. Strange juxtaposition, for her, where she could live in a country that had recently gained its independence but was in a relationship where she was still very much dominated and controlled by the English. So, yes, you're not the first to think my name doesn't quite fit what you see."

"I'm sorry, I didn't mean – "

Daniel cut her short:

"It's fine, trust me: you're not the first and you definitely won't be the last and there is a difference between someone showing me surprise and someone else demonstrating actual dislike. So, please don't worry."

"OK," replied Alba. Then, keen not to let go of the intriguing comment Daniel had previously made, she added:

"What is your normal type of missing person, then?"

"Oh, nothing so dramatic as you're probably already imagining; no military intelligence, 'black ops' or a police force's Missing Person Unit," stated Daniel.

"Are you a private investigator?" proposed Alba.

"No," he replied. "No, well not quite."

However, he consciously paused whilst Jed served Alba her food and topped up her water. Once Jed moved away, having cleared Daniel's plates and checked whether he wanted a dessert, which he did, the cheese platter with an extra pot of chutney, though to be taken up to his room later, Daniel continued:

"I work for a firm of solicitors in Bristol. I'm not one, to be clear, I simply work with them – history and ancestry are more my thing."

"How does that get you working with a load of legal bods, then?" queried Alba.

"Tracing beneficiaries to a will, primarily. That's where the bulk of my work comes from. However, the more interesting cases are when there is no will and seemingly no next-of-kin and I'm trying to trace one – someone, anyone, to inherit."

"How fascinating," said Alba genuinely.

"Oh, absolutely. But then – "

At which point, Daniel rested his elbows on the now empty table in front of him and precisely placed each thumb and finger-tip against its opposing one, fingers spread, giving himself the finished look that was somewhere between a calculating professor and a child trying to make a 'cat's cradle' but having forgotten the wool. He continued:

"The really interesting ones are those rare, rare cases, where we have no will but an obvious next-of-kin to inherit everything and then someone comes out of the shadows, as it were, with new evidence and suddenly we have a new beneficiary who trumps the previous one and so gets everything instead."

Daniel then lowered his voice before adding:

"Normally, the new information does come from the person who ends up being recognised as the new beneficiary – in that they are submitting evidence which favours them. However, occasionally it is someone with entirely altruistic intentions, someone just wants the truth to be told and for the 'right' outcome, even though they know they, themselves, will never benefit from their act."

Alba studied her dining neighbour and allowed him to conclude:

"Ah, yes. Rare, rare cases. Someone in my line of work might only get one, maybe two, such cases during an entire career but when they come along, it's as though you've found hen's teeth, King John's crown and Excalibur all at once. And if you do get such a case, you have to savour it."

"Savour it?" echoed Alba.

"Oh, absolutely: everything you've been working on, for that particular case, just gets blown away. The house of cards, so to speak, gets scattered by this unexpected gust of wind and you find yourself staring at a solitary upturned card that remains on the table, one you hadn't even seen before, and yet you know it outplays every other card that was there before."

With that, and as they both noticed Cecilia approaching the table to Alba's right, Daniel dropped his hands, folded his arms on the table and somehow, as far as Alba thought, lost his animation and his *joie de vivre*. He became once more the person he had been when Alba first started speaking to him about his meal choice. Still looking at Alba, he said far more unexcitingly:

"But I've taken up enough of your time and your food will be going cold; I should leave you to enjoy it."

As he stood, checking his pockets for the room key and some change, Alba asked:

"Are you here looking into such a case, then, or simply on holiday?"

He smiled, as he twirled the key and its cumbersome fob around one finger, and simply replied:

"I got here yesterday and already I think I'm going to have an enjoyable few days. I'm not one for the seaside normally – I mean, goodness me, I can't even swim – but yes, I sense an enjoyable few days. Good evening, Miss White. You made a good decision as to your choice of mains."

"Good evening. Maybe I'll see you in the bar later?" she said hopefully, still intrigued by his line of work.

"That is unlikely, very unlikely since I don't drink, plus I have plans."

With that, and having stacked a number of coins on the table, Daniel headed out of the dining area and into reception.

"How fascinating," said Alba quietly to herself as Cecilia apologised to her husband, Geoffrey, for forgetting to bring down his medication.

*

The fish pie was indeed excellent.

Alba had virtually finished it before she really started chatting to Mr and Mrs Constance. She was just about to launch into telling them about her day at Restormel Castle when Cecilia, realising Geoffrey should be taking his tablets with his food, insisted on returning to their room to collect his pills.

As Cecilia departed, Alba retrieved something from her jeans pocket and passed it to Geoffrey.

"Yours, I believe," she said as she handed him a little plastic coloured cribbage peg. "Found it this morning."

"Oh, bless you. We were looking for this earlier as we played – had to improvise and shave the end of a matchstick so we could score properly. Thank you for finding it; it's so much nicer keeping score with the original pegs."

"I'm sure," agreed Alba as she rearranged the remaining condiments in the rack on her table to restore some order to it.

"She beat me once again – I had a pretty good hand and a 'box' to come but she just pipped me as she scored well as we played our cards and then, as you may remember from us teaching you the game, she got to show her hand first, that round, and so reached one hundred and twenty one points just before I got to show my two hands."

"Never mind," sympathised Alba, "there's always next time and it's playing the game, not the winning, that really matters."

"Indeed," agreed Geoffrey. "Losing to my Cecilia is always a joy."

"Duck any good?" questioned Alba.

"It is but it is Alan's sauce that really makes it. Actually," said Geoffrey, "I really should be taking my pills with it. I wonder what's keeping her, for they should be by the tea tray. I should go and help her look if they are not there. Would you excuse me?"

"Of course. See you in a moment."

Alba watched him head out followed by the two local women, who had now finished their meals. With the 'barrier' between where Alba was sitting and the Detz family gone, Ben called across to Alba:

"You can come and sit with us if you'd like," he said.

Alba, more reserved than a ten-year-old boy, opted not to instantly call back. Rather, she got up and moved across to where the three were sitting and spoke, though only once she was standing by their table:

"You're kind," she said. "But it looks like you've finished."

"We've still got pudding to have," stated Gregory.

"What are you having?" asked Alba.

"Ice-cream!" announced Ben.

"Me too," declared Gregory.

"You two surprise me," teased Alba. "I had you both down for the fruit salad."

"Nah," they both replied in unison.

"I should be so lucky, getting them to eat fruit," contributed Gerry. "Would have thought you boys had had your fill of ice-cream today, with what Alba bought you earlier."

"Don't be daft, dad," came the predictable reply.

"Think I'm going to have the fruit," proposed Alba. "Shall I save you two lads the pieces of pear?"

"No thanks!" insisted Ben, on behalf of both of them.

"Would you like to join us and have pudding at this table?" asked Gerry. "You would be very welcome."

"Yeah," added Gregory. "We could play 'Top Trumps'" – whereupon he showed her a handful of cards with pictures of footballers on them.

"You're very kind. Can I have Chris Waddle if I play?" she asked.

"Waddle? Who's Waddle?" challenged Ben.

As Alba watched Gerry shake his head in disbelief, as he realised his own son was too young to know who one of England's finest midfielders was, Gregory spoke:

"I know who he is," he claimed proudly. "He used to play for Tottenham Hotspur and then some French team. There's a page on him in my 'Match of the Day' album: he's on their 'legends' page. Dad, can I go up to the room and get it to show Ben? Please!"

"Tell you what. As you two are talking so nicely to Alba and they're about to bring you your ice-creams, I'll go and get it. Where is it?"

"In my bed, I think," Gerry's elder son replied.

"Right, won't be long. And it was Marseille that he went to, Gregory." Then to Alba he added, "Join us if you'd like."

"Thank you but I'll head back to my table. I want to catch up with the couple who were to my right once they return. But I'll keep a distant eye on you two until your dad gets back."

With that, despite the boys' protestations, and as Gerry headed out, Alba returned to her table.

She had resumed her seat, and adjusted the bronze-effect buckle on her left boot, just as Martha, who had now also finished her meal, walked past. Martha was on her way to the snug door and thus her bedroom. As she passed, she very slickly slipped a piece of paper into the condiments rack on Alba's table. Martha made no attempt to speak to Alba and did not even make eye contact. She was past and gone before Alba had had time to process what the other woman had done.

Alba left the slip of paper hidden where it had been inserted. It went unnoticed by Jed, when he came to take her order for dessert, and, less surprisingly, given she departed via reception, by Annabel when she, in turn, vacated the restaurant area too, having also finished her meal.

*

"Seems like it's just you and me left!" announced the only other grown-up present, besides Alba herself, and over the sound of the increasingly heavy rain outside.

"Well, except for the two lads behind your right shoulder," corrected Alba. "Though I accept they are pretty quiet as they are eating their puddings."

However, with her fruit salad being served, her conversation with this other man lapsed as quickly as it had started. As she ate her dessert, in the relative quiet of the restaurant and still leaving Martha's note where it was, Alba listened to the rain outside.

For by now it was pouring. It was hard, Alba thought, to define the sound of rain, especially heavy rain. There was an intensity to it as each drop hit its own, almost pre-determined, spot on the ground and the noise of every single drop merged into one glorious cacophony.

The evening was dark – especially so due to the storm clouds – meaning she could not see the weather but hear it she absolutely could. She imagined the branches on the plants outside bend under the weight of the water, arching over as a result. Then, as she listened, she asked herself whether it had eased slightly in those last few minutes and whether that distant light that she could see through the window, coming from a boat out at sea, was just that little bit clearer?

If the rain had eased, though, it was momentarily. Still the rain cascaded down and another hundred thousand little droplets hit the ground and their combined glorious noise filled her ears once more. And part of her wanted to go outside and be bathed by the water, to be cleansed, almost baptised by it, to surrender herself to it. But she did not. Nonetheless, she remained lost to the mesmerising sound of the weather; she listened to the rain gutters struggle to cope and she told herself a dozen times that she had not left all her car windows open.

And still the clouds released their torrents and, if it were at all possible, to a greater degree than before. In that moment Alba wondered if this were how Noah had felt all those years ago and whether she too should regard the weather as an omen.

CHAPTER 9

Drops, corners and doors

"You know, the blasted thing had fallen right down between the bed and my bedside unit!" exclaimed Geoffrey on his return. "We had searched handbags, coat pockets, the tea tray, trouser pockets, the bathroom, twice as far as the bathroom was concerned, the drawer where the hairdryer is stored and even under the bed. Yet the pill box had wedged itself half-way down, meaning it wasn't visible from above neither did I have any success groping for it from beneath – well and truly lodged half-way, which we only discovered when I moved the entire unit in sheer desperation. Blasted thing!"

"You'll have to call it your 'Duke of York pill box' from now on," teased Alba.

"What?" said Geoffrey, distracted as he was as he finally took the much sought-after little pink tablet.

"Your Duke of York…"

"Oh, yes," he agreed, speaking over her. "Very good. That was always one of my favourite nursery rhymes when I was a little boy." With that, and it was as if the last six decades of his life faded in an instant and he was once more in shorts and with a scruffy but much-loved teddy bear held under one arm, he effortlessly and enthusiastically sang the rhyme's final line: "*And when they were only half-way up, they were neither up nor down*'."

As Cecilia took her seat also, Alba asked them:

"Good day?"

"Yes, thank you," replied Cecilia. "Geoffrey was at home, so he was available for the builders. Spent most of his time in the garden, mind you."

"That will have been a waste of time," contributed Geoffrey. "Just listen to that weather outside."

Alba, who had been doing exactly that over her dessert, simply acknowledged that she could hear it.

"Will have flattened everything I planted out," said Geoffrey despondently.

"Maybe you should have heeded the forecast," suggested his wife – unhelpfully, in Geoffrey's opinion.

"Well, yes but there are so many micro-climates down here I had a feeling this rain would miss us. Still, at least it didn't ruin Cecilia's afternoon; she was out meeting an old friend."

"Yes," continued Cecilia. "We had a lovely time in a little tea shop in St Buryan. We had the most delightful cream tea and – "

"Sorry to interrupt," said a somewhat damp looking Robyn, who had evidently finally made it into work, "but there's a telephone call for you, Mrs Constance. You can take it at the reception desk for quickness or I can keep them on hold until you get up to your room."

"Is there?" queried Cecilia, which simply prompted an affirmative nod from Robyn.

"I'm not expecting any calls but if you'll excuse me for a moment," she said, speaking to her husband. Then, to Robyn, added "I'll take it at reception for quickness."

*

"You're looking puzzled," observed Alba to Geoffrey, following Cecilia's departure.

"Is my face that readable?" he replied.

"I'm afraid so. The phone call?" suggested Alba, as she chased the remnants of the cream around her bowl.

"Actually, no. She's had one or two friends call her whilst we've been staying here, so not the telephone call. Rather, I'm sure, as we were playing cribbage before dinner, she said she had met her friend in a tea shop in St Just, not St Buryan. It must be me, getting my saints all mixed up and yet – oh, never mind, I'm keeping you. You've finished. If you scrape that bowl any more, you'll have the glaze off it. Feel free to head off – you don't have to keep this old man company. Cecilia will be back in a minute."

With Robyn's arrival, meaning Jed would have resumed his main duties in the bar, Alba keen to chat some more to him about his dad's garden, accepted Geoffrey's offer.

"Well, actually, if you don't mind me abandoning you, I think I'll retire to a window seat in the bar and marvel at the weather from there. Enjoy the rest of your meal."

With that, and having discretely retrieved Martha's note, Alba departed. As she was about to enter reception, Alba held the door open for the returning Cecilia and the two women passed.

"Was the fish pie any good?" asked someone as Alba then cut across reception to the bar.

"Pardon, what?" she replied, somewhat caught off guard, not having expected anyone to have been loitering in reception, given Cecilia had just taken a phone call there. Having processed it was Daniel, standing as he was by the wooden table, she continued:

"Sorry, yes, it was lovely."

"Good. Well, if you'll excuse me, I've got what I want," he said, as he tapped a couple of leaflets, side on, against the table – a brief tap and then, Alba was of the view, three slightly heavier ones, as if he was sending a message in morse code to someone. He then made his way up the stairs – tapping the leaflets once more, this time against the wooden hand rail.

As she settled herself at one of the window tables in the bar, Alba found herself wondering whether the rain, as it hit the window, was in turn sending out its own message in morse code.

*

"So, what do you reckon?" asked Alba to Jed, as he came over to ask her whether she would like something to drink.

"About what?"

"Our missing guest of course! Where have you been, Jed?" she joked.

Yet Jed did not hear the humour in Alba's question, meaning it was a very matter-of-fact reply Alba received:

"Well, I haven't been here. I've had a few days off, as I said, and wasn't meant to even be in tonight either but I got called in."

"Unlucky for you that you were holidaying at home!"

"It's fine. We're a team here and I don't mind mucking in. Plus, it was never really a 'holiday' as such; I was having some time off to sort out dad's stuff – the cottage, for one, that's being sold."

"Is it? From what you were saying earlier, I'd assumed you were taking it on – you were even asking after blackcurrant bushes."

"I know, I know," conceded Jed. "I wish, really wish I could keep it. It's my home too, which some people, not you though, seem to forget."

Jed looked for affirmation from Alba on that point, which he got in the form of several discrete nods. She then leant forward and patted the other seat at the table, angled her head and, with an encouraging look, invited him to sit down. His pause prompted Alba to speak:

"Come on Jed, sit for a few minutes. No one else is waiting for a drink, sit down for a bit and tell me."

He sat down – awkwardly and unnaturally. This was not his

domain and he was clearly feeling incredibly self-conscious. This tough weathered Cornishman seemed as unnatural sitting where he was as if he had been asked to blend in in London's Covent Garden, amongst all the cafes, boutiques and street artists. Jed's world was behind the bar, serving, engaging the guests but always with that wooden barrier between them. His world was one of half shadows, of being there but not really being noticed, of knowing what people wanted before they had even considered it for themselves. His world was behind the highly polished wooden defensive ring, cleaning the glasses, with their 'St Austell' or their 'Sharp's' logos engraved on them and checking stock levels. To be sitting in the bar, relaxing, chatting, was not him and his stiffness was not lost on Alba.

"Tell you what, I'll come and sit at the bar. You can serve me a drink and we can chat like that, if you'd prefer."

"Much," replied Jed.

*

Once Alba had settled herself at the bar and as she cradled her little glass of liqueur, she prompted Jed to continue:

"You were saying about the cottage – " she said.

"It's to be sold," Jed replied. "My home, all of my memories, our mother's ashes, which we scattered in the garden, all count for nothing apparently. It's not right."

His passion and frustrations were not lost on Alba as he continued.

"My home. All the repairs, all the maintenance, all the effort I've invested into the cottage, it's not right. I mean it's not dad's fault – he believed in fairness and being equitable. You know," he continued, with a moment's lightness in his voice, "dad always insisted, when it was Sunday lunchtime, that whichever of us three children got to slice the cake or serve into bowls the dessert, got to choose last. That got us to serve things out equally, I can tell you."

"Very good," agreed Alba. "You'll have to mention that to Gerry."

"Gerry?"

"The Detz family, who are staying here."

"Oh right. Anyway," continued Jed, "I always assumed dad would leave things equally between us three children – not that the other two need an inheritance as they're more than financially well off. And I guess I don't begrudge them their inheritance but why do Anthony and Eva – that's my brother, who's dad's Executor, and my sister – have to take their share as cash straight away? It's not fair and there's absolutely no way I can afford to buy them out: look at me, I'm a barman! As I say, they're both well off and neither needs the money right now – Anthony even has a second home in Italy. Why couldn't we keep the cottage and they let me pay them rent? I've suggested that, said I'd pay a fair rent as well. Eva said no before I'd even finished talking, said it was simpler – cleaner – to share things out as soon as practicable and Anthony agreed."

"All nice and clinical but lacking any compassion," suggested Alba.

"Exactly," agreed Jed. Grateful to have someone to offload to, Jed placed a white saucer in front of Alba and then, from a transparent ice-cream box which was out of sight under the counter, duly filled the saucer with circular foil-wrapped mint chocolates and from which Alba appreciatively selected one.

As Jed continued, Alba folded the first, of what would be several, pieces of gold foil into a tightly folded square and placed it back on the saucer.

"So, they just want everything cashed in," said Jed. "Anthony already has got a buyer lined up for dad's cottage, meaning as soon as Probate comes through, he'll be rushing ahead with the sale. It's just not right that they're taking my home away."

At which point, Jed slammed his damp tea towel down against the bar. The hefty thump and the scattering of several packets of crisps, as the towel caught the edge of a small wicker basket that had, up until that moment been a safe cradle for them, caught Alba off guard. The mini commotion, even though it was of his own making, caught Jed out, too.

"Sorry, Alba," he said apologetically, as he, and as Alba was doing from her side of the bar, collected the scattered crisp packets from the floor.

"It must be frustrating," she said sympathetically.

"Completely," he said as he replaced the final packet back into the basket. "There's nothing I can legally do to stop them. I'm not being robbed, as such. I'll get my share but that's not the point somehow. They're taking my home away. They both moved away a long time ago and their veins don't seem to run with the Cornish blood that I have. I mean, I'm not quite one for 'Cornish independence and all that' but my understanding is that whoever Anthony has lined up to buy the cottage isn't local and will be having it as a second home. That'll bring work for some local builders, for a few weeks at least, as they renovate it – strip its heart out more like – but after that it'll be another empty property for eleven months of the year, further eroding the sense of community that we have in Marazion. It would be slightly less painful if Anthony insisted on selling to a local family but no and my guess is, that my dear brother has had someone lined up to buy it and rip it to pieces well before dad died."

He paused, noticed there were now three tightly folded pieces of foil in the saucer, then added:

"They'll modernise it, no doubt. They'll pave over the garden – so dad's kitchen garden will go as it'll be too much maintenance for people who are hardly ever there. Then they'll take out an internal wall, to join up the living room and the small lounge to create a large modern living space, and the stone floors will get ripped out so they can have underfloor heating under some modern slatted shiny wood-effect flooring. If the cottage is lucky, the main fireplaces might stay but they'll probably take them out of the bedrooms and the coffin drop will probably get sealed up. That will be because of some modern-day squeamishness about death, though, no doubt, they'll claim it's down to a fear of little children somehow falling through."

"Coffin drop?" queried Alba. "What's one of those?"

"If I said it's so you can drop coffins, please don't think I'm being condescending but that is exactly what they're about. In tight little old Cornish cottages, like dad's is, and from a time when people probably didn't live as long but were blessed to be able to die at home, you couldn't – literally couldn't – get a coffin up and down the staircase. The solution is incredibly simple when you think about it – a section of the bedroom floor is constructed as a discrete trap door. The floor joists are positioned, from when the cottage is first built, to allow a rectangular panel in the floor to be hinged. A bit like, I guess, the panels you can have in the floor of one of those non-conformist churches, where they hide a baptistry, or like those compartment doors you have in the sides of modern caravans, which allow you to access the space behind in a more convenient way. So, whether it's a church floor, a caravan or in a little Cornish cottage, the discrete door is there simply as an access point."

"A coffin drop is a slightly grimmer example," mused Alba.

"I guess," agreed Jed. "But when you live with it all the time, it's just part of the structure of the house. You don't see it from the bedroom if you cover it with rugs and, from the living room, beneath, well, how often do you really study the ceiling above you? I mean, you see it if you look at it but really all you're seeing is a matching section of the wooden ceiling with some discrete brass fixings. And, on a lighter note, we did use it to move items of furniture from time to time between the floors – saved dismantling bookcases and chests of drawers."

"How interesting; I'd keep a feature like that," reflected Alba.

"But from what Anthony's inferred about the buyer he's got lined up, it won't be retained."

"Their loss," stated Alba. "Definitely not prevalent in my part of the world – I've never heard of such a feature before."

"Oh, there are a few such morbid features in old houses, if you know what you're looking for. Coffin drops are one, coffin corners are another and 'being at death's door' is a phrase that hints at a third – though that's more colonial."

A further blank expression from Alba told Jed he needed to explain.

"Well," he said as a fifth foil square appeared in the saucer, "coffin corners are those little alcoves you get part way up turning staircases. I tend to imagine them in Georgian or Regency homes – there were definitely some in Trelyn House. Mum took me round there quite a few times when I was a boy. She used to work there and often wanted to show me around. I remember her pointing out these little alcoves on the staircase up to the servants' quarters. The alcoves might have little ornaments in, such as an urn or a little flower vase, but their real purpose was to increase the angles you could manoeuvre a large object around as you tried to get something up or down."

"Something being a wooden coffin?" suggested Alba, having worked out where Jed was going with his explanation.

"Exactly, yes. On tight turning staircases you need those little recesses to give you the flexibility to manoeuvre a heavy rigid object – and his Lordship wouldn't want dead servants taking the liberty of expecting to be carried out via his main grand staircase, would he?" concluded Jed, with a wry smile on his face.

"And 'being at death's door'?" asked Alba.

"Ah, yes, as I say more of a feature in colonial homes out in New England. We use the phrase now as a way of saying someone is really ill but that is drawing on an architectural feature where colonial homes would have a door on the side of the house that gave direct access to the parlour. It was to allow people to pay their respects to the deceased without walking through more of the house than the grieving relatives would want. Also, that design of home with a central staircase and central chimney, meant manoeuvring a coffin in and out of the parlour – for the body had to be laid out in one room for people to pay their respects, especially as they didn't have morgues and funeral parlours as we do now, in our modern attempts to sanitise death – was physically very difficult. The result of which was to have that extra external side door to get the coffin in and out of the parlour. Ultimately, therefore, it was the door through which the deceased person left their home."

"How absolutely fascinating," said Alba. "So, 'being at death's door' means you're really quite unwell!"

"Deathly ill," echoed Jed in a melancholy voice.

"As I say, how interesting. And don't take this the wrong way, Jed, but you're almost wasted as a barman – I mean, you're not, as you're very good at your job and I'm sure the hotel would struggle without you – but with your building knowledge you should be an architect or something like that. You've got a real eye for buildings, it would seem."

"Thanks and no I don't take it the wrong way and I do enjoy wandering around the grounds of the now closed down Trelyn House and marvelling at it; it's as if sometimes it is speaking to me. But, as for architects, over-rated if you ask me. Unreliable – "

At that point, though, Alba cut across Jed:

"Actually, that reminds me of what I started to say to you, as I was sitting over at the window," and she needlessly gestured with her left arm to where she had first been sitting in the bar after dinner.

"Which was what?" asked Jed.

"Just what you thought about our missing guest – he's an architect. That was what just reminded me, us talking about buildings and architects and the like."

"Someone's missing, you say?"

"Yes Jed, of course. As I said fifteen minutes ago, where have you been, Jed?"

"Well, I haven't been here, have I? As I said, I've had a few days off sorting out dad's stuff, waiting on people who didn't…"

"So, you don't know?" Alba said, talking over what Jed was saying.

Jed simply raised his eyebrows and gave a brief shrug of the shoulders, making it clear to Alba that he did not.

She took the hint and continued:

"Joshua and Stella are staying here, at this hotel. I guess they checked in when you were already off. They're in room seven. I was at school with Stella – actually that bit isn't important, it just shows what a small world it is, that, completely randomly, we both happen to be staying here. Actually, it's a useful coincidence that I'm here at the same time because Stella's husband has gone missing."

"Missing?"

"Yes. He and Stella had done a boat ride yesterday morning, then back here for lunch and then visited St Michael's Mount in the afternoon…"

This time it was Jed who spoke over her:

"In an afternoon? That's an insult to the Mount – why do tourists think they can do such a mesmerizing place in just a few rushed hours? It's an insult to the island's heritage and the people who live and work there."

"And the flora," added Alba.

"Well, yes. Flipping insult all round. Still, that's the modern tourist for you."

"I suppose so. Anyway," continued Alba, "they then separated at the beach car park. As you live in Marazion, you'll know which one I mean."

A nod from Jed allowed Alba to maintain her narrative:

"Stella drove herself back here whilst Joshua went off for a site meeting. He's an architect, is having this mini-break with Stella to dovetail with this work visit he had arranged and yet didn't come back last night. Stella is beside herself with grief and worry and he still hasn't returned – she's up in her room now dreading a phone call but desperate for one nonetheless. It's not helped by the fact that she doesn't know the address of where he went off to."

"Flipping heck, another one!" exclaimed Jed, as he held a glass up to the light to check he had properly cleaned it.

"Another one?" queried Alba. "What do you mean another one?"

"Well, as I was trying to say a few minutes ago, architects are over-rated and unreliable. A flipping architect was meant to meet me yesterday late afternoon: he was due about half five. Never showed. Blooming waste of time – in part, that's why I had those few days off, as this bloke was meant to be visiting yesterday but he never showed. Complete waste of my time. I could have stayed on my allotment longer but, no, thought I should get back to the cottage in good time, in case the bloke was early, and yet he never showed. No respect for other people's time. Seems like that profession is full of unreliable, absent…"

But Alba did not listen to any further views Jed expressed about people wasting his time or what else he could have done on his allotment with the extra time. Rather she was up and out of the bar. In her haste she sent the packets of crisps in their little wicker basket flying once more. She attacked the stairs as aggressively as her still relatively recently eaten dinner would allow and as her limited sporting prowess would itself allow – she had never made it through the hockey trials at university after all.

A turning staircase is never the best staircase to take on, when going at it at speed. To be fair to Alba, she did make the first turn successfully. However, the number of stairs from the first ninety-degree turn to the second turn was one less than it was from the ground floor to the first turn. The effect of that subtle difference was that Alba's stride pattern was wrong and she did not make the second turn. Rather, she collided heavily with the wall. It was her shoulder which took the brunt of the impact. Had she been of a different build or wearing the type of jacket she had spent a good part of the nineteen-eighties in – during her teenage years – with their prominent shoulder pads, Alba would probably have put a 'coffin corner' into the wall at that point, such was the force of her collision.

Yet, as she built up momentum once again, for the final section of the ascent, she did not notice the pain for her focus was entirely on gaining her friend's attention:

"Stella, Stella, I know where he went! Stella, Stella, I've got news. He didn't go back onto the island. He stayed in Marazion. Stella…"

CHAPTER 10
Déjà vu

It was even earlier than Alba had agreed with Stella to be down in the breakfast area; the excitement of last night and the hope that Joshua might be found alive and well were all too much for Alba and so here she sat, at this ridiculously early hour. She stirred the pot of tea that had, thankfully, already been produced from the kitchen.

As she had made her way down the stairs – having glanced at the almost imperceptible scuff on the wall where she had collided with it the night before – she wondered whether the same sense of optimism would have prompted Stella to also be down at this hour. Yet she found herself sitting alone at the breakfast table and, from her friend's absence, Alba could only conclude that the developments of last night had given Stella a chance to sleep; to sleep either from a sense of peace or at least from a sense that things were progressing. Whichever it was, it seemed it had allowed Stella to sleep – hopefully to really sleep, neither flittingly nor as a succession of disjointed catnaps, interspersed with disturbed dreams, but to have that deep, deep sleep, where one feels immersed in one's bed, wholly cocooned by the quilt or as if one is floating on Aladdin's carpet wafting through the warm night sky of the Arabian desert.

As she stirred the pot once more, whilst deprived of Stella's company, Geoffrey and Cecilia Constance were present for breakfast – if Alba had regarded herself as being down early, her friends must have had a good half an hour on her at least. Once they had explained this was due to Geoffrey needing to be back at their home to meet with their project manager at eight o'clock, they asked Alba about the developments of the previous evening. Having poured herself a cup of tea and as she cradled it in both hands – savouring one of life's great simple pleasures, of that first morning brew – she attempted to explain.

"It seems wrong to admit it," Alba began as Mr and Mrs Constance listened eagerly. "But it was rather thrilling in those first few minutes. There was something to take to Stella, something to help, something that brought, well, if not an answer, then at least a lead. The path, the journey that lay before us was still far from clear but we at least knew, so to speak, which direction to head off in. Prior to that we had – "

"Nothing?" suggested Geoffrey.

"Exactly, nothing, nothing beyond the car park where Stella and Joshua separated. Gerry – that's Gerry Detz, the dad who's holidaying here with his two sons – had wondered whether Joshua had headed back to the island, St. Michaels' Mount itself, meaning our search, or at least the police's, should start off back on the actual island. At least now we know that Joshua was heading inland, more specifically to the other end of Marazion itself and – "

This time it was Cecilia who interrupted but she cut herself short before she really said what had 'jumped' into her mind:

"Does that make you think that Gerry was deliberately, no, sorry, I shouldn't say what I was just wondering," and with that, Cecilia fell silent.

"No, come on dear, out with it," said Geoffrey. "There's no one else here; just your dull old husband and dear young Alba. Plus, remember someone is still missing. So, if a thought has just come to you, share it, however 'left field' it is."

"I suppose you're right but it does seem a bit unfair to say," answered Cecilia, still unsure of whether she should divulge what was on her mind.

"Look, I'm sure it'll be fine – so long as you're neither about to accuse me of having this missing bloke buried under the folly we're having built in the garden nor that Alba is secretly in love with him and he is hiding in her room."

"Geoffrey!" exhorted his wife. She then further admonished him – "Don't you be so coarse."

Stern looks from both his wife and Alba brought a look of contrition to Geoffrey's face.

"Sorry," he meekly said.

"I should think so," Cecilia said. "Right," she added, "before you take our conversation further down the gutter, I will simply say what I stopped myself from saying a moment ago and, I might add, it is not nearly so crude as what we've just heard you expound."

"Sorry," Geoffrey said again.

The two women let him stew a moment longer before Cecilia spoke once more:

"Right, all I was going to say was – and this is in confidence between the three of us – I suddenly just wondered whether this Gerry Detz was deliberately trying to get you, Alba, to focus the wrong way? I mean, I don't know him and it seems a bit unfair to start throwing such wild accusations around but it suddenly struck me as a bit odd if he were getting you to fix your thoughts on properties on the island, when you had all of Marazion and beyond to consider – Gulval, Ludgvan, Crowlas and the like. Plus, in all honesty, what could an architect do to a cottage on the island? Surely they're all listed properties, meaning you could, effectively, only repair and restore? You could only replace like with like. I could understand a builder visiting an island property but an architect? Why would an architect have any kind of work on that particular island? So, I just wondered, in that moment you mentioned this Mr Detz, Alba, whether he is really as naïve as he made out or whether he was trying to throw you off the scent? After all, where was he Thursday afternoon, himself? As I say, a bit unfair of me to make such comments; I do not know him nor is he present to defend himself but at least my observations are not as coarse as your crass remarks, Geoffrey."

"Noted, my dear," said Geoffrey apologetically once more.

"I think," said Alba, feeling a need to defend her absent companion from the day before, "he was simply being naïve and, as for where he was himself on Thursday, I'd have to ask him – I think he mentioned it but I can't remember. They're interesting points you make though, Cecilia, I hadn't considered things through such practical eyes."

"No, nor me," concurred Geoffrey. "You'll have to sound this Gerry bloke out, Alba."

"Suppose so," agreed Alba. "But it's a bit like Jed, isn't it? We could sit here, the three of us all morning, and start expounding wild theories involving people neither present to defend themselves nor who have ever given us any grounds, be it over many years we've known them, such as Jed, or in the brief pleasant time we've encountered them, such as Gerry, to doubt their integrity and plain and simple goodness."

"I agree entirely," said Cecilia. "But if something has happened to your friend's husband – as opposed to him simply abandoning her – and an accident becomes less likely with each passing hour, someone else is involved. So, hypothetically speaking and before anyone else comes down for breakfast, what could one say concerning Jed?"

"Well," started Alba before pausing to take a sip of her tea. She was aware that, unlike her tea, what she was about to hypothesize would leave an unpalatable taste in her mouth.

However, the sound of footsteps on the staircase down to reception prompted Alba to speak quickly:

"Look, Joshua was due at Jed's father's cottage at half past five Thursday evening – Jed still had the letter from Joshua in his pocket and which he showed Stella and myself last night. So, there's no way we're talking about multiple missing architects: just Joshua not turning up for his appointment with Jed. Jed assured us last night – for Stella and I rushed down to the bar to talk to Jed – Joshua did not show up. Simple as that; Jed had taken time off work to meet the architect acting on behalf of the person that Jed's brother has got lined up to buy the property, once Probate is granted."

Understanding nods from the other two allowed Alba to continue: "But – and this is the bit that leaves a bad taste in my mouth – we only have Jed's word for that. Jed had been saying to me earlier in the evening how much he resented his brother forcing a sale through, a sale that is more than just his father's cottage but of Jed's home too. And there's no way Jed will be able to afford anything remotely similar here in Cornwall, inheriting, as he will, a third of his father's estate. Jed is naturally upset, feels powerless and that he is without a voice. He could well have been offended if Joshua was wafting through the cottage and perhaps talking about knocking down walls, paving the well-worked and productive little garden, ripping out fireplaces and adding a room in the loft utilising those ever popular 'Velux' windows. An argument could easily have started. It could have got heated and a fist could have been thrown. It's possible, that's all I'm saying – as unpleasant as it is to say."

"But he didn't try to keep the appointment hidden from you or Stella, did he?" offered Geoffrey in Jed's defence.

"No," agreed Alba. "Plus, as we phoned the police from reception to tell them of the development, Jed seemed neither troubled nor agitated. He really didn't seem to have anything to hide and he said he would be at home this morning if the police wanted to visit and check things out."

"But it's possible he did turn up. It's possible there was an altercation. Possible Joshua got no further than the front door because Jed refused to let him in. Possible something happened to Joshua after a 'failed' appointment that had nothing to do with Jed.

Don't worry, my young dear," said Cecilia sympathetically to Alba, "you are simply going over what's possible. I really don't think you're betraying Jed in considering what could have happened."

"Thank you," replied Alba, comforted by her friend's words.

Their discussion, however, was curtailed as the wooden doors from reception swung wildly open and two boys entered.

*

"Morning," called out Gregory.

"Hi Aunty Alba," added Ben, as he made his way to where Alba and Mr and Mrs Constance were sitting.

"How the blazes did I get that prefix?" asked Alba quietly to Geoffrey and Cecilia. "I spent a few hours with them at Restormel and suddenly I'm their aunt!"

"Enjoy the innocence of it," said Cecilia helpfully – just as Ben reached where they were sitting.

"Look!" said Ben to Alba, as he proudly showed her a 'Lego' fire engine he had been making in his room that morning.

Alba, going with Cecilia's advice, threw herself into the moment and entered the world of a young boy:

"That looks good. Is that someone sitting in the engine's cab?"

"Yeah," replied Ben. "And, see, he can come out. The doors open but to actually get the fireman out, you have to open the roof." Whereupon Ben demonstrated to Alba how, by lifting the ladder out of the way and opening the hinged red roof, a little yellow-faced 'Lego' figure, in a black uniform with precise gold buttons painted down his chest, could be retrieved.

"Look, he's holding a walkie-talkie. That's so he can talk to the other one when that one is up the ladder putting out a fire."

"Wow!" acknowledged Alba. "But should he really be holding anything when he's meant to be driving such a large fire engine?"

Alba hoped there was not any sarcasm in her voice – she had not meant it sarcastically, rather in a 'creative' way. She wanted Ben to think for himself, not just adorn the figures with their accessories because that was what the picture on the box 'told' him to do. She also felt that it was never too early to instil good driving practice in anyone.

"Oh, I hadn't thought."

Ben then turned the vehicle round and showed Alba a little compartment on the other side, revealed when he opened a pair of shutters – a 'Lego' component which, had the frame and pair of shutters been green or yellow as opposed to fire engine red, would easily be found in a 'Lego' house as a window with French shutters or, if blue and white, would have been a structural part of some space station with folding-out solar panels.

"We can put his radio in here," announced Ben. "Then he'll be just like dad when he's driving. He doesn't like any distractions – won't even have a travel sweet in case he coughs or chokes on it."

"That's impressive," acknowledged Alba. "Plus, with regards to your firemen, as one is driving it, the other is hardly likely to be up the ladder at the same time."

"Actually, the other one I've decided is a fire woman," announced Ben.

"Very twenty-first century," said Cecilia quietly to her husband.

"This one can be you, Aunty Alba," said Ben, pointing to the 'Lego' figure clipped to the vehicle's ladder, and dad can be the one driving. I've got some spare 'Lego' walkie-talkies up in the room, so I'll give your figure one so you'll always be able to talk to dad even if you're not near each other."

"Right," said Alba nervously – she was spared any further imaginations of the young child as his father, having first wished Alba a good morning, called him across to where he and Gregory were sitting.

"Quite a sweet boy," declared Geoffrey once Ben had gone. "Seems quite taken with you."

"Somehow this holiday of mine is becoming less and less solitary," reflected Alba.

*

The breakfast area was getting busier as Alba and Mr and Mrs Constance returned to their ruminations about Joshua's disappearance and the significance that it was with Jed he was meant to be meeting; Annabel, Daniel and the other solitary male resident – the one who had been alone with Alba in the restaurant the night before, following everyone else's departure or non-appearance – had all seated themselves at different tables and were served teas or coffees and were having their food orders taken by Lizzie.

"Gosh, look at the time," Geoffrey suddenly announced. "I need to be going."

"You not going too?" asked Alba of Cecilia.

"No. I mean I could but I've decided not to."

"I've said she's very welcome and this isn't just my building project," insisted Geoffrey.

"It is, Geoffrey. You know it is," she answered but then added, though to Alba rather than her husband:

"It's fine. It is Geoffrey's project and he's got a much more practical, spatial mind than I have and I completely trust him with what needs to be done. Plus," and a different level of energy was in her voice now, "if you've got nothing else planned for this morning, once you've spoken with Stella, I was going to ask whether you fancy a walk around the grounds of Trelyn House. But please don't think it's some posh gardens I'm proposing taking you to, with a delightful tea room and gift shop, for it is not. The house is now empty, there never was a tea room and the gardens are untended and have been for a while – increasingly lost to brambles, willowherbs and successive years of the unremoved dead stems of your *sedums*, *echinops* and *alliums*. And as for the rose beds and the *espalier* fruit trees, well, don't even look, it would make you weep! For all that, or because of all that, I find it quite an enchanting place still."

"Cecilia has always had an interest in that old house. She used to work there, for the late Sir Roger de Roches."

"I did but that was a long time ago," said Cecilia.

"He died quite suddenly a couple of years ago," Geoffrey explained. "His only child died young, Sir Roger's wife predeceased him and he had no brothers and sisters. Apparently, some distant firm of solicitors are managing the winding up of the estate."

"Geoffrey still desperately wishes he could have been Sir Roger's solicitor," stated Cecilia.

"I do," admitted her husband. "Wouldn't have retired when I did if I had been. Would have kept working until I had tidied up Sir Roger's affairs. But for reasons unbeknown to me he appointed some firm up in Bristol. I really don't know what's taking them so long – the estate clearly has to be handed back to the Crown."

"No will, Geoffrey says," contributed Cecilia.

"That's the rumour and with no known heir it seems quite clear to me that the whole place reverts back to the State. Why it's taking them so long though beats me – seems they're stringing it all out for as long as possible simply to claim as much as they can in expenses for themselves. Just because it must go back to the State doesn't mean they should be lining their own pockets out of it; not my way of doing things, not at all."

"Doesn't like people bending the rules," stated Cecilia.

"Well, there's a way of doing things. If – "

However, Cecilia, as she massaged that tiny area on her forehead between her two fine, perfectly defined, eyebrows and with her eyes shut, cut him short:

"Geoffrey my dear, it's too early for you to tell us your way of doing things once again. I'm sure the firm of solicitors from Birmingham – "

"Bristol," corrected Geoffrey.

"Yes, alright, Bristol, wherever. I am sure they are a decent firm and there's a good reason as to what is slowing them up."

"Well, perhaps," Geoffrey had to concede. "But I have my doubts."

"Geoffrey, you ought to be heading off," said Cecilia trying a different tack. "You'll be late for your meeting. It's fine if you go off without me, for hopefully Alba will be happy for me to show her Trelyn this morning."

"It does sound rather enchanting," agreed Alba. "Naturally, though, it all depends on Stella. If there have been any further developments, you'll understand my priorities are to my friend."

"Of course," agreed Cecilia.

"Right, I'm off," announced Geoffrey, as he placed a kiss on his wife's cheek. "See you at lunchtime, my dear."

"Drive carefully. Remember you parked in the bays at the front of the hotel – don't go and spend the next twenty minutes looking for our car in the main car park," said his wife to the departing figure of her husband.

"Thank you but I hadn't forgotten," professed Geoffrey. "And I do wish you'd let me forget that one occasion in St Ives."

As Geoffrey held the reception door open for Emily Hibbert to enter the breakfast area, Cecilia filled Alba in on her husband's embarrassing episode:

"We'd been to visit Tate St Ives and we couldn't find our car in the car park. Geoffrey was convinced it had been stolen and was about to call the police when I repeated my belief that we were in the wrong car park altogether. Thankfully he listened to me at last and, of course, we were in completely the wrong one. You see, just occasionally, he goes about things in a slightly gung-ho or rash way and gets himself in a bit of bother – I dread to think how far he would have escalated that 'theft' had I not been there. Bit like looking for his pill box last night. He was unnecessarily pulling out every drawer, turned the bathroom upside down and was about to start accusing the staff of throwing it away or even taking it. Why would Lizzie or Robyn steal some pills, I ask you? Finally, I was able to force him to sit down and calmly try and recall where he'd last seen them. Had I not, I dread to think where that 'crisis' would have ended. He probably would have had Cliff up and forced him to apologise for something his staff had never done. You see, my dear husband does occasionally jump to conclusions – the wrong ones – and start throwing accusations around before having all the facts at his disposal."

"We all have our faults and foibles," replied Alba.

"You're too protective of him. He can be a stubborn old boot at times," claimed Cecilia. "Anyway, as you've finished your breakfast, let me show you Trelyn House. There's a picture of it in reception."

"Is there?" puzzled Alba. "You've said it's somewhat dilapidated, has no gift shop, so, all in all, I doubt the late Sir Roger de Roches was producing postcards of his stately pile. And I've looked in the tourist information box in reception and there's definitely no leaflet on Trelyn in there."

"Trust me," said an assured Cecilia. "Come on, follow me – the picture is very much there and I reckon you've looked at it a hundred times yet never quite seen it."

As Alba followed Cecilia across the breakfast area towards reception, and having smiled at Gerry as she passed his table, Alba said to Cecilia:

"I thought I was quite an observant person and yet you're claiming I've seen it lots of times."

"Hundreds!" declared Cecilia. "And, therein, I've given you a clue."

However, as they stepped into reception, Stella was making her way down the stairs. Cecilia, recognising now was suddenly not the time to be teasing her young friend, quickly stated:

"Alba, it can wait. Your friend will clearly want to chat with you. Just to say, I'm around the hotel this morning, as you know, so if you still have time and fancy a trip to Trelyn, just come and find me. It's not too far to drive so even half a morning will allow me to show you it, which I'd like to. You will have to drive though, as Geoffrey has our car."

With that, and in contrast to Annabel who bustled out of the breakfast area and up the stairs, Cecilia discretely slipped back to her breakfast table, allowing Stella to speak:

"Alba, sorry, I overslept. We need to talk."

*

Sensing once more Stella probably would not want to walk through a busy breakfast area and that where they were in reception was actually quite a good place to sit and talk, Alba pulled the two grey high-backed chairs closer together and the two friends sat.

"I'm pleased you were able to sleep. But where are things at?" Alba simply asked.

Stella shook her head and looked once more at her friend with sad, searching eyes. Finally, she spoke:

"Nowhere, at least not where I thought they'd be. As you said yourself last night, it was exciting when you rushed up with what you'd found out. I guess we both thought it was all over."

As Alba massaged her bruised shoulder once more, she nodded her agreement.

"But, as you know," Stella continued "once I'd spoken to Jed myself, I then called the police. They took all the details I gave them and they said they'd call me back. You know, I assumed they'd rush round to the hotel and interview Jed. Then, I assumed, they would go over and search the cottage and the garden; perhaps even send sniffer dogs. Yet, as we learnt last night, no, nothing like that. They simply spoke with Jed themselves on the phone and allowed him to confirm everything he had told us – which was basically nothing."

"But if Joshua didn't show, there wasn't a lot for Jed to say," said Alba, feeling once more she needed to defend an absent participant in this troubling mystery.

"If!" exclaimed Stella, suddenly full of agitation and frustration. "If," she repeated. "But what if Jed's lying? Why couldn't they have gone and searched and checked things out for real – for themselves – last night? Surely their philosophy is 'trust no one'?"

"Perhaps. I guess, all I can say is, why would Jed, if he felt neither you nor the police knew where Joshua was going for this meeting, voluntarily disclose Joshua was meant to be meeting him? Better, for Jed, if he's involved, to hide the fact for as long as possible. But," Alba added, "I don't think he's involved; he just can't be."

"We'll see," replied Stella, a fraction calmer than a moment before. "All I know for sure, is the police said, when they did finally call back, once you'd gone to bed, that depending on any developments overnight – and once they've confirmed things with Joshua's office this morning – they may go and speak to Jed in person."

Alba could suddenly see the panic resurface in her friend's eyes. Yet Alba could not think of anything to say, realising that unlike the excitement of last night, once more it was to become a painful, drawn-out, frustrating and numbing waiting game for Stella – a realisation Stella herself put into words:

"So, I've just got to wait once more."

"Yes," agreed Alba.

The intensity of the moment was broken as the only hotel guest whose name Alba did not yet know, made his way out of the breakfast area and headed up the stairs. He spoke as he did so:

"Good morning."

His words were said more out of ritual than in an attempt to trigger a conversation and he was gone from sight before either seated woman had a chance to consider offering back a reply.

"He's the only guest I have yet to properly speak to since I arrived," said Alba. "He turned up Thursday dinner time, I recall. Also, he and I were alone in the dining area last night – well, alone save for the two young boys staying here – and we spoke briefly but nothing of interest. I think we simply commented upon how everyone else, even the boys' father, had found a reason not to be in the dining area at that moment. You see, suddenly it was just us two left."

"Oh, him," replied Stella. "I spoke with him yesterday as I was milling around the hotel whilst you were out visiting that castle. He's a university lecturer, Nicholas is his name, Nicholas Goodwill. He's down here doing some research for a paper he's writing for some journal."

"Yes, he had that look about him on Thursday evening: I remember thinking that then. Not quite casual enough to be truly just down here on holiday," said Alba.

"Did you notice anything else about him?" queried Stella.

"No, can't say I did. Well, I would hazard a guess he is a vegetarian, as he opted for a veggie lasagne, possibly teetotal as he had a glass of water but really, no, nothing stood out."

"Oh, OK," replied Stella.

"A bit like the other solitary man who is staying here at the moment. Neither of them has quite pulled off the holiday look." Whereupon Alba explained to Stella the type of job Daniel Jones did for a living.

However, their conversation was interrupted when Annabel returned to reception from her room and started to vigorously ring the reception desk bell.

"Hello, hello," she called out to empty space behind the wooden desk. "Is anyone there?"

"You might have to give them a minute," called out Alba. "Lizzie is serving breakfasts and I haven't seen Cliff, the manager, yet this morning."

Yet Annabel ignored Alba and continued to bang the bell and call out:

"Hello, hello. Can someone come?"

Thankfully, for Alba at least – for Alba was about to ask the other woman to 'Stop ringing that bell, can't you tell the staff are busy? You'll just have to wait' – Lizzie extracted herself from the breakfast area, where she had been clearing tables, discussing with Emily Hibbert what she could have as a packed lunch and supplying further pots of tomato ketchup to Gregory and Ben.

"Yes? Can I help?" said Lizzie before she had even got to the reception desk and trying her best to mask her annoyance at such an impatient guest.

"Ah, you're here at last," snapped Annabel. "Finally."

"Can I help?" repeated Lizzie – and as Alba and Stella watched, they could see the annoyance in Lizzie's eyes as her 'mask' started to slip.

"Yes, you can. I need you to tell me whether my companion has already checked out? She's not answering her door. We're both due off promptly this morning as we've got a long day's walking ahead of us. It's unlike her to not have anything for breakfast but maybe she ate in her room. But, whatever, she can't have left as we still have to hand over the car key so I can pick her up at the end of today's walking – we are walking in opposite directions, you see. So, she can't have left already. But she's not down here, all your rooms are en-suite, meaning she's hardly going to be having a wash in the toilets at the back of the snug, and she's not answering when I knock on her door. So, where is she?"

Alba could suddenly feel her heart racing and her senses becoming heightened. Stella, too, seemed on edge. It was Alba, struck by a sense of *déjà vu*, who spoke first; she spoke to Lizzie but effectively it was to the whole room:

"Lizzie, something's not right."

CHAPTER 11

Three enter

Everything then happened quite quickly. Cliff appeared from his office. Cecilia and Gerry appeared from the breakfast area – Gerry, sensing something was wrong, had thankfully persuaded his boys to help the absent Lizzie, by stacking all the dirty plates on one table and straightening the chairs. Their reward, he had assured them, would be an ice-cream at least, when they visited the tin mine later that day. Alan, too, having finished cooking people's breakfasts, appeared at Cliff's side.

A barrage of comments and questions established that no one had seen Martha that morning. Cecilia stated Martha had not been seen down at breakfast when she and Geoffrey had ventured down and this was confirmed by Lizzie. Annabel repeated her assertion that Martha would not have checked out without swapping keys with her. It was then established that Martha's room key had not been returned, in that it was neither hanging on the board behind the reception desk nor had it been dropped through the key slot within the desk itself – that feature which allowed guests to quickly and securely leave their keys when heading out for the day. It was therefore assumed she still had her key with her. Further, Annabel stated there was no point looking for Martha in the hotel's car park given she had journeyed to the hotel on foot.

At this point, Alba opted to withhold the technicality that Martha had got a taxi to the hotel on Thursday, wishing to protect Martha from Annabel's withering judgment were she, Annabel, to discover the fraud Martha had once more pulled off at her walking companion's expense.

"It is obvious we should get into her room," stated Cliff. "If she's fainted or knocked herself out by slipping in the bathroom because she didn't put the bath mat down, we must get in to help her."

He then paused and spoke quietly but firmly to Annabel. He was aware of the seriousness of the suggestions he was about to put to Annabel Lloyd-Kent – also that everyone else in reception would hear him and whatever answers were forthcoming – but knew this was not the time for discretion:

"Miss Lloyd-Kent, in case we need to get Lizzie summoning an ambulance before we even go up to the room, is Miss Martha Peacock, epileptic, diabetic or allergic to peanuts or anything else which might trigger an anaphylactic reaction?"

"No," was Annabel's immediate response.

"And, though in asking what I am about to ask please be assured I am not making any judgment on Miss Peacock's character, to the best of your knowledge does she have any history of misusing drugs, prescribed or otherwise, of excessive alcohol use or episodes of self-harming, episodes which you fear are escalating in severity? As I say, I am not judging her or anyone but we can't call an ambulance just because someone is not answering their bedroom door. However, as I hope you will all understand," at which point Cliff looked to the others standing further back than Annabel, "I feel we would be justified in making such a call immediately if you, Miss Lloyd-Kent, said 'yes' or even if you said you have your suspicions."

"Not to my knowledge," replied Annabel.

"Thank you," said Cliff.

"You were right to ask," said Gerry.

"Absolutely," concurred Alba – which prompted an agreeing nod from Cecilia.

Cliff nodded his thanks to those around him and then addressed Lizzie and Alan:

"Right, I'll head up with Miss Lloyd-Kent and we'll check the room. Lizzie, you stay here but don't phone for anyone just yet. Alan, if you could wait at the top of the stairs, if we need the emergency services, I'll give you a shout from the room and you can then call or run down or both to Lizzie to action that – I won't make any phone calls from the room itself as I almost certainly will be administering first aid."

"Got you, boss," said Alan.

"You stay with your boys down here and keep them out of the way," Alba discretely suggested to Gerry. "They're too young to see anything they shouldn't have to."

"I guess you're right but I have, over the years in subtle little ways talked to them about death and sacrifice," replied Gerry.

It was a comment which caught Alba out, somewhat. She was unable to reply before Gerry added:

"And yet, I feel I should go up and help as well."

"You will be helping by staying down here and protecting the innocence of your boys; we can't have them following you up and seeing goodness knows what," insisted Alba. Then, as she once more tried to drive the image of finding Vaughan from her mind, she added:

"There is a difference between talking about death and seeing it: I've seen death and it is not nice. It – if you'll forgive the oxymoron – lives with you and is there in your mind and you can never get it out. Protect their innocence by entertaining them in the breakfast area down here. Maybe time Ben on how quickly he can dismantle and rebuild his fire engine. Perhaps talk to Gregory about watching Chris Waddle, if you ever did, or who the best footballer you ever saw play was. Whatever, just do something, anything, with them just so long as you keep them out of all this – whatever 'this' is."

Alba, she would reflect later, was suddenly incredibly protective of her two self-appointed nephews and would have stayed with them herself but for Gerry's nod of agreement that he would do as Alba pleaded.

"Right, room ten," said Cliff as he took a duplicate room key from the drawer under the desk. The simplicity of where he had retrieved a spare key from and the jangling and clunking sounds, which emanated from the drawer as he did so, indicating that all the duplicate keys were therein, prompted Cliff to speak to no one in particular even though he was speaking to everyone:

"There's no real security here. If people only knew where to look for things in a hotel they could get in just about anywhere."

"Really?" said Cecilia.

"Indeed," continued Cliff. "Actually, that reminds me about one grand hotel I used to work in, in Somerset. The building was a bit like a figure of eight, if seen from above, for it had a couple of enclosed courtyards and it was a big enough building to have separate corridors and stairwells for staff to use to keep them out of the way of residents. Anyway, we had a guest who frequently stayed with us and I often caught him using the staff staircase, even though it was uncarpeted, scruffy and each stair window was whitewashed. They were whitewashed as the stairs equally looked out – would have looked out – onto one of the courtyards and we didn't want guests, who had rooms which looked into that particular courtyard, looking in on such a drab part of the hotel. Even though he should have been using the hotel's grand staircase, with its gold hand rails and plush carpet, secured by slender brass rods on every step, this particular guest just said the staff one was more convenient, brought him out right by his room and, he admitted once, that he liked confusing other guests, who were on the same corridor as himself, when they left their bedrooms at the same time as him and yet, despite him never technically overtaking them, he was always down in reception before them. I originally would tell him off and speak to him about health and safety matters and all that but in time it just became something I turned a blind eye to – he wasn't doing anyone any harm and he enjoyed his little scam he would pull off at other residents' expense. Still, enough of my ramblings. Miss Lloyd-Kent, if you would accompany me, let's see whether your friend has simply vacated the hotel or whether she is unwell."

'So, Martha isn't the only one who plays her little games', Alba thought to herself.

As Cliff moved round to the front of the desk and as Annabel readied herself to go as well, Alba felt a tap on her shoulder. She turned to Cecilia, who had suddenly positioned herself by Alba's side.

"I think you should go too," said Cecilia. "If Martha has collapsed and knocked herself out stepping out of the bath or if someone has got into her room and attacked her, she's going to need two women to help. As good a man as Cliff is, he is a man and Martha may well need two women to help her up, to put a robe around her, to bathe any wound or whatever. It might be me being old fashioned but I think you should go too."

Before Alba could answer, Cecilia said loudly and confidently to Cliff:

"Cliff, Alba will go up with you. You might need an extra woman if Miss Peacock is in some distress."

"Of course, right, makes sense," answered Cliff as he made his way up the first part of the staircase. Annabel, Alan and now Alba followed.

*

It was strangely unnerving for Alba to follow Cliff and Annabel towards her, Alba's, own bedroom. Alan had assumed his position at the top of the stairs but the others kept heading towards Alba's

THREE ENTER

room. Thankfully, once level with her room they kept going to the one room that was beyond her own. Martha's room, room ten, was the final room along this hotel corridor and beyond it was simply the fire escape which led to the metal staircase. If one went directly across the metal 'landing area' of the staircase, one was at the staff accommodation, where Cliff and Alan had a small room each, plus a small shared kitchenette area. Alternatively, in heading down the staircase, one got to that side of the hotel and the car park. It was at the bottom of these metal steps that Alba had twice been speaking to Martha the day before.

No one went through the fire escape, for Cliff, Annabel and Alba stopped in front of Martha's bedroom door.

Cliff initially allowed Annabel to knock once more and then to call through to her walking companion. With no response, he, in turn, banged on the door and then called out that he had a key and would be entering if they got no response. Without any response, Cliff turned to the two people at his side and spoke as he inserted the key into the lock:

"You have to be so careful in this business. You can't just walk into a guest's room because they're having a lazy morning, are drunk from the night before or are simply in a sulk and not wishing to talk to people."

"I think we're beyond that," commented Alba. "One of your other guests has been missing for almost two days and everything Annabel has said this morning about her friend's normal behaviour indicates that something has happened. We need to get in."

"Miss Peacock, Martha," Cliff called out, "myself, Annabel and Miss White, Alba, are coming in to check on you. We hope you are OK but with no reply from yourself we feel we must open the door and check on your welfare."

With that, Cliff opened the door – grateful the internal security chain had not been put on – and the three of them entered.

CHAPTER 12

"Take the sleeper"

Several hundred miles away, there was movement at another bedroom door.

"Sorry Reverend, didn't see you there," said Andrew as the two men almost collided in the doorway.

The Honourable Andrew Chapman had been too preoccupied with the tea tray he was carrying to notice the Reverend Matthew Quinn exiting the room Andrew had been trying to enter.

"Looks like the drinks have survived," replied Andrew. "Thought you'd gone. I would have brought you something up too, had I known you were still here."

"It's fine, Andrew. I must be heading off but thanks anyway."

"Sure?"

"Sure."

The room the Church of England minister was leaving, and which Andrew was about to enter, was Edward Chapman's bedroom. Edward Chapman, more formerly known as the 7th Lord Hartfield and the owner of Hillstone Hall, was Andrew's grandfather – Andrew would one day be the 8th Lord but that day thankfully seemed further off than everyone had feared just a few days ago when Edward had been rushed into hospital.

"TAKE THE SLEEPER"

"You've got to hand it to the doctors and nurses," said the Reverend Quinn. "As your grandfather has just said himself, he was very unwell. So, for them to have turned him around so quickly says much for their knowledge and level of care."

"Absolutely," agreed Andrew. "Thought I'd still be visiting him in the William the Fourth Memorial Hospital for several more days. Still, I'd have happily done that given how worried I was when he was rushed in to begin with."

"He was quite ill, I know," concurred the minister. "I'm just so pleased I could do my little bit and sit with your grandmother at the hospital until you could come and be with her – rather fortuitous that I was visiting another person there that morning. God works in mysterious ways sometimes. And it's been good to be able to come and visit your grandfather here this morning; I've just stayed a bit longer than I was perhaps expecting. Just as I thought I was leaving he suddenly asked after a passage in the Bible. He was asking why in the Easter story it is recorded that a curtain gets torn in two when Jesus dies. He said he kept puzzling over that image as he lay in his bed, looking out of his hospital window, as it seemed an irrelevance and a distraction to what was happening."

"OK," said Andrew.

"So, we've spent a few moments looking at a bit in Matthew's Gospel and Mark's and the significance of the curtain in the Temple tearing in two – tearing from top to bottom, mind you, and that, for what's estimated to have been a sixty foot high curtain, is key to understanding why that fact is recorded. I've suggested he looks up Romans 8: 38-39 but I sense he doesn't normally keep a Bible by him so he might, just might, ask you to locate one for him. I hope one of these books in here is a Bible."

With that the minister looked back into the room at the many bookcases therein, in the first part of the room, before adding:

"But I'm not so sure. Still, I really must be away, I've got so much to do – write some sermons for tomorrow, meet a couple who want to get married and, amongst other things, explain to them how 'marriage banns' work, offer home communion to two separate housebound parishioners and, if that wasn't enough, the Bishop has said he will be dropping by later."

"Blow, I thought I had a lot to do running this place," mused Andrew.

"It's fine and I take Mondays off, in order that I get my sabbath rest. Plus, it helps that I work for a boss who himself is very much hands-on and listens."

"The Bishop?" asked Andrew.

"No," smiled Reverend Quinn. "Not the Bishop, as nice as he is. Anyway, must away. It's good of you to be taking such good care of your grandfather."

"It's no trouble. We've given Barnes, grandad's butler, a few days off, grandma's not up yet and it's the least I can do. I just need to remind him to keep resting and not to overdo things too soon."

"Well, I've told him something similar. Also, that I'm happy to visit again."

"Do you want me to show you out or can you find your own way through all the corridors we have at the Hall?" asked Andrew.

"Happy to chance it myself. You take those drinks in before they get cold. See you Sunday, perhaps?" called out the Reverend as he departed.

"Perhaps," replied Andrew without any conviction.

*

Having watched the vicar of the parish disappear into the Hall's internal maze of corridors, staircases and doors which opened to reveal dumbwaiters, Andrew entered his grandfather's bedroom.

It was a bedroom befitting both an elderly Lord and the fading grandeur of Hillstone Hall. Unlike his wife's bedroom and dressing room, which were decidedly heavy in French styling and fragrance and which looked out over the formal gardens to the rear, his rooms belonged very much to a country gentleman. There was a two-poster bed, aged yew furniture, which carried their fair share of scuffs, knocks and scratches, and a thick, dark olive-green carpet. This room opened into what was meant to be the adjoining dressing room but which he had turned into his private study. The study contained a small open fire, two green leather chairs and several pairs of mounted antlers on the walls. It, as the bedroom itself did, looked over the front of the house and the usual smell of the room was not unpleasant, being a mixture of port, the occasionally used fireplace and 'Quink' ink, the latter emitting an aroma due to the Lord's inability to bother to put the screw top lid back on to the glass bottle of black ink that sat on his desk. The 7th Lord Hartfield had often wondered whether blue ink smelt the same as black but such was his abhorrence of blue ink – 'common' was his view of those who wrote in such a colour ink, whether they wrote with a fountain pen or not – he had never purchased a bottle of blue to make the comparison. However, since yesterday – and it would last for a few more days to come – the usual smell was dominated by numerous vases brimming full of freshly picked daffodils.

"Morning, grandad," said Andrew upon entering.

"Ah, Andrew, good to see you. Just had the minister here as you may have gathered. Something had been puzzling me as I lay in my hospital bed – something that had sat at the back of my mind since I was a little boy and some dreary Sunday School teacher had told us about it. As I lay there in hospital this week, I decided if I recovered, I'd darn well ask someone to explain it. Strange, I would say, how of all the things you assume you would think about as you lie ill on a hospital bed, it's the random and completely unexpected thoughts that fill your mind."

"Thankfully, I've yet to experience being in hospital myself, so I'll take your word for it. Still, pleased you're awake and even up to taking visitors. Hope you haven't overdone it," stressed Andrew.

"I'm fine, my boy."

A raised eyebrow from his grandson forced Lord Hartfield to correct himself:

"Well, I'm much better than I was."

"I'll say. You had us all worried for a moment, I can tell you."

"Me too," acknowledged the elderly gentlemen as he lifted himself slightly to force himself to sit more upright against the bed's headboard.

Andrew hastily put the cooling cups of tea down and helped his grandfather make himself comfortable once more.

"Better?" Andrew enquired.

"Yes, thank you."

"Tea," Andrew proffered. "It's in a mug, I confess. Couldn't really be doing with the fancy china for just the two of us."

"Thank you, I'm sure it will taste almost as nice," stated Lord Hartfield.

However, he promptly handed his cup back to his grandson as a further coughing fit took hold. Eventually, it eased and after several sips of water, he was ready to take the mug once more.

"And, anyway," the 7th Lord added, intent on making his point, "Barnes will be back this evening, meaning I can have tea in a proper drinking vessel then."

"Point taken, grandad," replied Andrew, happy to be chided by the other. "Grandma has overdone it a bit on the flowers, don't you think? There must be at least half a dozen vases full of them in here."

"It's her way of helping – though don't think she went and picked them herself, for she will have got one of the garden volunteers to gather them from the grounds. Look, talking of our garden helpers, you really didn't have to cancel your holiday," said Lord Hartfield. "The hospital staff were taking good care of me, whilst I was there, and now I am home your grandma and I could have muddled through until Barnes returns."

"Don't be daft, Grandad. There was no way I could have gone off and enjoyed the Cornish coast with Alba, knowing full well you were in hospital. And, as for now, with all due respect to dear grandma, you both still need someone else just to be around to keep an eye on things."

"We would have coped, my dear Andrew," stated his Lordship defiantly.

Andrew decided not to challenge his grandfather further on the point. Instead, he simply said:

"Well, I did stay, in order that I could visit or be overseeing your recovery here."

"It was kind of you, my boy. Please don't think I'm not grateful," replied Lord Hartfield.

"It was nothing. Alba understood and she was happy to go by herself. Apparently, it is almost like going home for her whenever she heads off to Cornwall – she says the small tight-knit group of staff always make her feel so welcome. She just added 'maybe another time'," said Andrew.

"Look," said Lord Hartfield in a firm tone. Then, having got his grandson's full attention, he added:

"It is good that you stayed but I'm on the mend."

"That doesn't mean you're fully recovered," countered Andrew.

"I'm on the mend," repeated the gentleman sitting up in his two-poster bed. "I have Grandma with me, Doctor Brierley will be visiting me later this afternoon and, as we've already mentioned, Barnes will be back later. You need a break yourself – so, go and get packed, get the train up to London, have supper at my club and then take the sleeper out of Paddington. You've lost part of your holiday, no need to lose it all. Don't tell her you're coming, just turn up and surprise her – make her day."

"She's too independent for anyone to make her day, Grandad," replied Andrew. "However, it would be nice to get away for a few days and I do enjoy her company. She's become a good friend."

Andrew placed his empty mug down on the tray and walked over to the window. As he looked out and down onto the empty plinth that stood in the centre of the grass circle, around which the front drive swung, he spoke again:

"I'm tempted and you are much better than you were; you really had me worried. But I'm not going to rush anywhere today."

"No?" queried Lord Hartfield, who sensed Andrew was keen to get away, despite his stated hesitancy.

"No," continued the man at the window. "Let's wait and see what your doctor has to say later today. If he has no major concerns and once Barnes is back and I've handed a few house matters over to him to follow up in my absence, then I'll head off tomorrow afternoon and do as you say – take the train up to London, eat at your club and then catch the sleeper train to Penzance. I'd be in Cornwall Monday morning. Only if Doctor Brierley is happy, mind you."

As Andrew took his grandfather's empty mug, collected yesterday's 'The Daily Telegraph' newspaper from the floor by the bed – noticing that both the quick and the cryptic crosswords on the back page had been finished – and closed a couple of bedside drawers, he wondered what Alba, his supposed holiday companion, was herself getting up to this Saturday morning.

CHAPTER 13

Just like Captain Briggs

But of course, whatever Andrew may have imagined Alba to be doing this Saturday morning, it definitely was not what was unfolding in the dining area of 'The Jupiter Hotel'.

*

It was a bit unfair on Gregory and Ben, who had so meticulously tidied the furniture in the restaurant at their father's instruction and who were now up in their hotel bedroom, that so much furniture had subsequently been moved around. However, the eclectic mix of people were not really thinking of the two young lads or the people – the day trippers, the walkers, the locals – who might be in later for lunch. For the residents and staff had rearranged the chairs and tables in order that they could sit around in an approximate square. They sat and looked at each other, completely at a loss as to what to make of things, as Cliff had just relayed to them. The only movement was Alan as he brought out some pots of tea and placed them on one of the two dark mahogany tables which had been dragged into the centre of the square. The tea was to accompany the already present coffee pots, a jug of water and some glass tumblers and a not unsubstantial batch of Alan's ginger biscuits.

"Bit harsh on my boys," commented Gerry, unable to think of anything else to say. "I asked them to tidy up in here, to distract them as much as anything, in case something tragic was unfolding upstairs and look at what we've now done to their efforts."

"Can't fault their work ethic," contributed Lizzie.

"Thanks. However, it would have been simpler to have asked them to build a desert Legion camp out of the furniture. They'd have known exactly what to do and saved us all the hassle of rearranging stuff ourselves. That said we've made a pretty good job of pitching camp – a defensive square, provisions and supplies stacked in the middle and the prioritisation of drinks."

The randomness of Gerry's reflections was lost on everyone as they helped themselves to a drink and a biscuit – which generated a universal nod of approval from each person in turn as they took a bite. As Alan sat himself down in the last vacant chair, still no one knew what to add to that which Cliff had just described to those who had not been present during the search of Martha's room.

Of those present, save for Gregory, Ben, Mr Constance, who had gone to meet his builders, Joshua and Martha, every guest – Emily, Daniel, Nicholas, Cecilia, Gerry, Stella, Annabel and Alba were seated around. Whilst save for Robyn and Jed, who were on late shifts, the remainder of the staff were also present and interspersed amongst the guests – Cliff, Alan and Lizzie. Lizzie was seated closest to reception in case the telephone rang.

"It just doesn't make sense," said Annabel.

It was a comment which was on everyone's lips but which she gave voice to first. For indeed, things did not make sense given what she, Cliff and Alba had seen.

As Alba sat there, she discretely felt once more the business card for a Truro taxi firm, 'Three Diamonds taxi service', which she had secreted in a pocket of her jeans, having 'lifted' it from Martha's room.

It had been almost entirely underneath some Ordnance Survey maps which had been laid out on the coffee table in the room they were searching. The moment Alba saw it protruding from underneath the maps, and before Annabel herself noticed it, Alba took it in the belief it was what Martha would have wanted her, Alba, to do: to protect the other's fraudulent behaviour from 'The Empress'.

Eventually, it was Alba who felt compelled to re-iterate what Cliff had already told everyone, as if by repeating their discovery – or more accurately, non-discovery – some clarity and reason would cascade down upon the square within which they were sitting:

"No trace, just no trace of her. It was as if we had stepped onto the *Mary Celeste*, in that all her belongings were still there exactly, so it seemed to all of us, as she had left them. All her belongings were still there," Alba repeated. "She clearly hasn't done an early morning disappearance trick to avoid paying her hotel bill, having just grabbed the basics and fled as she suddenly realised she couldn't pay for her room. Her toothbrush was still in the holder in the bathroom, her maps were still open on the coffee table and her hiking boots were still sitting there together, on top of a plastic bag."

"In any case, we paid for all of our guest houses and hotels when we originally booked our trip," contributed Annabel.

"Well, that definitely rules that vague theory out," replied Alba – who was somewhat frustrated because she could not offer the group who were gathered around her, especially Stella, a solution. That, somehow, she, Alba White, should be able to see through all the 'fluff' and irrelevancies and grasp just exactly what was going on at 'The Jupiter Hotel' and thereby explain it to the others. Yet, she could not and the fog was as much swirling around her as it was everyone else.

"And no indication of anyone breaking in or, even if not breaking in, getting in and rummaging around her possessions?" asked Emily.

"No," replied Cliff. "It was just as Alba described – as if we had stepped on to the deck and into the cabins of that infamous nineteenth-century ship. Martha's possessions were neither ransacked, nor, conversely, packed away perfectly in her large rucksack nor missing in their entirety. It was as if she had just stepped out for a moment and never returned; just like Captain Briggs, his passengers and his crew."

"And you're certain nothing is missing?" Emily challenged Cliff.

Alba studied the artist for a moment. Emily was again in a long flowing dress, this time more eastern Mediterranean in feel, than either gypsy or Spanish. The burnt umber dress, with its leaf motive, slightly oversized sleeves and, for this time of morning thought Alba, a surprisingly deep V-neck, was instantly stylish and made Alba, in her jeans and washed linen top, feel rather drab in comparison. Alba had the impression that Emily would command whatever room she was in. There was, though not only from her style, a presence about her. In consequence, her challenge to Cliff was not treated lightly by the manager of 'The Jupiter Hotel' and he only answered after he had mentally replayed to himself what he had seen in Martha's room.

"No," he said. "I'm not certain. Not because I sense something is missing but rather, I suppose, by not being familiar with Miss Peacock or her possessions, I really couldn't tell if something wasn't there that should have been. To ask if I'm certain *nothing* is missing, requires too high a benchmark for me to say 'I'm certain'. All I can say, there was nothing out of the ordinary to suggest something was missing."

"Or even that someone had been in and been looking for something to take," added Annabel.

"Exactly," concurred Cliff. "There was a pair of walking boots, as opposed to just one, and there were two trekking poles which were intact, as opposed to broken in half because some master criminal had been on the hunt for a missing diamond. Equally, the boxes of plasters and foot gel in the bathroom were in an orderly manner, as opposed to scattered over the floor or emptied out because someone thought something was hidden in the box or submerged within the gel itself."

"And looked at from the other angle, there didn't seem to be anything in the room that shouldn't have been there," said Alba. "There were maps laid out of the Cornish coastline, as opposed to of the Kent coastline, there were lady's toiletries in the bathroom but no men's ones and the nightwear laid out on one pillow and the T-shirts slung over the back of the chair, from my impression of Martha, were her sizing."

"Did anything about the room seem staged?" queried Daniel.

"No," replied Annabel – which prompted nods of agreement from Cliff and Alba.

"Everything was entirely natural," added Annabel.

*

As she felt once more the card in her pocket, Alba wondered whether she should tell those assembled around her that she, Alba, had removed something from the room. However, Alba held on to the belief that a business card for a Truro taxi firm related only to Martha's deception which was solely and, all things considered, harmlessly targeted at Annabel. Alba pushed the card to the depths of her pocket and wondered whether Cliff or Annabel would at least comment on the presence of a half full hip flask in Martha's room but, if they had noticed it, neither made any reference to it.

"No one rushed past me as you were searching. Nor did I hear any odd noises or doors being worked when I first got into the kitchen this morning," contributed Alan.

"The *Mary Celeste* was bound for Genoa when she was discovered; I wonder where Martha was bound for this morning and why?" pondered Cliff.

"We were scheduled to resume our coastal walk but she wouldn't have just started it without all her gear," said Annabel.

It was then Cecilia who spoke. She did not develop Annabel's comment, rather she gave voice to what everyone had tried to bury deep within their own psyches, fearing that by mentioning it, it would come true. However, for Cecilia at least, it became too uncomfortable to keep deep within and, perhaps feeling Geoffrey's absence more acutely than normal, she spoke – quietly but somehow heard clearly by all:

"So, are we all going to go missing one by one?"

"Only one person is missing, this lady's husband" said Nicholas as he pointed at Stella. "This Miss Peacock is currently 'whereabouts unknown' but is that really missing?"

"Sounds like being missing to me," suggested Gerry, which generated a murmur of approval from the majority of the group.

"Who will be next then?" said Cecilia – Alba could sense a level of fear was beginning to take hold of her friend.

"Please, no one," insisted Stella. "This is no time for joking."

"I wasn't joking," insisted Cecilia.

"It's probably just an unfortunate coincidence that someone else is unaccounted for. Within an hour or so the missing woman will have returned from wherever she's been," said Nicholas, trying to continue his theme of de-escalating the tension that was beginning to fill the room.

"But I thought Joshua would be back after an hour or two and that was Thursday evening and now we're Saturday morning. What if Miss Peacock equally doesn't come back any time soon?" said Stella.

"Maybe she's an attention seeker," suggested Daniel. "You know, the type of person who begrudges, in their slightly warped way, all the attention Stella is getting – and rightly so, I might add, please don't misunderstand me there – and so tries to re-create some similar scene for him or herself."

"Possible," said Lizzie. "We do have our share of guests, in any given season, who always want the spotlight to be on themselves; people who believe some drama is forever unfolding around them or are able to generate crisis after crisis out of nothing just to be the centre of things."

Knowing looks and nods from the hotel manager and chef followed.

"It's technically possible but, knowing her, I would say that's not her style," proposed Annabel. "If anything, she's the exact opposite, always trying to sit out of the limelight and away from the camera. She hid her talents very well and it was a loss when she resigned as my 'Events Manager' – we worked at the same London gallery, you see."

Alba, from the few times she had spoken to Martha in her time at the hotel, felt Annabel had captured Martha's character exactly in that assessment of her.

"Any indication that your husband previously knew Miss Peacock?" asked Cliff of Stella.

"No," Stella firmly replied. "We had never met her prior to staying here."

It was then Daniel who spoke:

"Assuming there is no connection and that this is a freakish coincidence, can anyone shed any light at all on what's happened this morning? Otherwise, someone simply needs to take responsibility and alert the police to a further missing person."

In the silence, as everyone else did mental mind games as they tried to come up with a theory as to what had unfolded or where Martha might be, Alba took the opportunity to stand up and refill her cup from one of the teapots on the table in front of her. Having done hers and having added just the right amount of milk, she turned to Cecilia and was about to offer her a refill when a sudden realisation flashed through Alba's mind – which she immediately gave voice to:

"Has anyone actually seen Martha this morning?"

"No," half a dozen people replied, which was followed up by Nicholas, who added:

"And that is why we've been discussing her whereabouts. I think you should be drinking something stronger than tea to wake you up," he added with just a hint of sarcasm. "You do understand, the very simple fact that none of us have, don't you? Hence why we, especially her walking companion, are worried for her."

Even Cecilia was puzzled over Alba's naivety until Alba replied to Nicholas – although, in that moment she felt she was defending herself to the whole group, not just to Nicholas:

"Yes, thank you. I do understand that, that none of us has seen her this morning. What I mean is, given that, how do we know she hasn't gone missing before today. When did anyone here last see her? She arrived at the hotel on Thursday, after her day's walking."

"We had a rest day, yesterday, Friday," confirmed Annabel.

"And she was around the hotel yesterday, during the day. I chatted to her a couple of times, most recently outside the hotel just before dinner, as she took in some air and as I was collecting something from my car. Who saw her after that? Who had the *last* sighting of her?" asked Alba, with as much emphasis on 'last' as possible.

Alba knew she had seen Martha in the restaurant area, after their conversation on the metal staircase by the hotel's car park, at dinner time but wanted someone else to develop her theme. Annabel took the prompt:

"We had dinner together last night in here as you all saw. She finished before me, said she hadn't finished looking at the route she would be doing and hadn't decided what she would be wearing."

"Hence the maps and clothes about the room," observed Cliff.

"I guess so," replied Annabel. "She went up and I haven't seen her since."

"So, did anyone see her after dinner?" asked Cliff. "If I'm going to call the police, we'd better be precise on when we did last see her."

Shakes of heads and several 'No, didn't see her after that' came back in reply. Annabel needlessly summed up people's replies:

"She had dinner, went up to her room and has literally disappeared. How can someone seemingly disappear walking up the stairs to their bedroom? There are no mysteriously locked doors part way up the hotel's turning wooden staircase, there was no logic in going out the front door if she were heading up to her room, meaning the only place she could have diverted was into the bar or the kitchens."

Suddenly everyone's eyes fell on Alan.

"She didn't come in, promise," Alan stated.

However, it was evident to Alba, equally to Alan himself, that not everyone believed him.

"Look, I didn't see her," Alan added.

"Well, where else would she have gone?" challenged Stella.

"I don't know; why would she have come in?" Alan retaliated.

"Maybe we should search the kitchen and the cold store. If she didn't go into the kitchen, you won't mind us looking," stated Daniel, whereupon he stood up and looked around him for support.

"I won't mind," responded Alan. "Just don't expect any evening meals, let alone lunches, here today as I'll be spending the rest of the day cleaning and wiping down everywhere you lot will have been and everything you'll have touched – good hygiene doesn't just happen!"

"Maybe we should look," said Nicholas reluctantly. "Let's at least rule this unlikely option out and then," as he gestured to Cliff, "the police will have to be contacted."

"Boss," pleaded Alan, as he could see his whole day being wasted and food already prepared having to be thrown away due to the risk of contamination. "Boss," he repeated but he knew it was futile as it was clear the mood of the room had changed and several people, including Daniel, Nicholas, Gerry and a slightly more reluctant Emily headed for the door to reception and thereby the kitchen.

Stella and Alba briefly exchanged glances, as they both wondered whether to follow too and then, as Alba watched Daniel open the door, she suddenly remembered something, something significant, from the night before. She called out, standing as she did so:

"No wait!"

Then, having got everyone's attention, continued:

"If she didn't return to her room, she either went out the front doors or into the kitchen. The front doors seem, at best, unlikely as she neither had a car nor the need to go for a walk given it was raining heavily and that's what she should have been doing all of today."

"Bucketing down," stated Alan. "Robyn told me she got drenched coming in for her evening shift."

"Right," continued Alba. "So, the kitchen is logical if she went out of here that way but she didn't. I've just remembered. As I saw the group of you heading that way just now, I suddenly realised Martha didn't exit the restaurant that way last night. She, as she had done the night before – Thursday night – went out via the snug door."

"Why would she have done that?" asked Stella. "You just said she was hardly likely to have gone for a walk – I'm puzzled."

"Me too," added Lizzie.

"Two-fold, maybe three," replied Alba. "Initially, to get to room ten, her room, it's quicker that way."

"But it was pouring, she'd have got wet," insisted Stella.

"Well, yes," answered Alba. "Only for a moment though and for an experienced walker as she and Annabel are, she'd hardly have noticed or cared. Further, she was heading towards the snug door in any case as she came to my table to leave me a note, which related to something we'd been talking about earlier. So," Alba concluded, "I guess Martha just instinctively then took the shortest route to her room, which was out via the snug door. I watched her go."

"What note? Did anyone follow her?" asked Stella, suddenly sounding worried.

"No one followed her," replied Alba, deliberately not wanting to say anything more about Martha's note.

"That's right," agreed Nicholas. "I remember now, the missing woman did leave as Alba has just said and, no, no one followed her as it was just myself and Alba still eating."

"And Gregory and Ben," added Alba.

"Oh, yeah, the two lads as well and I can vouch for Alba not going after Martha and she can vouch for me. As for everyone else," continued Nicholas suddenly looking around inquisitorially, "only each of you knows where you individually were."

"I was looking for Geoffrey's tablets," insisted Cecilia.

"She can't still be in the car park, she hasn't got a car," observed Emily.

"So everyone keeps saying," said Cliff. "Still, if none of us has been in or out of the snug door since Martha vacated the restaurant, someone had better go and see if she dropped something on her way up to her room. Maybe then we'll have something to hint at where she then went – maybe but I'm not hopeful."

As was always going to be the case, though, it was not just one person who went. Everyone went.

*

It was better it was not just one person who went. Better it was not just one person having to rush back in and alert everyone else. Better, somehow, given the two boys were not present, that it was a shared experience of finding Martha crumpled at the foot of the metal staircase. Crumpled, contorted and tragically still.

No one needed to ask whether Martha was dead or not – the staring, unblinking eyes, her sodden, twisted body and her hair matted with blood was all that anyone needed to know.

Cliff, trained as he was in first aid, knelt to formally check for a pulse in her neck.

"Nothing," he said. He turned her slightly, looking for where all the blood had stemmed from. As he did so, he said:

"*Rigor Mortis* has set in and, given how sodden her clothes are, it's clear she's been here since last night."

Turning her a fraction more revealed to all who chose to look a severe gash to the far side of her head.

"Poor soul," said Lizzie. "She must have slipped on her way up the stairs."

"Look," said Emily somewhat randomly and as she pointed to a few feet beyond Martha's lifeless body, "there's her room key. She must have dropped it as she fell – she never made it to her room."

"That's why, when you went to look for her in her room, it was as if you had stepped into the *Mary Celeste*; for she hadn't packed up and left the hotel, she simply came down for dinner, obviously expecting to return but never did," said Daniel.

"And why the security chain wasn't on," added Cliff. "She'd locked her bedroom door from the outside, not the inside."

"But why hasn't anyone noticed her lying here this morning?" asked Nicholas.

"I was just wondering the same, too," added Stella.

"Well," offered Lizzie, "my husband dropped me off at the front of the hotel this morning, Robyn and Jed won't be in until later and, of course, Cliff and Alan live on site."

"That's the staff accounted for then. As for me," continued Nicholas, "I haven't been to my car this morning."

"Geoffrey went off to meet our builders but we'd parked in one of the spaces at the front of the hotel," said Cecilia.

From what the others then added, no one had been to their vehicle this Saturday morning.

"So," summarised Nicholas, "had Miss Lloyd-Kent gone off walking, assuming Miss Peacock had already left, then until some other day visitors came to the hotel, Geoffrey returned or one of us headed off, she could have lain here all day – unnoticed and unmissed."

"That's a sad, frightening observation when you put it like that," said Lizzie.

"I just hope my Joshua isn't lying somewhere himself because no one has noticed him," cried out Stella. With that she burst into tears and rushed inside with her head in her hands, highly distressed.

"I need to go and be with my boys," Gerry suddenly said. "Can't have them wandering out here by themselves and seeing this poor woman." With that he rushed back inside, too.

"I need to go in, too; I have seen enough," said Emily, who herself was now keen to detach herself from what they were all witnessing. As she moved away, she part covered her eyes with her hands – hands wrapped up as they were in her dress's baggy sleeves.

Cliff followed her in but then almost immediately returned with a large tablecloth and, with Alan's assistance, covered Martha's broken body.

"I'll watch over my friend," said Annabel. "The rest of you can go in as well, if you want, but I'll stand beside her until the ambulance comes."

Cliff took the hint and went to make the appropriate telephone calls. The rest of the group, save for Annabel, dispersed too. Some went to be alone in their own rooms, alone with their own thoughts on the fragility of life, some went and sat in the bar, Lizzie and Alan returned to the restaurant, Cecilia went to telephone Geoffrey and Alba, in that strange way that some people do when confronted with unexpected tragedy, sought out a routine task to do. Thus, Alba went round to the front of the hotel and started to weed the stone troughs by the front doors, picking out the spurges and the shepherd's purse from amongst the young sea holly plants and the saxifrage.

CHAPTER 14

Rod of Asclepius

As Alba stood and wondered whether to now weed the red valerian seedlings, which were growing under one of the hotel's bay windows, Cecilia came out of the front of the hotel just as an ambulance turned into the hotel's drive. The two women listened to it struggle for the correct gear as it climbed the steep drive and then watched as it passed them.

It did not arrive with its blue lights flashing nor its siren blaring, for there was no emergency, not now. The vehicle – though perhaps more accurately, this was how Alba and Cecilia regarded it – had an air of the macabre about it, for it was not here to save life, to treat the wounded or to care for the injured. Rather it was here to collect the fallen. It was as if a hearse had just pulled in, though one decked out in florescent yellow and dull green panels along its sides, yellow and reddish-orange chevrons on its rear doors and displaying the blue six-pointed 'Star of Life' symbol. There was no rush about the vehicle's approach. It was a solemn, almost processional, arrival of the emergency vehicle.

"The 'Rod of Asclepius' isn't going to help her now," said a dejected Alba, as she referred to the image of the snake entwined around the rod which formed part of the 'Star of Life'.

"No," agreed Cecilia. "It's just so tragic."

"I was only talking to her just before dinner yesterday. We had a pleasant chat and I think it lifted her mood somewhat," said Alba.

"Strange to need to have your mood lifted when you're on holiday; how odd," commented Cecilia.

"She probably had walked one too many miles at the instruction of her companion," said Alba.

"A holiday friendship that was past its sell-by date?"

"In a sense but they knew each other through work originally; worked in the same London art gallery, Annabel is the curator and Martha was on the events side but she resigned not so long ago."

"Did she? Why was that?" asked Cecilia.

Not having proof of Annabel's fraudulent activities concerning forged works of art, only Martha's account, Alba did not quite feel able to relay to Cecilia all that Martha had told her when they had sat on those, now tragic, steps yesterday. Alba offered up something approaching an overview:

"Martha felt there were some questionable business practices going on and that works of art were not being handled as Martha felt they should have been."

"Must have been pretty serious failings for Martha to actually resign over," observed Cecilia. "Did she talk to Annabel about it?"

"I'm not sure," Alba replied and she hoped her evasiveness would not be challenged by the other; she was therefore relieved when Cecilia instead asked after the note Alba had referred to:

"Just now, when we were all trying to work out where Martha had gone – though of course we now sadly know – you said she'd exited the restaurant the way she did as she was leaving you a note."

"That's right."

"What was that all about; you didn't say at the time," pursued Cecilia.

"Oh nothing, just her contact details as I said she could come and visit me at some stage," explained Alba.

"Oh, right, never mind then."

With that, Cecilia paused – a pause which allowed Alba to kneel once more and pick out a couple of seedlings of herb bennet, which had just caught her eye. She spoke as she effortlessly plucked the young plants from the soil and scrunched them up in her hand:

"These are really annoying plants – *Geum urbanum*, herb bennet. I know they're wild flowers and once upon a time the plant was hung over people's doorways to keep the devil out but their seeds are *so* annoying: they catch on your clothing, your gardening gloves, anything and spread themselves around your garden so easily."

Alba then stood once more as Cecilia spoke again:

"I came out looking for you."

"Really?"

"Just to talk to, I guess. You see, I couldn't get hold of Geoffrey on the phone but I'm sure that's because he's busy chatting with our project manager and I didn't like sitting in the room by myself, especially as I could hear Stella sobbing, albeit quietly, to herself. I did knock on her door and ask if there was anything I could do or whether she'd like to sit with me but she said no. I did also ask whether she wanted me to go and find you, so she could be with you but she said she'd taken enough of your time."

"Oh, that's silly, no she hasn't and, even if she had, I don't mind," stressed Alba.

"I know," agreed Cecilia, "but sometimes it's best not to force yourself on someone when they're stressed and worried. Sometimes, as strange as it might seem, they just need to be alone to process what's going on for themselves. I have no doubt she'll want your company a bit later today."

"Well, the police should be giving her an update this morning, especially once they've got through to Joshua's office."

"Well, there you go. So, probably best you don't press yourself on her until lunchtime."

With that, Cecilia fell silent and a visible shiver went through her body, starting at her neck and shoulders and then working its uncomfortable way down to her ankles. The sensation gone, she spoke once more:

"Actually, I can't stand here, knowing there's an ambulance round the other side of the hotel. I suggest we drive the few miles to Trelyn House and go and have a quiet walk there together. It would somehow seem wrong to go shopping in Helston or Penzance or to go to some idyllic café in Cadgwith but to have a stroll around the abandoned, semi-derelict Trelyn would not be unfeeling – you'll have to take my word for it but once you get there, you'll see what I mean."

"Trelyn?" said Alba.

"Yes."

"I assumed that was miles and miles away."

"It's not as far as you think," replied Cecilia. "It probably seems a long way away to you as you've never been. Also, I suppose, by having been in private hands and so not managed by the National Trust or English Heritage, there aren't multitudes of brown road signs around telling tourists how to find it, which, had there been, would have highlighted that it is really quite close by. But it's in decline now and the sad thing is, the house would probably have survived if Sir Roger des Roches had brought one of those organisations on board. However, he was a private man and wouldn't accept help from anyone. Maybe had his wife still been alive, it might have been different but she wasn't and, in the end, he didn't even want the involvement of the Historic Houses Association. That is an organisation which supports owners of historic properties without seeking control or ownership in return. And now, he's gone and the house, though to be fair it had been going that way for a good few years, is falling into ruin, too. It's a sad, pathetic sight now – fitting for an hour's walk this morning, of all mornings."

"Well, so long as neither Stella nor Annabel think we're off enjoying ourselves – not that I'm in any mood to even try. This is proving to be a horrible few days but," Alba added reflectively, "you're probably right – standing here isn't going to achieve anything."

"You'll have to drive," stated Cecilia. "Geoffrey has our car."

*

"That's a wry smile you just had on your face," said Cecilia as she buckled herself into Alba's car.

"I was just thinking, as I turned the key in the ignition, whether I had left the radio on. It would have just been my misfortune for the radio station to be playing some upbeat, lively song that was full of optimism or spoke of love, when here we are just metres from Martha's broken body."

"Oh, poor Alba, you feel responsible for too much."

"But it could have been Gloria Gaynor or 'Yazz and the Plastic Population' or – "

"Yazz and the what?" queried Cecilia.

"Never mind. And it's definitely not too far, Trelyn?"

"No. And look," stressed Cecilia, "there's nothing you can do here; this tragedy is not for you to sort out. Let's go and have an hour or so meandering around the former home of the des Roches family and try and get you to switch off."

Alba nodded an acceptance and, with that, put her car into first gear, lifted the handbrake fractionally, in order to depress the button, and then lowered it and pulled out of her parking space. Neither woman glanced across to where the paramedics were going about their sombre business and were relieved to pull on to the lane that would take them back to the main road and then the few miles to Trelyn House.

*

As she stood at her bedroom window, which overlooked the front of the hotel, Stella watched Alba drive away. Stella ran both her hands through her hair and wished her own life to be different to what it was and this thing that she was enduring. She wished she was accompanying Alba – wherever she was going – and not tortured in the way that she was experiencing right now. Stella wished she could be innocently heading off as well. Yet here she was, waiting for a phone call from the police that she somehow would rather not come, waiting on news of her husband's whereabouts that she feared getting, waiting even on Joshua's office contacting her as well, once the police had contacted them.

Stella then found herself thinking of the times she and her old school friend would head off to the local corner shop, as they used to during their school lunchtimes, to go and buy a bag of sherbet-filled flying saucers and pineapple cubes, a can of 'Fanta' or a four-fingered 'Kit-Kat'. She wished for, craved, the innocence of those long-lost days; days which normally lived obscurely in her memory but somehow now came screaming back to the front of her mind. The feeling of innocence was there, almost, but still impossible to truly grasp; as if she were trying to take hold of a rainbow or trying to gather back in the ripples you make as you sit on the side of a swimming pool and gently move your legs back and forth. Or, as if she were trying to gather back all those little bubbles that suddenly escape from the spout of a bottle of 'Fairy' washing-up liquid as you put it down, even though you put it down in exactly the same way every other evening and do not get bubbles then. Yet she knew, she very much knew, the innocence was gone and it, like the rainbow, the ripples or the bubbles would be forever out of her reach.

She wondered, if there were no developments today, whether she should travel home tomorrow; could she face being there now, alone? She wondered whether, if she went home, it would look like she had given up hope on Joshua being found alive – no, she must stay at the hotel, she told herself, for she would never want anyone saying she had abandoned him. Yet her brain started spinning once more with 'what ifs' and she desperately tried to dull those thoughts by focusing on Alba's disappearing car.

Once she could see it no more, Stella went and uncomfortably sat down by the room's telephone and waited.

*

Gerry Detz was also waiting. He was waiting by one of the windows in the snug as his two boys looked through it. Believing, as he did, his two boys were old enough to hear what had happened, he had gone and told them. Shortly after that, he brought them downstairs. Having got them to wait in the dining area, staying out of Alan and Lizzie's way, he first went and checked what could be seen through the snug windows and, reassuring himself that Martha's body was not visible, had allowed his boys to come and quietly look at the emergency workers through the window and to watch how they calmly and efficiently went about their task. Gregory and Ben watched as the two paramedics collected equipment from the rear of the vehicle, sat in the cab to check something on a clipboard and, at times, to simply stand a few steps away from everything to agree what their next task was.

Having assured himself they would not see anything they absolutely should not, it was a life lesson Gerry felt they could handle. Whether Tania, his wife, would have agreed with him, he very much doubted it. However, she was not here, being in prison as she was, and so it was his choice. He knew, though, that when they did go and see her in just over a week's time and the boys told her, he would be severely criticised by her for allowing the boys to see what little they could but, he reminded himself once more, she was not here; 'was it so wrong that he didn't miss her as much as people assumed he did?', he wondered.

"Right, lads. That's probably long enough. You've seen them go about their work and I'm trusting you not to joke about this all later. Probably best now if we go and put our boots on and go for a walk.

We can head up into the fields behind the hotel. Let's take one of the footpaths and see how far we can see along the coast from being a bit higher up."

"But dad, we're still watching," answered Gregory.

"I think you've watched for long enough; the hotel staff," he added as he glanced to his left into the restaurant area, "have already finished setting the room out for lunch, so you've definitely been watching for long enough here. Then this afternoon, we might head off to the tin mine after all – we probably didn't need a whole day there in any case."

*

Emily, once she had got back to her room, from being part of the huddle around Martha's crumpled body, found herself much calmer. She stood up from where she had been sitting on the side of the bed, suddenly aware that her need to flee the scene had now been replaced by a need to capture that scene within her art. Not the whole scene, not absolutely everything but aspects of the whole and some of the finer details that had caught her eye as she and the others stood about the metal steps. Nor to use in every future work she ever did but definitely in some and she would need sketches and drafts to refer to.

Emily was conscious how, as much as she had stared at Martha, she had stared at everyone else too. Emily was intrigued how she had been able to detach herself from the tragedy in front of her, not because she was recoiling from it, rather so she could study those around her – to see their reactions. She had noted the furrows in their brows, what they did with their hands, how they angled their feet, whether they wrapped their arms around themselves for comfort or not, the look of horror on some, of worry on another, of panic, of relief – 'was there relief on someone's face?' she found herself wondering, 'why would someone be relieved?' – of sadness, of loss.

All these emotions and reactions as people witnessed death, which she had just seen for herself, she now had to capture.

She suddenly wondered whether that was how war photographers operated, with that ability to somehow detach themselves from the horrors of what is going on about them in order that they can search out and capture that perfect 'shot', that unique image that says infinitely more than a thousand words. Or was that how the great war poets worked she wondered; to see, to feel what was around them but somehow to be at the same time, even if only momentarily, removed from it – to be wholly immersed in a situation and yet to be able to see it from without at the same time. For her, Emily felt that would be something like being both the painting and the painter simultaneously. The war poets and photographers had created works of beauty – sad, poignant and full of grief but beautiful for it. Now, too, Emily had witnessed death at close quarters and she must record what she had seen in other people's faces.

Somehow all she had just seen had opened a window within her mind on how the living interact with the dead, how, in certain moments, being alive and being dead are so intricately entwined and how truly, overwhelmingly fragile everything actually is – and Emily realised even more, she needed to capture all of this within her artwork. Emily felt a photographer, as skilled as they are, once they have got the shot, they kind of have it, their task is complete, whereas she, Emily, knew this was now where her task began, in that she had to get onto canvass the images she had just stored in her mind; what she had just seen within people's faces, within their poses, within their demeanour, she had to paint and she had to begin now.

She moved her easel into the centre of the room and placed a new canvas upon it. She was grateful as she did so that, by having an easterly facing room, she still had the morning light coming in through the window and so would not be working under electric bulbs. She set her little stool to her right side and placed her artist's box upon it.

She held her hair back within a curved silver hair clip, which she retrieved from its compartment within the top of her painting box and she lifted her long flowing dress off over her head. She slung it over the bed and, such was her haste to start painting, did not bother to put more clothes on. She stood there, in her peach-coloured matching underwear, palette in one hand, three brushes held within the other, each perfectly balanced and positioned between her fingers so that any could be used without having to put the others down, and began to paint.

*

By contrast, Cliff had spent his time on the telephone. First to the hotel's owners and then to the insurance company. He was able to inform both owner and insurance person that there were the appropriate signs up, concerning the staircase – 'Slippery when wet', 'Not for guest access' and 'Staff only'. Phone calls made, he then asked Lizzie to 'book out' room ten for the next few nights so that he or a relative of Martha's, if they could get to the hotel at short notice, could clear Martha's belongings. He then went and joined Annabel outside the hotel.

*

Annabel was standing exactly as she had been when Cliff had gone in. As he came and stood by her side, he asked:
"Can I bring you out a drink?"
"No but thank you. It's really not that long since we were all sitting inside having our teas and coffees wondering where she'd gone."
"But it seems ages ago, doesn't it?" reflected Cliff.
"I'll say but probably only half an hour or so." She then turned to the man next to her and asked, "What am I going to do now? All our

accommodation, as I was saying, along our route is already booked. I can't stay here, as I have no booking, and ought to move on but somehow it seems wrong just to keep going with my walk. Plus, I ought to be here in case Martha's brother or sister turn up – I assume you or the hospital will be informing them what has happened."

"I'll check with the paramedics when they are ready but I'd assume it would be the hospital. As I say, I'll check. As for where to stay tonight, and as Lizzie has just mentioned to me and I tend to agree with her, she's not sure you should be walking the coast path after the shock you've had, particularly not the stretch along our bit of coastline."

"I don't have a lot of choice – I've got to collect the car and stay somewhere tonight and I can't stay somewhere where I have no room, can I?"

"Actually, fortuitously, the bad weather that we had yesterday led to a number of last-minute cancellations – we really ought to charge people a deposit when they book but we don't as we operate on a goodwill basis. However, people tend to abuse our goodwill when they anticipate getting bad weather when they would be here and so cancel. The band of rain that hit us last night has put people off for the whole weekend even though it was always going to clear us by this morning and we're now set fair for a lovely spring weekend."

"Lovely?" reflected Annabel.

"Weather-wise," stressed Cliff. "What I'm saying, is the person who was meant to have your room has cancelled, meaning you can stay an extra night or two. You'll have to inform where you're meant to be tonight – though in the circumstances I'm sure they will understand and might offer you a refund. I can get Lizzie to call on your behalf if you'd like. So, you can stay until you're ready to walk or take a taxi to where you were meant to be at that stage."

"That's kind of you. I'll just have to come back and complete this section of the walk another time. You're right I probably shouldn't be doing it today."

"No," agreed Cliff as he realised his hotel was, in a bizarre way, collecting guests unable to move on both physically and emotionally – 'The Jupiter Hotel' was becoming more akin to a safe house, a refuge and a sanctuary. Yet, he felt, was not that what he was always striving to create, somewhere where people could come and stay and escape from the world around, feel safe and be unhurried?

They lapsed into silence as Cliff waited for one of the ambulance crew to come and speak to him and as Annabel simply watched.

*

Once Lizzie and Alan had rearranged the dining furniture for a further and they both hoped final time this morning, they paused and spoke to one another.

"Thank goodness I didn't have everyone tramping around my kitchens," said Alan.

"I could see the frustration on your face when it was first suggested by that bloke in room four – Mr Jones."

"Well, yes," agreed Alan. "Still, they didn't, thank goodness. Are we all done here or do you want help laying the tables?"

"No, it's fine. I can do that later this morning. I'd better go and clean a few rooms now."

"I sense you can leave room ten, Miss Peacock's, for a bit," reflected Alan.

"Suppose so," said Lizzie. "Well, I ought to pop in and get the damp towels and empty the waste bin at least – wouldn't want the room smelling bad when whoever it is comes and collects the poor lady's stuff."

"I really don't think you need bother," said Alan.

"I should," Lizzie said firmly. "I ought to just tidy it a bit," she added.

"OK," said an unconvinced Alan. "Right, if you don't want any extra help here, I think I'll make a drink. If I do one for Cliff and myself, can I make you one?"

"Oh yes, coffee please," replied Lizzie. "Actually, before I do the rooms, I ought to give Robyn a call to let her know what has happened, otherwise she'll wonder why everyone is quiet and withdrawn this evening when she comes in on shift."

"That's a thought – I'll ask Cliff to call Jed for the same reason."

As the two exited into reception, Gerry used the fact that Lizzie and Alan had completed their task as reason for why he felt his boys had watched the ambulance crew for long enough.

*

"Are you on holiday?" asked Daniel Jones of the other man in the bar, who up until Daniel spoke had been standing at the window, lost in thought. "Join me, if you'd like," added Daniel.

"Not really on holiday," replied Nicholas. "I mean it's nice to have someone else cook for you but, have you noticed, the time you save by not cooking for yourself you lose as you have to wait to be served or because of the dead time between courses? That's why I'll never have dessert, much rather just a piece of fruit in the room – you save so much time that way and it's healthier than all that sugar."

"Surely the odd pudding is fine," suggested Daniel, as he patted his somewhat portly stomach.

Nicholas felt the other man's visible greater weight was all the evidence he, Nicholas, personally needed to keep foregoing the sweet course. However, he chose not to be confrontational as he replied:

"Well, I have to keep my fitness up as I'm into my triathlons – that's running, cycling and swimming all within one race."

"Rather you than me." Not wishing to discuss physical activity, Daniel instead pursued his opening question he had put to the other man. "So, if you're not down on holiday – " he said, leaving his comment 'hanging'.

"Well, I'm trying to fit in a bit of exercise whilst I'm down here, open water swimming for example, but I'm really down here to finish off a research paper I'm doing. I'm a university lecturer – lecture in marine biology at the University of Southampton – and I'm doing a piece on the inter-tidal zone along this stretch of coast."

"Why not a stretch closer to your academic base, if that's not a daft question?"

"We have so many students covering what's closer – at times you can hardly walk along the Hampshire or Dorset coast without bumping into our students undertaking some piece of study. At times I do worry we're taking on too many students. We might be getting a lot of research out of them during their three or four years but I fear the university, in enrolling them all, prevents us from discovering the really brightest amongst them."

"Ah, finding the Private with the Field Marshall's baton in his or her rucksack, you mean?" pondered Daniel.

"Exactly, the 'diamond in the rough' and all that. Plus, with so many students, I'm forced, if I want to progress my own academic career, to find a new, relatively unresearched stretch. So, I head west. However, that has its own challenges; the stretch around St. Ives is too well documented, as people are naturally drawn to the town anyway, the Bristol Channel is also a popular choice, as is the bit around Land's End. Thankfully, this bit, nearer to 'the Lizard' as we are, is relatively untouched by academic hands. And I always try, just before submitting my paper, to revisit the area, not to re-take samples nor re-interview people, rather to re-immerse myself in the geography, literally, by walking, swimming and sitting and observing it, for fear of having missed something so obvious that I'd be the laughing stock of the Faculty. Plus, it's somehow fitting to proof read what I have written down here. Another day or two and I'll be done. You, what brings you here? Like me, you're not really on holiday, are you?"

"Me, no, though I sense I'm appreciating the indulgences a bit more than you." Then, as he glanced to the bar itself, said, though as much to himself as to Nicholas, "I wonder if someone will be around shortly to serve me a 'choco mocha'?"

"You might have to wait for a bit," stated Nicholas, as he too looked over to the highly polished wooden bar, devoid as it was of anyone standing behind it.

"Shame. But to answer your question, I work for a firm of solicitors. My role is sort of to do with wills and inheritance. We've had a bit of a lead on something which has brought me down here to follow up on a few things; primarily, to have a chat with the person who contacted us, to look at the corroborating evidence they were unwilling to post to us, for fear of it going astray, and then to spend a bit of time, if it all seems to be plausible, which I might say it does from the letters I've now seen, at the local registry office and perhaps the Town Hall to cross-reference a few things myself."

"Bit of a Poirot, are you?" teased Nicholas.

"No, not at all. He was a detective genius, and what a literary creation on behalf of Christie he was, whereas I'm just a dullard, an administrative plodder – more Inspector Japp than Poirot and that's doing a disservice to Japp. However," whereupon he leant towards Nicholas, precisely placing his spread-out thumb and finger tips together, and spoke noticeably quieter:

"I must say this is proving a most interesting few days."

"Really?"

"Oh yes."

However, the chinking of glasses and the running of a tap behind the bar broke their conversation as they both looked over to see Jed. Jed had decided to come in early as he personally wanted to oversee a delivery from the brewery, keep an eye on a couple of electricians who were coming in to look at the lights on the outside of the front of the hotel, which had been flickering since the previous night's storm and unable to be turned off, and to tidy what was, to anyone else, an already immaculately organised bar. He spoke as he went about his work:

"Morning, gents. I wasn't expecting anyone to be in here quite so early this morning. I can start up the coffee machine if you'd like and get you something just as soon as I can. And just to say, a couple of electricians are coming along shortly – which is good of them as it's Saturday morning but we do look out for each other down in this little part of the county – and they'll be checking the lights outside the front here so just be careful of ladders and any wiring that they may have trailing about."

"Looks like you might get your 'choco mocha' sooner than you expected," commented Nicholas to Daniel.

"Actually," replied Daniel, "I ought to be reading through some papers in my room. As tragic as this morning has been, I should be making some headway with them; after all, as we've been saying, we're not down here on holiday, are we? Please excuse me."

With that, Daniel made an unexpected exit for someone, Nicholas felt, who had so recently been craving a sweet sugary coffee from the machine behind the bar. Left alone, Nicholas caught Jed's eye, ordered a black coffee for himself and then went and resumed his position at the window and lost himself in his own thoughts once more, as he gazed out across the calm sea.

*

"You're going to have to give me directions to Trelyn," stated Alba to Cecilia, as they approached the main road.

"Of course. Right onto the main road, then once we're through the village, it's first left just before you hit the forty-mile-an-hour road sign. I'll give you the bit after that once we're at that point."

"Makes sense."

However, in seeming contradiction to what she had just said, Alba shook her head and uncurled her fingers from around the steering wheel and, by keeping pressure on the steering wheel through her palms, moved her fingers about in random, almost agitated, movements in the air just above the wheel – as if she were playing the piano really badly. She was aware that for the first time, in all the times she had been to Cornwall, a county she loved and was enchanted by, she found herself missing home – missing the tile-hung cottages, the Downs, the oak trees dotted as they were throughout the countryside, 'The Sun and the Moon' pub, the worn, sagging chair she would sit in in the gardeners' bothy at Hillstone Hall, where she was a volunteer gardener and which she would occupy during her tea break, the Reverend Quinn, her mustard yellow 'Denby' teapot, Neale, Andrew, definitely Andrew.

"I can tell you again if I didn't make myself clear," offered Cecilia, thinking Alba was struggling with the directions.

"No, sorry, it's fine – right, left, I got it. No, it's just that I was thinking this is definitely not the holiday I was hoping for."

"Well, I'd be surprised, not to say a little bit worried, if you had been hoping for what has been going on these past few days."

"Oh, well, yes and I know this suddenly sounds selfish on my part but I was really hoping for a lovely holiday."

"I understand," said Cecilia supportively. "And didn't you say your friend was meant to be here with you as well?"

"Andrew, yes. Yes, it would have been delightful to have him here with me but I do understand why he couldn't make it," and with that Alba shot Cecilia a quick glance before looking at the road once more.

"His father was taken ill, you said," commented Cecilia.

"Grandfather," corrected Alba. "Andrew's father died a long time ago. And please, don't get me wrong, I am quite happy here and you and dear Geoffrey and Lizzie and Robyn and Alan and all the familiar faces are just lovely. It's just, oh how shall I put it? I know this makes me sound horrible and all selfish, with what's happened to poor Martha and Joshua being missing as well but I can just see my holiday slipping away before my eyes. I'm almost minded to pack up my holdall and rucksack and head home this afternoon."

"This morning has been upsetting for everyone," said Cecilia sympathetically. "You're probably suffering from a degree of shock – are you sure you're up to driving?"

"Yes, I'll be fine driving." Then after a pause, though that was in part due to Alba concentrating as she needed to slow down in order not to overtake a cyclist, as she was upon the next turning she needed to take, Alba added, "It's sad in a different way too, if I'm allowed to say something else. Just that – "

Yet, having taken the left turn just before the road sign, Cecilia was obliged to cut her short:

"So, that was the turning you could have missed if you hadn't been paying attention. Now, then, follow this road for a couple of miles and when we get to a grass triangle, due to the road forking, and where there's a red telephone box and one of those old fashioned black and white road signs, we want the right fork. Then a mile or so down that lane we get to the old stone gates of Trelyn House. Sorry, you were saying."

"No, it's fine. Thanks for saying – two miles, fork right, a mile. Am I parking in the lane near the gates or can we get through?"

"We should be able to get through. The metal gates are still hanging on their hinges, just, but they're wide enough apart so we'll be able to drive through – I could yesterday – unless last night's bad weather has brought a branch down across them."

"Yesterday?" queried Alba.

"Yes. Anyway, you were saying something about 'sad in a different way'," said Cecilia.

"Was I? Oh yes, and I know this sounds silly and irreverent, just that all this trauma is happening at 'The Jupiter Hotel', which is in itself kind of sad. It's such a lovely, friendly hotel and I always feel so at home there whenever I come back, it's just a shame Martha's accident and Joshua's disappearance are always going to sour my memories. It was always so idyllic up until these last few days."

"Don't worry about whether you sound irreverent or not," reassured Cecilia. "It's a way of processing what you've just witnessed. Plus, you've been supporting your friend Stella – you were at university together, were you?"

"No, secondary school."

"Oh, yes, you did tell us the other evening. Anyway, you've been investing a lot of time and emotion in being with her. Also, you've hinted you'd been chatting to Martha yesterday as well, so a bit of irreverence is fine – almost a coping mechanism, as you allow your brain to see it all slightly differently, in slightly lighter tones almost. The hotel's idyllic, you say?"

"Yes, with its bay windows, chiming grandfather clock and the old map hanging in reception."

"Oh, yes, the map," said Cecilia.

"The leather chairs in the snug," continued Alba, "and the views from the hotel. Actually, I like the room I always go for – not too close to the staircase you see – but the views from the rooms which look out from the front of the hotel, with their large windows, must be spectacular."

"They are; you should come in and look out from ours one morning," offered Cecilia.

"Ah, thanks. I can never justify booking one of those four rooms for myself though, being family rooms or suites, and I am quite content in the room I ask for each time. All I'm saying is, all in all, it's kind of sad that all this misfortune is happening at such an idyllic hotel," opined Alba.

"Idyllic?" mused Cecilia. "Have you noticed how long you have to wait for hot water to come through when you are trying to run a bath? Have you leant over the reception desk and noticed how worn the carpet is on that side? Doesn't the posh coffee machine in the bar drive you absolutely mad when you are sitting in there, trying to do a crossword and someone orders a latté. As for the large bedroom windows on the front of the hotel being all impressive and offering fine vistas, all I saw as Geoffrey and I returned on Thursday afternoon, as he turned up the drive, was a pair of swimming trunks draped over the open sash window of one of them to dry, so idyllic I think not," said Cecilia.

"I won't hear a word said against my hotel," joked back Alba as she turned off the lane between a pair of stone pillars with their metal gates thankfully still wide apart and free of any fallen trees.

"Here we are," said Cecilia, "Trelyn House. Let me show you around."

CHAPTER 15

Trelyn House

You would not have known it was the drive to Trelyn House they had just turned into. The once proudly engraved name on the stone pillars, which you passed through as you left the lane, were weathered and worn – in no small part to frost-shattering and an inexperienced stone mason who did the work originally. The 'T' and 'E' were gone from the left hand one and all but the final character on the right-hand pillar had to be guessed at.

The gravel drive still afforded that pleasant 'scrunch' sound effect as you drove along it but, to the naked eye it was as much pineapple weed, clover and last autumn's leaves, as gravel. The once clearly defined sweeping curve of the drive was gone, lost to the encroaching grass from both sides. The curve was repeated by squat stone posts, set back from but running up each side of the drive; each post was about four feet apart and originally would have had a metal chain linking each one. The original idea, in having the stone posts set back from the edge of the drive, was in order that there was enough width to get a hand push grass cutter once up and once down the width. With its turning cylindrical cutting blades and roller, the effect of taking it up and down the strip of grass between the posts and the gravel was to create alternating grass stripes and therefore to further highlight the grand sweep any approaching visitor to the house would see in making their way through the once fine entrance gates.

However, the chain link was long gone, surrendered following the war-time government's request for scrap metal, and the weeds and the encroaching grass broke the eyeline of the curve before one had even noticed that many of the little stone posts – posts about half the height of your average staddle-stone – were leaning at irregular angles. The only continuity which the drive afforded was of the tiredness already offered up by the entrance gates.

Off to the left of the drive, beyond the stone pillars, were terraced lawns which fell away down the hillside. They too were unkempt. They were the victim of several years of infrequent cutting by all too often inexperienced gardeners, told to work there unsupervised by the owner of the grounds maintenance company Sir Roger des Roches had ill-advisedly taken on to tend the gardens, and with mowers that were the oldest and least well maintained of the ones the maintenance company had. Completing the look – not that Alba could see them from the car – was a set of stone steps, between the second and third terrace, that had succumbed to subsidence and were therefore giving that same look as one got when in a cemetery looking at chest tombs, where the sides are coming apart and you can see between the sections of stone. A self-seeded *buddleia* – butterfly bush – within one of the gaping cracks in the set of steps completed the sorry scene to the front of the house.

"The terraced lawns used to drop down to a lake but the man-made dam failed several years ago. So, all that now remains is the original little stream; pleasant enough but not the look that one used to have from the house," said Cecilia.

The sense of neglect, followed by abandonment, in the lawns to the front of the house was a portent of what Alba saw once she had parked and stepped out of her vehicle, whereupon she allowed herself a proper look of the house itself. However, it's level of dereliction was not the first thing Alba commented upon:

"Of course, of course."

"Told you," said Cecilia.

"Yes, I've seen this place before, just as you said I had after breakfast this morning."

"Was it only breakfast time this morning?" reflected Cecilia. "It seems longer ago than that."

"A lot has happened since then."

"Yes."

"As for Trelyn House, you were absolutely right – I've seen it plenty of times before."

"*Hundreds*, in fact," teased Cecilia one final time.

Alba smiled at her friend's joke, which she now got. With her hands inserted into her jeans pockets, Alba looked up and over Trelyn House – the House which featured, due to its once fine grandeur, as an inset image in the early nineteenth century map of the Cornish Hundreds which hung, as it always did, in the reception area of 'The Jupiter Hotel'.

"I'd looked at it a hundred times or more and yet I'd never seen it – shame on you, Alba White," said Alba out loud to herself.

"Well, what do you make of the House, now you're seeing it for real?" asked Cecilia.

"Atmospheric," said Alba kindly. "Especially so, I'd imagine, on an October morning as the mist hangs about the place and you have the last of the autumn leaves catching the weakening morning sunlight before they too fall. You'll have to tell Emily about this place and, if it hasn't sold by then, let her come and paint in the grounds."

"Oh, I think I'll be able to get her in, even if the new owner is in by then," offered back Cecilia.

"Really, how so?" asked Alba of her friend even though she did not look at her, for Alba was still studying the house itself. Alba observed sections of missing guttering high up – although, they were not all strictly missing, for a rather substantial section was quite visibly lying across the stone steps up to the front doors. 'If not missing, then at least probably not where that piece is meant to be', thought Alba to herself as she waited for Cecilia's reply.

"Just a hunch. And you are right, Emily would love to come and put brush to canvas here. Have you seen any of her work, by the way?"

"No."

"You should. She really is quite accomplished; you should ask her one evening to have a look at some of the works she's brought with her. We've offered to let her come and paint in our garden."

"Why bring stuff she's done? Blank canvases and half-finished works I can understand but completed stuff?"

"She said she was wanting to show some of her work to a gallery or to a curator or some such person, I can't remember which now, in the hope of getting some future commissions out of her. She was quite happy to show Geoffrey and myself; when was it now, Wednesday evening I think."

"The day before I got here," threw in Alba.

"Yes, I think it was. As I say, I think she's very accomplished. You should ask to have a look as well before you or she leave."

"OK. Anyway, if she does come and paint here, later in the year, I wonder how much of the house will be left by then," said Alba. "Just look at it, cast iron guttering lying about for starters; round my way the local scrap metal scavengers would have had that by now."

"I fear our local lot have been more pre-occupied with the roof lead and the cabling – better returns for lead and copper than cast iron," reflected Cecilia.

"Yes, that's my fear for this place, having seen it, that they've got to the lead. Then, once the roof fails and water gets in, what up until then may have been a slow, almost graceful, decline of a once beautiful house becomes a rapid and brutal end. I mean rain getting in fractionally through broken windows," whereupon Alba pointed up to a couple of first-floor examples, caused, in almost all probability, by bored teenagers throwing stones at them, "is one thing but when the rain that falls onto an entire roof, especially a roof of this size, starts to permeate its way into the fabric of the house because sections of lead are gone, that is quite another. This place really needs a new owner now, doesn't it before it starts to resemble Kirby Hall."

"Kirby Hall, where's that? Haven't come across that one," said Cecilia.

"Northamptonshire," replied Alba. "It's a grand country house and it was once owned by Sir Christopher Hatton, one of Elizabeth the First's Lord Chancellors. It's a wonderfully romantic place but that, in a large part, is because of its semi-ruinous state. There are echoes of that sensation here already. However, I'm not wishing such an end on this property which we're currently looking at. It desperately needs someone to care for it, doesn't it?"

"Yes."

"It's in the hands of solicitors, you say? And that they are dragging their heels," commented Alba.

"Yes, it is with solicitors but only Geoffrey, to be precise, says they are dragging their heels. As for me, I think 'Chatteris, Corby and Lane' are an excellent Bristol based firm."

"Oh, but you, I mean, I thought – " but Alba, not quite sure where she was going with her sentence, lapsed into silence.

"What?" queried Cecilia.

"Nothing really," said Alba after a pause. "Just that you seem pretty certain all of a sudden."

"Of what?"

"Well, the firm of solicitors. I'm sure over breakfast you said you thought they were based in Birmingham and Geoffrey had to correct you. It was," whereupon Alba paused once more. For a moment she studied the stone urns placed at regular intervals in front of the house, full of dying plants in nutrient starved soil, and then at the climbing rose, which was in desperate need of pruning, if only to prune out the 'three D's' – the dead, diseased and damaged branches – and of being retied to the supporting wires. Only then did Alba resume:

"It was as if you wanted to appear vague in front of Geoffrey about 'Chancery, Corby and whoever'."

"'Chatteris, Corby and Lane'," corrected Cecilia.

"But not of their work ethic," Alba suddenly realised. "You seemed keen to instil in Geoffrey your belief that whatever delay he felt there was in proceedings it was with good cause – though without wishing to let on that perhaps you knew more about it all than he thought you did. And, I sneakily suspect," at which point a knowingly wry smile crept across Alba's face as she looked at her friend, "next time Trelyn gets mentioned and Geoffrey speaks of the solicitors you'll no doubt make out that you think they're based in Bedford, Brentwood or Beaconsfield."

Cecilia, however, did not respond to her friend's observation. Instead, she simply said, "Let me show you the gardens, well, what were the gardens."

As they walked past the large double front doors, Alba glanced above them and read the still legible family motto of the des Roches family – *Deo Confidimus* – and wondered what comfort '*We trust in God*' had given the successive generations of those who had resided therein. However, she did not linger for Cecilia was keen to take Alba round to the left of the property and show her what lay beyond.

*

"Thank you, Dr Brierley," said Andrew.

He put the receiver down, grateful the doctor had confirmed that he still wished to visit Lord Hartfield that afternoon and had only been calling to move the time back by half an hour. Andrew placed the morning's newspaper – just dropped off by the person who ran the village shop – on a tray alongside a fresh cup of tea to take them up to his grandfather. 'He'll like today's 'Matt' cartoon' thought Andrew as he made his way along the first corridor.

*

As they made their way round the far side, the north side, of Trelyn House, the dampness from last night's rain permeated Alba's nostrils and the thick, evergreen, leaves of a now overgrown laurel hedge still hung heavy with water.

There was more depth to the house than Alba had first appreciated and so it took fractionally longer than she had expected to walk to the rear of the property. Yet, what awaited her there was exactly what Cecilia had forewarned her about – a garden but one increasingly abandoned to time.

"Oh, I see what you mean," said Alba.

Alba could make out the dead stems of *sedum*, *echinops* and, what she could guess at were probably *rudbeckia* – cone flowers – and *solidago* – golden rod – within their respective beds within the formal *parterre* garden. The surrounding box hedging, once so immaculately trimmed, was now shaggy and the gravel paths, like the drive, were succumbing to yet more pineapple weed. Alba bent down and 'harvested' a couple of the weeds and pressed the flower heads between her fingers and placed them under her nose.

"It's a delightful innocent fragrance," said Alba. "It always takes me back to my childhood and an aunt who first showed me this plant."

Alba stood still for a moment and closed her eyes and smelt the plant once more. In her mind's eye she could see herself as a young girl, dressed in a bright yellow hand-knitted jumper, kneeling down beside her aunt in her aunt's garden as she was introduced to this wild flower. Her aunt had shown her numerous others besides over the course of Alba's many visits, be it enchanter's nightshade, scarlet pimpernel or sun spurge – though told to always be careful of the milky sap of any spurge – but the pineapple 'weed' was her favourite.

Once Alba was back in the present, Cecilia kept walking. They left the *parterre* behind them and ignored the croquet lawn until they were both looking down into the substantial rock garden.

"I won't show you the rose beds or the trained fruit trees for, as I said over breakfast, it will only make you weep. However, here," said Cecilia, "well, the rock garden almost gets away with the neglect. If you try not to notice the brambles which are arching over some of the boulders nor the nettles, then it's not too bad."

"No," agreed Alba.

"We can head down into it, if you'd like," offered Cecilia.

"Maybe, perhaps in a bit," replied Alba, for she was aware that, unusually for her, the house itself seemed as interesting as the gardens. She turned to look at the bit of the house that was still in view. "It's a much deeper house than I was expecting."

"They had quite a few servants at the house's peak, so they extended it backwards to allow more to live on site – sacrificing the grand terrace as they did so. Obviously, the servants lived in the tiny little rooms up in the roof, whilst the des Roches occupied the expanded first floor rooms and, naturally had the additional ground floor rooms to entertain in, including a billiards room, a morning room and a new drawing room. And, of course, some tight little staircases allowing the servants to discretely move about between floors."

"Oh, yes, Jed was telling me about those and an easily missed design feature they had."

"Ah, Jed."

"Yes, said his mum used to take him round; said she used to work here."

"Did he?"

"Yes, you did too, didn't you?" asked Alba.

"Yes. Many years ago, I might add and definitely not when it looked as it does now."

"It must have been a fine home in its day. Were you here at the same time as Jed's mum?" asked Alba.

"For a time. I was just a teenager, helping at events, waitressing, that kind of thing. Whereas Jed's mum worked here full time. She took me under her wing but left when she became pregnant with her third child, Jed as it turned out."

"Yes, Jed was telling me about being the youngest of three."

As the two women strolled back in the general direction of the house, Alba commented further that it was sad that the family line had died out and how the book, so to speak, had been closed for Trelyn.

"You always want, I mean I guess it's human nature," Alba found herself adding, "for a happy ending, the story to continue, the family name to survive, someone to come in and love this place. But it's not always like that, is it? His only child died young, Geoffrey said, didn't he?"

"Yes, there was an undiagnosed condition. Probably the child, as well as Sir Roger and his wife, had a happier life not knowing until that tragic day – probably but who knows. Do people want to be reminded that they are mortal, who am I to say? But it broke Sir Roger's wife and she died of a broken heart not long after and Sir Roger lived a lonely life from then on and his servants became his *de facto* family. He took comfort in – "

Yet Cecilia cut herself short and fell silent.

By now they were back at the rear of the property and Alba was able to peer in through some tall, once elegant, French doors.

"You can't see a lot, can you? Dust sheets covering furniture, one or two pictures gone from their hangings and I'm sure that's a telephone sitting in the middle of the floor all by itself, with a long trailing wire heading off to some obscure socket. As you said, they're probably not selling postcards of the place."

"Sir Roger was never into that kind of thing – he was a private man. And in its dying state there is something endearing, almost romantic, about the place."

"Tragic, definitely," offered up Alba.

"Yes, tragic, for now at least, but maybe something good will emerge; it's a waiting game."

Yet Alba's puzzled look was, if not missed by Cecilia, definitely ignored.

"We ought to be heading back. Geoffrey should be back and Stella might appreciate your company by now," said Cecilia.

"Yes, you're right," agreed Alba. "Although, just before we leave, once we're back round the front of the house, I'd like to drop down onto the terraced lawns; it would be nice, just for a moment, to see the house from the viewpoint the artist had. The viewpoint he or she had when sketching it so it could be included as an inset into that map of Cornwall."

"Of course, sorry, I should have taken you down there initially; we need to be down on the third, the lowest terrace, just by a now very uneven set of stone steps. I'm sure Stella can manage without you for another five minutes – what can happen in five minutes after all?"

CHAPTER 16

A grand Tudor kitchen?

They hardly walked in joking and laughing but, compared to how they had felt when they had set off, it was a definitely more relaxed Alba and Cecilia who walked into 'The Jupiter Hotel' upon their return from Trelyn House.

"Thank you," said Alba to her companion. "That was a good idea to go and have some time there; a change of scenery for an hour or two was definitely needed."

"Yes and it was nice to show you the place."

"Strange to think you used to work there."

"Is it? Still, as I said, it really was a long time ago," replied Cecilia.

"I can't really imagine taking you round the place where I used to work," replied Alba. "Round Hillstone Hall, where I volunteer in the garden, oh absolutely, but not where I worked once upon a time. I have no desire to go back there."

"Well, whatever is behind that comment doesn't apply to me. I liked my time at Trelyn; I was young and carefree and the other staff were nice, especially Jed's mum, and it was a lovely place in its prime," said Cecilia.

"I can imagine," replied Alba. She took a brief glance at the old map on the wall as they made their way to the reception desk before continuing with what she was saying, "I will enjoy coming back down to study the picture of it once I've collected my key, had a cup of tea in my room and spoken with Stella."

Neither Cecilia nor Alba had noticed the pained look on Lizzie's face as they made their way to the desk but they did as soon as Lizzie spoke.

"Stella," said Lizzie. "You won't be able to speak to her right now."

"Why, what's happened? Is she OK?" responded Alba, instantly worried.

"She's had a phone call from the police."

"That's good, isn't it?" said Alba. "Stella was waiting on a call because they were speaking to Joshua's office this morning – it was open, you see, having been shut yesterday. The police were going to confirm the address of where Joshua was going on Thursday after he and Stella had walked back from the island and separated at their car. So – "

"But he was meeting Jed at his father's cottage. Everybody knows that – even Jed has confirmed he was waiting for an architect to turn up but didn't," cut in Cecilia.

"Well, yes," agreed Alba. "But it would still be good to have it formally confirmed. With everything that's been going on, especially what's happened to poor Martha, I think Stella and I still wanted it formally corroborated by the police speaking with Joshua's secretary just to rule out any strange coincidence where a second professional man has gone missing in this remote part of Cornwall. So, a call from the police was what Stella was not only expecting, but, kind of, wanting so she could 'tick that box off', if you see what I mean."

"Well, yes," agreed Lizzie. "But – "

"But what?" said Alba before the other could finish. "Maybe I should just go up and speak with Stella and see what this call was all about and what has got everyone worried." Alba shot a glance at

Cecilia who nodded in agreement with what her younger friend was proposing.

Lizzie though shook her head.

"Why can't I? What's happened, Lizzie? Surely Stella is up in her room – I was expecting to catch up with her now I'm back. What's happened?" Alba repeated.

"You can't," said Lizzie weakly.

Alba chose not to push the young mother the other side of the wooden counter. Alba could tell she was close to tears and clearly worried. They waited until she had composed herself and taken a moment to calm herself. Drawing on some source of courage and composure from somewhere deep within, Lizzie finally spoke:

"You can't because Stella is not here. She's had a phone call from the police. A body has been found, washed up near Kynance Cove. Cliff is driving her over to Helston police station now. Oh, it's horrible, just so horrible. First Martha and now Mr Mallory: it's just so – "

Yet with that, Lizzie broke down and the tears came. She slumped into the little black swivel chair behind the counter and sobbed. Stunned, Cecilia and Alba could do no more than listen to Lizzie's tears until she spoke through her sobs once more:

"It's ghastly. What is happening here? One accident after another. It's just so horrible. Why is this all happening? She's an old friend of yours, isn't she? Well, so Robyn told me."

With that Lizzie looked up to Alba. Deep down it did not matter to Lizzie whether Stella and Alba were friends or not, it was just something, anything to say as she fought to regather her composure. She looked up to Alba for an answer.

"Yes," said Alba. "We were at secondary school together – she was always such a good friend to me."

"It's a shame you weren't here five minutes ago," said Lizzie. "If you had been, you could have gone with her."

"What?" exclaimed Alba.

"You could have gone with Stella," repeated Lizzie. "They only left five minutes ago. Obviously, she's not driving herself and Cliff felt someone should go with her – she could hardly take a taxi, so he went with her. As I say, it's a shame you weren't back five minutes ago; I'm surprised you didn't pass them in the lane."

Alba looked at Cecilia and the two women exchanged a frustrated look, whereupon Alba placed her own hands to her own face and then spoke through them:

"Five minutes – to think we said what difference would five minutes make to our return."

With that, Alba, hands still masking her face, shook her head in disbelief that she had not returned in time to go with her friend in her moment of absolute need. She shook her head once more. She was unable to see Cecilia move round to the other side of the reception desk and kneel down on the section of carpet which Cecilia regarded as rather worn and give the still crying Lizzie a motherly embrace.

With her hands lowered, Alba, not realising the effect she was about to have on Cecilia, asked Lizzie:

"The police are sure it's Joshua I assume."

"Oh, my word, no!" exploded Cecilia. Her cry was to both of the other women, in one sense, and, in another, to no one but herself. She immediately spoke again:

"Not Geoffrey, please not my Geoffrey. Please."

It is one of those strange, totally tragic, human characteristics, where, in pleading for the safe return of one's own loved ones, one is, in one sense, asking it to be someone else who instead does not return; asking for the burden of grief and perpetual loss to fall on the shoulders and the heart of someone else, someone almost certainly unknown. It is done because the other person is exactly that – other – and so desperate is one to be spared loss, that one almost pleads for it to be someone else.

Naturally, in the cold light of day, one would not want loss to fall on anyone. Yet the human heart is, within that single moment, wired to hold its nearest and dearest not just close but within the heart itself; the love you have for them is as much part of your own heart as the muscle, valves and the blood which courses through it, are part of it. It was inevitable then, in that moment, that Cecilia's first, only thought, was for her husband – her husband of so many years. She thought of the father of her children, the person she wanted to walk through old age with and the person, if ever it was to be this way round, who would sit at her bedside in her final moments and hold her hand. Cecilia then panicked that she could not remember the colour of his eyes nor suddenly whether it was redcurrant or crab apple jelly which was his favourite accompaniment to his Sunday roast dinner.

"Please, no. Not my dearest. I know he's only been away since breakfast but with all the craziness that is going on at the moment, please not him," continued Cecilia. With pleading, darting eyes she first looked to Lizzie and then to Alba and, had she not already been kneeling down at this moment, would almost certainly have slumped to the floor.

"No," stated Lizzie as confidently as she could. "No, not Geoffrey." Whereupon Lizzie, through her own tear-filled eyes, embraced Cecilia as much as the other way round.

"No," repeated Lizzie through the embrace. "Well, although the police are not one hundred per cent certain on who it is, they did specifically ask for Stella to be taken over to them. I think the body, no, I mean the person, no, the, oh, what do I mean? It matches, the err – "

"Don't worry," said Alba calmly. "We both know what you're trying to say: that the body of the person they have matches the description Stella gave them when she reported Joshua as missing."

"Yes, that's right," said a grateful Lizzie. Then to Cecilia said:

"So, I can't promise but it can't be, just can't be Mr Constance."

"Come on, 'C', let's help you up," said Alba. "Let's get you onto one of these chairs here in reception."

Between the now more composed Lizzie and Alba herself, they

escorted Cecilia to one of the grey high-backed chairs the reception area offered.

"Blast the time of day, can we get her a brandy?" asked Alba to Lizzie. "I'll pay," added Alba.

Lizzie nodded and went into the bar to get Mrs Constance the drink.

"I won't believe it until he walks in," said Cecilia.

"No, I know," agreed Alba as she held her friend's hand with one hand whilst at the same time dragging the other grey chair closer so she too could sit down.

As they sat there, Alba exhaled a long, slow breath and wondered whether she too needed a drink.

"Everything alright?" asked Alan as he emerged from the kitchen. "What's been going on? I was on the phone to our fish supplier about what I'd like – though of course it's always determined by what they can land. But forget that, I thought I could hear crying."

However, as Alan moved round to stand in front of the seated Cecilia and before Alba could reply, he could more than see for himself that everything was far from alright.

At that moment Lizzie returned. She passed a glass of cognac to Cecilia, allowing her to sip from and then cradle the bulbous beautifully cut lead crystal glass in her hands.

"No charge," said Lizzie to Alba quietly as Cecilia took a further sip.

Then Alba and Lizzie filled Alan in on the latest developments, from the police call to the distress Cecilia found herself in.

"I've got a pot of tea brewing – seem to always have here," commented Alan. "I'll bring some hot drinks out. Looks like you need to sit down for a moment, too," he said to Lizzie. "Look, you sit here. Alba and I can go and sort out some hot drinks."

He gestured with his head for Alba to follow and the two of them made for the kitchen – Alan just pausing *en route* to step in behind the reception desk and switch the hotel telephone to answerphone.

*

Despite all the times she had stayed at 'The Jupiter Hotel' Alba had never been into the kitchens.

She had hardly expected them to be something akin to the Tudor kitchens at Hampton Court Palace or the, arguably grander, one at Burghley House. There, within a great rib-vaulted room, the 'Old Kitchen' was located; where walls were flush with highly polished brass cooking pots and dishes and which was dominated by a large spit rack over an open fire. A rack large enough for an entire pig to be slowly turned. 'The Jupiter Hotel' was, by contrast, simply a small Cornish coastal hotel.

Yet, somehow nor did she expect to enter a highly modern space, glistening with nothing but highly polished stainless steel work surfaces and units, that would not look out of place in some glitzy London or New York restaurant. A kitchen where every utensil and cooking vessel hung or was arranged in perfect alignment, with everything so pristine it was as if one had entered a hospital's operating theatre and one felt one had to be 'gowned up' before entering. An area sterile because every escape of steam from a saucepan or gust of heat from a momentarily opened oven door was sucked out through deafening bulky extractor fans – meaning it was devoid of the aromas that should permeate any proper kitchen.

Rather the kitchen was, to Alba's delight, exactly as she had always imagined it to be. There were inevitably the industrial sized fridges which were stainless steel but somehow did not dominate the kitchen. The double, perhaps triple, width matt black range cooker, was glorious in its understatement. Alan had clearly sought functionality over glitziness and the food he could produce on it or in it, indicated it was more than up to the job of any top of the range one. A working top along one wall – with cupboards underneath – was evidently where the sweet dishes and puddings were prepared, whilst still providing enough space for a couple of kettles, teapots, a coffee machine and several plastic containers, filled to varying degrees with homemade biscuits and jam tarts.

In the centre of the kitchen were two adjacent wooden tables. They were overlaid with colour coded chopping boards and had knife blocks strategically positioned along them. Also, there were several shelving units replete with the numerous bowls, overflowing with fresh fruit and herbs, a whole array of different size ceramic flan dishes, trays of varying sizes and a multitude of lever-arch files. Finally, there was an archway through to where Alba assumed the freezers and a well-stocked larder would be. This then, was Alan's kitchen.

However, as homely and functional and 'just so' as it was, it was the aroma, or perhaps more accurately, the mix of aromas that took hold of Alba's soul. For there was a mix of citrus and those freshly picked herbs but that fragrance was caught up in some recently prepared fresh fish – now, no doubt, sitting in one of those two large fridges, marinating in some sweet sticky sauce – coupled with just a hint but no more than a hint of garlic and, as Alan was about to confirm, spiced parsnip and apple soup.

"This soup smells divine," commented Alba as she stood by the range cooker to get the full effect.

"Thanks," said Alan humbly. "It's the last of the parsnips and a tub of stewed Bramley apples I had in the freezer."

"It's got to be more than apple and parsnips, surely? Just from the aroma there's a bit of a kick to it."

"Ah, well, in addition to some vegetable stock, some onions, coriander and fresh cream, there's just a little curry powder."

"A little? I'm not so sure on that," joked Alba.

"Well, enough to just surprise the unsuspecting," conceded Alan. With that he rustled in one of his utensils pots and retrieved a medium sized wooden spoon. "Have a taste," he enthusiastically added. "Let me know what you think."

After a couple of blows, then gingerly placing her lips to the very tip of the spoon to gauge the temperature, followed by just one further blow, she did.

"That's excellent," she said as she nodded her head in further appreciation. "Excellent," she repeated. "I'm not even going to joke it needs more salt or a dash of freshly ground pepper – it's just perfect."

"Thank you," whereupon Alan, with a further spoon, took a taste, too.

"Yes, happy with this. Actually, you talking of adding salt and pepper reminds me of a friend of mine, Edoardo, he's got a restaurant out in Ravenna, Italy, and he refuses to put salt and pepper out on his tables for diners to use."

"Why is that?"

"He says he's spent a lifetime learning and perfecting his culinary art and therefore feels perhaps he knows how much salt or pepper is actually needed in a dish. It used to annoy him, so he told me, when he would serve people their food, watching them automatically add salt and pepper without even tasting the dish first. He said he would stand there and wonder why he had bothered creating something for them in the first place if, as their actions suggested, they knew how to flavour the food better than him. As I say, he eventually removed the condiments from the tables – if they were coming to his restaurant, they jolly well had to eat his food his way!"

"Wonder what he'd make of Gerry's two boys – Gregory and Ben – and their craving for tomato ketchup."

Alan rolled his eyes before responding:

"Don't get me started on ketchup and as for barbecue sauce, let's not even go there. Our culinary artwork is ephemeral enough and the flavours, textures, appearance and aromas are all so finely balanced, why do people think they know better and immediately cover their meals in such strong flavours. I won't even mention how quickly some people eat – savour it, I'd say. Then you get the people who are looking at the desserts board as they eat their mains, so they're probably not even tasting what's in their mouths at the time, rather always thinking about the next course. You know, sometimes I'm tempted to serve people a mouthful of food at a time in an attempt to get them to slow down and truly taste what they're eating. Yes, a mouthful at a time," repeated Alan.

"Edoardo might approve," replied Alba.

"Yes, I think he would," answered Alan. Then, with a rueful smile on his face, added:

"Guess I should check I've got enough tomato sauce ordered for next month's delivery – this is a battle I will never win!"

"I don't think you will," agreed Alba. "People are very regimented in their tastes and like predictability."

"Yes," concurred Alan. "Normally guests are very predictable – even after their first meal here I can usually tell what 'parameters' guests will order within."

"Always?" mused Alba.

"As I say, normally," reflected Alan, "but there are always exceptions aren't there?"

"For example," said Alba as a leading statement.

"Let me think. Hmmm. OK, for example the guy who's gone missing, the first night he was here, he was obsessed with how his steak was cooked – had to be medium rare – and then by the following lunchtime, I heard him, as he and his wife were ordering a lunch for their room at reception with Robyn, ask for something vegetarian. What's that all about? It was a quality steak I served him the night before. Why change your tastes so suddenly? I found it odd, that's all. Anyway, the bloke hopefully is still just missing but perhaps the body the police have just found is him. Who knows. It's strange," added Alan all reflectively, "how random people's decisions or behaviours seem when you suddenly look back over what might have been their final day."

"Strange," agreed Alba. "Actually, I was in reception Thursday lunchtime. I can even remember their order – it was cheese sandwiches or rolls, with some Cornish blue, but if not available egg. I remember it vividly as that's when I realised I was standing next to my old school friend. I was definitely meant to be staying here this week so I could support her as best I can."

"They had cheese," confirmed Alan, who was unimpressed with tales of old school friendships, having himself had a disjointed school experience due to a father in the diplomatic service. Alan had been to more schools than he cared to remember. On the other hand, Alan's numerous schools in numerous countries had exposed him to the cuisine of the world and instilled into him a love of cooking; for cooking gave him a sense of peace and order during his teenage years which were, to all other intents and purposes, lived too frequently out of suitcases and within compounds in frequently unsafe countries.

"Yes, cheese," repeated Alan before he continued:

"Then there was the one morning Lizzie forgets to note how Mrs Constance wants her eggs done that breakfast time. So, inevitably I assume I'll do them as she's had them every other morning she's been here, but for some reason she'd fancied a change – well, so she said to Lizzie when she sent them back. I had to do the order again, differently, but strangely Lizzie said she really didn't remember Mrs Constance being specific in the first place: seems something had got to that guest that day, too. Actually, that was Thursday morning – clearly a portent of what was to come these last couple of days. What was it with people on Thursday, pernickety or what?"

"Not the day any of us expected, nor is today," offered back Alba grimly. "Come on let's get some hot drinks to Cecilia and Lizzie."

"Yes, of course, and there's me moaning about people adding salt to my cooking. Right, grab one of the trays from the shelves over there. Any that are stacked on the left will do. This pot," continued Alan as he lifted the one with a blue tea cosy on it, which had a procession of puffins around it, "is freshly made and there are cups in the cupboard over by me which I'll lift out once you bring the tray over."

A GRAND TUDOR KITCHEN?

As Alba reached and retrieved a tray, a little cylindrical white pill box fell off the shelf. She bent down and picked it up before it rolled under one of the central tables.

"Yours?" proffered Alba as she passed it and the tray to Alan.

"Oh, thanks," said Alan, pocketing them instantly. "Just some paracetamol. Don't tell Cliff – I'm not meant to have medication stored in here but they're just a few tablets and it seems daft to have to go all the way back to my room to get some if I have a bad head whilst cooking."

"OK, I won't tell," replied Alba.

"Thanks. I do keep them on a shelf away from any food so they could never get into a dish. Right, I'll take the tray and you can bring some more of those ginger biscuits that we had earlier."

"I won't say no," said Alba as she reached for the tub Alan had indicated. "They were rather moreish."

With that, the pair of them rejoined the others in reception and then all four went and sat in the bar.

*

As they sat in the bar, before they had really discussed anything in particular and before any of them needed their cups refilled, Cecilia saw Geoffrey's car pull in off the lane and, just as the ambulance had done earlier that morning, struggle for the correct gear as it came up the steep drive.

"Oh, he's back," almost screamed Cecilia. "Oh, my word, oh my goodness me," and with that she got up. She looked at the other three, briefly, said her thanks for sitting with her and hurried out.

The remaining three could hear the hotel's front doors open as Cecilia headed out.

"The snug door would be more direct to the car park," observed Alan.

"Bit heavy for Cecilia, I would dare to suggest. The glass front doors are much lighter," commented Alba, which got a nod of agreement from Lizzie.

"Suppose I'd better get back to work," said Alan, given the reason for his sitting down with the other three had now gone.

"Me too," added Lizzie. "Don't rush yourself, Alba. You finish yours and leave the trays and cups, I'll collect them shortly."

With that, Alba suddenly found herself sitting there alone.

*

She looked out of the window and gazed across the sea and watched a large container ship, seemingly on the very horizon itself, move imperceptibly slowly west, bound for the great Atlantic Ocean.

Her sudden solitude caught her off guard. She half expected Jed or Alan, perhaps Robyn or Emily, maybe Daniel, Lizzie or Nicholas to come and disturb her. Such had been the intensity of the last few days, her being alone became almost unsettling and she was aware that she was half wanting to hear Gregory or Ben rush in and show her something they had made or bought in a toy shop in Helston, Newquay, Penzance or wherever.

Yet no one came in in those moments. Thankfully, her feeling of being unsettled by being alone, passed as quickly as it had arrived and, for the first time since she had sat in the snug of 'The Jupiter Hotel', Alba felt a stillness wash over her and she felt connected to the chair she was sitting deep within. Connected too to the room itself and even with the view – and the ship that seemingly had still not moved – through the window.

Alba heard Cecilia and Geoffrey enter reception. They spoke with Lizzie at the reception desk. Alba did not hear what was said, rather she heard the tone and the relieved laughter and felt everything – everything as far as Mr and Mrs Constance were concerned – was alright. Alba did not mind that they did not come in and speak to her. They simply headed up the stairs to their room once they had spoken with Lizzie. Alba reckoned she would catch up with them shortly no doubt – 'Let them have some moments together' she thought to herself.

With that Alba rested her head back against the chair and breathed deeply.

*

In time, perhaps forty minutes, maybe it had been an entire hour, Alba roused herself. Aware Stella might return shortly – brought back by Cliff – Alba felt she should be ready for her. Alba did not quite know how 'ready' would manifest itself, if indeed it was Joshua's body which the police had found, but 'ready' almost certainly did not involve 'dozing in the chair in the bar, warmed by the spring sunshine flooding through the window'.

Despite Lizzie's assurance that she, Lizzie, would come and clear the tea trays, Alba tidied the cups and saucers and picked up the fuller of the two trays to return it, if not to the kitchen, to the reception desk. She glanced at the ship on the horizon one final time and, as when one watches the moon in a clear night sky and knowing it is hurtling westwards, from her perspective, nonetheless, in that moment, it seemed entirely, wholly, still.

Back in the reception area, with the tray left on the desk, instead of heading up to her room, the framed map caught Alba's attention once again and she moved to stand in front of it once more. She studied the jagged edge of the coastline, the nautical imagery and then the inset picture of Trelyn House.

"Aunty Alba," cried out Ben as he clattered in through the front doors. "You should have come with us. What are you looking at?"

"Hello, Ben. Oh, just this old map of Cornwall. It's – "

"Don't like old stuff – it's boring," decreed Ben without letting Alba finish. "You know, in dad's car you actually have to wind the windows up by a handle on the door. How boring is that. Mum's car is so much cooler 'cause in her car you just have to press a button and 'whoosh' up it comes; makes my arm ache does dad's car."

"Your dad has a car too?"

Ignoring the question, Ben bounded over to the reception desk and announced his arrival there by repeatedly ringing the bell – seemingly lounder each time.

"That's enough Ben," called out Gerry as he and Gregory themselves entered. "That'll do." Gerry then turned to his elder son and finished what he had been saying to him:

"…so that's why sticking with your piano lessons will be worthwhile."

"Yeah, I guess," answered a clearly unconvinced child, whereupon he joined his brother at the counter. "Hi, Aunt Alba," he added without looking around to her. "We've been out for a walk with dad. You can see for miles from…"

"Key, please" almost demanded Ben upon Lizzie's appearance and drowning his brother out in the process.

With key in hand the two brothers bounded up the stairs desperate to get to the television and any sports programme that would tell them the West Ham United line up for the afternoon's game.

"I feel like a pair of mini-whirlwinds have just blown through," said Alba to Gerry who had come and stood by her side.

"They like you and are still excited to be out of school for a few days," offered back Gerry.

"Oh, don't get me wrong, they're sweet boys; just lots of energy." She then turned to Gerry and asked a direct question:

"Why have you taken them out of school? Yesterday, when we got back from Restormel Castle Ben had said it was so you could use his mum's car before the courts seized it – well, he didn't say it quite that succinctly as he spoke a lot about confetti. Yet he's just told me you have a car as well. An older one apparently but one nonetheless. I'm just puzzled," and with that she half tilted her head and pulled a

A GRAND TUDOR KITCHEN?

half smile, "for surely you wouldn't take them away from their lessons and their friends just to make use of an 'Audi' car."

"My one is a 'Ford'," answered Gerry. "But you're right, that's not why we're here."

"But if it's because of your wife – "

"Tania."

"Yes, sorry, Tania is in prison, why not wait just another week or two and bring the boys to Cornwall then? Easter in Cornwall is not crazy busy – I mean busy-ish but nothing like St. Ives gets in August. Why cost them a week or so schooling and time with their friends by bringing them now? I don't get it."

However, Alba's face changed from puzzlement to almost one of apology as she added:

"Sorry, you really don't have to answer. I've known you just a matter of days and here I am prying into your affairs. Why you're here shouldn't be any of my business – your boys are lovely and you clearly think the world of them and, whatever has been going on that I don't know about, you've clearly been through a bit with them. If you're having a good holiday with them, then that's what matters – just don't take them out of school when it's their exam years that's all I'd say."

The stern look that came to Alba effectively forced Gerry to promise not to.

"Promise. I think I should – "

With that, though, Gerry was prevented from continuing for the reception telephone rang. There was something about it – even though it was exactly the same ring as it had always had – that seemed to offer a portent. In the way that a telephone ringing in the small hours of the night sounds darker, heavier and almost unnatural, the sound now emanating from the reception desk seemed to warn everyone present of tragedy.

Lizzie lifted the receiver.

"'The Jupiter Hotel'. This is Lizzie, how may I help you?"

"..."

"Oh, hi Cliff. Where are you?"

"..."

"Still?"

"..."

"And?"

"..."

Cliff gave a much longer response this time. What he said, however, prompted Lizzie to sit, though a slightly less elegant description would be to say the young mother, slumped down into the chair behind the reception desk – stretching the telephone cable to its limits as she did so. Alba and Gerry were stationary as they listened although Alan did emerge from his kitchen, sipping at a glass of water as he did so.

"Hold on," said Lizzie to Cliff, "let me update Alan who's right beside me."

"..."

With Cliff evidently agreeing to fall silent on the other end of the telephone line, Lizzie spoke to Alan but audibly enough for the others to hear as well:

"It's Cliff. He's at Helston Police Station still. Mrs Mallory has just identified the body they found at Kynance as her husband. Oh, it's just so awful." Lizzie paused, calmed herself and then continued:

"He says he doesn't know how long he'll be there with her. Clearly he can't just leave her."

In that split second, Alba bitterly regretted not having returned from Trelyn House those few minutes earlier. Had she done so, she could have been with Stella rather than Cliff. As good a man as he was, Alba felt she should have been there with her friend.

"So," Lizzie continued, "he'll be a good while. He says, practically, as for here, we're not to take any more bookings and to ask any day trippers who want food to eat outside."

"Why's that?" enquired Alan.

A GRAND TUDOR KITCHEN?

"A police request. They're treating it as an unexplained death at the moment; Cliff says Mr Mallory took a knock to the head and then drowned but that the police have told Mrs Mallory they're treating it as unexplained rather than accidental, which is what Miss Peacock's was. Apparently, they – and Mrs Mallory herself I can only imagine – are puzzled how, for someone last seen at a car park in Marazion, where there are no cliffs, his battered body gets washed up near Kynance Cove."

"Well, yes," agreed Alan. "That's got to be a good twenty miles."

"So, Cliff says the police are curious and ask that we keep things simple here just in case they come and have a look round."

With that, Lizzie turned her attention back to the person on the telephone, who would have heard what she had relayed to the hotel's chef –

"Anything else, Cliff?"

"..."

"OK." With that Lizzie repeated out loud everything Cliff had just said as her way of remembering:

"Don't let anyone other than Mrs Mallory access their room, room seven, have a simple lunch plated up for her in case she is hungry on her return and tell the other residents they are not obliged to stay at the hotel today if they don't want to: two unconnected deaths are just that." Lizzie then concluded the conversation with Cliff. "Right you are. Alan will see you when you get back and I'll probably see you tomorrow, since I'll be off shift and I have to pick my children up. Robyn will obviously be here."

"..."

"Yep, bye, bye."

With that she stood up and replaced the receiver and, in doing so, eased the tension in the cable that had still until that moment been at full stretch.

As Lizzie turned once more to Alan, Alba turned to Gerry to see what he made of it all. Gerry, however, was not at her side. He had not 'gone' gone, for he was over against the other wall, perched against the side table that had all the tourist information leaflets on it.

"You alright?" asked Alba, as she moved across to talk to him. "You look ghostly pale."

He looked up at her, almost childlike, and spoke:

"I need to tell you something."

"Go on then."

"Not here," Gerry replied.

"Well, where? Outside?"

"No, not here," repeated Gerry. "Look, I've promised to take the boys to the nearest tin mine this afternoon. In light of what we've just heard, I've definitely got to take them – get them away from everything that's going on here. We won't be that long. Please come with us."

"What?"

"Come with us. I need to say something but not here. Come, please," pleaded Gerry.

"You serious?"

"Yes. You must come and the boys would love to have your company too."

"Look, as nice as they are, I can't. Stella needs me to be here. I can't just be getting on with my holiday and all that whilst my dear friend is mourning her husband. I can't."

"But Alba, you just heard yourself, they'll be at the police station a long time yet. I need to talk to someone. No," Gerry corrected himself, "I need to talk to you. Come, please."

"Gerry, I don't know what this is all about, I really shouldn't."

"Please."

Alba did not answer, not straight away. She turned and looked out through the front doors as a shadow fell across the hotel due to a passing cloud. She shook her head, once, twice and wondered what the blazes was going on. She turned back to Gerry:

"You want to talk?"

"Yes."

"But not here."

"That's right."

"And you're not mucking me around."

"No. Wouldn't dare."

Alba thought for a moment. She shook her head once more – though more out of puzzlement than defiance – and then asked:

"And you'll buy me an ice-cream, if I come?"

"Of course. And a fridge magnet."

"Please, no," replied Alba.

"Thank you," offered back Gerry. "If we head off in a few minutes, you should be back in good time for Stella's return."

"We'd better be," said Alba. "I can't miss her a second time today."

*

Minutes later Alba was back in reception waiting for the arrival of the Detz family. By her feet was her rucksack containing a quickly made flask of tea and a scarf grabbed at the last minute. She studied the map of the Cornish hundreds once more – though this time more out of a desire not to stand by the wooden table with all the tourist leaflets on, fearing she would succumb to picking up leaflets on sites she really had no intention of ever going to but taking the leaflets nonetheless.

"It's a fine old map, isn't it?" said Daniel as he came down the stairs.

"It is," agreed Alba.

"And it's a fine old country house, they've used as an inset."

"Yes. Cecilia took me there this morning, incidentally. Trelyn House."

"Is it?" offered back Daniel. "Well, as I say, it's a lovely sketch the artist has done of the place. Nice angle they've got of it – suppose someone just needs to add in a butterfly bush in the foreground, growing through the stone steps."

"Yes, guess you're right," agreed Alba. "I'll have a word with Emily, our resident artist."

"Anyway, better not keep you. I sense you're waiting for someone. As for me, I need to rush over to Porthleven to meet a local historian. Might see you over dinner."

"Perhaps," answered Alba as Daniel headed out.

As she waited by herself once more, she straightened the strap of her little bag which was looped over her shoulder and unfolded and refolded her light cotton jacket which she was also holding and which, according to the magazine she had first seen it in, was 'seafoam blue' in colour.

Two boys then bounded down the stairs, followed by their father.

"You're coming with us," announced Gregory.

"Brill, Aunty Alba's coming, Aunty Alba's coming," declared Ben on a seamless loop.

"Yes, she is," stated Gerry. "Ready?" he asked Alba.

"Yes, I think so."

"Good. We'll be back in good time. Trust me."

"We have to be," insisted Alba as she picked up her rucksack.

With that Ben grabbed Alba's right hand and pulled her towards the dining area and the snug door that led out to the car park.

"My school jumper is that colour grey, too," said Ben as he continued to pull her. "Just like the jacket you're holding."

CHAPTER 17

Stannum

For those who love Cornwall, the setting and the view afforded by it was near perfect. Alba and Gerry were sitting at one of the randomly placed picnic tables, located as they were around the site, and marvelled at the view.

"It's the way the sea is the backdrop to all this that gets me," offered up Gerry.

"And me. They say the light is different around St. Ives, which is why it is such a draw for artists, and I'd suggest it's similar here. Everything is just so clear, so defined; there's a sharpness to it."

"Absolutely," agreed Gerry. "And it's not just a dull browny-grey sea either which we're looking out on, is it? It's a deep rich heavy blue – almost Prussian blue. And all that," whereupon he spread his arms out to replicate the broad horizon that lay before them, "is simply the backdrop to this amazing site we're at – this once sombre, industrial, no doubt dirty, grubby, noisy, dangerous, yet now completely silent, tin mine."

With that, as is the way when someone tells you what a wonderful view you are looking at – though, to be fair to Gerry, he was completely right in his opinion – Alba looked over the whole setting once again.

She saw the roofless engine house, built of rich brown blocks and great granite lintels over the square or rectangular openings where doors or windows once would have been. She noted other openings built into the thick walls, which had curved tops – tops defined not by great hulks of Cornish granite but rather by curves of bricks. Those discrete faded reddish curves gave a subtle softening to the whole. She looked at the mighty, perfectly round and tapering chimney stretching up into the clear blue sky, then at the surrounding undulating ground, with lush grass paths meandering between the gorse and the heather.

Alba's eyes then went beyond the mine workings and the routes around it which the modern day sightseer could take, to the landscape beyond. She could not properly see the cliffs, for Alba and Gerry were up above and the cliffs dropped down to the sea, but she could see hints of them due to the occasional dip in the ground. Plus, the smell of the sea, the taste of salt on her lips, the sound of the sea gulls and the buffeting effect of the wind at this exposed site, meant she could 'see' them in their entirety in her mind's eye – her other senses more than compensating for the lack of vision as she observed the cliffs beyond the mine.

The hardened Cornishmen who once worked the mine were now long gone and Alba wondered what they would make of her and Gerry sitting at a wooden picnic table – her sipping at her cup of tea, Gerry his coffee and with the boys' half-drunk cups of hot chocolate, purchased from the vending machine in the little ticket office-come-shop, left to go stone cold. Or what those long-gone men would have thought of the discretely placed information boards located at relevant points around the site or of the simple ticket office-come-shop itself. A hut big enough to sell the requisite items: fridge magnets, postcards, multicoloured rubbers, fifteen-centimetre-long rulers for children of primary school age, also chocolate bars, locally made fudge, bottles of Cornish ale, a choice of fruit or chocolate-coated flapjack bars and, to Gregory and Ben's relief, ice-creams –

which had been promised to them if they went off and completed the children's quiz by themselves.

Alba hoped those men from a time past would have appreciated the fact that their heritage and livelihoods had not been forgotten and, perhaps, had they been sitting next to her on this spring morning, would have lost themselves in the view as well. Perhaps, too, they would have been baffled by some of the things for sale in the little shop – the multicoloured rubbers, which all too frequently left a smudge on the paper where you had tried to erase your pencil markings, rubber eggs and magnets to go on a kitchen appliance that had yet to be invented in their time and an appliance which, ultimately, would put the local milkman or woman out of business.

*

"We could have stopped at a village store on the way back to the hotel for a bottle of beer for you," offered Gerry. "It would have been cheaper than what you've just paid."

"Oh, I know," agreed Alba. "And don't get me wrong, I'm not against village shops and I do my best to support the one in my village back home but, equally, I feel I ought to support these heritage sites; they need revenue, too."

"Fair enough."

"And it was either a bottle of 'Tribute' from the St Austell brewery or, as you've just bought for Ben, a garish red plastic pencil sharpener, saying 'Cornwall' on it, for my friend Neale."

As she repacked her rucksack, with the said bottle now wrapped in her burnt-gold coloured scarf, Alba went on to explain that Neale was an author who lived in the same village as her.

"He's favoured to have you as a friend," reflected Gerry.

"You'd have to ask him, I guess."

"I think he is," stated Gerry. He paused as he heard a distant 'there's another board over here', from one of his boys desperate as they were to earn their reward. Gerry then added, "I hope I can remain in contact after your holiday has – "

"Holiday?" interjected Alba. "Some holiday! I mean, don't get me wrong I enjoyed Restormel and here, well the scenery is just stunning, but 'holiday', are you serious? You can recall what's been going on, can't you?"

"Break then?" mused Gerry but Alba's look suggested he was still off the mark. "Time away? That's the best I can offer."

"OK, let's go with 'time away'," she conceded.

"I hope," rephrased Gerry, "we can stay in contact after your time away in Cornwall has ended. Gregory and Ben really like you and they – "

"Don't!" stated Alba and she stared at him, suddenly angered.

"Don't what?" asked a completely taken aback Gerry, as Alba's eyes continued to bore into him.

"You know exactly what I mean," Alba declared. "Don't bring your boys into this, whatever 'this' is all about. They're good boys and you clearly love them to bits – please don't think I think otherwise – but don't start playing with my heart strings by saying how much your two lads like me."

"I'm not. Really, I'm not," he insisted.

Yet Alba's look still said she was not convinced.

"Please, all I was trying to say was, clearly very badly, it would be nice to stay in touch once our time here in Cornwall is over. Nothing more, nothing less. I'm sorry for not being more articulate," Gerry added, "but I have enjoyed your company in the few days we've been here. That's all."

"But it's not that simple, is it? What would your wife make of it? Of me popping round for a pizza on a Saturday evening or taking a Sunday afternoon walk with you? Might not she – "

"Tania," prompted Gerry.

"Yes, I know," said Alba. She did not quite 'snap' back at Gerry but she was not far off.

It resulted in an awkward silence. Gerry did not know what, if anything, to say and Alba was embarrassed for how she had just spoken. She shut her eyes, pinched the bridge of her nose and lowered her head as she did so – and, in those moments, all that could be heard was the distant sound of seagulls as they followed a solitary fishing boat, out of sight, way down below them.

Finally, she lifted her head. She looked at Gerry once more and spoke:

"Look, sorry. I didn't mean it quite so bluntly as that."

"It's alright," replied Gerry weakly.

"No, it's not. I'm sorry. All I was getting at, in a sort of blunt way, was I know your wife is Tania. However, if I start calling her that, it's too much, too soon. If all this friendliness gets too personal too soon, we'll be swapping birthdays, inviting each other round for meals and meeting up in London to 'take in a show' together. You're a good guy but where does it all end – you're married after all. What will Tania think, if you, if your lads even, start talking about me in front of her and expect me to call in when I'm passing or she finds you having long deep meaningful telephone calls with me on a Sunday evening?"

This time it was Gerry who almost snapped back – even if he did not snap, his language was at best rich:

"I know I'm married. Bloody hell don't I know it." He paused then, in a more refrained manner, added, "I've never kept that from you – in fact, I told you I was. You didn't discover it from my boys or from someone else but from me. In asking if we could stay in touch, I wasn't asking for, wasn't inferring, anything else – I've realised I've enjoyed your company and, even given the last few minutes, would have regretted not asking you. That's all. And as for what Tania would make of you, of it, of whatever, well, to be blunt, I don't really care at the moment after what she's put me and the boys through – and they don't know ninety-five per cent of what's gone on."

Gerry looked at her and the sadness in his eyes was clear for

Alba to see – the sadness from maintaining a façade in front of his two boys, a façade of loyalty and love towards their mother, because that was what two young children needed to see, even if it was many, many miles from the truth.

"What's gone on?" said Alba. "I won't judge – we've all got skeletons in our closets after all, haven't we? And, you do know at least one of mine, which concerns Stella."

"Ah, Stella, yes," replied Gerry.

Somehow, for reasons she could not quite deduce in that moment, Gerry's reply unsettled her, even unnerved her and it prompted her to suddenly ask:

"Why are we here?"

She did not rush him for an instant answer but her tone and unwavering eyes made it clear, as clear as the view they had just been enjoying, that she expected a proper answer; not some glib *'why are any of us here?'* or some weak jokey reply along the lines of *'because we were looking for a tin mine to visit for a jovial day out'*. She allowed Gerry to pour himself another cup of coffee from his flask whilst she, without looking down at her hands, folded her empty crisp packet lengthways several times and then tied a knot in it to prevent it from blowing away.

Yet still he did not speak. He cradled his coffee cup and stared deep within its warm brown contents and found it impossible to answer. Once, possibly twice, Alba thought he was about to speak but the moment passed and still he studied his coffee. Alba was surprised at herself that she was not finding herself getting cross with him for not speaking, for she sensed there was a serious answer within him but somehow it was such a burden that still he could not quite formulate it; still, she felt, he needed prompting.

She stood up and then calmly spoke to Gerry:

"Look, I'm going to go and throw our little bit of rubbish in the dustbin over by the car park and then I'm going to come back and sit down and you are going to tell me. Whatever it is must be serious –

there's no way you'd have brought me all the way here just to say *'can we stay in touch?'* and serious enough you don't want anyone else at the hotel overhearing. But – "

At which point Alba paused, as she decided whether to say what she was about to say. In that split-second pause she decided she would – she would bring Gregory and Ben into it but into it on her terms:

"But," she repeated, "if you don't tell me upon my return, I will call your two lads over and you can tell me in front of them; your call."

As she strode over to the bin, leaving a visibly shocked Gerry sitting at the table, she thought to herself that that man needed a rather hefty kick up the backside and, she hoped, her threat – which she knew she would never follow through on – would provide that kick.

*

"I've returned," stated Alba as she sat down opposite Gerry at the same picnic table which she had left just a few moments ago.

"I see," answered Gerry as he lifted his eyes to meet Alba's look. His apprehension was not lost on Alba.

"So? Shall I call them over?" she asked.

"No."

"Good," she said – privately relieved her bluff had not been called. That said, she chanced it once more, as she added:

"I didn't want to but would have done. I think, having brought me here, I'm entitled to ask why."

"Yes, I know. It's just hard to work out where to start and it all sounds like madness when I go over it in my head – madness."

"Try me," Alba offered. "It probably won't sound quite so mad when you say it out loud."

"It will."

"Try me," repeated Alba.

"I didn't do it," stated Gerry.

*

"I beg your pardon?" replied Alba.

"I didn't do it," said Gerry once more.

"Do what?"

"Murder Joshua."

"Sorry, what did you just say? Murder Joshua?"

"Yes," said Gerry. "I didn't."

"OK, that's good," said a completely taken aback Alba. Her words did not quite capture the whirring of her brain, a brain trying to process what Gerry had just said. "Sorry, what?" she added. "Why on earth would you have? Assuming he is dead, which seems almost certain."

Alba's comment received a nod from Gerry, whereupon she continued:

"Assuming that, it probably was an accident after all. Suicide, well, perhaps, after all who really knows what pressures any of us are under at any given moment. Murder, though? Why have you suddenly jumped to that conclusion – though, I acknowledge, it is a puzzle why he was found so far from where he was last sighted – and why, perhaps more worryingly, are you so quickly feeling you have to rule yourself out?"

"Remember please, after you've heard all I have to say," pleaded Gerry, "remember I didn't do it."

"I'll try."

With that, Gerry began:

"I've wanted to often enough, mind you."

"You've wanted to?" repeated back a shocked Alba. "But you've never met him before. Stella clearly doesn't know you and there's absolutely nothing to connect you to them or even to Jed, who's cottage Joshua came to visit on Thursday. Nothing. You're just here on holiday with your boys."

"Yeah, just here on holiday," mused Gerry as he allowed himself a glance out to sea – relieved that he had at least started his discourse. A moment later he fixed his eyes once more on the woman opposite him and continued:

"Don't tell the boys anything else – we are here on holiday, that's it. This isn't their flawed battle, it's not their misadventure, nor is it their self-cleansing – understand?"

"Not really," said Alba.

"You will, when I tell you. For Gregory and Ben, though, it's a holiday by the sea, making use of mum's car one last time before the courts confiscate it."

"'Confetti-it'," offered back Alba – allowing Gerry just a moment of lightness and her assurance that she would protect his boys.

"Ah, yes, Ben struggles with the correct word," said Gerry and a faint, relieved half-smile crept onto his face.

"Yes," agreed Alba. "Some big-wig judge-man is going to take it for himself – well, according to your son's understanding of how the court system works. Ben says you should just hide the key from the judge-man!"

"Hadn't thought of trying that – oh, bless the innocence of youth. Wish I knew something of that innocence," continued Gerry, "rather than those horrible, dark nights, where I'd lie in my bed thinking of bad, horrible things to inflict on Joshua Mallory. In my defence, though, sometimes I would also wish Tania would come home and that we might just be a normal, happy family."

"Well, she'll come home once she's served her time – sooner if the appeal is successful," offered up Alba.

"Actually, I'm talking of a time before she was arrested and convicted; she worked long hours."

"In love with her job, was she?" threw in Alba.

"If she had been, that would have been fine. She always had the better job than me and I loved – still love – being with the boys. I was quite happy in my role working part-time and being a full-time parent. Quite often we had their friends home from school too, when their parents were stuck in traffic or held up at work. I didn't mind and it was nice to help out; perhaps, though, as they progress through secondary school and they have lots of homework that will have to reduce. Who knows? But up to now it has always been a happy, bustling home – well, happy until you put Tania into the mix. Each evening, well, the evenings when she did come home, she would come in all stroppy and resentful. Moody about seemingly anything and would find fault with everything that was going on at home."

"Well, if she was focussed and career-minded perhaps she found it hard to unwind each evening. Maybe she found it hard to switch from a world of high-pressured board meetings, business travel and supply chain issues to one of colouring crayons, school plays and children's five o'clock tea-times and she didn't know how to communicate that to you. She probably loved her job more than she could admit," suggested Alba sympathetically towards a woman she had never met.

"She didn't love her job. I mean, she was good at it – though not quite as good as she thought but I'll come back to that point shortly – but it allowed her to pursue her actual love."

"Which was what?" enquired Alba.

"The question you need to ask is who not what," responded Gerry quietly.

"Oh."

"Yes. I didn't know to start with. Actually, in a way I still don't but I'm certain she had fallen in love with her boss. Whether he returned her affections I don't know but she did work late a lot and was often on, what she said were, business trips; whether he was complicit in it all I don't know – she could just as easily have been stalking him as in an actual relationship. I don't know as I never found any actual proof as such. I guess it just got to a stage where she was too vague about too many things to do with work and travel for me not to suspect something. It broke my heart when I first reached that point – I mean I loved Tania after all, still do in one sense and my wedding vows meant something to me. I've kept them and still intend to, well, at least until she divorces me."

"But you're not wearing your wedding ring," stated Alba.

"Don't have one, never have – so, please don't think I slipped it off the moment I saw you at the hotel."

Yet Alba's unconvinced look forced Gerry to expand:

"My dad never wore one and was happily married for over forty years. I never wanted one either; told Tania the day we got engaged so there was never any misunderstanding. I was never one for boyish necklaces or chunky rings as a teenager either. My view, as it was my dad's, is that a wedding ring is just a ring, no more no less. It's often a misleading symbol in fact, whereas actual commitment, love and loyalty can only be found within. Given Tania wears one but I don't, well, I rest my case."

"OK," said a more convinced Alba.

"Anyway, I played the innocent unsuspecting husband as best I could after my realisation, for the sake of the boys. Then her arrest and conviction happened. In a way, for me, though definitely not for Gregory and Ben, it was almost a God-send. That was because, with hindsight, I was almost at breaking point. With her being in prison, well it has almost been a release-valve for me."

"I'm told she's in 'The Queen's Prison Faraway'," said Alba.

"Ben again?" queried Gerry.

"Yes," said Alba. "I'm assuming it's HMP Holloway."

"That's right. I'm taking the boys to see her in a week's time. It's a bit of a train ride from where we live – hopefully we can get a train into London Waterloo and then get the tube to where the prison is in north London. Otherwise we have to go via Clapham Junction before we even get on the tube and that just makes it messy."

"I got caught in the rain outside Clapham Junction station once – that was a memorable day, I can say," recalled Alba absent-mindedly. "But not relevant. So, you're not travelling into London from my corner of the country, if you're hoping to get in to Waterloo; I go into Victoria or London Bridge. And if you're travelling down from the north or midlands isn't that Kings Cross and Euston respectively? Waterloo to me suggests travelling from the west country."

"Very good. Wiltshire, specifically Salisbury," replied Gerry.

"Salisbury?"

"Yes."

"But that's where – "

However, a knowing nod from Gerry meant Alba did not need to continue voicing the connection she had just made.

"That's where Joshua's office is, yes. I assume you learnt that from Mrs Mallory?" said Gerry.

"Yes, over breakfast yesterday. As I said, we'd not been in contact for several years."

"As you explained to me at Restormel," said Gerry supportively.

"Right, yes. I didn't previously know where they were living or working – Stella told me yesterday. She also said, one of the firm's employees was done for fraud a while back and wondered whether Joshua's disappearance had anything to do with that."

With that, Alba paused. She studied Gerry for a reaction. Almost to her disappointment there was not really one at all – which she somehow found frustrating. She wanted, hoped for something, anything, be it shock, defiance, anger, pride, something but he offered nothing. Alba suddenly felt Emily would struggle to paint Gerry in this moment, or Neale, her author friend back home, would struggle to write him into a story because he too frequently offered nothing for the artist to capture or the author to describe – Gerry just sat there, in effect allowing Alba to continue. She did:

"I didn't really pick up on it at the time as being of significance."

With that, though, Gerry did react. His eyes became more

focussed, slightly smaller, a flash of colour darted across his cheeks and he sat more upright, having straightened his back. He did not let her continue:

"It's not of significance," he stated.

"No?" challenged Alba.

"No," stated Gerry determinedly. "No," he repeated. "There is a connection, in one sense, a background detail but significance, no. I was getting to it; was about to mention it."

"Blow, in a protracted, drawn out, laboured way," said Alba.

"Perhaps. It's not easy saying my wife, Gregory's and Ben's mother, is in prison for fraud, for stealing from the very company she was working for. As I say, she thought she was a cleverer accountant than she actually is, for the partners eventually worked out what she was up to. She stole because her love affair with one of the senior people in the firm ended or, maybe, because he told her it had never started and only existed in her head – who knows, who cares – but steal she did."

With that, Gerry slung the contents of his cup across the grass to his right side.

"It's gone cold," he said angrily. "Sorry," he immediately added, "that was said in anger to Tania, not you."

"I know," offered back Alba. "Can I go and buy you a hot drink from the little shop?"

"Thank you but no. Well, maybe but not yet. Let me fill you in on the rest and, fundamentally, why I am here, why I've brought my boys out of school and why I have brought you here, away from the hotel, to speak with you."

"I'm listening," she said as she refilled her own flask lid with the remaining contents of her own flask. Yet, knowing he was not the most direct of talkers, she gave him a prompt:

"She worked for the firm of architects where Joshua was a partner, I take it. Fallen for him, too?"

"Yes. When Joshua Mallory spurned her or ended it, she hated him and started helping herself from the company's bank accounts to have her revenge."

"But her appeal?" mused Alba.

"Complete waste of time," said Gerry. "She's guilty, guilty as, well, you know what. The appeal is a futile waste of court time in my opinion. Her lawyers should just tell her to accept her guilt. However, they tell her they've spotted a technicality and are basing an appeal on that. I hope the appeal fails as she's guilty; plus she'll be insufferable if she comes home upon appeal, chirping on about being innocent after all – she won't be innocent, just let out on a technicality over some date on a letter."

As Alba sipped her tea and broke off another bit of the fruity flapjack bar, she had bought herself, Gerry continued – having declined the final chunk of her flapjack which she had just proffered him:

"And no, Tania hasn't slipped out of prison and come down here to take her revenge and murder him. Well, not to my knowledge. If she has, it's been without my involvement. More pertinently, nor have I done him harm. I am connected to him, in that my wife worked for him. My fear though is, now we have heard a body – his body – has been found, the police are about to view me as very much involved and that, in turn, will see my two lads taken into care. The police will believe I have followed him down here to take my revenge because my wife has been falsely imprisoned upon his evidence. That is my fear. Further, the police will claim" Gerry continued, "I learnt from Tania about this booked trip he had – she signed the costings off, after all – and plotted to avenge my wife when I knew he would be alone, on his way to or from a little Cornish cottage."

"Jed's cottage?"

"So it would seem," concurred Gerry.

"But you didn't do it, so you tell me," Alba succinctly summarised.

"No."

"And yet," said Alba calmly, "you just happen to be here on holiday at the same time as your wife's former employer. Here rather brazenly making use of a car she financed, so I'm surmising, out of money she, perhaps even both of you, siphoned off from his company. All a bit of a coincidence, don't you think? And, if one viewed you very unkindly, you're shielding your murderous acts by having your two children around you."

"Is that what you think?" asked Gerry. There was no anger or hostility in his voice for he knew the ice he was figuratively on was thin, so thin as to basically be not there – he sensed he was in fact closer to treading water and aware the sharks were beginning to circle.

"No," replied Alba. "And yes. It's hard to explain – kind of both."

With that she paused. They both listened to the sound of a young boy, closer this time, calling to his brother that they had just two more questions to answer before they could claim their ice-creams; the other child's reply was lost within a gust of wind. Alba continued:

"Sort of both, I suppose. That's not just me sitting on the fence because I can't be bothered to think. Rather, there are things in your favour and things which are not so favourable to you. For example, I don't have you down as a cold-hearted killer but you've got motive."

"Agreed," confirmed Gerry.

"Then although you're here with your boys ever present – so surely couldn't have done Joshua harm – actually you had the opportunity," stated Alba.

"Did I?"

"Yes. Shall I tell you where you were on Thursday from lunchtime onwards or do you want to tell me?" asked Alba. "I know, by the way," she added, "I'm not bluffing."

She was not – not this time.

"I can see you're not," replied Gerry. "We were at St. Michael's Mount – how did you know?"

"You didn't tell me yourself. However, when we were at Restormel yesterday you were telling me about how you'd got me in on your family ticket."

"That's right."

"And that," continued Alba, "how you have a family ticket for both English Heritage and the National Trust."

"Yes, as I said our respective presents to each other."

"But you went on to say, though you didn't say which property it was, because the National Trust had sent you the wrong ticket, the ticket attendant wouldn't let you in and that there was a bit of a scene as you contested the fact. You see, I know it was on the island because Stella witnessed it all. She must have been in the queue that had built up behind you as you argued your case to the attendant. Stella relayed that fact to me inadvertently over breakfast yesterday when I got her to go over hers and Joshua's movements on the day he went missing. You see, she was telling me how they were fitting in a rushed visit to the island in the afternoon, how she didn't really like the 'Blue Drawing Room' and that it was an even more rushed visit because they got stuck in the ticket office queue because some bloke ahead of her and Joshua was being refused entry because he was trying to get in on his wife's ticket."

"Ah, I see," noted Gerry. "Unfortunate," he added.

"Unfortunate you were spotted?"

"In part. Not that I did Joshua any harm."

"So you keep saying," observed Alba.

"More, unfortunate that either you or she will inevitably tell the police I was there and that will be another piece they'll wrongly fit into the puzzle and have me arrested."

Alba closed her eyes and shook her head in frustration once more at the man opposite her:

"Look, come on Gerry, I'm minded at the moment to arrest you myself – you've followed Mr and Mrs Mallory down to this remote part of Cornwall. Once here, you probably heard them discussing their plans over breakfast on Thursday, heard they'd be going to the island, and followed them there. Furthermore, you've got opportunity, as I say. I've seen for myself how well behaved your boys are and how they can be left – like here, like at Restormel – to entertain themselves for quite a while; easy, then, for you to leave them playing somewhere whilst you slip off and attack Joshua, knowing he was going off to a site visit by himself about five o'clock. Maybe you left Gregory and Ben on the beach at Marazion, there are hardly dangerous waves there after all. Maybe on the zip-wire at that rather good children's playground the town has or you gave them money to go and get an ice-cream each. It's all very very possible, you see."

"Yes, I can see that. I accept we were at the island because I did overhear their plans at breakfast that day. We were behind them on the causeway walking over in fact. Well, to start with but ended up ahead of them as the boys ran ahead as they were getting nervous about the incoming tide. I mean, it wasn't about to come over the causeway for another quarter of an hour or so I reckon but it made them nervous enough to insist we had to run the last bit; hard to run over those cumbersome boulder stones that make up that beautifully snaking causeway."

"Yes, no doubt." Then, her voice heavy with exasperation, Alba asked:

"Why are you here, Gerry, I mean in Cornwall, this week?"

Gerry forced himself not to glance out to sea once more as he prepared his answer in his head. Rather, he kept his eyes upon Alba – a face he already knew he found hard not to look at whenever he saw her.

"I wanted to see for myself this guy my wife, my children's mother, had fallen for. I was curious about him. You see I didn't want to simply hang around his house in Salisbury and watch him leave for work one morning – I wanted to observe him over a period of time, to see for myself what kind of guy he is. Yes, I admit there were nights when I would lie in bed and wish him harm, ill-health and untold horrors. It's strange how such thoughts can take hold of you in the cover of darkness, isn't it?"

Alba did not respond, keen not to break Gerry's flow – thankfully he continued:

"But each time morning rolled around I was able to bury such thoughts and the joy my two boys give me kind of gave me a re-birth each new day. I knew after a while, be it weeks or months, I would never actually do anything to Mr Joshua Mallory. That was never really me but the thoughts and the depths of anger which I had were real and scary at the time – all I can say is thankfully they never took hold. Don't get me wrong, mind you, I don't like the guy and he should either have never had an affair with my wife or allowed an 'atmosphere' to arise that played on her feelings. Either way, I was interested in him and, as much as it pains me to consider, he might one day have become my boys' step-father. You see, maybe he was actually missing her whilst she's locked up, maybe they agreed to part for a bit and maybe the affair would one day resume. Maybe and it breaks my heart that it might be so but, for the boys' sake, I thought I should see the man for myself, over a few days, not just a snatched view from behind his dustbins as he steps out of his front door in Salisbury. Rather for a few days to see *who* he is – does he have a sense of humour, even if not my sense of humour, does he tip the waitress, does he get visibly irritated having other people's young children around him, you know, a thousand and one silly little things that make up who a person is."

"Like a leather hat, a pair of secateurs, a red rose, a recipe and an old battered journal," mused Alba ever so softly to herself, thinking of a time past.

"Pardon?" said Gerry.

"Nothing. You said you came to watch – to observe, if you like?"

"That's right, not to stalk, well, not in a nasty, controlling way. I just wanted to see the man for myself. If I came away thinking but for his involvement with my wife, he seemed an OK-ish sort of bloke then if, but please may this never be so, he became the boys' step-dad one day, it might, just might, break my heart a little bit less. So, I went through Tania's work bag, found the bill she'd signed off for this business trip Joshua had arranged to Cornwall and booked myself into the same hotel. And – "

"And?"

"And yes, I did choose to come in Tania's Audi car because it's a better car than mine. Ben is still blown away by the fact that he has buttons to work the windows in the back of the car and that it has a compact disc player; we listened to Roald Dahl's 'The Fantastic Mr Fox' on CD on the way down. If we'd come in my car, Ben would have complained about the windows making his arms ache and we'd have had to have listened to my crackly audio cassettes and, you know what, I thought they'll be taking the car very soon, why not 'take it for a run' so to speak? Blow, I'll never get to drive a car like this one ever again."

With that, Gerry looked around him to see his wife's car glistening – glistening as best a grey car can – in the spring sunshine.

"No," he continued as he still looked at it, "I'll be back to my old car. But," he added quickly, looking once more to Alba as he heard two boys come bounding up, "I didn't do it. I promise you, I didn't. Whatever has happened to him, it wasn't me. You must believe me – it wasn't me!"

"Wasn't what?" asked Gregory, as he collapsed across the picnic table between Gerry and Alba. "Cor, he added through his hoodie top, which had flopped over his head as he fell onto the table, "you two have been sitting here ages. What have you been talking about?"

"That it wasn't your dad's turn to buy you an ice-cream. Apparently, it's my turn once again. I think I've been hood-winked," said Alba – choosing to step back into the world of child-like innocence. "But only if you've completed the quiz."

"Brill," said Gregory, as he stood up and proudly retrieved his scrunched up but completed children's quiz from his pocket. "You buy us the best ice-creams – thanks Aunty Alba. The final question was the hardest. It was about why tin has the letters SN on the periodic table."

"Blow, that's a hard question for a children's quiz," said Gerry. "Thankfully you've been studying the periodic table in your chemistry lessons, haven't you?"

"Well, yes but I still didn't know the answer," conceded Gregory. "So, we had to go back to the ticket office and ask the nice lady there where the answer was. We missed one of the boards she said. She told us where the board was and that had the answer – it's its Latin name so the board said."

"Which is?" pressed Gerry.

"Oh, dad, I can't remember. All I wrote down was that it was from the Latin. Something like 'stanley' I think."

"Never mind," said Alba reassuringly to Gregory. "Your answer is good enough for me. If anything, 'stanley' is better than the actual Latin name for tin."

"So, we'll still get our ice-creams?" asked Gregory in hope.

"Of course," said Alba.

"We'll look it up in your school books when we get home," insisted Gerry.

Yet Gregory chose not to hear his father's latest comment. Instead, he spoke to Alba, who would be supplying the ice-creams:

"Thanks Aunty Alba. Do you know, on the same board it also said the patron saint of Cornwall – "

"St. Piran," offered back Alba.

"Yeah, that's right. Well, it's his cross on the Cornish flag so the board said. It also claimed some people think the white cross on the black background is a picture of Cornish tin stuck in black rock."

"That's interesting," said Gerry.

"It had it on the board I just read," said Gregory, keen to show he had not just made it up. "Also…" but he was drowned out by Ben's loud protestations upon his return:

"Aarrghh, not fair," decried Ben. "You do cross-country training at school, I don't. You were bound to get back to the table before me. Not fair. Not fair," he repeated to his dad.

"Never mind," said Gregory to his brother, "Aunty Alba is buying us an ice-cream; you've got to show her your completed answers, though. Come on, race you to the freezer in the shop. I'm going to have a 'Fab'!"

Whereupon, after a second scrunched up piece of paper was proudly presented to Alba, two boys ran their hearts out once more – this time to be the first to the ticket-office-come-shop.

As Gerry and Alba followed, Alba decided the breeze was now just too much for her and that she needed her burnt-gold coloured scarf on. As she wrapped it around herself, she accepted that Neale's bottle of ale would have to take its own chances within her rucksack. Once Gerry saw she had finished untangling her silver necklace from the scarf, he spoke:

"Thank you."

"Please don't thank me. I would like you to take me back to the hotel as soon as they've had their reward, in order that I can think through all you've just said. Until then, rest assured, whilst I am still here with them, for your boys' sakes I might add, not necessarily yours, I will continue to play along that we are here having a fun time out. To that end, you're about to buy me a cup of tea and a bag of chocolate fudge. I guess I'm simply now at the stage you are, in that I'm maintaining a front to protect two young boys. I might add, though, you should never have come."

She stopped and turned to Gerry and repeated her last comment – keen that the seriousness of it was not missed by the person at her side:

"You should never have come. You were, you are, a fool. You should have stayed a hundred miles away from Joshua Mallory but you didn't."

CHAPTER 18

Eve

On the drive back, Alba had said to the two children behind her that she had indeed had a lovely time with them but, once back at the hotel, she had a few things to attend to in her room, such as another sewing job, flasks and sandwich boxes to wash out in her sink and her own postcards to write. She did add, however, that perhaps she would see them in the restaurant for dinner.

Gerry Detz was aware of the 'distance' Alba was discretely trying to put between herself and his family, in order that she could think over all that he had just revealed to her, and added his own contribution, to ensure that Alba would get some space. He did so by asking the boys to help him check the fixings for the car's roof box once they got back. The subtlety of what was going on was thankfully lost on the two children, who seemed far more interested in who their 'Aunty Alba' would be sending postcards to.

Surrendering herself to their unrelenting badgering, Alba informed them that one would be to her own mother and a few would go to friends. Those friends included Sally, Helen and David, who were garden volunteers at Hillstone Hall like herself, and Terry, a university friend who now lived in Uzbekistan; Alba had already decided Neale would not get one as well, for he was getting a present that thankfully was still intact in her rucksack, and she remained unsure whether Andrew would get one as well as the present she wanted to get him from St. Ives. She did not want to appear to be 'swamping' him with things.

However, in return for all the personal disclosure about her friendship group, which she had to share with Gregory and Ben but which she really wished she had not had to share in front of Gerry as well, given everything whirling around in her head following his disclosures, Alba at least elicited promises from the two young boys sitting behind her that they would indeed write their own postcards, which they had bought at Restormel Castle, to their grandparents.

In all other respects it was an uneventful trip back. Unbeknown to the other three, Alba noticed the turning off the main road which she and Cecilia had taken that morning on their way to Trelyn House – given they were driving back to the hotel, on this occasion the turning was just after the speed limit sign and just before they got into the village. As Alba turned to look down that turning, she thought once again of the declining garden, the damaged structure of the house itself and the uneven stone steps in the terraced front lawn, with their requisite buddleia now growing through them. She wondered what Cecilia's involvement really was with 'Chatteris, Corby and Lane'.

Alba fell silent as she continued to think about Trelyn, the weed-infested drive, the smell of pineapple and of pictures missing from their hangings, which she had observed when looking through a set of French doors, into a room containing dust sheet covered furniture.

Presently, as they turned into the hotel's steep drive, Gerry spoke:

"Right, we're back. Say 'thank you' to Alba for coming with us and remember not to pester her until dinner time as she's got things to sort out."

"Thanks, Aunty Alba," said Gregory.

"Thanks," echoed Ben. "The ice-cream was great and you gave us some of your fudge that dad bought you. You're the best. Please come out with us again, pleeeaaassseeee!"

"Yeah," agreed Gregory. "Dad says he might take us down to the cove after tea to build a sandcastle. Please come down with us. You're good fun."

"And you make dad smile," added Ben.

"Yeah, dad likes you. So, please come and build a sandcastle with us after dinner."

"Pleeeaaassseeee!" pleaded Ben.

"Boys, I've said Alba needs some quiet time, so leave her be now. Let's not," he concluded, having parked and turned the engine off, "swamp her. You might get to see her later but she's got things to do now."

"Oh, dad, you're such a spoiler," responded Gregory.

"Anyway," said Alba, as she turned to look at the boys as she got out of the car, "you've got your own important things to do, once you've helped your dad, haven't you?"

"Have we?" answered Gregory on behalf of both of them.

"Yes," stated Alba. "Postcards are to be written, aren't they? To some very special grandparents, I believe; I will hold you to your promises that they will be written today."

"Yes, Aunty Alba," they both replied to Alba – they each, for that moment at least, decided she was not such a wonderful aunt after all.

"I expect to see them before they are posted," Alba added.

And with that, Alba headed into the hotel by herself.

*

As Alba entered, Mr and Mrs Constance were already at the reception desk. Having collected their room key from Robyn they turned and saw Alba waiting behind them.

"Ah, it's lovely to see you both," said Alba. "Your absence had us a little bit worried earlier, Geoffrey."

"More than a little bit," confessed Cecilia as she linked her right arm through Geoffrey's left and visibly pulled him closer. She then turned and looked at him and added, for not the first time that afternoon, "I was so worried, I'm not ashamed to say – you were gone such a long time."

"I didn't think so," suggested Geoffrey. Then more to Alba than to his wife, for he had already given this explanation to Cecilia several times upon his return, he added, "I was meeting with the builders and there was a lot to discuss but, I might add, the exterior brickwork is coming up a treat – should have had it stripped back years ago."

"It seemed such a long time, though," stressed Cecilia once more, "what with the phone call about a body being found – I was beside myself with worry."

"We were all worried for you," said Alba, keen to relieve Cecilia's self-consciousness.

"I'm touched. I was just caught up in a few things and time – "

With that Geoffrey fell silent as the grandfather clock began to chime the hour. Once the final chime began to die away, he continued:

"And time just ran away from me a bit. Anyway, my dear Miss White we had better not keep you. We're just heading up to our room for a little nap before dinner."

"We've been taking in the sea air down at the cove – holding onto my beloved the whole time," said Cecilia, sounding as if she had stepped out of some Georgian period romantic novel.

"Did you go for a swim whilst down there as well?" asked Alba.

"Oh, goodness me, no," replied Cecilia. "Geoffrey can't swim and I wouldn't go in without a lifeguard around and, as you know, our little cove is much too small for it to be patrolled by a lifeguard."

"Just never could get the hang of swimming," said Geoffrey keen to defend his 'failing'. "I love the sea to look at, have a healthy respect for it, admire its majesty but appreciate it all the more for having *terra firma* beneath my feet. Well, we'd better not keep you, see you over dinner, I guess."

"Have a nice rest. I'll see you later."

As they headed up the stairs, with Cecilia continuing to hold Geoffrey ever-so tightly, Alba turned to Robyn, who was the other side of the reception desk and already offering up room nine's key.

"Thank you," said Alba as she took it.

"Been out somewhere nice?" enquired Robyn. "Sorry," Robyn immediately added, "it's not the day for pleasant holiday chit-chat, is it? Sorry," she repeated, "it's kind of a stock phrase you use when handing over a room key to a returning guest."

"Don't worry – I think everyone is falling over themselves with what they're saying today, what with first Martha and then that further telephone call just before you came on duty. I don't suppose you've heard anything from either Cliff or Stella?"

"Well, they're back, if that's what you mean. She's up in her room."

"And?" asked Alba simply but a multitude of questions were encompassed in that solitary word.

"Yes," replied Robyn. "It was her husband. She told me herself as Cliff brought her in – almost as if the gravity of it hadn't yet hit her. Well, it did as we got her to her room; I reckon the reality of seeing his clothes, his papers on the bedside unit, a piece of jewellery he'd apparently just bought her from the gift shop on St. Michael's Mount, was all just too much."

"I'm sure it was but you must excuse me – I've got to go and see her."

"Yes, yes, of course," agreed Robyn to the already disappearing Alba. "If there's anything…"

Yet Robyn's subsequent words were lost to Alba as she made her way up the stairs.

*

Alba could not hear anything emanating from room seven – Stella's room – as she made her way along the corridor. Having reached it, she stood in front of the bedroom door and wondered what to do; to turn the handle and stride in or to knock and by so doing give Stella the option of whether she wanted company. Or should she, Alba wondered suddenly to herself, just walk past and leave Stella all alone. Yet, Alba felt she surely could not go with that final option and leave her friend to her own private grief – they were, they are, or perhaps more accurately, are once more good friends and she could not simply walk past.

She would knock gently – not brashly or bang out some little musical ditty, just gently. If Stella were sleeping, for maybe a police doctor had given her some pills to help her sleep until a family member could get to Cornwall and be with her, Alba did not want to wake her from any sleep she was able to get. Yes, just loud enough for Stella to hear if she were awake; they were friends after all and Alba wanted to be with her.

Alba though remained motionless and silent. She was aware of the fact that neither Stella nor Cliff, had left any message for Alba at reception; a message Robyn was to pass on to Alba upon her return to go and be with Stella. Maybe Stella just craved solitude. After all, Alba thought to herself, what could she, Alba, actually offer her? Embarrassed silence or meaningless words of sympathy, for what does one say to someone who has just had to identify their husband's broken, blood-stained, sea-soaked body? Or hollow words about the future and how 'Joshua would want you to live on', 'to be strong' and other wholly inappropriate pap?

Still she stood unsure. Eventually she raised her hand to knock and then, with her clenched fist four or five inches away from the white bedroom door, uncertainty crept in once more and she was once more motionless.

"Come on Alba, get a grip," she said out loud to herself. "I can't just ignore her. If she doesn't want company, she'll simply tell me so."

And with that, Alba knocked three times.

Alba could hear movement the other side of the bedroom door

and a weak 'hold on' being offered up before finally Stella opened the door.

"Oh, Stella I'm so so sorry. You poor thing."

However, before Alba could say anything else or even for Stella to offer a reply, be it through words or, more probably, through tragically sad eyes, a bedroom door was widely slung open at the other end of the corridor, off to Alba's left.

*

"Finished!" exclaimed the room's occupant, as she stood in the doorway, silhouetted against the window behind her. Her near-perfect figure was lost within the bulky, though marvellously warm and cosy, hotel-provided white dressing gown which she had around herself.

Such was the thrill with which the announcement had been made, that Alba and even Stella, who had taken half a step out of her room to look, turned and then made their way down the corridor to find out what the unexpected cry was all about.

"Emily," said Alba, "are you OK?"

"Yes, yes," said a thrilled Emily. "Come in and see."

"Has something happened to you as well?" asked Stella quietly as she took hold of one of Alba's hands for comfort.

"Yes, yes," Emily repeated. "All day, since we discovered that poor woman at the bottom of the metal staircase, I've been driven to paint."

"Have you?" said Alba on behalf of herself and Stella. "Seems an odd way – " with that though Alba fell silent, not quite wanting to finish saying that it seemed an uncaring way to process grief or show respect to Martha. "All day," Alba simply added.

"Yes, yes. Come in and look – look at what I've painted. I don't normally show off my work like this but I'm thrilled with it. Come in and see." With that she actually tugged at the sleeve of Alba's linen top to usher the pair of them in.

EVE

*

There, in the centre of Emily's bedroom, stood her easel. To its side was a little stool with her artist's box upon it and her dress was still strewn across the bed. On the easel, on a large canvas, was a picture of a man, walking away from something – the something had not been painted, it was, quite literally, a blank on the canvas off to the man's right, the observer's left, and the rest of the picture just faded into this missing oval of nothing. The picture was of high quality; the sky exquisitely captured, or perhaps reflected, the feel of the picture, the feel Emily wanted to convey, and the foreground offered enough, in a way only an artist of Emily's ability could do, to take the observer's eye in towards the man's face – for it was his face that 'held' you, it was that which this picture was all about. The man's face held your attention.

Neither Alba nor Stella had seen any of Emily's work before but Alba suddenly understood Cecilia's assessment of Emily as being quite accomplished. Such was the composition, the brush strokes and especially the man's face, Alba felt it would surely not be long before she would be travelling up to London to see Emily's own work on display.

"It's just a sketch," declared Emily.

"A sketch?" puzzled Alba. "It's brilliant."

"Why thank you, my dear," came the reply in an airy-flighty way that only an artist, comfortable in their own work, can. "It's taken me all day and, even though it's only a sketch, I've clearly got a bit, perhaps, to fill in but I've finished what I had to get onto canvas – that look, that expression on the person's face. That's what's been driving me today, the man's expression. The missing bit, kind of, isn't important, it's the look I had to record and now I have got it I can keep this sketch and refer to it in future works. I doubt I could capture it again but I've been driven to record it today because it's intriguing."

"It is," agreed Alba.

"Yes," said Stella quietly who then went and sat herself down on the room's solitary chair that was situated by the dressing table.

"His expression holds you, doesn't it?" added Alba. "It's sort of wrong, no, I don't quite mean that but there's something about it, isn't there?"

"Yes, that's why I had to capture it; it's not right," replied Emily.

"Yes, not right, that captures his look."

"You see, he shouldn't be walking away from whatever is going on behind him, whatever that thing is – it could almost be a different thing for everyone who sees the picture. For one person it might be a car crash, another an animal caught in a snare and, for someone else, a dying friend. As I say, different for each person but whatever it is, he should be going the other way, going to help or, if not going to help," stressed Emily, "because the animal or person is dead, at least not walking away from the scene with that expression on his face. Sadness, regret, anger, fear but not – "

"Relief," interrupted Alba.

"Exactly," agreed Emily. "That's why it's so mesmerising, that's why I had to spend the day painting. Now though, I need a shower and then I need to eat and drink something – I've done nothing but paint all day. Plus, I'm staying at a basic bed and breakfast in Hayle tonight as I want to paint Godrevy lighthouse in the early morning literally as the sun comes up and hits it – the landlady is doing me breakfast when I've finished my painting."

"Are you about to check out of here, then?" asked Alba.

"No, here for a few more days but tonight I'm staying away. I'm leaving most of my stuff here and the hotel are kindly only charging me half-rate for tonight as I won't need breakfast in the morning or my room cleaned; I'm back Sunday evening."

With that, Emily stepped into her bathroom. Then, through the pushed-to door, she called out:

"You don't have to go: quite happy to chat through the door until the shower starts."

"Is it someone you know?" called through Alba.

"Who?" called back Emily.

"The man in your painting?"

"No, not quite, not in the way you'd expect."

"No? You've lost me and Stella probably," said Alba. "What drove you today to paint this composition?"

"As I say," called back Emily between the noise of the bathroom cabinet doors being opened and closed, as she retrieved all that she wanted to take into the shower with her, "it's not someone I know but the expression is. I saw it this morning, you see."

"Did you?"

"Yes," called back Emily. "Oh, can one of you throw me through a bath towel? I've forgotten to grab one from the bed."

"Of course," said Alba – whereupon she picked one up from another corner of the bed and, with arm outstretched, held it through the ajar bathroom door.

"Thanks," said Emily as Alba felt the towel taken from her. "Saw that look this morning," continued Emily. "As we stood looking at that poor lady at the bottom of the metal staircase."

"Martha, you mean?" offered back Alba.

"That was her name, was it? OK, Martha. As we stood looking at her poor frame, I found myself, I'm afraid to say, looking at the crowd gathered around, studying their faces, their expressions and postures – I'm an artist, after all, life is my subject matter. And whilst some simply looked sad, others confused, others still pity, one, one person's face showed relief."

"Relief?" answered Alba, keen to ensure she had heard correctly.

"Yes, relief. Someone looked relieved and that intrigued me more than I can say."

"I didn't notice," replied Alba, "and Stella was there only a moment before she rushed up to her room." With that, Alba turned and offered a sympathetic glance to her friend, who was sitting quietly, lost in her own thoughts, sitting on her hands, rocking herself ever so slightly.

"You wouldn't," called back Emily. "You, inevitably were looking at Martha, whereas I wanted to look at how people were looking at Martha. I can't remember who's face it was but I definitely observed it this morning. It'll come back to me, no doubt; I'll probably remember in due course, in a day or two – it wasn't Stella though as she'd already gone by the time I was studying people's faces."

With that Emily turned on her shower and Alba and Stella could hear the glass shower-screen door open and close as Emily stepped in.

"Whoa!" Emily exclaimed. "That's not warm – whhheeerrr! Should have waited for the hot to come through. Oh my – come on, come on," she pleaded. However, the hot water system ignored her.

*

As Emily showered, Stella spoke:
"I'm heading back to my room."
"Of course. I'll come and sit with you – that's what I was coming to do anyway."
"You'd been out again?"
"Yes," conceded Alba. She felt guilty and felt compelled to offer some explanation:
"When I got back from having a look at Trelyn House – "
"Trelyn?"
"Yes, Mrs Constance took me this morning," said Alba.
"Oh, that's where you were going – I watched the pair of you drive off."
"Did you?"
"Well, yes. As you've just said to errr – "
"Emily?" offered Alba.
"Yes, Emily. I was up in my room unable to look at Martha's body a moment longer and watched you and that older woman leave," said Stella.

"I guess," replied Alba, still very much on the defensive, "we were all trying to process the horrible accident in our own unique ways."

"And yours was to go off to a country house?" reflected Stella coldly.

"Err, yes," answered Alba weakly.

An awkward silence followed – broken only by further exclamations about the state of the hot water system coming from the bathroom.

"I was coming to see you just now," stressed Alba.

"My," responded Stella – and the sarcasm was not lost on Alba – "you were out a long time. Big country house, is it? Did you have a nice cream tea whilst there?"

"No, actually. Small, as country houses go; it's now abandoned, semi-ruinous, and we were only there an hour or so."

"So, where have you been this afternoon? For you weren't here when Cliff brought me back from seeing my poor, poor Joshua, were you?"

With that, Stella burst into tears. She sobbed. Angled over the dressing table, as she now was, she pushed Alba away, upon Alba's attempt to comfort her. Through her anguish and despite having her head buried within the angle of her own elbow, Stella spoke to Alba again:

"Been out again this afternoon, have you? Somewhere nice, I hope?"

Alba did not know how to answer and offered nothing back. Stella was not about to relent and repeated her last question:

"Been somewhere nice this afternoon, have you? Went out with another of your hotel chums, did you? Let me guess, was it this bloke Gerry, you know that guy who was all over you yesterday breakfast time? Take you somewhere nice, did he?"

"Err, well, yes. It was Gerry and his boys; he took me to a tin mine but it's not…"

Alba's further attempt to explain herself, to add context, was drowned out by Stella's angry reply; Stella ceased burying her head in her arms and looked up and round at Alba, with contempt in her eyes – she virtually screamed at her former school friend:

"At a bloody tin mine? Bloody hell, you're a joke. So, if I've got this right," with that Stella paused. It was not a pause for Alba to speak into, rather a pause for Stella to convey her anger and disappointment towards Alba. The purpose of the pause over, Stella continued. "You weren't here when I needed you this morning; for you didn't come and find me when I fled to my bedroom having seen that woman's body, did you?"

"No," offered Alba weakly, "but Cecilia, Mrs Constance, said she'd knocked on your door to check on you and that you didn't want my company."

"Did she?" shouted Stella. "Did she? Strange, I don't remember her knocking."

"But she said she did," offered back Alba softly – but Alba felt completely on the back foot.

"Oh, that's all right then! It must be me having it all wrong," Stella angrily stated.

"I don't understand," said Alba. "She said you didn't want me with you."

"As I say, it must be me being all wrong about it." However, Stella's sarcastic, hostile tone did not suggest for one moment she felt she was wrong. To make the point, though, Stella added, "But I don't think I am. Anyway, enough of this morning, may I remind you, you weren't here for me this afternoon either – you were off on another little jolly with your new boyfriend. Had an ice-cream there, did you? Bought you a little present there, did he?"

"Err, yes. Actually, Gerry bought me some fudge but it's not as it sounds, really, it's not," pleaded Alba.

"For pity's sake, I've had enough of this; of you actually, Miss goody-two-shoes White. I've just seen Joshua's body laid out on a mortuary table and you've been eating bags of bloody fudge with your latest bloke. You weren't here for me this afternoon, you weren't here for me this morning and you weren't there for me on the day of my wedding! You're a joke, a pathetic joke. Tell you what," whereupon she went and physically poked Alba in the chest, "you keep your boyfriend, your snacks, your pathetic little holiday romances. So long as you're having a nice holiday, I guess that's all that matters!"

"But it's not like that," offered back Alba – yet her energy to justify herself was gone and she slumped onto the corner of Emily's bed. As she weakly pulled Emily's long, flowing dress from underneath her, Alba tried a final time to explain but her words died in her own throat:

"It's not like that, Stella – please believe me."

As Stella moved to Emily's bedroom door, she turned a final time to her once best friend and spoke words which cut Alba deeply:

"But it is, isn't it? The world has to fit itself in around Miss bloody White. You've never been there for me – you abandoned me on my wedding day, you abandoned me this morning and this afternoon." With that, Stella threw her head up and laughed, a cold, mocking laugh, "Yes, when I needed you most, on my return from looking into the face of my dead husband, you abandoned me even then. My poor Joshua is dead – dead I tell you – and all you care about is having some guy buy you ice-creams. Well, I've seen through you. I thought I had five years ago but I definitely, completely, one hundred per cent have now. I can see what you are and, no doubt, your latest *beau* will see through you all too quickly as well. I never want to see you again, Whitey, and I rue bumping into you at this hotel."

Alba watched Stella walk back to her, Stella's, room – though not before Stella turned, half-way along the corridor and virtually spat through her grief, tears and anger – "And as random as this seems, I bet it was you who played that joke on me all those years ago with the banana which ruined my school blouse on the day of the whole school photograph; I was so embarrassed. Yes, that's the type of thing you would do, isn't it? Oh, come, don't look at me all blankly like that – it would have been the nasty little thing someone like you would have done."

With that, Stella just looked at Alba – anger, hatred in fact, towards her. Stella spoke just once more:

"Now, though, I must wait. Wait until my sister comes and picks me up on Monday – she's getting the train down so she can drive me back in my car. I have to wait until then, crying, almost certainly not sleeping and sick with grief. But I will endure, I will; by myself, alone. I am strong enough to keep myself going until Monday and then I will break down in my sister's arms. So, let me say this – don't you even bloody think about coming and knocking on my door! Just stay away from me Whitey!"

A moment later Stella slammed her bedroom door shut behind her.

With that, Alba slumped into her own lap and broke into tears.

"It's not like that," she said to herself in her distress, "Cecilia wouldn't lie."

*

Five minutes later Emily stepped out of the bathroom, her bath towel wrapped around her, tucked in and secured tightly under her left arm. Despite her still dripping hair, being devoid of all make-up and the fact that she was simply wearing a plain white towel, she still commanded the room. She was far from gaunt looking in her facial features and had a pleasant curve to her cheek bones and naturally full lips. Healthy-looking skin, be it on her face, her arms or her legs, from days spent painting outdoors, and her perfect, unblemished ankles simply added to her beauty – as if she were Eve, prior to being driven from Eden. This, however, was all lost on Alba, who was slumped on the corner of the bed, crying.

"Oh, my that was cold! Is it like that for you, in your room? Maybe you're on the other side of the hotel and the hot water comes through quicker for you, eh?" said Emily, who had yet to notice Alba's distress, given the strands of hair matted across her, Emily's, face and water still dripping into her eyes. "I know I'm still dripping but I need a smaller towel for my hair."

Only once Emily had collected a suitably sized towel – from where she had remembered leaving it on her pillow – and dried her face and pushed her hair off her face, did she notice Alba and, more pertinently, notice Alba's disposition.

"What's the matter? You're distraught," said Emily.

She knelt in front of Alba. The soles of Emily's feet were upturned and her toes, three of which were adorned with silver rings, each ring beautifully handcrafted, each displaying its own unique Celtic weave, were outstretched behind her. Emily, as she wrapped her hair up in the smaller, equally predictably white towel, said once more:

"You're distraught."

For a time Alba could not find the words to offer any kind of reply. Emily, as compassionate as she was beautiful, waited. As she waited, she went and shut the still wide-open bedroom door, to afford Alba some privacy from any other guests moving about in the corridor as they went to or from their own rooms. Then she went and refilled the white plastic kettle that sat on the hospitality tray. Calling from the bathroom, as she stood by the sink, as the water filled the kettle – and as she wished, yearned for, for the towels, the quilt cover and the pillow cases, also the kettle, the hotel-provided face flannels and so many other items to be any colour, just any colour other than white – Emily said:

"I'm going to make you a tea or a coffee. I think it will do you some good."

Grateful for something specific, simple and unemotive to consider, Alba was able to muster a response:

"Tea, please."

"OK," came back the reply.

Once Emily had returned the kettle to its base, watched it boil and then added the water and two tea bags to the white teapot, she once more came and knelt in front of Alba. She rested one hand on Alba's right knee and simply said – "Want to talk?"

Through her tears and curled frame, Alba managed to convey a nod.

*

It took two cups of tea, all three custard creams, that had been in the little packet upon the hospitality tray, sufficient long pauses – pauses long enough for Emily to swap her towels for a vest top and a pair of stone-washed denim shorts and to run a brush through her hair – plus many hugs and squeezing of hands from Emily to Alba, for Alba to talk. Alba spoke about her broken friendship with Stella, how this particular Saturday had unfolded, her puzzlement over why Cecilia, that morning, would have misunderstood what Stella had said through her bedroom door, Alba's desire to somehow still help Stella but that Emily was not, absolutely not, to go and knock on Stella's door on Alba's behalf. Alba also spoke of her own self-loathing because she realised, deep-down, that she had rather enjoyed her afternoon trip to the tin mine and was, completely unexpectedly, growing rather fond of being an honorary aunt to Gerry's two boys.

Emily listened to it all which allowed Alba, if not to regain her composure, to at least stem her tears.

*

"Look," said Emily, as she stood by Alba's bedroom door, having walked Alba back along the corridor to Alba's own room, an hour or so later, "if you want to talk some more, before I head over to Hayle later tonight, or you want to go for a walk together, just come and knock; maybe we could go for a walk along the cliff path together.

Give me time to do something properly with my hair and to pack for my night away, though!"

"Perhaps," replied Alba, "but for now I think I'm just going to lie down."

"Good idea."

With that Emily took her leave only to return a few seconds later to ask whether Alba had accidentally picked up her, Emily's, room key as it was not where she thought she had left it in her room.

"I thought I'd left it on the dressing table," said Emily, "but it's not there nor can I find it anywhere else obvious; thankfully I had the door wedged open when I walked you back."

"Sorry, no," offered back Alba.

"Oh, well, never mind. It must be caught up in some clothes or something. If I can't find it, I'll pop down to reception when I'm dressed more appropriately and borrow the spare."

*

Alba, with her own bedroom door firmly shut and with its security chain on – such was Alba's desire to lock the outside world out for a time at least – slumped on the side of her own bed. She pointlessly rearranged her alarm clock, loose change, her Lancôme Poême fragrance bottle and jar of face cream. She then picked up the postcard which was lying on the unit also. It was a postcard Gerry had bought her, when buying the fudge, at the little shop at the tin mine. Still red-raw from all Stella had hurled at her, Alba opened the top drawer of the bedside unit and placed the postcard under the Gideon Bible that was already in the drawer and slammed the drawer shut.

Feeling woefully alone and upset more than she could describe, and for reasons she could not define, she suddenly found herself slowly opening that same drawer once more and taking out the Bible.

She permitted herself to half-drop it onto the bed to her left. She wanted, as bizarre as it might seem, to be linked, just for a moment, to someone who, unlike Stella, did like her; someone who had shared meals with her in 'The Sun and Moon' pub in her home village and someone – as if to prove a point to Stella – was not her boyfriend, rather simply someone who liked her. Alba wanted it to fall open on a chapter from Matthew's Gospel; Alba wanted to be reminded of the Reverend Matthew Quinn.

She glanced down at the now open Bible. It had fallen open at Deuteronomy chapter one. She read for a moment about spies being sent out but it meant nothing to her, spoke nothing to her. Yet, she was suddenly struck by a thought. It would allow her to help Stella work out what may have happened to Joshua. Plus, it would allow her to help without, for the moment at least, necessitating her to go and speak with Stella. It would involve soliciting the Reverend Quinn's help by asking him to go and visit someone, someone in prison but – from past experience – she knew he was rather adept at getting in when the circumstances demanded it. With that, she reached for her little shoulder bag in the hope that she may have the Reverend Quinn's number on her. She hoped she had made a note of it in her little pocket diary.

Diary retrieved, she turned to the last page, hoping she had indeed written 'Rev Matthew' alongside a telephone number there.

CHAPTER 19

Mission call

The Reverend Matthew Quinn did not choose to leave writing sermons until the day before he was due to give them, let alone the afternoon of the day before. However, he had run out of time earlier in the week due to no particular reason, beyond his efforts to be engaged in his parish as much as possible – be that through talking to parents at the toddler group which met in the church hall every Tuesday morning, being available on Wednesday for the ecclesiastical insurance assessor who came to undertake his annual site visit, attending a whole day 'child protection' seminar run by the Diocese on Thursday, visiting a number of housebound parishioners throughout the week and being asked to lead a couple of assemblies at the village primary school on Friday. As for this morning, a monthly men's prayer breakfast had been followed by his visit to Hillstone Hall, to visit the unwell Lord Hartfield, and then the Bishop calling by.

All in all, it had been a busier than usual week and his sermon preparation had been pushed back and pushed back until the Saturday afternoon. It was a far tighter turnaround than he was comfortable with but he had trusted it would be enough and had committed the task to prayer. He was immensely grateful – but consequently not surprised – that no telephone calls or crises came his way during the afternoon and he had been able to write a sermon for the morning service he was pretty happy with. The shorter evening sermon he planned to write after dinner. As for the one he had just completed, it was a talk on the Gospel of Luke, chapter fifteen, verses eleven to thirty-two – the parable of the lost son. He had preached on this passage before but such was the richness of it he had been able to find an entirely new focus to it.

Previously, he had spoken about how far the prodigal son had fallen, how the father only needed to hear the first half of the son's rehearsed speech and how the older son, because of the hardness of his heart, stayed outside at the end. This time, however, aware that if he just preached to the unconverted in his congregation, he would not be sufficiently feeding those who were and, if he went too far the other way, the reverse would be true, he felt he had found a beautiful way to speak to his whole flock – be they in the sheep pen already or sheep still lost. His sermon, then, considered the obvious necessity of turning to the father to seek forgiveness but, once so turned, how the father thereafter seeks to convey blessings upon his child. The Reverend Quinn had drawn out how the father makes the prodigal son more like him, by dressing him in his own robe and presenting him with jewellery. 'Yes', thought the Reverend Matthew Quinn to himself, 'I have covered repentance, salvation and sanctification within a single, manageable talk'.

With that, as he placed the lid back on his fountain pen, closed his Bible and commentary on that particular Gospel, he offered up a prayer of thanks – thrilled with the sermon he had just prepared.

However, it was a sermon he was not destined to give; at least, not tomorrow. Perhaps because he was just a bit too thrilled with himself, a bit too self-congratulatory or perhaps a different plan was always destined to unfold about him. Either way, it was a sermon that would remain unpreached on the morrow – for at that moment the telephone rang.

"The Vicarage, good afternoon. Reverend Quinn here."

"..."

"Oh, hi Alba. Back from your week away, are you?"

"..."

"Still there, are you. Good for you otherwise that would have been a very short break. Nice of you to call but you didn't need to."

"..."

"You need to talk to me? Everything's alright, isn't it?"

"..."

"No?"

"..."

"Yes, yes, I've got time to talk. Actually, I've just finished a little thing I was doing and had nothing planned for an hour or so other than to check how my football team did this afternoon, so, yes, have time to talk – always have for you. Cornwall is lovely, I think – you did tell me the name of the hotel before you went."

"..."

"'The Jupiter', that's right. But what's up, you sound tearful?"

"..."

"Alba, Alba, whooooaa, slow down. You're going much too quickly and you're crying. I mean, you're allowed to cry, it just, rather, somewhat makes you hard to understand. So, just pause, for a moment. Take a breath. I'm here and I'm not going anywhere but you've got to stop for a moment – look I won't mind the silence down the line. Just start up again when you're ready."

As he waited, Matthew Quinn sipped at a cold cup of tea, twirled his pencils and pens around in his desk-tidy and glanced out of his study window. He watched a pair of bullfinches, the male with its glorious red – brick red he decided – chest and the less ornate female, with her shades of grey, jump between some branches in the apple tree nearest to the house and then at a female blackbird as it hopped across his lawn.

It was a good half a minute before Alba spoke again. She was more composed and more fluid in her words but Matthew still needed to cut in occasionally to both slow her pace and because what she was telling him was, it was fair to say, unexpected:

"Someone went missing?" he queried.

"..."

"But they've been found now, have they? You're talking in the past tense, after all."

"..."

"That's good then, isn't it?"

"..."

"Oh, I'm so sorry."

"..."

"Well, of course it's very upsetting: you're allowed to be upset."

"..."

"You know the wife? That's good – you'll be a wonderful support to her in these horrible few hours and days. Whoooa, what's up, you've started crying again. Don't worry. Just start again when you can."

As he listened to Alba's tears once more, he looked down at a framed photograph on his desk of himself and his wife standing on York's city walls – with a heavenly blue sky behind them and with them both smiling, the happy, innocent smiles of young love. He ran his finger along the top of the frame, picked it up, to allow himself to look into his wife's eyes, and then placed it back down. In his ear he heard Alba's voice once more:

"..."

"Oh, that's not great; she's blaming you, is she?"

"..."

"I guess all you can do is respect her wishes for now and not try to force an explanation on her. I might add, though, knowing you the little I do, I don't think for one moment you meant to be insensitive or selfish – I suppose in her distress she is seeing it differently. My counsel is don't try and resolve it now. Maybe in a week or so you could write to her – show me the letter by all means if you'd like, a second pair of eyes might be prudent in the circumstances – and explain how today unfolded from your perspective. For the here and now, well, you'll just have to give her the space and solace she has asked for."

"..."

"Yes, I know you are a good person; try not to worry. I know that's easy for me to say and you've had a tough day."

"..."

"Sorry, did you say someone else went missing?"

"..."

"Like the *Mary Celeste*?"

"..."

"An accident? Found at the foot of a metal staircase, how horrible."

"..."

"Oh, you poor thing! And you were so looking forward to some time away. I have no doubt, you're not the only one in tears in their hotel bedroom at this very moment; if anything, I'd like to drive down and be with you all to offer some pastoral support. Well, I would offer if tomorrow wasn't Sunday but it is and I have three services to take tomorrow; I can't just abandon the parish and leave it to the curate."

"..."

"What do you mean you're puzzled? Puzzled about what?"

"..."

"His body was found somewhere else?"

"..."

"Well, I'm not a seafaring man but I'd guess the tide took it if he fell in near to where he was last sighted; that would seem the obvious answer. Have you anything else to cause you to be puzzled?"

"..."

"Sorry, Alba, you need to slow down – you're going ten to the dozen all about butterflies, cheese sandwiches, pill boxes, Cecilia not passing on the correct message to you, then something about another hotel resident, Jonah did you say his name was?"

"..."

"Oh, Gerry you said, not Jonah – Gerry, then. May I suggest we start with the last thing you just said and tell me about him – why is *he* puzzling you?"

"..."

"His wife worked for the same firm of architects as the dead man; a random connection you think? Not in itself necessarily puzzling."

"..."

"Pardon? She's in prison for fraud; yes, that is interesting."

"..."

"Fraud against the firm itself: more interesting still."

"..."

"Yes, I agree. As I said, interesting but I'm not sure how far you can run with that, so to speak. What can you do with that bit of information, after all?"

"..."

"Sorry, what?"

"..."

"I can do something, did you say?"

"..."

"Well, naturally, I'll pray for you and for your poor friend – never underestimate the power of prayer."

"..."

"Well, of course I'm being all 'vicarish', I'm a vicar. And if I might say, too many people leave prayer as their last option when it should be their first."

"..."

"Yes, I know it's not quite your thing but you could always give it a try. You – "

"…"

"Yes, alright, a discussion for when you're back. So, I'll do the praying but I don't see there's anything else I can do – Cornwall is such a long way from here."

"…"

"London?"

"…"

"North London?"

"…"

"What's in north London? I mean, well, obviously a lot is in north London – Camden, the RAF Museum at Hendon, the beginning of the M1 motorway, the Brent Cross shopping centre, Epping Forest – but I sense you're being very specific."

"…"

"A prison? What prison?"

"…"

"Holloway? That's a women's prison, I believe."

"…"

"Sorry, to go and visit someone, did you say? Who? A guard, someone from the Board of Visitors, oh, hold on, the prison chaplain, perhaps?"

"…"

"A prisoner?"

"…"

"Yes, of course. Sorry, there's just quite a lot to take in – you're telling me about so many things, people and places, I'd already forgotten her. So, if I've got this right, you want me to go and visit Gerry's wife in Her Majesty's Prison Holloway? Is that right? Why?"

"…"

"Well, I get the fact you still want to help your friend whose husband has just died but I don't get why you're sending me to Holloway."

"…"

"OK, that makes sense."

" ..."

"Right."

" ..."

"Interesting angle, like your thinking. Actually, in that case, what about – "

" ..."

"I agree, that's what I was about to suggest."

" ..."

"So, assuming she hasn't escaped of her own accord, let me recap why I'm going. Initially, to enquire, with the prison itself, whether they allowed her out on a temporary licence last week, specifically last Thursday."

" ..."

"Yes, I agree, as she will be assessed as low risk of harm, given her crime was financial rather than violent, she may well be let out from time to time on short-term release during her sentence; perhaps even an overnight release. However, if we can establish she hasn't been lawfully let out and got down to Cornwall to do harm to this Joshua bloke herself – "

" ..."

"Yes, unlikely but possible. So we need to rule it out. If we can rule her out, you'd like me to find out from her what her relationship with Joshua was, so we don't just have this Gerry bloke's word for it. Then what she thinks of her two boys and, and this is where I like your thinking, what her view on her husband is – including whether he is the murderous type, taking revenge on his wife's lover or, alternatively, if this Gerry bloke has spun you a yarn about a difficult marriage, taking revenge because the testimony of the architect led to his wife's imprisonment. Also, and, to that end, whether the two boys are good at telling fibs at their parents' instructions."

" ..."

"Yes, of course I'll go about it all discretely – it won't get me anywhere if I ask '*Have you brought your children up to tell lies to help shield their murderous father?*' so I'll have to play it better than that, so of course I'll be discrete."

"..."

"Well, yes, thank you. Right, I'll contact the prison early next week and try and get a visit booked."

"..."

"Pardon?"

"..."

"What do you mean next week won't do?"

"..."

"If it's not a daft question, Alba, when do you expect me to go?"

"..."

"This weekend? You're joking, right?"

"..."

"You mean you're serious?"

"..."

"But it's late Saturday afternoon now and north London is a bit of a trek from here. Even if I left now, I wouldn't get there 'till evening, probably late evening."

"..."

"You realise that. Good – that's something at least. So, it'll have to be next week, won't it?"

"..."

"Tomorrow? You're having a laugh!"

"..."

"Tomorrow – you're serious?"

"..."

"You do realise tomorrow is Sunday, don't you? Sunday, as strange as it might seem, tends to be a working day for a vicar – I can't just slope off to London because Alba White has asked me to run an errand."

"..."

"Yes, I know, I have demonstrated an ability to get into prisons against the odds but – "

"…"

"Yes, Alba, I know. Please don't misunderstand me, for I would do it – will do it – willingly for you but tomorrow is Sunday. Look, I'm not adverse to people travelling to anywhere, even London, on the sabbath but tomorrow is the sabbath – the LORD's day – and my place is here in the village, more accurately in St. Mary's church. I have three services to lead and I have communion to give at two of them. I have written, literally just finished writing a sermon for one of them as you called me in fact, and, if I may say, it is a rather excellent sermon. Not only all that, also I will be the one certain parishioners will want to talk to as they leave the church after the service. I have worked hard since coming to this parish and I have set a standard and I – "

However, the Reverend Quinn's voice died in that moment and he fell silent. Alba, too, on the other end of the telephone line, was silent, unsure why he had stopped himself mid-sentence. As she waited, she twisted the coiled telephone cable around her fingers, listened to two seagulls argue over a scrap of food on the hotel roof and then she studied the business card for the Truro taxi firm, which she suddenly remembered she had put in her trouser pocket, having found it in Martha's bedroom. 'Was it only this morning that I picked this up?' she thought to herself, 'it seems such a long time ago'. With that, she turned the card over in her hand and saw Martha's note on the reverse – 'Jack, safe driver, fair fare, would use again'.

Finally, the Reverend Quinn spoke:

"Sorry Alba. I was just struck by something."

"…"

"No, not about the goings-on in Cornwall, rather, I just had it placed on my heart how many times I had just said 'I'. How frequently I had referred to myself as I told you all about what I have lined up to do tomorrow: I will be preaching, I had written a good sermon, parishioners wanted to talk to me, my role in the parish and so on. I was suddenly struck by the danger of pride, self-importance and forgetting that whatever good is going on in this parish is, ultimately, nothing to do with me. Didn't Moses fail at Kadesh for similar failings, amongst other things, and didn't James and John get above their station a millennium later?"

"..."

"Yes, alright, I'll give you the references when you're home but in case you have a Gideon's Bible in your hotel room you could always have a look at Numbers, chapter 20 and Mark, chapter 10 one evening. Anyway, what I'm saying is, on reflection, 'yes'. Yes, I'll travel up to north London tomorrow and try and get in to see this prisoner – what's her name again?"

"..."

"Tania Detz – unusual surname, is that German? French, perhaps?"

"..."

"No, sorry, not important. Where was I? Yes, I'll try and see her tomorrow. I can't promise I'll get in as I haven't booked, the visits hall might be fully booked and something else might rile the guards about me. However, if I'm meant to get in, I will get in."

"..."

"Tomorrow's services?"

"..."

"No, they won't be cancelled. The curate can step in and lead them – if anything, it will be good for him and maybe I should be encouraging him more than I currently am; so church life will continue in the village tomorrow; don't worry yourself on that score."

"..."

"No, Alba, dear Alba, please don't thank me – first, I haven't actually done anything yet and, second, I've been taught a very good, and definitely much needed, lesson during this call. It has made me realise 'I' am not this parish, rather I am simply a servant of this parish and you, one of the people who live in the parish, have tasked me with a mission."

"…"

"Yes, yes, of course and as soon as I have any news I will call you – what's the hotel's number?"

"…"

"That was 035 to finish, was it?"

"…"

"Right, good. I'll call you tomorrow evening."

"…"

"Bye, Alba, I'll be praying as well."

"…"

"Of course I need to and it's what we vicars are good at. We'll speak tomorrow. Bye."

With that, he carefully placed the receiver back onto its base. He then moved to the side of his study desk, knelt and spent the next few minutes in silent prayer – after which he went to his hall table and found his train timetable – hoping it was an up-to-date one – and then went to find his curate to give him the good news that he had three sermons to write for the following day.

CHAPTER 20

'Haslam's Faithful'

Alba never made it down to the cove beneath the hotel the evening before – despite Gregory and Ben having begged her to do so – for a combination of exhaustion, sadness and, though she would not recognise it herself, the peace she gained from her conversation with the Reverend Quinn on the telephone, meant, when she put her head down on the pillow to rest for a bit, she slept.

She did not sleep through the night, for she woke shortly before midnight. She made herself a decaffeinated cup of tea and nibbled on the pack of biscuits on her hospitality tray – which were oat crumbles. She spent a moment or two trying to decide whether they were the better biscuit than custard creams, before deciding they were worthy of being deemed equal. As she sipped at her tea, she went and stood at her window. The darkness meant she struggled to make out any features, that was unless she looked straight down, where the glow emanating from the restaurant and snug windows beneath her meant she could make out the hotel's drive and some of the nearer parked cars. She tried to look for Gerry's car but its colour was such that it was lost to the weakening glow of electric light.

Her tiredness returned and she took herself back to bed. Grateful that even the seagulls had decided to sleep, she drifted off once more – thinking, as she did so, of biscuits and appreciative that, putting the competing merits of custard creams and oat crumbles to one side, neither were digestives.

*

Nor did she make it down for breakfast this Sunday morning – perhaps, technically she had made it down but she did not linger and did not take a table. Rather, because it was a 'Sunday breakfast', where the hotel laid out many of the breakfast options as a buffet on a side table, she grabbed at a banana, a pear, two Danish pastries, serviettes to wrap them in, and three spoonfuls of dried fruit and nuts, which she put in one of her own food bags. Food sourced and with a flask of tea, which she had already made up in her room, she ignored those who were present for breakfast – Daniel, who was having a full English, with extra fried bread, Annabel, who was having toast and black coffee, and even Mr and Mrs Constance, who had yet to order – and headed down to the cove, to breakfast by herself.

*

She laid out her travel rug just above the high tide mark – just far enough above it so, were she to stretch her legs out, she would remain free of seaweed, driftwood and the inevitable bits of jetsam. However, the cove was sufficiently quiet all year so, jetsam aside, there was very little actual litter; those who did frequent the cove somehow between them, be they locals or those, like Alba, on holiday, respected the signs to 'take your litter home with you'. Maybe the cove was just too tranquil, too encompassing and too captivating not to heed the signs or, maybe, the lack of fast-food outlets and invasive supermarkets in the vicinity meant those who did bring food down to the beach with them, and who had, by definition, carefully prepared it at home – or in a hotel room – had also thought about how to take the detritus away as well.

Equally, somehow, the cove, because of how the currents moved around this stretch of coastline, remained relatively free of an excessive quantity of jetsam – there would always be some, the sections of broken fishing nets, the occasional flip-flop, plastic milk bottle tops and the odd wooden pallet but it always seemed to be a tolerable quantity. The pallets, at least, were recycled, in a fashion, by some of the locals who would break them up and burn the wood when having a beach barbecue.

As Alba enjoyed her maple and pecan Danish – a pastry which always seemed too extravagant for breakfast – she looked at the cove before her. It was far from matching the absolute perfection of Lulworth Cove in Dorset. Neither was it Robin Hood's Bay in North Yorkshire, where an aura of smugglers and high seas derring-do still intriguingly hovered over the place. Neither was it on a par with the relatively close by cove at Durgan, on the Helford River below Falmouth, a cove which oozed picture-postcard charm and where Alba had suggested Gerry take his two boys, when she had been chatting to him at Restormel Castle two days previously. However, this cove beneath 'The Jupiter Hotel' was endearing and Alba kept coming back to it; for what it lacked in the out-and-out beauty, intrigue or innocence of those other places, it more than compensated for by its relative unknownness, meaning that here one could enjoy peace. One was seldom alone down at this cove – it always got a steady trickle of people – but it was peaceful.

The peace it afforded was somehow greater because there were normally always a few other people around. It was a place where, as if to truly experience a sense of peace, certain sounds were in fact needed. They might be the sound of children playing at the water's edge. Or of their laughter as they ran up the beach with buckets of water to fill the moat of a sandcastle which they had started to build but which they got their parents to finish off. Or perhaps the sound of a retired couple as they quietly discussed the wrongs of his golf club and her worries over the cleaning rota for their local chapel. Or, perhaps, the sound of a hard rubber ball against wooden circular bats. It was as if the human soul needed to hear those noises to tell itself it had found peace here at this cove. However, such was the earliness with which Alba got down to the cove, that type of peace was absent and what she was instead experiencing was solitude – this was because, for a moment at least, she was alone and, apart from the sound of waves breaking and the gulls overhead, all was quiet.

Out of habit, rather than necessity on this calm day weather-wise, she had already scooped a couple of handfuls of sand onto each corner of her rug. She had then levelled a patch of sand on which she placed her flask and, having taken her sandals off, placed them on the sand to the other side of her. Beyond her sandals was a sandcastle or, at least, the remnants of it. Alba noted it was not of traditional design, where British seaside beach convention dictated that a keep was built in the centre of a surrounding curtain wall which was itself enclosed by a trench-come-moat. The 'castle' Alba found herself looking at this Sunday morning had a thick perimeter wall with a square turret on each corner and the impression of buildings crafted against the inside of the walls. However, it lacked a central keep – as if it were the Tower of London without the White Tower. Being wholly above where the high tide reached, this sandcastle, though it had more of a feel of a wild-west fort than a medieval castle, had not been reduced by the sea to be little more than a rounded off mound. Rather, it had suffered from the drying breeze, which had brought down three of the four corner towers, and from at least one dog and a smattering of seagulls scratching around within it.

Just before she lifted her eyes from the sandcastle, something caught her attention; something protruding from one of the fallen turrets. It did not get her attention by glistening in the early morning sunshine, for it was obviously plastic, but it intrigued her nonetheless – it was as if it had been buried within the castle during the construction. It had an oval base and then two things protruding from it but the rest was still buried within the sand.

Alb reached, sort of half rolled, to her left side to lift it out of the sand. She did not retrieve it believing it would be of value, rather to liberate the beach from one further bit of plastic, assuming it was a gnarled, part-shredded plastic bottle top or plastic spoon. However, as soon as she had pulled it out of the sand with her right hand, stretching as much as she could over to her left to reach it, it was clearly neither a bottle top nor a spoon. As she sat back up, she studied what she was now holding, which was a figure – a little purple plastic person standing for all eternity on an oval plastic base. She was not an expert on children's toy soldiers but her cousin's young son was and she had dutifully paid full attention when he had shown her most of his collection one long wet Sunday afternoon a few months back. So, now, with a trained eye, she looked to see if the figure were moulded to be wearing shorts, which would have suggested the British Eighth Army. Then she looked to see if it had been given a curved, bulbous, helmet which, if the figure had been green, would have indicated an American infantryman or, if grey, a German soldier. But it was none of these and Alba's cousin's son did not have one in this colour in his collection and Alba did not know the 'secret' code of plastic toy soldier design as to what country purple represented. The figure seemed to be wearing a tailed coat, almost Napoleonic, but lacked an accompanying tall tapering hat. It was holding a gun, as opposed to a bow and arrow or sword and had a round little hat that seemed to extend down to cover the back of the figure's neck; definitely not the hat she had been repeatedly shown that Sunday afternoon, of an 'ANZAC', an Australian and New Zealand Army Corps soldier. Alba wondered if the little purple figure she was holding was Italian, based on an unfair stereotype of its elaborate fashionable long coat, or from some African country. However, she was only really going with the African continent because it gave her quite a few chances of being right, were she to ever find out the figure's supposed identity.

She placed it between her two sandals, feeling just a tiny little bit sorry for whichever child had lost it. However financially cheap it might have been to buy, it was still one of some child's toy soldier collection.

*

Alba turned her attention back to the view before her and to having her breakfast. Once both Danish pastries were finished, she sat at the edge of her rug, hugging her knees, which were bent up before her, and allowed her feet to work their way into the soft sand. She watched the waves break and gazed out to the group of rocks that broke the water a good distance out from the beach. As she sat there, having tied her hair up, she felt the gentle breeze across the back of her neck and lost herself to the sensation of the fine sand working its way between her toes.

She had her one-piece swimsuit on, with its grand palm leaf design set against a cream background. It was underneath her cropped baggy, duck egg blue trousers and loose-fitting white blouse, were she tempted to go for a swim – a tightly rolled white hotel towel having been brought down too for that eventuality.

As she pondered whether to strip and venture into the sea, she heard someone behind her making their way down the last few roughly-cut stone steps of the path that brought you down to the cove. She chose not to look round but attuned herself to the person's arrival as she sensed them stepping onto the sand. The person was probably alone as no accompanying conversation could be heard. He or she, Alba felt, was probably in relatively good health as there had been no sound of a metal walking stick 'clinking away' against the stone steps nor had the footsteps routinely paused between steps, as the person assured himself or herself of their own balance before stepping down once more.

Alba challenged herself to guess who it might be – Emily was staying away and not back until later today. If it were Gerry, the sound of his footsteps would almost certainly have been drowned out by cries from Gregory and Ben of 'Morning Aunty Alba'. Daniel, Alba felt, did not quite have the physique to be descending such a steep path so swiftly and Mr and Mrs Constance would have given a double sound, being the two of them. Lizzie would be serving in the restaurant and Robyn would not be on shift yet. Consequently, given Alan and Cliff were probably working too, Alba was left with a choice of Annabel, Martha's walking companion, or Nicholas, the university lecturer; Alba felt the experienced walker that Annabel was, would have had a trekking pole with her out of habit as she descended the steep path and, given there was no sound of an accompanying walking pole, on that basis alone, Alba speculated that the person coming up behind her – if it were anyone from the hotel – might well be Nicholas.

*

"Good morning, Miss White," said Nicholas Goodwill as he came and stood to her right, just by her flask and in her field of vision. "Fine morning, isn't it?"

"Yes," answered Alba, slightly ill-at-ease with how close the other was standing.

The cove was deserted apart from the two of them and whilst it would have been odd had Nicholas stood significantly further away, somehow Alba felt he was just that bit too close – that he had breached that undefined social convention of not standing in someone else's personal space. Although between the pair of them they had the whole cove to share – in that he had everything off to his right, Alba everything off to her left – he was, Alba felt, too close. Perhaps eighteen inches, maybe as little as a foot, further away would have been sufficient to not invade her space but he had not done so. He had, Alba was certain, stood too close deliberately and that made her feel uncomfortable – they were, after all, the only two people down at the cove this early.

Alba did her best to mask her nervousness, striving to be all confident:

"Yes," she repeated, "it is a lovely morning. I knew it was you coming down just then."

"Did you? How so, for you didn't look round – I was watching you?"

"Ah, a woman's intuition."

"You've lost me," responded Nicholas.

"Never mind. Have you come down to breakfast on the sand like me?" asked Alba.

"No, just to swim."

With that, Nicholas kicked off his flip-flops, unzipped his shorts and slid them down his legs and quickly whisked off his red polo shirt, with its 'Crew Clothing Company' logo of three letter 'C's' and crossed oars. It was all done very slickly, by a man used to adjusting his attire quickly due to his triathlon races, but all done, Alba now felt even more, too close to where she was sitting. He had the broad shoulders one might associate with the best swimmers, also muscular thighs, prominent calves and defined stomach muscles but Alba was not expecting to be studying him quite so closely quite this early in the day. As he stood there in just his tight black swimming trunks, he continued:

"Would you mind watching over my stuff, if you're sitting here? There's nothing valuable but it would be an uncomfortable walk up to the hotel if some dog or child ran off with one of my flip-flops; my bag just has my towel and some protein bars in it."

"I think you're OK concerning dogs and children at the moment," observed Alba.

"Just in case?" pressed Nicholas.

"Yes, alright," conceded Alba. Then with a bit more energy in her voice and infused with a dash of holiday spirit which suddenly welled-up within her, added, "I'll fight off the hordes to protect your stuff." With that, she made some sweeping movements with her arm, as if she were wielding a cutlass and driving back a group of rampaging pirates. "Be having you, you scallywags, don't do your plundering here," she added for effect.

"Thank you. Very impressive – I've definitely left my stuff in a safe pair of hands. Won't be long."

With that, Nicholas strode off down to the water and Alba tried but failed to not look at his departing figure.

*

He was in the sea for a long time and he went further out than Alba strangely felt comfortable with. At times she had tried to read her book, she had rummaged in the sand for other little toy figures and had watched some of the seemingly precariously nesting birds part way up the cliffs but each time she quickly found her gaze returning to the swimmer out before her.

If he had got into trouble there would have been little she could do – Alba could swim but would never risk venturing that far out and it would be pointless to return to the hotel to raise the alarm, for he would have drowned long before she had even got to the reception desk. So, she just sat and watched and hoped that a person she did not know, apart from being her sole dining companion on Friday evening, and who seemed, just now, to make her feel just a little bit on edge, would return from the water safely. The longer he was out and the further away he swam, the more she wanted him safely back.

Finally, and to Alba it was as if ice ages could have come and gone in the time it felt she had sat and watched and feared for him, he started to swim more to the shore than away from it. Each loop brought him that bit closer till, in time, he actually stopped and was able to stand on the bottom and look around him. Alba could tell he was looking at her, then up at the hotel, way above both of them, at the descending path down the cliff and then back at her. He did not swim any more, rather he strode, as one does when wading through water, slowly and with visible effort having to be put into each step, towards the shore.

Then, suddenly, he was free of the water altogether and its pulling, sucking power. He effortlessly now made his way up the beach, beyond the high-water mark and came to stand by Alba once more – and suddenly his closeness was not an issue for Alba. She did not mind him standing there once more, for the relief she felt with his return washed her earlier awkwardness away. Then, without thinking, she patted the blanket she was on and said:

"You can sit down if you like."

"Thanks."

With that he sat down to Alba's left, with his large beach towel wrapped around his shoulders. He made no effort to dry his legs or to rub off all the sand which was now 'stuck' to his feet and ankles.

"You went out much further than I expected," stated Alba, as matter-of-factly as she could, trying to hide the concerns she had just had.

"Did I? Actually, I was tempted to go further still but thought I should return in case you were heading off and worried about abandoning my clothes to all the pirates hidden about these parts."

"I'm pleased you didn't."

"Do you swim, err – "

"Alba," replied Alba.

"Well, Alba?"

"Yes, to a degree but nothing like you've just done."

"Oh, I'm sure you're much better than you're letting on."

"I'm not, really," replied Alba.

"I don't believe you," teased Nicholas. "Come on," he suddenly added as he jumped up and held out a hand towards Alba, inviting her to join him. "Come on, we can head in together and swim, perhaps to – "

With that he turned round to look out to study the sea and the coastline before him. Having chosen his spot, he continued speaking to Alba even though still facing away from her:

"Perhaps to that point there. What do you think? Up for giving it a go?"

"Where?"

"There," repeated Nicholas. "Can you see those rocks breaking the surface? We could swim out to them, perhaps even around them. I swam out to them the other day and they're not jagged at all and we could quite safely climb up on to them and get our breaths back. What do you say – fancy the challenge?"

"That group of four or five all the way out there?" said a taken aback Alba. "You're joking right? There is no way I could reach those, let alone go beyond to swim around them: no way!"

"I think you're putting yourself down, Alba," offered back Nicholas, as he turned back towards Alba and held his hand out once more, in the belief she was about to take it and he could help her to her feet. "Come on," he continued, "you're dressed for it – I can see you've got a costume on underneath."

"I'm really not sure," said Alba in uncertain tones. "That's so much further than I've ever been out before and I wouldn't be able to touch the bottom."

"You're right, there; the bottom has gone, so to speak, well before then."

"So, I would be too fearful."

"Fearful? Surely not you and anyway, we'd be going out together. You could either hold on to me if you needed a breather or, as I say, we'll take one when we reach those rocks."

"I really don't think I should," answered Alba – feeling she was figuratively and literally being taken out of her depth.

"Oh, come on," responded Nicholas. "Live a little and confront the fear but I'm sure it'll dissipate the moment your foot touches the water. Look, you're dressed for it, so clearly you came down this morning hoping to go for a swim and we'll be together so nothing can go wrong."

"I'm really not – "

Nicholas cut her short again, though:

"Look, too many people come to the seaside but never really engage with the sea itself. They seem to think that an ice-cream, laying out a travel rug, staking a windbreak or playing with a couple of wooden bats with one of those annoyingly bright pink rubber balls, is what the seaside is all about. But the seaside – that is the beach you are sitting on – is but a gateway to the inter-tidal region. The beach, the seaside, the sand, call it what you will, is an open door to the world that lies just a step or two beyond. You have to get your feet wet but too many people choose to stay on dry ground."

"It's so far out," said Alba still doubting her ability.

"Not as far as you think – not as far as it looks."

He stretched his arm and his hand just that little bit more towards Alba and then added:

"You can be a boat that never leaves harbour and looks the real deal but which is slowly rotting away underneath or you can lift anchor and explore and live. It's the world beyond the beach and I'm passionate about it – it's why I'm a university lecturer specialising in the coastal zone. To experience it, though, you've got to step away from the sand, away from your cosy, safe rug and flask of tea and away from children's sandcastles," and with that he took a step to his side and knocked the fourth and final turret down of the sandcastle to Alba's left.

"I'm not – " Alba started to offer up.

"Please," said Nicholas. "Look, what if I say we'll turn around the moment you say you've gone too far but, I promise, you'll thank me for enticing you out. Plus, once we're back on dry ground, a drink from your flask will taste divine because you'll have earnt it."

"I'm really…"

Nicholas was not listening, for he leaned towards Alba to lower his hand and said:

"Come on – you'll regret it if you don't."

Against her better judgment and to her surprise she lifted her hand, tentatively, towards Nicholas' hand. Then suddenly she felt his strong grip and him pulling her upwards – suddenly she was standing before him and, a moment later, stripped down to her cream and palm leaf swimsuit.

"Ready?" he asked.

"No," replied Alba, "but we'll try."

"Great, you won't regret it."

"And we can turn back as soon as I give you a shout."

"Absolutely – actually, if I think you're struggling more than you realise yourself I'll signal for us to return to the shore."

"Promise?"

"Promise," answered Nicholas.

With that, side by side, they stepped over the bits of plastic, the broken sections of fishing nets and other random assorted bits of jetsam, which, along with the seaweed, denoted the high tide mark and made towards an outcrop of rocks – known locally as 'Haslam's Faithful' – that lay out in the English Channel.

CHAPTER 21

Sandcastles by 'The Jupiter Hotel'

They made their way down the beach.

They had gone beyond the warm, dry sand and were now on the damp sand and it was noticeably cooler under foot. Alba once more wondered what she had just agreed to – to swim to an outcrop of rocks, an outcrop that only a few scant minutes ago had looked unreachable.

Thoughts rushed round her head. Thoughts of excitement, of foolishness, of disbelief she had so casually stripped down to her swimming costume in front of her hotel companion, of excitement again, and then of fear, fear as deep as the sea in which she was about to swim.

Yes, she could swim a bit, preferably, though, with the surety of knowing the bottom was within touching distance but what she was about to do was real swimming. A slight breeze moved across her and it instantly brought her out in goosebumps; she folded her arms over her chest in an attempt to keep herself warm. Hugging herself for warmth, she told herself that she would not be alone and that Nicholas had promised they would turn back – she only had to ask – or he would turn them back if he felt she was struggling. In any case, she then thought, had not she just been watching him swim where the pair of them were now heading, admiring his stroke, his composure and stamina, meaning if anything went wrong – though he had assured her nothing would – he was the best person to have by her side. Anyway, nothing would go wrong.

Nothing.

The sand was not just damp now. Rather, they were beginning to splash with each step, for underfoot the sand was rippled and little rivulets of sea water snaked their random but beautiful paths around their feet. In a moment they would be wading into the sea itself. She knew she was being reckless, that she should never have agreed to it and wished, truly wished, not to go any further. Yet she had agreed to give it a try – to swim out to 'Haslam's Faithful', a group of rocks which were much too far out for her. She was a fool and yet she did not know how to stop. How does one get off a roller-coaster that has started? How does one stop one's dive once one has sprung off the board? She had left the 'safety' of her travel rug, still laid out neatly on the beach behind her, which had her little scoops of sand on each corner to weigh it down. She had left her comforting flask of tea, her clothes, her sandals, even her newly found little toy soldier behind her, to embark on a scary journey that she did not know how to stop, for she had agreed to give it a try. She had willingly stripped and here she was, to all outward appearances, willingly walking into the sea.

Yet she really, really, really, did not want to.

Alba glanced down and directly behind her at her footprints. Each one, as they got closer to the sea, was filling more quickly than the one before with sea water. Then she started to feel the water lapping at her ankles and, as she nervously ran her index fingers under and around the leg cuts of her swimsuit, in an attempt to stretch it down a fraction more on each side, she looked out once more to where they were now heading. Somehow, even though she was now technically closer to them, the rocks looked even further out than before.

*

Suddenly, out of nowhere so it seemed to Alba, she heard them. Then, in the next moment, one of them was grabbing at her left hand.

"Aunty Alba, Aunty Alba, don't go!"

Ben yanked at her hand in an effort to stop her – continuing his pleas as he did so:

"We thought you were coming to play with us yesterday evening down here on the beach but you didn't come. Gregory and me wanted to build a sandcastle with you but you didn't come!"

"Gregory and I," offered back Alba, almost by rote, but her words were lost on Ben as he immediately continued his pleas:

"You can go swimming later. We want to show you one of our sandcastles that we're about to build."

Mirroring the way the sea seemed to be pulling her out – as the water enveloped her ankles and a little bit higher still – Alba experienced another of Ben's pulls, as he tried to get her back to the beach.

Alba stopped and spoke to Ben:

"Ben, dear, I've just said to Nicholas that I'll go out swimming with him. We can play on the beach later."

"No," responded Ben. "You can play on the beach first and then go swimming – we want you to be with us. I want to show you the sandcastles we make: they're special ones."

"Well, I think I was just sitting by the one you built yesterday. I guess you ran out of time to build the keep bit of the castle," said Alba.

"No, we finished it and it's not a castle!" Ben said defiantly. "It's a fort – a Foreign Legion fort and that's why you've got to come and watch us build one."

"The Legion?" commented Nicholas – who reluctantly had also come to a halt.

"Yes, the French Foreign Legion. Great-grandpa, no wait, err, great-great grandpa or was he great-great-great, oh bother, I'll have to ask dad again, anyway, he served with the Legion out in north Africa a hundred years ago," said Ben proudly. "Corporal Detz, my great-great, maybe great, grandpa was very brave. He won a medal."

"How interesting," said Nicholas. "Maybe you can tell us a bit more about him later, after our swim." Then to Alba he added, in purposeful tones, "Come on, swim first," before adding quietly:

"Then you can play on the beach with the little children – but let's go on our adventure first."

With that, he took hold of Alba's other hand and gently encouraged her out further.

However, he had not been as quiet as he had hoped:

"I'm not a little child. I'm ten years old!" exclaimed Ben. "Gregory is twelve and we want to build a fort with Aunty Alba. And anyway, the sea is dangerous, dad says so, so we must stay on the beach."

"See, what did I say?" said Nicholas to Alba. "People come to the beach but never engage with the sea itself. They build their silly little sandcastles and get no further. Come on let's go swimming."

Alba was literally being pulled in two directions and she wanted to keep both people pulling at her happy but she knew she could not. She glanced at both and could see the passion in both of their eyes as she stood, now unmoving, calf-deep in the sea – aware that for Ben the water was above his knees – and she could feel the draw away from the shore of the water underneath the surface.

"Ben! Ben!" called out Gerry. "You're out much too far, come back this instance."

"But dad, I'm waiting for Aunty Alba."

"No, Ben – come back now!"

Yet Ben froze. He was rooted to the spot due to a combination of not wanting to let go of Alba's hand and suddenly realising how far out he already was.

"NOW, I said!" Then, feeling he needed to justify himself to the adults out with Ben in the water, Gerry added, "You know I can't swim, mum can, I can't, so we have to be careful, don't we?"

"He can come with us," suggested Nicholas to Alba. "He'll be fine with us – we'll look out for him."

With that, Alba's mind was made up. Later she would reflect on what a great burden had instantly been lifted.

"Don't be a fool," she said to Nicholas. "There's no way he can come out with us – I shouldn't be going out with you, let alone young Ben coming as well. You've enticed me to try going much further out than I've ever been before and I'm incredibly nervous – fearful even, I'm not afraid to say. Now, I know you've promised to look out for me but you can't look out for both of us; what if we flounder at the same time? You're being reckless."

With that she forcibly retracted her hand from Nicholas'.

"It'll be fine – trust me," offered back Nicholas, as he gave a reassuring smile. "It's really not that far out."

"For you perhaps but not us and definitely not Ben; you're being reckless. And things go wrong when people are reckless and we've had a string of tragedies this week already. Come on Ben," she continued but now addressing only Ben, who was still lovingly holding her hand, "let's do as your dad wants – let's go back to the beach and build a sand fort."

She did not let go of Ben's hand. Mostly it was because she wanted to keep him safe – for they were out deeper than he was clearly comfortable with – but partly to visibly demonstrate to Nicholas her genuine concerns. In that moment, Alba felt an immense bond to the young child at her side and she suddenly knew she would derive deep joy from building a sandcastle with him and his brother.

"Your loss," threw back Nicholas.

With that and as if somehow the water now offered him no resistance whatsoever – as if it were welcoming one of its own – he strode out effortlessly another fifteen yards before diving in and striking out for 'Haslam's Faithful'.

*

'Nicholas is a fool' thought Alba to herself, as she and Gerry's younger child dropped to their knees onto her travel rug.

As she retrieved her towel from her rucksack, to allow Ben to dry off his legs, and as she proceeded to put her arms and head through her blouse, before pulling it down over her, Gerry spoke. He was stern at first, as he knew his fatherhood role demanded, before softening in order that Ben did not just have a telling off.

"Ben. It was very dangerous, you going out that far."

"But dad, Aunty Alba – "

"No 'buts' Ben and please don't involve Alba. It was wrong of you to go out that far; haven't I told you before, never above your knees unless mum is here. So, I'm not impressed. You will write twenty-five lines when you are back in the hotel room, is that clear?"

"Yes, dad," said a resigned child, knowing not to argue with his dad any more and feeling very embarrassed for being told off in front of Alba.

"But," Gerry added in a gentler tone, "I did notice you were holding Alba's hand the whole time you were out that far so I will reduce the amount by eight if you promise to write them without a fuss – understood?"

"Yes, alright dad," said Ben, suddenly feeling liberated from an impossible burden.

"Good. Right, help your brother with building your fort. You might as well show Alba what you can do, now we've got her company for a bit."

"Yeah! Thanks, dad," said Ben.

As Ben got up and took a spade from his brother, who was already building out from the first corner tower, Gerry spoke to Alba:

"We have got you for a bit, haven't we?"

"Oh, yes," replied Alba.

"Good. You don't mind us sitting right by you?"

"Not at all – it's my pleasure." With that a random thought crept into Alba's head, which she instantly voiced. "Why eight?"

"Sorry?"

"Why reduce the lines he has to write by eight? Five or ten I can understand but eight seems so random."

"Exactly. I'm just giving him a tiny little maths lesson in the bargain – twenty-five minus multiples of five is easy but he'll have to think about deducting eight."

"Sneaky," offered back Alba.

"Can I take that as a compliment?"

"I think so," said Alba and she then thought to herself that if Ben got good with his 'fives', 'sevens' and 'eights', Mr and Mrs Constance would have him joining them for cribbage each evening.

"Thank you for keeping him safe and for not letting him go out any further," added Gerry.

"I kind of feel somehow your Ben has just kept me safe."

Alba's comment, for he had not seen the emotional turmoil that had been taking place within Alba's mind prior to Ben grabbing at her hand, was not understood by Gerry. If anything, he felt he should offer her a chance to return to the sea.

"Actually, if you'd like to join your swimming companion – "

"Nicholas," cut in Alba. "Another hotel guest."

"Oh, right. Well, if you'd like to go out with him the boys can show you what they're building on your return."

"No, it's fine. I want to watch as they build – they might even ask me to help. I'd like to keep them company. Blow," added Alba as she suddenly glanced out to see where Nicholas had got to, "he's not even half way to those rocks he wanted me to swim to – my stamina would already have been going."

Alba decided to withhold Nicholas's suggestion that Ben swam out with them as well – Alba felt it would only worry Gerry how close Ben had been to real danger.

"He's swimming all the way out there!" offered back Gerry, having realised where Nicholas was headed.

"Yes and that is definitely too far for me," announced Alba, as she wondered why she had agreed to even try it – why she had allowed Nicholas to tempt her in that way. "And, anyway, I'm curious to know a bit more about why your two boys are so obsessed with building forts and not sandcastles; something to do with a far-off relative was it?"

With that, Alba reached into her rucksack to search for a hoped-for second cup, in order that she could offer Gerry a drink whilst he told her.

*

Many miles away from this remote Cornish cove, there was the sound of several heavy metal doors being slammed shut almost simultaneously. Then, with a final slam of a single door, as one passenger realised they had not quite pulled it to with enough force the first time, and a blast of a whistle, the London-Victoria bound train pulled away from East Croydon station.

Sitting upright in his seat, the Reverend Quinn turned once more to look out of the window. With no one sitting opposite him, he was lost in his own thoughts. He wondered whether it had been fair to leave everything to the curate at the last minute. He pondered on his chances of actually getting into HMP Holloway, given he had not booked a visit in advance. Mostly, though, given it was the stretch of line between East Croydon and Thornton Heath, which offered up little more than the rear ends of small industrial units, unused piles of concrete railway sleepers, mounds of surplus dull grey gravel, that ragwort, herb-robert and common mallow were beginning to colonise, and the inevitable drink cans, plastic bottles and abandoned and now rotting high-visibility jackets, he wondered why he was bothering to look out of the window at all.

*

"Sugar?" asked Alba.
"No thanks," answered Gerry.
"So?"
"So, so what?" replied Gerry.
"What's with the Legion? They're building a Legion fort out of sand. Also, when we were all sitting in the dining area yesterday morning, just before we discovered Martha's poor body, you described how between us, the residents and the staff, we'd rearranged the furniture as if it were a Legion camp. How did you describe it? A defensive square and something and something?"

"Oh, yes – a defensive square with provisions in the middle and the prioritisation of drinks. You've got a good memory, Alba."

"It helps – sometimes," mused Alba out loud.
"I guess."
"So, what's with the Legion? Normally boys at their age are into 'The Beano' comic, football and whatever the latest trading card game is, not the French Foreign Legion. That's a bit niche, isn't it?"

"Oh, they're into all that other stuff as well – they read their fair share of comics, though in my day, I always thought 'Buster' was an even better comic than 'The Beano' or 'The Dandy'. But back to my boys. Gregory and Ben love their football, they are very worried for West Ham this season and you've seen them with their 'Top Trumps' card games but the Legion is part, a distant past, of our lives so I don't discourage their interest. That said, I do try and ensure they don't just glamorise it all."

As Gerry paused to have some of Alba's tea, Alba glanced to the boys' progress. Three of the four corners were built and whilst Ben packed damp sand into his bucket, for the construction of the fourth,

Gregory was carefully shaping the top of one of the walls with two halves of a broken Perspex school ruler.

"Nice crinkly top you're giving that wall, Gregory," teased Alba.

"I'm making the battlements, silly. It's so the soldiers can shoot out but have some protection."

"Very good. I'll come and inspect it all when you've finished building – your dad's just explaining why you're so interested in the Legion."

Taking the prompt, Gerry continued:

"My paternal great-grandfather served with the French Foreign Legion – *La Légion Étrangère* – at the beginning of the twentieth century out in modern day Morocco and Algeria."

"A land of sand, heat, dust and flies I guess," suggested Alba.

"Yes – well, it was for him but, over the years having read into the history of the Legion, many a Legion regiment or battalion also served in Tonkin, in – "

"Tonkin, where's that?" interrupted Alba.

"Oh, sorry, now it's north Vietnam. So, Tonkin, Madagascar, the Levant, even on the western front during the Great War. Obviously, not all at the same time. Troops went out to Tonkin in the 1890s, Madagascar in 1895 and to the Levant following the collapse of the Ottoman Empire, so that was the 1920s. All-in-all, a *légionnaire* was as likely to die from drowning in a jungle swamp as from heat exhaustion in the desert. Equally, they were as likely to die from a jungle disease as from hostile action. Do you know, of the twenty thousand French troops who served in Madagascar, six thousand of them died but only twenty-five died as a result of being killed by the enemy? Twenty-five!"

"No, I didn't know as surprising as that seems," said Alba.

"Well, why would you? But twenty-five out of six thousand is incredible – every other poor soul died from disease. From the Legion battalion which served during that campaign, of the over two hundred who died, only five were a result of the enemy. Tragic, absolutely tragic. To be clear, when I say the 'enemy', I ought to say the islanders, for I'm not convinced the French really should have been there at all. Anyway, my great-grandfather was spared the jungles and instead served in north Africa."

"How interesting," said Alba genuinely.

"It is rather. Predictably, it caught the boys' imagination from a young age. So, they could talk to you about the open country of Morocco – the *bled* – the dangers posed by raiding parties, called a *djich*, and the importance of knowing where the rivers, the *oued*, were. Or I could talk to you about some of the wonderfully romantic sounding towns and villages such as Figuig, Fes and Meknes. Then there was the intriguing figurehead of the whole colonial campaign in Morocco, General Hubert Lyautey. Suffice to say, when my boys first learnt their distant relative served with the Legion and won a medal for his bravery during an engagement with local warriors at a place called El Moungar, the *Médaille Militaire* no less, they were hooked. It means, whenever we come to the seaside, they want to build forts, not castles, and pretend it was somewhere where he served."

"Why did he enlist?" asked Alba, more interested in the personal story than tales of battles and conflict.

"He came from the Alsace-Lorraine region, as did his parents. It was French until the newly formed Germany acquired it after the Franco-Prussian war of 1870. Growing up and unable to find work, he enlisted with the Legion as he regarded himself as French and not German."

"And you?" queried Alba. "Detz sounds quite a German name to me and, when we were at Restormel Castle and I was showing the boys the little flowers, colloquially called 'soldiers and sailors', and then we got talking about the battle of Waterloo, you were quick to say how the Prussian General Blücher saved the day for Wellington."

"Did I? Well, he did. I guess there's some German blood in me as well but it's mostly French, a little Dutch and British – suppose I'm quite the European."

Gregory and Ben were adding the final touches to their fort and Alba knew they were about to announce it was ready for her inspection. As a result, she threw out a final Legion-related question to Gerry:

"You hinted that you try to stop the boys glamorising the fighting and the conquest. How do you achieve that?"

"It's not clever but it does seem to work and before you tell me off for littering the beach, I do ensure I pick up two other bits of litter in return."

"OK," agreed Alba.

"From their bag of plastic soldiers, which they will garrison the fort with once they've finished building it, I will insist one is selected to be buried within the fort just as we leave. It's a way of showing them – without being graphic – that war and fighting is a terrible thing and sadness and loss follow in its wake. There is a Legion saying, which is *À nos amis sous les sables*. Translated that's *'To our friends beneath the sand'*, which is their way of remembering fallen comrades. By getting Gregory and Ben to bury one of their toy soldiers each time seems a way to bring home that not all the soldiers come back – great-grandfather did, lots of his comrades didn't."

"Subtle," agreed Alba. "Clever way to bring it home to them," she added.

She then reached across to a little purple figure, which had fallen over between her sandals and thus had been out of sight, and passed it to Gerry.

"One of theirs, I believe. You'd better have it back."

"No, thank you," replied Gerry and he gave the figure straight back to Alba. "Please re-bury it or keep it otherwise yesterday's lesson won't be learnt."

"Right," admitted Alba as she dropped the little légionnaire into the breast pocket of her blouse – unwilling to rebury the little figure.

*

"We're ready," announced the boys in unison. "Come and have a look aunty Alba. Come on, up you get and come and see it!"

"OK," agreed Alba, still relieved to be on the beach and not out with Nicholas – who was now, finally, at the rocks and sitting up out of the water, with his back to the beach and looking out to the vast openness of sea before him.

"You can be Captain Vauchez. He was great-great, err, great, maybe that's one too many, grandad's commanding officer. You must come and inspect the fort."

As Alba made to get up, the two boys stood soldier-like to attention – Gregory kicking one of his brother's feet to get Ben to put his ankles together.

"Actually boys," said Gerry, as he placed his hand on one of Alba's bare knees to discourage her from standing up, "come and have some water to drink first then show Alba. Her inspection might take a while and you'll be telling her all about mountain passes, oases and camel trains no doubt, so come and have some water first like all good *légionnaires*."

As the boys stepped around their fort, Gerry added:

"Whilst you're having a drink, perhaps you can show Alba the postcards you've written to your grandparents – show her that you keep your promises."

The two boys, thrilled to have someone other than just their dad to engage with and to whom they could try and present themselves as all grown-up, were as happy to come and sit by Alba as to show her their sand creation.

"And you've written them yourselves?" enquired Alba. "Dad didn't help, did he?"

"No," answered Gregory.

"No!" answered Ben. "I did mine this morning when dad was in the shower."

"I wrote my one last night when dad was helping Ben find two missing 'Top Trump' cards," said Gregory.

"And you haven't just made up anything to write? Haven't copied each other's? Haven't just copied what's written on one of the leaflets on the table in the hotel's reception?"

Two resolute pleas that they had not – coupled with an affirmative nod from Gerry that whatever Alba was about to read was their own work – allowed Alba to say:

"Good, I look forward to reading them; who's first?"

"Me!" Ben almost screamed in desire, desperate as he was to impress his 'Aunty' Alba. With that he passed his postcard from Restormel Castle over, which Gerry had a moment before pulled from the family beach bag. "See?" he added. "This is my one!"

"I haven't read them myself, yet," offered up Gerry.

Alba glanced at the aerial shot of the perfectly circular castle keep before turning it over, whereupon she read Ben's account of his holiday so far:

Grannie and Grandpa, On Thursday afternoon we went to a castle on an island. We walked to it but had to get a boat back as the sea had covered the path. That was cool. It made dad feel funny and he had to take some pills to make him feel better. Got you this postcard from a castle we went to on Friday – it's really round! Love Ben xx

"Very good and all spelt correctly," said Alba, as she passed it back to Ben.

"Now read mine," insisted Gregory.

"But of course, dear Gregory," said Alba, as he passed her his.

It was a different picture on the front – in fact it was not a photograph of the castle at all, rather it was an artist's impression of how the castle looked in the fourteenth century, with timber buildings in the bailey, a perfectly dug moat and people walking around with bundles of firewood or tethering a horse. Alba turned it over and read Gregory's methodical holiday record, in his very tiny, neat handwriting:

Dear Grannie and Grandpa, Dad took us to a tin mine today (a bit boring), a castle on Friday (that was OK as a woman from the hotel came with us and she was nice) but the bestest bit was Michaels island on Thursday afternoon. We walked to it over a path made of big stones and got over just in time as the sea covered it up very quickly. We had to get a little boat back when we wanted to leave as the sea was still covering the path – dad said he felt sea sick and took some tablets. Silly dad as it was only a short boat trip. I liked the boat. From Gregory

"Very good," said Alba once more. "Well, a couple of little mistakes but – "

"Awww, no there's not," protested Gregory.

"Just a couple but don't be cross with yourself. It's sweet of both of you to write the cards. Well done."

"Yes, well done," added Gerry, keen to reinforce Alba's praise.

"So, you both liked the castle out in the sea – St. Michael's Mount – best of all," observed Alba.

"Yeah," said Ben.

"Yeah," echoed Gregory. "It was really cool, 'cause we walked there but had to get the boat back. The boat trip made dad feel seasick."

"No, that's not possible," said Alba suddenly. "It couldn't have."

"But it did," said Ben. "Dad was feeling all funny."

"Yeah, he just sat there. Looked all weird, dad did."

"No," repeated Alba, "that's not possible."

With that, Alba put the interlocked palms of her hands on the top of her head and looked in turn at her three companions. The two children could not explain the odd look in Alba's eyes. Gerry would have described it as a distant, confused look or, if pressed for a different description of it, as an uncomprehending, puzzled-giving-way-to-anguished look.

No one spoke to Alba for a whole minute such was the 'distance' that was suddenly between them. Eventually, Gerry felt he had to say something:

"But it did, made me feel all queasy, I'm afraid to say. I mean, I know I can't swim but it would seem I don't have any sea legs either; decided to take some travel tablets to try and help."

Yet Alba did not offer anything back following Gerry's embarrassed admission – she just sat there unmoving, seemingly unblinking, as if she were lost to this world and somewhere entirely different, somewhere remote and other-worldly. It was a look that Emily, had she been present, would have desperately sought to capture on to canvas, in the way she had of the person's face from yesterday morning, when they had all been standing round Martha's body.

Still, Alba sat motionless. Gregory and Ben started to feel awkward and worried they had just upset her. Gregory started to pick at his fingernails and Ben shuffled along the travel rug to snuggle into his dad's chest. Still, all three waited for Alba to do or say something.

They waited. Still Alba's hands were atop of her head but her eyes at least offered movement, as they darted from side to side. Finally, she let her hands come down from her head and as her left hand pulled at one of her own ear lobes, she spoke:

"Postcards. Can I see your postcards again?"

Once more Gerry retrieved them from his bag and he somewhat uncomfortably handed them back to her.

"You alright?" he asked as he did so.

"Yes, no, no, I don't know. It's not possible. Sorry, I need to see these again."

She took them from Gerry's extended hand and studied them. Unspeaking, she held them, studied them, read them, re-read them and kept turning them over in her hands.

"It's not possible. It just can't be, because that – "

"What isn't possible?" cut in Gerry. "It was a short boat trip yet it was a bit choppy and made me feel sick."

"But it doesn't make sense," answered back Alba and she knew there was panic in her eyes, visible now for the others to see. "It just can't be but – "

"But," said Gerry. "But what? What's got to you?"

"But," said Alba. "But, if it is, but it can't be, but if it is – though I don't know how the switch took place – she's in danger. Her life is in danger!"

"Are you sure?" asked Gerry, trying to inject some calmness into the situation.

"Yes," replied Alba. She suddenly then added:

"And mine – both of us. I've got to go; I've got to think. I fear I've got to start again but what I do know is she's in danger and I am as well."

"What?" said Gerry. "What are you talking about?"

"I've got to go; right now. I'm not safe and I've got to get to her in time. I have to, just have to!"

Then, as she tried to lay a hand on her sandals without actually looking at them, for she was just fumbling with one hand, she spoke directly to the two young children by her side:

"Boys, I have to keep these postcards for now. But I've got to go; I'm sorry, I've got to go. I'll buy you some replacement cards, boys. But I've got to go – I'm in danger. Stay together – don't go off by yourselves. Get up to your room as quickly as you can. But I have to run off ahead as someone else is in even more danger and I have to go and find her first – just get yourselves to your room and stay there. When you're up in your room, imagine you're trapped in some desert fort and you have to stay there until relief comes; don't leave the safety of the fort and don't let anyone else in. You'll be safe if you stay on the inside. I mean it, don't go wandering off, even just for a moment – always stay together until it's all over!"

With that, without waiting for any response from Gregory or Ben, Alba, whose hand had at last fallen on her sandals, for she needed them on her feet to aid her ascent up the cliff path back to the hotel, got up and ran as fast as she could and as the soft sand beneath her feet would allow. The remainder of her possessions, her blanket, her trousers, the remainder of her breakfast and even her rucksack got left behind, for they would only hinder her speed.

"Dad?" asked the boys simultaneously. "What's going on?"

"She didn't even look at our fort," added Ben.

"Dad?" repeated Gregory, "I'm scared – Alba says we're in danger and have to hide in our room. Dad, dad, what have you done?"

"I'm frightened," added Ben. He then began to cry.

CHAPTER 22

Cecilia is caught out on the rocks

She had not run all the way up, not even most of it. However, she had run when she could – when her breath allowed and when the path permitted it– and walked as fast as she could when she could not run. Whilst she would have liked to have made it in even quicker time, she knew she had done the best she could. Every other time she had climbed the steep path up from the cove, she would have stopped once, probably twice, to admire the view, to listen to the waves and the gulls and to consciously smell the sea air but not this time; this time she had not stopped.

She was paying the price for it now, though, as she slumped against the reception desk, exhausted, taking deep breaths and feeling physically sick because of her exertions. She had never been good at running on the flat, let alone what she had just done, which was something closer to fell running. Slumped, as she now was against the desk, she wiped the sweat from her forehead and from around her neck. She banged on the desk bell and looked over the counter top to see if Lizzie or Robyn, whoever was on shift, had left themselves a glass of water – for Alba needed a drink – but they had not.

In any other given scenario, she would not have dared to enter the hotel bar dressed as she was – she was feeling awkward enough where she was in reception. However, still without any response to her frantic ringing of the desk bell, she knew her natural reserve had to be overcome. Embarrassed and feeling immensely self-conscious she stepped into the bar.

Yet that too seemed empty.

"Oh, for pity's sake, where is everyone?" cried out Alba.

"You alright Alba, dear?" offered back Cecilia, who had been sitting at one of the slightly screened window tables and therefore effectively out of Alba's vision as she had entered the room.

As Alba stepped towards Cecilia's table, it was evident that Cecilia had been in conversation with Daniel and studying some old letters, which he promptly turned over.

"No, well yes – sort of. Actually, no. Oh, bloody hell, what am I even doing in here? I've got to get up to her room."

With that, Alba was out of the bar and chasing up the stairs as frantically as she had two days before. She caught her shoulder in exactly the same spot as before – having misjudged the stairs once again and yelped as she did so.

Worried for her young friend, Cecilia apologised to Daniel for cutting their discussion and reflections short and, having promised to pick things up with him later before Geoffrey returned from his day playing golf, hurried after Alba.

As she got to the top of the stairs, Cecilia could see Alba off to the left. As she made her way to find out what was going on, Cecilia bumped into Lizzie, who came out of Gerry's room having just finished cleaning it; together, for Cecilia beckoned Lizzie to follow, they went and stood behind Alba, who was still knocking.

As she knocked, Alba spoke through the door:

"Open up, please. I need to know you're OK."

There was, though, no response.

She knocked once more, which again generated no response.

Suddenly fearfully conscious of people behind her, Alba turned slowly. She knew she would not be able to defend herself for any length of time if attacked but, tensed and holding her arms tight to her chest – with a kind of instinctive desire to protect her rib cage – she turned.

"Oh, thank goodness it's you two," said Alba. "Oh, thank you, thank you. That's such a relief – it could have been – no, that can wait. Lizzie, please, you've got to open the door and get me in to her bedroom – I've got to check she's OK or whether she's been attacked and we've got to get paramedics to her. Or, she might be – oh, no, no, no! Lizzie, please let me in; we've got to check on her."

Maybe it was because she had got to know Alba over the years that Alba had been holidaying at 'The Jupiter Hotel', maybe it was because the worry was all too evident from Alba's voice or maybe it was because of Cecilia's calming presence that Lizzie did not for one moment consider not letting Alba in to another guest's bedroom.

Once more, Alba found herself entering, within a group of three, albeit a different three, another guest's bedroom and once more the person whose room it was, was nowhere to be seen. Emily, whose room it was, was not lying deathly still on the floor or in the bed, she was not slumped in a chair by the window with a bottle of pills spilt on the floor about her nor was she prostrate on the bathroom floor having received a fatal blow to the back of her head – nor was there any sign of a disturbance, which may have suggested Emily had been forcibly removed by some assailant.

"Thank goodness for that," said an immensely relieved Alba. "That's such a relief. I'm hoping she hasn't got back yet from her night away; she was staying in Hayle for a night so she could paint a lighthouse on the north coast as the dawn broke. That's good, that's something, that gives me some thinking time and the painting is still here."

"Alba, what's going on? Why are we in here?" asked Lizzie.

"You're dressed as if you should be on the beach," observed Cecilia.

"What? Oh, yes – yes, I was. The rest of my clothes are still down there, I guess. Oh, and my room key – all down on the beach. But she's not here; that's good, I think."

"Alba, what's this all about? Why come knocking on Emily's door? Why get Lizzie to open up and what are we looking for?" enquired Cecilia.

"Yes, sorry," replied Alba to both of them. "It's like this," Alba continued but it was noticeable to the other two women present that Alba was now slightly calmer, slightly more composed and definitely speaking less quickly, "Emily is in danger. Not vague and obscure, such as 'isn't life dangerous?' or 'isn't driving on the A30 back from Hayle a risk if a lorry decides to overtake a tractor?', not that type of danger. No, rather, she is in imminent danger of being killed by someone with, as the old saying goes, malice aforethought."

"Pardon?" said Cecilia, which was quickly followed by a 'what?' from Lizzie.

"Yes, I know, it all seems a bit unreal. It's because now I don't think – I really don't think – Joshua's death was an accident nor suicide. Also – "

"What?" repeated Lizzie, cutting Alba short.

"I believe," replied Alba in an almost courtroom manner, "someone murdered him. I also am beginning to think Martha's tragic accident was no such thing but I need to work through everything in my head to try and make sense of it all."

"Alba, where has this all come from?" asked Cecilia.

"It's sort of hard to explain. However, if different people recollect an event differently, that's possible because we all see things differently and they can both be right. However, when it's recalling a simple yes-no fact, they can't both be right, nor can they both be wrong – the light bulb is either on or off, so to speak, it can never be both. Someone has to be right and someone has to be wrong when it is a simple yes-no or X or Y event. All this time I've assumed the first account I heard was the right one – well, why wouldn't I? But it wasn't and that means everything else thereafter is built on a false foundation."

Confused, Lizzie looked to Cecilia, to see if Cecilia had just understood anything of what Alba had just said. Cecilia equally had not – she held out a hand to Lizzie to take for comfort, which Lizzie gladly accepted.

Alba's calmness, she would later reflect, derived from the fact that it was highly likely Emily was still out painting by herself or having her late breakfast at the accommodation where she had been staying last night and that, if she was there, she was safe.

"Right," Alba said, "we have time. I don't know how much but whilst Emily is away from here, she is safe. When she gets back though, she will be in real danger. Lizzie, I haven't got time to explain everything now because I need you down in reception to catch, as it were, Emily the moment she gets back – preferably, the moment you see her drive into the car park, we've got to get to her. I can't hang around the car park by myself as, after Emily, I think I'm the next person most at risk – it's because, no, explanations can wait. Just, please get down to reception and keep a good look out and tell Robyn to do the same when you see her."

Cecilia let go of Lizzie's hand and gave her a brief smile and an encouraging gentle nod of the head.

"OK," said a trusting but still uncomprehending Lizzie.

"Cecilia, would you stay with me?" asked Alba. "It would help me to have someone to talk things through with. Plus, I'd feel safer – if voices can be heard coming from my room, I'm less likely to be attacked."

"Of course, of course my dear."

"Right, Lizzie," concluded Alba, "we need to lock up here, I need you to let me into my room – as I say my key is down at the cove – and then please go down to reception and wait and watch. As soon as you see Emily, call me in my room and you or Robyn walk her up to her room. Don't leave her alone for a moment and I'll meet you in

CECILIA IS CAUGHT OUT ON THE ROCKS

her bedroom and then we will wait. They will have to come for her before the morning, they just have to because they can't risk leaving her any longer and allowing her to remember what she has currently forgotten. They will come, I'm certain."

"Right," said a visibly nervous Lizzie.

With that, they quietly vacated Emily's room and moved along to Alba's.

"Lizzie, I'm not just saying this but you are safe. Yes, there's a murderer afoot, actually two I think, but they are not crazed or irrational. They had a reason for killing both Stella's husband and Miss Peacock and they have a reason for wanting to do harm to Emily and myself – but not you. They're not going round just killing people randomly – there is a reason, a link, a chain, call it what you will, but because of it you are safe, as is Robyn. So, it's vitally important you treat everyone, I mean everyone, just the same as you always do; you mustn't alert anyone that we're on to them. Just try to be your normal bubbly self."

Alba then embraced Lizzie, asked her to get some rolls made up for herself, Alba, and Cecilia and for the Detz family upon their hoped-for prompt return and to have Jed, Jed but no one else, deliver them to the respective rooms in due course.

"Oh," added Alba, "I'm expecting a phone call from a Matthew Quinn. It won't be a hoax, it's a call he'll be making some time today. Please put him through and don't let him do anything daft like saying he'll call back tomorrow; I need his news today."

"OK, Alba," said Lizzie.

"Good, good," repeated Alba, "Go, go now," she instructed.

As Alba softly closed her bedroom door, Cecilia spoke:

"Dear Alba, what is happening – what's this all about? There have been two tragic deaths this week but you're speaking as if they were planned and that there will be more."

Alba turned and looked at her friend and calmly answered:

"Yes, I know. I'm certain now one had been planned a long time.

However, I'm not sure of everything, especially how Martha fits into it all, but some things are clear now and, I think, the rest will fall into place if I work through them carefully as we wait for Emily's return."

"I'll be your sounding board," offered Cecilia, "and I'm here to ensure you're as safe as can be. Let me put the kettle on and make us a nice cup of tea as you tell me."

Yet with that, Cecilia suddenly looked tense and spoke once more:

"We have got time for a drink, have we?"

"Until Emily returns, we have," stated Alba.

*

"Good of you to call in again, Dr Brierly," stated Andrew.

"It's no trouble, really. The church service finished much quicker than usual. It was taken by the curate unusually; not sure where the Reverend Quinn was. Anyway, nice short sermon – almost as if he didn't have a lot of time to write it – on the shortest verse in the Bible, John 11: 35, and how it shows how wholly human Jesus was. Yes, a nice short sermon so I got away quicker than I expected, so thought I'd call in here before heading home for lunch."

"It's kind of you to do so. So?" pressed Andrew, keen to know the doctor's latest assessment. "Grandfather's still saying he's fine and I've nothing to worry about."

"I think that's pushing it a bit," replied Dr Brierley.

"Right," acknowledged Andrew, trying to mask his personal frustration at seeing his chance to escape to Cornwall after all disappear.

"However," continued the village doctor, "your grandfather has said you cancelled your holiday to help look after him and I think you were right to do so. What I would say now though, is he has improved and between your grandmother, his staff here and myself, we can safely manage, meaning you'd be fine to get away now. If it would put your mind at rest, if you were still unsure, I'll call in after surgery for the next couple of days and check up on him in person."

"Really? Oh, that's excellent news. I could do with a few days away."

"Well, in that case, you definitely should go – you have to look after your own health as well. Somewhere in the west country, was it?"

"Cornwall – the Lizard Peninsula," stated Andrew.

"Very nice. Trerice is a nice place to visit – National Trust I believe. That's not too far from the Lizard."

"I was thinking more of relaxing on some quiet deserted beach with a friend who's already down there and I was meant to be holidaying with."

"Oh, oh right you are, I get you though I'm not sure there are any deserted beaches in Cornwall."

"I'm told she knows of one, a little cove that nestles down a steep cliff path which only locals and those who regularly stay at the hotel, which is up on the cliffs above it, know about."

"In that case, I'd better take my leave and let you go and get packed. So, yes, go and enjoy yourself and try not to worry for his health; between the rest of us, we'll look after him."

"I'll walk you out and thank you again."

"Don't be daft – this is what being a GP is all about – and if you trust me to find my own way out of this rabbit warren that is Hillstone Hall you can go and get yourself packed. Driving down?"

"No, I'll take the train up to London this afternoon and then the sleeper out of Paddington."

*

"Take this," Cecilia simply said to Alba as she passed her younger friend a much needed cup of tea in a white ceramic mug.

Alba, whilst the tea had been brewing, had changed into her

jeans and a sleeveless top, with its frill detailing, under a turquoise coloured hooded top.

"Thank you," offered back Alba.

"That top looks good on you – a bit too youthful for me but it suits you," commented Cecilia. "Looks new."

"It is – I got it from 'Weird Fish' just before I came away. I treated myself to a couple of new tops as I didn't want my friend who was meant to be here with me seeing me in my normal scruffy attire. As I was just changing, I thought 'blow it' might as well put it on now given I might be dead this time tomorrow."

"You're genuinely worried, aren't you?"

"Yes," stated Alba.

Cecilia had, on one level, understood everything that Alba had already said to her and Lizzie but somehow it had all been abstract or make-believe, as if they were all actresses caught up in a drama. Only now, with that 'yes', did she grasp the gravity, the seriousness and the reality of the situation – that there was genuinely a murderer within the hotel.

"Oh, my. So, Emily is in real danger too? You really think these events haven't been a string of unfortunate accidents?"

"No, not now."

As the two women sat in the room's two armchairs – armchairs with such wide arm rests Alba was able to safely place a coaster on her chair's left arm and sit her mug upon it – Alba repeated herself:

"Not now. Obviously, to begin with, yes, like everyone else I thought they were simply two tragic unrelated accidents one upon the other. Stella's husband, being unfamiliar with a coastal path, could easily have fallen to his death or perhaps he got hit by a car on his walk back to the hotel and the driver panicked and, assuming it took place in a quiet country lane, dragged his body to the cliff edge and rolled him over; that, if it happened, would be negligent in origin, becoming callous, and heartless but not murderous. Then Martha simply, tragically, slipped down those metal stairs Saturday evening during the storm that hit us. Two accidents, or perhaps one accident and one moment of awful driving. Well, something like that, so yes, that's what I thought to begin with."

"But not now?" asked Cecilia, who was surprised at how calm she, herself, suddenly sounded.

"No."

"Why? You were talking about a light bulb being on or off but you lost both myself and Lizzie at that point."

"Did I? Sorry. Well, I'm no electrician but to me a light bulb is either on or off – and that's true even with dimmer switches, surely? It's binary if you like, zero or one, on or off, yes or no, X or Y but not a bit of both, half and half or whatever you want it to be. It is producing light or it isn't."

"I'm following so far," offered back Cecilia.

"Good. And I'm not talking about the light bulb being on but wondering how much light it is throwing out – that's subjective and everyone's opinion can be equally true, for what is dull to one person is too bright for the next. No, I'm talking about an objective event – was the event possible or wasn't it?"

"What event?" asked Cecilia.

"Someone feeling sea sick on a boat trip," replied Alba. "Feeling so sea sick he had to take some pills."

"But isn't that a subjective thing?" said a puzzled Cecilia. "People have different tolerances, one person can cope with anything the ocean throws at them, the next feels queasy looking at the boating lake in Helston. Aren't you a bit muddled about it all, already? Maybe they were accidents, after all."

Yet before Alba could explain further, someone was outside Alba's bedroom door, trying the handle.

The room's two occupants looked at each other and then Alba spoke:

"Jed, I hope, with some food. But in case it's not him, quick, Cecilia, get out of sight so you're behind the bedroom door when I open it."

"If you're sure," said a very unsure Cecilia. "But what if he sticks a knife in you the moment you open the door?"

"No one has been knifed yet, have they? If the person gets in my room, I'll be clobbered over the back of the head but not knifed to the front – both victims have been attacked when their guard is down, that's the *modus operandi* here. Right, quick, hide, someone is trying the door again."

Cecilia moved silently into position as Alba released the security chain and opened the door.

*

"Oh, it's you," said a relieved Alba to the person in the corridor.

"Lizzie asked me to bring you up some food," said Jed. "There's quite a lot here, almost enough for two. Your early morning swim must have given you an appetite. Sorry," added a suddenly blushing Jed, "I saw you rush back to the hotel in your swimsuit just as I was heading down into the cellar. Everything's alright, isn't it, for you were almost running up the hotel drive?"

"Yes, thank you," replied Alba. "I was just keen to get back in time for a telephone call I'm expecting – hence having some lunch in my room."

"Would you like me to bring it in and place it on the coffee table? The tray is heavy, after all."

"No, it's fine, thank you, Jed. I can take it from you."

"Right you are," he said as he handed over the well-stocked tray. "Don't worry about the telephone call, for I've finished in the cellar so I'll be around reception as well in case Lizzie suddenly disappears herself."

"Thanks, Jed. I'll bring the tray down later."

She closed the door, put the security chain on once more and proceeded to place the tray down on the small table.

"Lizzie's done us proud," said Alba, "she's provided just enough for both of us without making it too obvious."

CECILIA IS CAUGHT OUT ON THE ROCKS

*

As they shared the bowl of spiced apple and parsnip soup – Alba having her portion from a washed-out mug – Alba spoke:

"Cecilia."

"Yes."

"I'm not getting confused – whether the sea was rough enough to cause someone to get sea sick is, if looked at a certain way, an objective question. But I'll come back to that as first I want to clear one thing from my head. You see, I'm sure it's not ultimately relevant but, at the same time, it is what brought several of the guests here so I need to clear it up. To do that, I need you to tell me the truth."

Cecilia placed her bowl down, dabbed at a corner of her mouth with a serviette and looked back at Alba in nervous anticipation.

"Trelyn," stated Alba.

"Yes, what about it?"

"I'm so pleased you took me there, yesterday."

"Because?" asked a still nervous Cecilia.

"Because I would otherwise have missed a comment another guest made about it, which showed he had been there very recently, too."

"What other guest?" asked Cecilia.

Yet Alba did not answer, rather she put a statement – something approaching a challenge – to the other:

"You really ought to tell them."

"Pardon?"

"Both of them. For different reasons but you really ought to share your secret with both of them. You're a dear friend to me – and I was thrilled, truly thrilled, when I saw you at dinner on Thursday evening, my first day here – and I have no doubt you mean well by it all but you really should tell them both."

Cecilia was lost for words herself – the years of keeping the secret had conditioned Cecilia not to voice it. Yet she knew what Alba was about to say.

"You will hurt Geoffrey's pride if you don't start involving him in this," Alba stated. "Yes, I know he's retired but he would love – dearly love – to be involved in such a case as this; he does love his country houses after all. For him to discover you've been doing all this behind his back, well, I know in one sense you're allowed to and Geoffrey has no monopoly on such matters but I really don't think he'd just take over and push you out of the affair. I really think he'd be thrilled to help you, to be your consultant, your guide if you like and I'm sure he'd stay in your shadow more than you think he will."

Still Cecilia was too conditioned to acknowledge anything.

"But most of all," Alba continued, "you must – absolutely must – tell Jed."

"Tell him what?" asked Cecilia.

Cecilia did not ask in hostile or dismissive tones, rather it was as if she needed Alba to voice it – as if, if someone else would say it out loud, then she would suddenly be freed from the secret after all these years.

"That Sir Roger des Roches was his father and he is the heir to Trelyn."

*

"How did you know?" asked Cecilia finally.

"Oh, it's easy to speculate over other people's lives, isn't it? That Jed didn't look like his supposed father, that Jed's personality is, it would seem, so different to those of his brother and sister, that Jed's mum used to work at Trelyn but left when she became pregnant with her third child, how she would take Jed to look around Trelyn more often than a small child probably would have wished to, things like that. But that's all conjecture, speculation, gossip almost. What 'told' me though, was something you said to Geoffrey over dinner on Friday and then something Daniel let slip in reception yesterday.

You see, you got all confused over where you had supposedly gone to meet a friend for afternoon tea on Friday, didn't you?"

"Yes," acknowledged Cecilia.

"Earlier in the day you had told Geoffrey you had met her in a tea shop in St Just but then over dinner it had changed to one in St Buryan. Geoffrey said to me you must have got your saints mixed up but that's not you, you're too sharp, too precise, about things – you even comment on people hanging swimming trunks out of a window at the front of the hotel – so you wouldn't have got confused had you actually gone to one of the two villages, would you?"

"No," said Cecilia. "Slipped up there, didn't I?" she added with a wry smile.

"Yes. Thankfully for you Geoffrey didn't make anything of it but it lodged in my brain. Instead, you took Daniel Jones to Trelyn House on Friday afternoon, didn't you?"

"Yes. I felt he ought to see it for himself. He's been doing so much work on the investigation I felt he ought to come down and visit it. Plus, there were several further letters I wanted him to see, letters I really didn't want to go astray in the post."

"Documents the two of you were studying again in the bar when I rushed in just now?"

"Yes. But Alba, how did you know I'd taken Daniel to Trelyn?"

"Simple really," said Alba. "I was in reception looking at the framed map of the Cornish Hundreds and the inset picture of Trelyn within it. I was waiting for Gerry to get ready to take me to a tin mine. Daniel came and looked at the picture at that moment and, as we stood side by side, he commented that someone should draw in a butterfly bush in the foreground of the picture of the house to make it more accurate. He had to have been there in person to be able to make that comment – and he only turned up at the hotel himself on Thursday."

"Very good, Alba. Very observant of you," conceded Cecilia.

"Well, I try to listen to what people say; especially when it's a throw away remark when they're not really concentrating on what they are saying. Their guard is frequently down in such moments, you see. So, all in all, given Daniel's an asset investigator, he's been to Trelyn during his time staying at the hotel, you had a 'missing' afternoon and, despite never letting on to Geoffrey why you felt this, you were consistently protective of the solicitors working on the disposal of the Trelyn estate, I would say you are trying to unravel a secret you have been keeping for a long time. Now though, you've got to trust Jed with the truth, however painful it will undoubtedly be to begin with for him. Plus, you've got to include Geoffrey – he'll be so hurt if you don't."

Alba paused before summarising all she had just said:

"I think the secret has been a secret for long enough, Cecilia."

Cecilia closed her eyes and her head slumped. She held her hands together incredibly tightly, causing the knuckles to whiten and entwined her ankles and feet almost as tightly as her hands. Eventually, she spoke through her still closed eyes and twisted, almost knotted, hands and feet.

"It's been almost fifty years – fifty years, that's a long long time. Jed's mum was a fine woman and, as I said to you when I took you round Trelyn yesterday, she took me under her wing when I started working there as a teenager. She worked there full-time and was already married to who Jed thinks was his father and she had two children with him but then she fell pregnant again – with Jed as it turned out. She never told me whether it was a consensual long-term relationship, succumbing to a single moment of temptation or rape by Sir Roger des Roches. She never told me," Cecilia stated.

With that, Cecilia opened her eyes and looked at Alba as she continued:

"She knew I knew but made me promise I would never tell. And of course, I did promise – she was only ever kind to me so why wouldn't I? I believe, I genuinely believe, she did tell her husband the child wasn't his. He stuck by her and treated Jed as his own son – I think Sir Roger tried to help financially over the years and tried to get Jed into the best schools but Jed's father, I mean adoptive father, oh it gets so messy."

"Don't worry, I know who you mean and I think you are right to call him father – for he was to Jed and Jed loved him as such and is still mourning him."

"Yes, he is isn't he. Well, Jed's father refused all financial help and would not allow strings to be pulled. He brought Jed up as one of his own; it was always so touching to see and hear they were as father and son, even more so in Jed's father's later years."

"Yes," agreed Alba. "Jed said as much himself."

"And over all the years I kept my promise. For half a century I kept my promise, kept it even after Jed's mum died. You see, I couldn't bear the thought of ruining Jed's family with the truth."

"Sometimes beauty is better than truth," said Alba for the second time this holiday.

"That's a lovely way of putting it," said Cecilia.

"What changed?" asked Alba.

"It wasn't that, with Jed's father dying, I felt free of my promise," insisted Cecilia. "Nor was it the thrill of wanting to tell a secret, nor even the desire to see Jed come into untold wealth as the sole heir to the Trelyn estate."

"I know," agreed a sympathetic Alba. "Jed loves where he lives and is at peace there – it is his home."

"Exactly," concurred Cecilia. "But when I heard his brother and sister – siblings who left Cornwall a long time ago and have more money than they know what to do with by all accounts and, and this is what really upset me, did nothing, absolutely nothing to care for their father in his final years and then have the temerity to insist on the cottage being sold in order that they could get their share of the proceeds – well, I couldn't stand by any longer and say nothing."

"I understand his brother and sister are entitled to their share but, well, somehow – " Alba started to say until Cecilia cut in.

"Somehow it feels wrong, doesn't it? Why couldn't they allow Jed to stay living there but retain joint ownership or charge him rent or come to some long-term arrangement but to force him out months after their father died, well, I felt I suddenly was doing Jed's mother more of a disservice by staying quiet than not. I felt this was now a scenario she had not foreseen and that somehow the circumstances released me from my pledge."

"So?"

"So, when I had a weekend visiting my sister in Bristol – needless to say Geoffrey didn't come – I looked up a firm of solicitors I'd heard my dear husband speak favourably of over the years."

"Chatteris, Corby and Lane," suggested Alba.

"Yes," agreed Cecilia. "They put me in touch with Daniel Jones, who they bring in for cases such as this, and he's been investigating since. I've supplied him with letters Jed's mother entrusted to me from her death bed, he's got hold of Sir Roger des Roches staff records and he's beginning to build a very plausible case. But – " with that though, Cecilia fell silent once again.

"But," Alba continued, "it will break Jed's heart when he's approached by an unknown firm of solicitors to go for a blood test or whatever they now do."

"I know – and I'll have been the one who instigated his broken heart. Yet, I couldn't see him lose his father, his home and driven out of the community, perhaps even Cornwall itself, that he loves."

"No," agreed Alba. "You had to speak out but I think he would cope better – recover better, too – if he heard it from you to begin with. Can you imagine if he heard it first through a solicitor's letter which fell on his doormat one morning?"

"I'd rather not imagine," agreed Cecilia quietly. "You really think I should tell him?"

"Yes. Not now – don't go rushing down this very moment. There are other pressing matters currently going on but maybe, once this is all over, could you not find a quiet time to tell him? Don't drag him over to Trelyn itself and go *'Look, all this will be yours'*, that could be a bit blunt. Rather, I suggest, find a reason to pop over to his cottage – take him a cake or something – and tell him at his own kitchen table over a cup of tea. It won't be easy and one, probably both of you, will be in tears but there will be compassion behind your tears and you'll only be saying lovely things about the parents he still deeply loves – even if Jed is a gruff, rough-round-the-edges middle-aged Cornishman. And once you've told him, ask his permission to share it with Geoffrey; that way, it will sound as if you planned to include Geoffrey all along and were just waiting on Jed's agreement."

Cecilia nodded softly to herself before standing up and going to the window. Despite looking out she spoke to Alba:

"For fifty years I've watched Jed grow, from baby to child to man. Through it all, I kept my promise to his mum but then things changed and I had to act. But you're right, telling him over a slice of cake and a cup of tea will be the better way. Also, not to include Geoffrey at all would be insensitive – I can see that now. You've got a very wise head on your young shoulders, Alba my dear."

Cecilia fell silent once more until she turned back to face Alba and spoke through already flowing tears:

"Thank you for catching me out about Sir Roger des Roches."

CHAPTER 23

'Two for his heels'

Then, much sooner than Alba could have hoped for, the telephone rang.

Nonetheless, it was a nervous Alba who went to the unit on the far side of her bed and picked up the receiver. She spoke into it:

"Alba here."

"..."

"That's excellent, thank you Lizzie."

Then there was silence.

Then the faintest of faint clicks preceded the sound of the Reverend Quinn's voice:

"..."

"Yes, it is," said Alba, as she confirmed to the Reverend Quinn he had got through to her. "Thank you so much for calling so early in the day," she continued. "To be fair, I wasn't expecting a call until late afternoon. I am amazed you're home already."

"..."

"Oh, you're not; you're calling from the prison chaplain's office," said Alba, repeating his words.

"..."

"Well, yes," agreed Alba, "I did want to hear as soon as practical. You got in, then?"

"..."

"Well done you – you can tell me how another time, if I'm not one of the next victims here."

"..."

"Thank you. So, you got in and met with Mrs Tania Detz?"

"..."

"And?"

"..."

"Right, yes – claims she hadn't been released on temporary licence overnight or even for a day. OK but have you been able to confirm that with the prison?"

"..."

"You have – with both the gate staff and a prison-based Probation Officer. Gosh, well done you for being so thorough. Well, that completely removes her from any direct involvement in two murders. Not that my money was ever on her. So, next, what did she say about any relationship with the architect Joshua Mallory, for whom she worked?"

"..."

"Well, yes, I can only imagine it might have been a bit awkward and embarrassing being asked such a question by a man of God whom she had never met before. But you persisted, I trust?"

"..."

"And?"

"..."

"OK, that's honest of her to admit that – that they did have an affair which he ended. Well, that confirms what the husband, Gerry, told me. Separately and maybe I'm just being nosey here, is that why she stole from the firm and therefore, ultimately, why she is now in prison?"

"..."

"Oh, yes, says she has an ongoing appeal and has been instructed by her solicitor not to comment further. OK, never mind as I really don't think it is relevant either way. So, the issue becomes is Gerry the type of man who would take murderous revenge against his wife's former lover? Did Mrs Detz give any pointers to that question?"

"..."

"She said, whilst he used to get angry with her over her disinterest in him and her lies about so-called business trips away and working late, he was never violent, controlling or abusive. He was angry, annoyed and upset but nothing more sinister. OK, good."

"..."

"And, to cope, would lose himself in time with their two boys. Can't argue with that – so, how did she summarise him, if at all?"

"..."

"A good father but monotone as a husband. Actually, my assessment of him wouldn't be that far off. But truthful – does she believe her husband to be truthful?"

"..."

"Hates deceit – which is why he especially struggled when he realised she was having an affair – and to that end has instilled it into Gregory and Ben to always tell the truth themselves. And do they? Reverend Matthew this is critical, so, please, only tell me anything their mother actually said, not what you'd have liked her to have said or what she may have said – I need her words. So, does she believe her children routinely tell the truth or do they exaggerate, tell fibs and concoct stories between themselves to play their parents off against one another?"

"..."

"Trustworthy you said? Trustworthy – you're sure? She used that word when describing her own two young sons. That's a big word when describing a ten and a twelve-year-old."

"..."

"Definitely her word, you say? Says Gerry has brought them

up well and she's both proud of the fact and shamed that that isn't because of her efforts. Trustworthy," Alba repeated before adding, "yes, I think they are and that means they have, together, told me a very important fact."

"..."

"Yes, sorry, that last bit is probably a bit lost on you. Can I tell you another time?"

"..."

"What? In 'The Sun and Moon' one Tuesday night? OK but my treat – for I'm incredibly grateful for what you've done today. You've been a godsend."

"..."

"No, that wasn't me being all theological; it was just a word I used."

"..."

"Yes, I'll call if I need you to do anything else – you're so kind. Thanks again and – "

"..."

"Pardon?"

"..."

"Oh, yes, you will continue to pray for me. Thank you and, yes, I'll call you when I get home. Thanks again and bye."

With that, Alba replaced the receiver.

*

"Good," she said to Cecilia. "I am amazed he was able to get in and see her. It means I have now learnt from Mrs Tania Detz what I had hoped to learn from her – that's just invaluable."

"I'm lost again," replied Cecilia, "but what is your next step, Alba?"

"Don't worry, I'll fill you in in a moment. As for next steps, well, I feel the pieces are almost aligned on the chess board. Almost but not quite – for there's something Martha said to me shortly before she died, where she was relaying a conversation she had had with someone as she first arrived here Thursday lunchtime, which proves a switch took place. If a switch took place, all was not as we thought it was."

Yet Alba paused.

"I sense there's a 'but' coming," offered up Cecilia.

"Yes," agreed Alba. "A significant one – but Martha is dead. She was killed for what she had unwittingly seen – so I can't prove what she said to me. Her comment to me is now something closer to, at best, hearsay and, at worst, something I'll be accused of making up to fit my theory. Damn it!" Alba suddenly added, "I can't see a way forward. In my head, I keep going through all the guests staying here and all the staff to see if any of them may, just may, offer any kind of corroboration to what Martha observed but I draw a blank each time. Damn it!"

Alba went and stared out of the window. Cecilia felt lost and somehow inadequate, wishing she could somehow help her friend.

"Right," Cecilia finally said to the unmoving, simmering, person at the window. "I'm not sure I'm going to be much help but I'm going to put the kettle on and make us another cup of tea. We can then share this sizeable slice of Victoria sponge cake Lizzie cut for us and then, as we wait for Emily's return, we can play a game or two of cribbage. I think, Alba dear, you just need to switch off for a while; lose yourself in something else for a bit and you might see things differently."

"I guess," Alba offered back despite still looking out of the window at nothing in particular.

Once the tea was brewing and the cake roughly divided into two, Cecilia added:

"I haven't got our cribbage board, that's in my room still, but fortuitously I have a pack of cards in my handbag and we can easily score on paper – it's really not too onerous to tally up to one hundred and twenty one."

With that, Cecilia took the initiative and, having shuffled the fifty-two cards, dealt six cards to each of them. Having looked at her own hand she quickly, knowing it was her 'box', discarded the jack of clubs and the queen of hearts.

"I need you to discard two and then cut the pack, Alba dear."

Without speaking, still lost in her own mental maze that consisted of nothing but dead ends, Alba came and sat opposite Cecilia. Alba glanced at her six cards and quickly, logically, placed two cards – the three and king of clubs – into the 'box'. Two cards which, in conjunction with Cecilia's two and with the card Cecilia was about to turn up, would give Cecilia eight points from her 'box'; it would have but the game was going to be abandoned before they got to that point.

"Cut," instructed Cecilia, once Alba had discarded her two.

Alba dutifully 'cut' the remaining cards in the pack allowing Cecilia to turn over the next card.

"That's very kind of you to cut me the jack of diamonds," said Cecilia. "*'Two for his heels',*" she added and scored herself two points on her sheet of paper.

"The jack of diamonds," repeated Alba. "The jack of diamonds – I wonder." She looked at Cecilia and just stared for a moment before continuing:

"I wonder, I wonder. The jack, the jack of diamonds. Oh, flip, where did I put it?"

She instantly jumped up and went and looked on both bedside units, then she tipped the contents of her little shoulder bag out onto the bed. Next she opened the drawer in the bedside unit which contained the Gideon Bible and held the book by its spine and vigorously shook it but nothing fell out.

"Oh, where the blazes is it?" she said to herself.

"What?" enquired Cecilia.

"A business card for a taxi firm," replied Alba.

"What's that got to do with anything?"

"I'll tell you when I find it – actually, it was in my trouser pocket. Oh, blazes, don't tell me I've left it down on the beach along with everything else. No, wait, I wore a different pair down this morning to the beach."

Suddenly she was searching the pockets of the jeans she was once more in, for a small, thin business card. As was always going to be the case, it was in the final pocket she rummaged in and then – as if she had drawn Excalibur from the stone – she withdrew it and held it up almost triumphantly.

"Got it. Got it!"

"You're going to have to explain," demanded Cecilia.

Alba was almost too excited with the find to be able to answer and it took a further prompt from Cecilia of 'Alba', for Alba to speak:

"Martha," said Alba.

"Yes, Martha," echoed Cecilia. "She was doing a walking holiday with the other lady, Annabel, but what about Martha?"

"She cheated."

"Cheated at what?" pressed Cecilia.

"She was supposedly doing a walking holiday but as often as not she got a taxi most days. She was meant to meet Annabel here on Thursday evening after they'd each done a day's walking from their respective start points. Yet, she got a taxi having only walked the first few miles."

"So, she doesn't like walking long distances. How does that help us in our search for a murderer?"

"She saw someone at the cove she was picked up from. Someone whose presence there doesn't make any sense until you fit it into a bigger picture. Someone she recognised later but who didn't want to be recognised and for that reason they killed her but I can't prove she did see someone there unless – "

"Unless?"

"Unless Jack the taxi driver, from 'Three Diamonds Taxi service' in Truro has a good memory for faces or vehicle number plates or both. If he can remember then I've surely got my proof of what Martha said to me. And it fits – fits with what two young boys wrote on their postcards to their grandparents, an observation by Alan and your comment, Cecilia."

"My comment? What comment?"

"Oh, just about this hotel not being as idyllic as I think it is," replied Alba. "What with the hot water system, the noisy coffee machines, the worn carpet in reception and people hanging their swimming trunks from hotel windows at the front of the hotel."

"Yes, I stand by all that. Don't get me wrong, I like this hotel but I do stand by all that I said – so what? What relevance does all that have to anything?"

"None of the men with rooms overlooking the front of the hotel had been swimming that morning. In fact, none of them can even swim. That means we have to factor in someone else."

"Do we?"

"Yes – and I know who. But now," said Alba as she weaved and twisted the business card over and through her fingers as if it were a casino chip she could rotate and roll across the top of her fingers, "I must phone this taxi firm and hope I can get hold of Jack."

*

As Alba telephoned, Cecilia gathered the cards from the abandoned game of cribbage together. She looked at Alba's cards, the two red eights and the six and ace of diamonds, then at what Alba had put in the 'box' and silently agreed with Alba's card selection.

"Excellent," announced Alba, as she put the receiver down once more. "It wasn't Jack who answered, rather I got through to someone in the control room, but I've booked Jack to pick me up from the hotel tomorrow morning."

"Why? Where are you going?"

"Nowhere. I'm not going anywhere but what I have done is got Jack to come to us – I'll pay him for a lost fare and his time spent here. Now, though, we wait. Wait for Emily's return and then, with Emily, wait in her room as I am certain they will come for her tonight, for they can't wait any longer in case Emily remembers."

"Well, I'm pleased Geoffrey is out of this. He's playing thirty-six holes of golf today and then staying over with one of his golfing buddies as he said he'd be too tired to drive back – don't know about too tired, more likely he'll be too embarrassed to admit he shot over two hundred for the two rounds," teased Cecilia. Then she turned serious and added:

"Alba, who's coming tonight for Emily and perhaps even you?"

Alba came and sat back down opposite her friend and told her – told her who, told her why and told Cecilia how she, Alba, had been able to align the chess pieces in a way to make sense.

"So," concluded Alba, "now we must wait. Wait for a telephone call from reception to tell us Emily has returned and then wait with her."

*

Several hours later, it had played out just as Alba foresaw it would.

Thus, upon Emily's return to the hotel Lizzie telephoned through to Alba to alert her of Emily's return. Then Lizzie had found a reason to just happen to walk up the stairs with Emily as she made for her bedroom. They met Alba and Cecilia at the top of the stairs, who relieved Lizzie of her escort role, and then Alba and Cecilia safely got Emily those last few yards to her room. Once ensconced in Emily's room, Alba shared with the artist what she had earlier shared with Cecilia and the three of them waited. They waited in nervous anticipation, for someone to come for Emily.

*

Dinner time came and went. Evening supper time came and went. They waited beyond bedtime, past midnight. In fact, they had to wait until two in the morning.

At two am, Emily's bedroom door handle turned and the door opened. In the darkness, softly, quietly someone crept in and stood over the shape of someone asleep in the bed. The standing figure brought a metal wheel brace down on the sleeping figure's head once, then twice.

From the shadows, out of sight for they were behind the partially open bedroom door, and despite expecting this to happen, Alba and Cecilia were still shocked at the savagery of the blows that were rained down upon the sleeping figure. Alba did not feel she needed to see a third blow. She turned the desk lamp on, which was on the dressing table to her side, and spoke into the scene before her – where a red stain, as if it were something as innocent as red paint, quickly spread through the bed sheets and across the pillow upon which the crumpled form lay deathly still:

"Morning Stella – couldn't sleep either?"

CHAPTER 24

Monday morning

"To her own husband! That's unbelievable," exclaimed Gerry.

*

Of the staff and hotel guests who were gathered round in the dining area, bleary eyed and stunned by the overnight development, it had been Gerry who had first given voice to what everyone was thinking. It was Monday morning still but now a slightly more sensible time of Monday morning.

Alba, Cecilia and Emily had waited from two in the morning until they first heard movement from the staff coming on shift downstairs, just before the grandfather clock in reception had struck seven, before alerting people. The three of them had just felt, after the emotional turmoil of the last few days, that everyone else would benefit from an undisturbed night's sleep – Alba feeling this particularly towards Gregory and Ben. So, they had waited until they heard the hotel 'wake up' as staff came on shift. Specifically, whilst Alba and Emily had remained guarding Stella, it was Cecilia who went and alerted first Lizzie, then Alan and finally Cliff. Shortly after that, the residents had been invited down to the dining area.

MONDAY MORNING

This time it was not as it had been two days previously. Then everyone had sat within an organised square of chairs, staff and guests intermingled as a collective, wishing to share in the common mission of locating Martha. On that occasion there had then been a sense of oneness, of being a group united in searching for one of their own. This time it was different. The sense of being together had gone, the unifying quest had ended, for they were gathering not only as the dawn was breaking on them but also breaking on them was the claim that one of them was a murderer. As a result, the staff – Cliff, Alan and Lizzie – sat together at one table but everyone else sat individually at separate tables.

It was also clear to everyone that Alba was now in charge of things; for one, she was the only one to remain standing.

Of those absent, Jed and Robyn had been contacted by Cliff and told to come in straight away and Cecilia had got hold of Geoffrey on the telephone and he was now equally on his way back from his night away with friends. Conversely, Gerry had persuaded Gregory and Ben to stay away by remaining in their room. He had done so on the promise of bacon sandwiches on the beach for breakfast once some grown-up discussions had taken place downstairs – the two boys, who were mightily sick of 'grown-up discussions', be they between their mum and dad, their mum and solicitors, their mum and police officers or whoever else their mum had had to talk to recently, readily agreed and so were happily occupying themselves with some 'Lego' sets in their room, including a major rebuild of a certain 'Lego' fire engine, which was the result of being dropped from Ben's top bunk bed.

*

"You're sure?" continued Gerry.

Cecilia glanced at Alba and just dipped her head ever so fractionally to indicate she was happy for Alba to answer.

"Well," said Alba, "at two o'clock this morning, Cecilia and I witnessed Mrs Stella Mallory enter Emily's bedroom and pulverise some artistically arranged cushions and an art box. The box, I might explain, plus a selection of tubes of red and orange paint, was wrapped in a hand towel to give it a slightly more oval, head shape, look when covered with a bed sheet and viewed in the dark."

"So, based on that, yes," said Cecilia, succinctly.

"But where was Emily, then? I thought I heard someone say, as I came down the stairs, the three of you had been in the bedroom together," queried Annabel.

"Oh, I was hiding in the shower room. Not overly comfortable sitting on the shower room floor for hours on end but we couldn't all hide behind the bedroom door when it was opened," explained Emily.

"And we agreed more than one of us should be in the room to witness any attack, to ensure multiple witnesses," stated Alba.

"So, you got the short straw sitting on a cold shower room floor," suggested Nicholas to Emily.

"We had to keep her as safe as possible," stressed Alba. "We didn't want to risk her being seen or heard leaving her bedroom once she'd entered it. If someone had been watching and listening for her return to the hotel, they would likely have been watching and listening as we 'ghosted' her out shortly afterwards. We couldn't jeopardise our plan; we had to keep her as safe as could be but somewhere within the bedroom itself."

"Yet your plan," observed Nicholas, "seemed to be little short of enticing someone to come and attack the person you were trying to keep safe. What if this woman, who you are claiming now to be a murderer, had come with a gun or a knife? No offence to the staff here," at which point Nicholas held up his right hand, palm outwards in an act of showing there was nothing personal in what he was about to add, "but the doors to our bath or shower rooms here are far from solid. In fact, the catch on mine barely holds it shut at all. Emily was hardly safe in the shower room. If you were genuinely worried you should have got Emily out of there pronto."

"Yes," agreed Annabel. "Maybe you three are making this all up as your holiday here was proving rather dull and you've decided you want the spotlight on yourselves for a bit – grown tired of Mrs Mallory having all the attention, have we?"

"Perhaps," added Nicholas, "you rigged up this dummy in the bed and enticed Stella to come and investigate in the small hours. Maybe one of you tapped on Stella's door and started groaning a little and then another of you called for help, which got her running and, in the dark, she tripped against Emily's bed and broke some tubes of paint which you'd placed for dramatic effect."

"I'm not quite sure I'd go that far," said Cliff. "I have known Mrs Constance for many years and Miss White for quite a few as well. However, I do agree it seems incredibly reckless not to have got Emily somewhere safer – if Stella had, if what you three say is true, come to kill, you had done no more than put Emily in a small room from which she could not escape. What if Stella had got to her?"

"It was a joint decision," responded Emily. "I'm not going to say I wasn't fearful but once Alba had explained it to me, it made sense and it was right I stayed."

"Sorry, what did she explain?" asked Annabel.

"That," replied Alba, "Stella wasn't going to come at her, at us, with a gun, a poison arrow, a ligature or knife. No, her *modus operandi* was to hit people over the head when they weren't looking. So, Emily was at some risk but it was containable and – "

"Containable? How?" interrupted Annabel. "Sounds pretty dangerous to me, bashing people over the head with some heavy instrument."

"First," stated Alba in reply, "there were three of us. Second, we had sodden bath towels under our chairs to wield ourselves in defence if she turned on us and, third, as I say, her pattern was to attack when someone was not looking. I didn't think she would have the courage to attack Cecilia and myself face on."

"She dropped the metal wheel brace as soon as we challenged her and she seemed pretty compliant once Alba made clear who was now in charge. Alba did that by quickly turning a desk lamp upside down and holding it as a club, were she required to go on the offensive against Stella," said Cecilia.

"Don't get me wrong," said Emily, keen to stress the point, "I was still in fear."

"Don't belittle yourself, Emily," said Gerry. "It is not wrong to feel fear. Soldiers going into battle feel fear – what they show, as you seem to have shown last night, is bravery. My great-grandfather, in his Legion journal recorded something a captain had told him, that being brave is when you overcome your fear; last night you were brave."

"Gosh, was I?" mused Emily. "I didn't feel it last night."

"But you were," repeated Gerry.

"So, where is she now – Stella, I mean?" asked Nicholas.

"Still in Emily's room – I've sort of tied her hands behind her back and then to the headboard," announced Alba. "In this part of the country, I guess the local fishermen would claim to be the best knot-tiers but I've tied together my fair share of bamboo and hazel structures to grow my runner beans, nasturtiums and sweet peas up to be pretty deft at tying secure knots myself."

"She's comfortable," stated Cecilia. "We offered her some water before we tied her up and she's sitting on the bed so she's hardly in some Soviet gulag."

"And she won't be there for too long before we call the police," added Alba.

"Sorry," said Cliff. "Why haven't you called the police already or come and spoken with me and asked me to contact them on your behalf? May I remind you, I had been meeting with them as recently as Saturday lunchtime. That was when I took Mrs Mallory over to the police station to identify a body – her husband's body. I might add, she was beside herself with grief and visibly distraught – everything you'd expect in the circumstances, having just identified her dead husband. Yet you're now claiming she was the one who killed him. If that is the case, then, well, all I can say is that she is the most accomplished actress I've ever seen."

"She was always very good in school productions. Plus, I was always surprised when she went on to study interior design at university instead of going to stage school – we went to the same secondary school," confirmed Alba to anyone sitting around who might not have realised.

"I'm sorry to labour the point," said Nicholas, "but you can't just tie someone up based on the fact she was good in a school performance of 'Grease' or 'King Lear' fifteen years ago. All I've heard this morning, having been woken up early by your own dramatics I might add, is you've tied a woman up based on what you claim you saw in the dark. Seems to me you've enticed her into someone else's room, stuck a foot out to trip her which caused her to fall against some conveniently placed tubes of paint. This is nothing more than a sham which the three of you – for reasons that will come out later perhaps – seem to be deriving a lot of fun from playing. I imagine you all have rather dull lives at home. Right," asserted Nicholas to those around him, "I think we should go up to this bedroom where you've tied her up, untie her and hear her version of events."

As Nicholas stood up and gestured for others to do likewise, Cliff spoke once more:

"Alba, Cecilia," he said, "I do think it is odd you didn't call the police. If you witnessed, as you say, an attempted murder, I think you need to give a very good reason, otherwise Nicholas is right and we should go up and speak to Mrs Mallory."

Emily and Cecilia looked at each other and then at Alba – the pair of them were suddenly doubting everything they had discussed throughout the long hours of waiting and then seen with their own eyes and heard with their own ears in the small hours of the morning. Yet Alba remained calm and confident and gave them each a reassuring nod, followed by a mouthed *'It's alright'*. She then answered Cliff but was, in effect, speaking to all who were gathered, including the still standing Nicholas:

"The reason I haven't called the police is because I feel I have a greater chance of flushing out her accomplice without them. You see, if…"

Yet her words were then lost in a flurry of comments of *'pardon'*, *'what?'*, *'accomplice?'* and several other comments besides. Calmly she waited for a hush to descend before she continued:

"Yes, an accomplice. Stella – Mrs Mallory – can, thankfully do no further harm tied to the bed as she is. However, I felt if we'd called the police at two in the morning, the subsequent arrival of police vehicles, the banging of numerous doors, heavy boots on the staircase, needlessly loud conversations, informing Cliff and then, on top of all that, forensics crawling all over the place, her accomplice would have sufficient warning and flee."

Again, Alba was confronted with a plethora of comments which she could not possibly answer as they all came at once. What stopped everyone from talking over everyone else, was the heavy sound of the metal handle on the snug door being worked and two people entering.

*

"Ah, Jed, Robyn, thanks for getting in so quickly," said Cliff.

"You need to thank Robyn for my arrival," conceded Jed. "She very kindly gave me a lift."

After a nod of appreciation to Robyn, Cliff continued:

"Well, sit yourselves down. Just to fill yourselves in, Alba, Emily and Cecilia have detained Mrs Stella Mallory upstairs after they witnessed her attack what she thought was Emily asleep in the bed;

to be clear, Emily wasn't in the bed it was a mock-up made out of cushions and towels."

"Oh, my!" exclaimed Robyn.

"Further, Alba believes Mrs Mallory is responsible for her husband's death and Miss – "

"Pardon," voiced Jed. "What, the man who never showed up at my cottage on Thursday?"

"Yes," stated Cliff, "and also for Miss Peacock's death. Alba doesn't now believe Martha Peacock slipped down the metal stairs."

"Oh, my! Oh, my goodness me," said Robyn in agitated tones – whereupon she crossed herself twice.

"Some of us," contributed Annabel, in support of Nicholas, "are a bit uneasy about a woman being tied up, alone, upstairs and had just suggested we brought her down to hear her side of the story as it all seems a bit far-fetched."

"Yes," agreed Cliff. "However, we were just waiting a few moments whilst Alba explained why she hasn't already called the police."

"An accomplice – apparently there's another guilty party within our midst," stated Lizzie, who probably would have burst into tears but for catching a supportive look from Alba.

"Yes," stated Alba, keen to progress matters.

However, she got no further as another door was heard being worked, this time the front door.

"She isn't escaping, is she?" questioned Emily, afraid that her would-be attacker was now at large.

"I don't think so," said Alan. "I can see into reception from where I'm sitting and she hasn't come down the stairs."

"Well, who is it, then?" asked Emily.

She got her answer in the form of Cecilia rushing to the door to reception and throwing her arms around Geoffrey, who had now himself made his return to the hotel.

As Cecilia, Cliff and Annabel filled Geoffrey in, as they had just done with Jed and Robyn, Alba suggested to Alan he might as well go and make up some pots of tea and coffee for everyone. It was not as part of some clever plan that Alba made the suggestion, it was simply that she fancied a cup of tea.

Finally, once everyone who needed bringing up to date had been and once hot drinks had been supplied, Alba began once more.

*

"Yes," Alba began, "an accomplice. One of us here is as guilty, I believe, of two murders and complicit in an attempted third as the woman currently tied to a bed upstairs. I might add, the lady I have tied up, was my best school friend. We grew up together, revised together and celebrated our exam results together, so I, of all of us here, really – I mean really – do not want to be right about this."

"Well, maybe you're not," suggested Annabel.

"But I am."

"But you can't prove it," added Nicholas. "All you've so far given us is a 'coming together' in the dark."

"There is a hint of 'entrapment'," contributed Geoffrey, drawing on his distant knowledge of the criminal law.

"There was no entrapment – no one enticed Stella to enter Emily's room in the middle of the night and no one prompted her to smash a metal bar down onto what she thought was Emily's sleeping body."

"So you keep saying," challenged Annabel, "but you've offered no actual proof."

"And here we still are, meekly doing as this woman, Miss White, tells us to do. I've truly had enough of this," announced Nicholas.

With that Nicholas got up and headed into reception and straight up the stairs, making for Emily's room.

Annabel followed as did Cliff and Alan. Gerry, too, stood to follow. He looked to Alba, almost as if to ask for her permission to follow the others up. All he got back was a shrug of her shoulders to indicate it was his decision. Yet something within him told him to sit down, that he did not need to undermine whatever Alba was up to – as if he could hear Gregory and Ben saying to him, *'Dad, it's alright, you can trust Aunty Alba'*.

Thus, Gerry and everyone else stayed where they were in the restaurant – well, other than Alba, who went and sat down next to Emily and calmly drank her cup of tea and waited.

It did not take long for those who had gone to return.

"Bloody hell, she's gone," announced Nicholas.

CHAPTER 25

Alba shows her hand

"She's gone," repeated Nicholas.

"No trace of her," added Annabel. "Clearly everything else that has been described to us this morning took place up there – pillows laid out under a bedsheet to create the impression of someone asleep, some disconcerting stains on the pillows, which if I hadn't been told they were battered tubes of paint, I would have found very sickening. Oh, and there are some sodden bath towels still on the floor."

"Are there?" said Alba. "Oh, sorry Robyn, Lizzie, we've probably left you a rather wet bit of carpet."

"But no Stella," continued Annabel. "So, Miss White, not so good with knot tying after all, are you?"

"She's not there," added Cliff needlessly.

"Oh, dear," said Emily as she turned to Alba who was still seated at her side. "I think, Alba, we've got confused, haven't we? We've been saying we left Stella tied up in my bedroom."

"Oh, yes," agreed Alba. "How silly of us."

"When all along," continued Emily, "we had her tied up in room eight, where we moved her to."

"Room eight?" queried Robyn.

"But room eight is empty," added Lizzie. "Has been all week."

"Exactly," said Alba. "Andrew Chapman couldn't make it to Cornwall as his grandfather was taken ill the day before he was due to come away with me. Now, some of you might be thinking 'why cancel a holiday because a grandparent is poorly?' To that, I would say two things. First, and most importantly, that's a bit callous but second, when your grandfather is the 7th Lord Hartfield and you are heir to the title and the estate, then duty requires you to stay. Thankfully, Andrew would have stayed purely for the first."

"Oh, my, we could have had a Lord-to-be staying here! How exciting," exclaimed Lizzie and she prodded Alan in excitement.

"Wouldn't have treated him any differently to anyone else," stated Jed.

"Good," replied Alba to Jed. "He wouldn't want you to. If I remember correctly, the first time I spoke to Andrew, I swore. Anyway, none of that is important other than the fact that I knew room eight was empty."

"How did you get in?" queried Lizzie. "We don't leave bedrooms unlocked."

"No, I should think not," said Alba. "But remember back to when we were looking for Martha on Saturday morning and we wanted to get into her bedroom but her key was not on the board behind reception; well, Cliff just came along, opened a drawer behind the desk and took out a duplicate key – he even said something like 'there was no security if only people knew where to look' as he did so."

"Thus," continued Emily, "we quietly came down in the night and got the key to room eight and moved Stella before we woke everyone up."

"Why?" asked Gerry.

"Partly," said Emily, "I didn't want her in my room a moment longer – how dare she come in and bludgeon my sleeping form. I wanted her gone."

"But mostly," added Alba, "I was curious as to who wished to get to her, if they had the chance, before the police came and perhaps help her escape."

"Are you basing your claim that one of us is her accomplice solely on the fact that several of us went to check on her welfare?" said Annabel.

"Oh, no, not at all. I have all the evidence I need. Plus, some more will shortly be arriving so, no, not basing anything on who went to check but it was a telling experiment nonetheless."

"What evidence?" asked Geoffrey.

"Oh, it's all so confusing," added Lizzie. "This used to be a quiet, normal hotel."

"Yes," agreed Robyn. "Up until Thursday evening, when Mr Mallory went missing, everything was normal."

*

It was almost the cue Alba had been waiting for. It was as if Robyn had acted as the Master of Ceremonies and, with that observation, had invited Alba onto the stage to explain.

Calmly Alba stood up, went and refilled her tea cup and then moved to stand by the empty table nearest to the snug door.

"Good," she stated as she glanced at her watch. "Almost perfect timing. I have about ten minutes to explain before Jack turns up."

"Who's Jack?" asked Geoffrey.

"Well, she mentioned someone called Andrew a moment ago but, yes, who's Jack?" said Annabel to Nicholas, whom she was sat nearest to. Her words, though, were heard by all.

"All in good time, all in good time," said Alba. "To begin with, though, perhaps it would help if I took you back to the beginning of our little mystery here, when we all thought Mr Joshua Mallory went missing."

"Yes," contributed Jed. "He was due at the cottage I shared with my late father at five o'clock Thursday evening but he didn't show."

ALBA SHOWS HER HAND

"Says you," said Annabel but not quite under her breath. "Odds are you were involved in his disappearance – got some secret cupboard in your cottage where smuggled goods were once hidden though, this time, perhaps a body? Hidden until you could dump it at sea?"

"Drop your Cornish stereotypes before I come and whack you one," said Jed angrily.

"Jed – easy now," said Cliff.

"Bit of an anger management issue, have we?" came back Annabel. "Had an argument with this architect, did you? Your rage get the better of you?"

"He didn't show," repeated Jed forcibly. Then, slightly calmer, he added, "I'd had a few days off so didn't know that the guy who was meant to be meeting me at my dad's home was actually staying here; I only learnt that when talking to Alba on Friday evening. But whether I knew he was staying here or not doesn't matter. What matters is he never showed up as arranged – he never arrived to knock on the front door."

"So, if he never made it to the appointment, Mr Mallory's been missing, probably dead, since shortly before five o'clock in the vicinity of Jed's cottage," said Cliff in support of his barman.

"Jed would never be involved in killing Mr Mallory," added Cecilia with emotion in her voice, wishing to also defend Jed in front of everyone else. "I knew his parents, I've seen him grow up, I know his character – I never thought he was involved in what's been going on this week."

"But it is in the vicinity of his cottage when and where our mystery starts and which, Alba, you're about to shed some light on. Well, I hope you are," stressed Cliff.

"No," replied Alba.

"No?" challenged Cliff.

"No," Alba repeated. "Admittedly, it was the cottage that brought Joshua Mallory to Cornwall. In fact, the cottage brought a number of you here this week. Joshua and Stella Mallory came as he had an appointment to view Jed's father's cottage. That trip was booked by someone from Joshua's office, a Mrs Tania Detz."

"But that's the same surname as – " began Lizzie.

"Yes," continued Alba, keen to keep her explanation of things on track, "as Gerry and his boys."

"Correct," confirmed Gerry Detz to all those gathered about him.

"You're here, with your boys, but without your wife?" said Annabel. "Isn't that a bit odd?"

"Yes, it is but I ask all of you here that whatever you think of me and whatever else comes out this morning, please, please, not a word to my boys. They've had it tough enough as it is, let alone with what's been happening here this week, so please not a word to them – just let them stay innocent of all of my inadequacies."

Despite the tension, confusion and level of mistrust between everyone in the room – as they all continued to wonder who Alba would claim the second murderer to be – the collective silence that followed conveyed to Gerry that people would respect the welfare of Gregory and Ben. It allowed Gerry to continue and, to Alba's relief, far more succinctly than he had when talking to her at the tin mine:

"My wife did work for Joshua Mallory but she is not here on holiday with us as she is currently serving time in prison. She stole from Joshua's company after he ended an affair he was having with her. The boys know nothing of the affair," stressed Gerry. "However, I was curious about who my wife was involved with and so, having gone through my wife's papers, I learnt which hotel she had booked Joshua into and duly booked myself in as well. But, as much as this man, Joshua, was slowly ruining my family, I didn't kill him, nor the other lady."

"But you did follow him and Stella to St. Michael's Mount on Thursday, didn't you?" asked Alba. "Even to the point of your boys overtaking them on the causeway; your boys running past them as Gregory and Ben were fearful of the incoming tide."

"Yes," conceded Gerry. "But you know all that, Alba. I've

already confirmed all that myself with you. To be clear," he added to everyone else in the room, "I wasn't reckless about the sea coming in, just to save paying a boatman. We had a good fifteen minutes before the causeway would have been completely covered and impossible to walk across."

"Thank you," said Alba. "Yes," she confirmed to everyone else, "Gerry had told me all that but I wanted you to hear from him about getting over to the island and that he saw Joshua and Stella there. Interestingly, earlier in the week, Stella confirmed she had seen Gerry and his boys in the queue for tickets on the island."

"So," summarised Cliff, "Gerry here can confirm Mr and Mrs Mallory got to the island, so the last sighting is still about five o'clock at the beach car park but we still don't know what happened thereafter."

"Nothing happened thereafter because Joshua was never there at the car park to begin with," stated Alba.

"What?" asked Geoffrey.

"Flipping heck, now I really am confused," admitted Lizzie.

"So was I to begin with," admitted Cecilia – which got an agreeing nod from Emily. "But when Alba explains it, it will all make perfect sense."

"He was never at the beach car park," stressed Alba.

*

"But that was the last sighting of him," reiterated Cliff.

"Seemingly it was. However, ask yourself, who stated he was there?" said Alba.

"Well, his wife told us when he was last seen alive – he went missing after they'd parted having left the island she said," relayed Lizzie.

"So Stella said – exactly!" announced Alba. "Don't you see? We – I – never corroborated that 'fact' with anything else. I just took

Stella's word for it. Well, why wouldn't I? She's an old school friend. Why would I think to cross-reference what she said to me about her husband vanishing? I never considered whether I had any other bit of information to confirm what Stella told me."

"So, you're saying he never left the island, are you?" said Gerry. "See, didn't I suggest that to you, Alba, when we were at Restormel Castle? I said the police should widen their circle of search to include the island itself."

Alba paused, took a sip of tea, then spoke calmly:

"Actually, he never went to the island to begin with."

"What?" said Cliff.

"But we passed him on the causeway," asserted Gerry.

"See his face did you as you ran past to catch up with your boys who were running ahead, frightened as they were of the incoming tide?" asked Alba.

"Well, err, no, as I come to think of it," said Gerry. However, desperate to base his claim of having seen Joshua Mallory on something, he added, "it was the same hooded top that he was in as he had been at breakfast – same crest or logo on both sleeves."

"Yes," agreed Alba. "It was the same type of mistake I made when I thought I saw Joshua here at the hotel. I didn't see him either. You see, I arrived here Thursday lunchtime."

"That's right," confirmed Robyn. "I was on duty and it was such a lovely surprise to see you back, Alba."

"And, as I was speaking to Robyn, Stella and Joshua rushed in from their morning boat trip. Stella asked for lunch to be had in their room whilst Joshua rushed upstairs to go and have a shower because he got splashed by sea water whilst they were out on their hired boat. I never thought at the time that it seemed a bit excessive to need a shower after a boat trip – he must have got really wet! But it took me days to realise, like you Gerry, I never actually saw Joshua. I heard someone come in with Stella, I heard two people speak as husband and wife and I saw someone, hood up, rush up

ALBA SHOWS HER HAND

the stairs. I never saw Joshua. You know," continued Alba in almost confessional tones, "I have never seen Joshua Mallory. I was friends with Stella at school but then, having gone to different universities, never saw her boyfriend and, when invited to her wedding to be her sole bridesmaid, I fled the event before I ever saw her husband-to-be. I still couldn't tell you what he looked like in the flesh because I never saw him. All I saw this week, as Gerry did on the causeway, was someone pretending to be Joshua Mallory."

"Did he ever exist?" asked Lizzie. "Well, I mean, did he come here at all or was someone pretending to be him the whole time?"

"Oh, he did arrive here," confirmed Alba. "Checked in and was alive until he left the hotel Thursday morning after breakfast – Stella had to get the real Joshua Mallory here so she and her lover could enact their murderous plan."

"So, it was him we saw at breakfast, that day?" queried Gerry.

"Yes," confirmed Alba. "But, when we disregard my 'sighting' of him Thursday lunchtime, given I never actually saw him, it was only Stella's sighting of him thereafter that we were basing our search upon. Take that card away and the whole structure comes tumbling down and you have to start rebuilding from the bottom upwards – from Thursday morning. It is from then our hunt should have begun, not hours later when he was already dead."

"So, if someone pretending to be him and Stella was complicit with that, I can see the time of his murder can be moved to earlier in the day," stated Geoffrey. "You will tell us when and where, I trust."

"Of course," confirmed Alba. "It was out on their morning boat trip. Stella hit Joshua over the head and he would have fallen or subsequently been pushed over and drowned, if he were not already dead. As we know, his body was washed up on Kynance Cove two days later."

"It's possible," reflected Cliff.

"Lots of things are possible," commented Annabel.

"Indeed but you don't seem to have proof, Miss White. You're speculating. It seems to me you don't actually have proof of anything.

You haven't even explained why you started to doubt what Stella had been telling you," challenged Nicholas.

*

"Two postcards," stated Alba simply.

"What, the ones my boys wrote to their grandparents?" asked Gerry.

"Yes," confirmed Alba.

"What on earth have they got to do with anything? They're not involved in any of this; what are you alleging?" Gerry added, suddenly incredibly protective and worried that not just someone but Alba no less, was trying to draw his two sons into a man's disappearance and subsequent murder.

"Don't worry, Gerry," said Alba sympathetically as she brought out the postcards. "I'm not trying to drag them into this other than to say that what they wrote on their postcards about their holiday, told me a very important detail."

"OK," said Gerry nervously, which allowed Alba to continue.

"Let me read them," she said. "Well, specifically their final comments."

With that, Alba read out what Gregory had told his grandparents:

"The bestest bit was Michaels island on Thursday afternoon. We walked to it over a path made of big stones and got over just in time as the sea covered it up very quickly. We had to get a little boat back when we wanted to leave as the sea was still covering the path – dad said he felt sea sick and took some tablets. Silly dad as it was only a short boat trip. I liked the boat."

Alba placed Gregory's card behind Ben's and proceeded to read what the younger child had written:

"On Thursday afternoon we went to a castle on an island. We walked to it but had to get a boat back as the sea had covered the path. That was cool. It made dad feel funny and he had to take some pills."

Alba looked around the room having read from both, then spoke once more:

"See? Innocently, independently of each other, and in their own handwriting, they have both told us a critical fact."

"Yes, that I get seasick very easily," offered up an embarrassed Gerry. "They weren't exaggerating," he added. "I felt quite rotten as I stepped off the boat which brought us back from the island to one of the concrete jetties."

"You're not the only one to suffer from seasickness," said Geoffrey. "It affects me, too, probably not helped by the fact that I can't swim either."

"Forget about seasickness. The postcards tell us something else, something more basic, something so objectively sound that it made me realise what Stella had told me at breakfast on Friday couldn't be true," said Alba. "They tell us, not that the boat trip from the island made Gerry seasick but that they were on a boat."

"So what? How's that relevant?" asked Annabel. "I mean, if the two boys had been describing a morning boat trip, maybe we could link them and their father to following Mr and Mrs Mallory out to sea and him taking the other's place. Yet you're talking about a completely different time of day – late afternoon, in fact."

"Yes, late afternoon," agreed Alba. "That's the key point in all of this. In late afternoon, in Mount's Bay, they had to be on a boat to get back to shore from the island. Now, compare that to Stella's version. She told me about a boat ride in the morning and lunch in the hotel bedroom. She described walking over to St. Michael's Mount in the afternoon, visiting the castle, walking back and parting from Joshua at the beach car park around five o'clock. In doing so, however, she had unwittingly revealed to me, not that I realised at the time, that her movements from mid-afternoon were all made up."

"But how could they be?" puzzled Gerry. "We literally passed right in front of Stella and her husband or the person pretending to be her husband but we did pass them. They were there."

"Yes," agreed Alba, "but you're missing the point. They didn't stay. They went to the island to get an admission ticket, to prove she was where she claimed to be all afternoon: in fact, they were right behind you and your boys, Gerry, as you tried to get entry on your wife's ticket. However, as soon as they'd got their 'proof', they were off. They headed straight back to the mainland, to Joshua's car in order that she could return the person, who had been impersonating her husband since before lunchtime, to where he had left his car miles away from Marazion. We know they must have left immediately because Stella, not realising she was making a mistake each time she relayed her movements to me, stated she walked off the island late afternoon and yet, by then, the tide was in."

"That's right," confirmed Gerry, "we made it to the island shortly before the tide covered the causeway – that's why the boys ran across, fearful as they were of the sea. Reckon the water would have been across it altogether in another fifteen minutes."

"Exactly," stated Alba. "Just long enough to queue up for a ticket to be able to prove to the police she was there all afternoon but then dash back over the causeway to carry out the final stages of their murderous plan. As I say, that part was to get her lover back to his own car in order that he could turn up at the hotel later as himself. Whereas, if she had really been on St. Michael's Mount all afternoon as she claimed, she would have – "

"Come back by boat," offered up Geoffrey in bright realisation.

"Yes, yes," agreed Alba. "That's what Gregory and Ben told me on their postcards. Not that the boat trip from the island made Gerry seasick but that they were on a boat. If Stella had been on the island all afternoon, as she claimed, she could not have walked back, just couldn't, for the sea was covering the causeway. Stella couldn't even have waded through the water back across as the tide was so far in by five o'clock it was making Gerry seasick as he came back by boat."

Alba paused, took a further sip of her tea and continued:

"So, you see, as I sat down at the cove yesterday, as I read the two postcards, it dawned on me if Stella's account of her and Joshua's movements on Thursday were correct, Gregory and Ben had lied on their postcards to their grandparents. But why would they do that?"

"They wouldn't," expounded Gerry.

"That's what I felt, too. They had absolutely no reason to lie and no one had written the cards for them. Plus, from the time I've spent with them this week, I'd describe them as good lads. That said, up until very recently, I would have described Stella as a good friend. So, not wanting to base anything on my feelings for anyone, it became important to ask someone else for a character reference, if you like, for Gregory and Ben. Someone who knows them but is not here; someone who knows their characters but, sadly, does not care for them much."

"Who?" asked Gerry. "Their Scout Master is pretty positive about them. Their youth club leader is perhaps a bit more uninterested in them."

"I asked their mum," answered Alba simply.

"You did what?" said Gerry in utter bewilderment. "How? Where? She's currently in – "

"HMP Holloway, yes," continued Alba. "Well, I didn't ask her myself, rather a trusted friend travelled up by train from Sussex at my request at incredibly short notice but he got to see her."

"How is she?" asked Gerry, suddenly struck that his family did have, for the moment at least, a fourth member and whose welfare he was concerned for.

"My understanding is that she is alright. I can get my friend to call you later, if you would like. However, what's important to us here, is that Gregory and Ben's mum, despite being absent from the boys' lives for too long, equally described her children as trustworthy. Meaning, as they wrote their postcards to their grandparents, they had no false story to weave; they were simply telling grannie and grandpa what they were doing in Cornwall and we can believe what they wrote – specifically that they enjoyed a boat trip on Thursday afternoon because it made their dad seasick."

"Because she was there such a short time," added Emily, "Stella forgot about the movement of the sea. That's what makes coastal painting so challenging – it's why I've been spending so long at Kynance Cove this week. Not only do you have the changing direction of light, as the sun moves, which plays havoc with where the shadows are, and the movement of clouds across the sky as the wind blows them across, you also critically have the sea itself changing position. One moment you're mixing up your yellows and your browns to paint expanses of damp sand then, in no time at all, you're having to paint over it with blues and greens as the tide has come in. Yet you miss that fact if you are only making a fleeting visit somewhere."

"So, I knew Stella had lied to me because of what Gregory and Ben had inadvertently revealed to me," summarised Alba. "Enough people here saw the real Joshua Mallory at breakfast on the Thursday but then his wife took him on a wildlife watching boat trip. I've spoken with the boat owner and he's confirmed two people took the boat out and two people returned in it – seemingly impossible then for a switch to have taken place out at sea. The boat owner said two people went out and two people, in the same clothes, came back. It's not easy to pick up a replacement person out at sea."

"It wasn't me swimming out," joked Geoffrey.

"Nor me," added Daniel.

"And we already know Gerry isn't one for the sea," said Alba. "What about you, though, Nicholas? You're a pretty good swimmer."

"Not bad," offered back Nicholas, suddenly conscious that everyone was now studying him.

"Better than 'not bad', I'd say, having watched you yesterday morning swim out to 'Haslam's Faithful'," said Alba.

"Alright, pretty good – perhaps I'd even go so far as to say if the boat were even two miles out to sea, I could have swum to it. Please don't drag me into this based solely on the fact that I'm the best swimmer here. I got here Thursday evening after all these comings-and-goings had taken place, I'm here to do some academic research on the inter-tidal zone and if you're looking for an accomplice for Mrs Mallory, why not choose Daniel, who perhaps can swim, the chef, who's been pretty quiet this morning, or the barman, who we know to have a grudge against Mr Mallory."

"Perhaps," conceded Alba. "Perhaps but I really don't think so on any count. Plus, none of them had a reason to kill Martha nor to try and kill Emily – whereas you did."

"Sorry," said Nicholas. "Are you accusing me of being involved in all this?"

"Yes," stated Alba.

"May I remind you, when Martha Peacock fell to her death on Friday evening – "

"She was clubbed over the head and then fell," interrupted Alba.

"Alright, someone bashed her on the head first. Have it your way. May I remind you, though, I was in here having my evening meal. Apart from the two young boys, you and I were the only two people still in here when Martha was attacked on the metal staircase. I have an alibi and you – Alba White – are it. Furthermore, though this hardly needs saying, the person you're claiming came and attacked Emily in the small hours of this morning wasn't me. Even if it happened, as you three women have described, it was Stella who is the murderess, not me."

With that, Nicholas stood up – as if he wished to challenge the fact that Alba alone was the one who had been standing.

*

At that moment a car could be heard turning into the hotel's drive. As was almost customary, due to the steepness of the drive, the driver struggled to change down the gears quickly enough to avoid stalling.

'Good, he's here on time' thought Alba to herself.

"OK," conceded Alba, addressing Nicholas once more. "I am not accusing you of actually killing Joshua, Martha or the attempted killing of Emily. No, Stella alone is responsible for delivering the fatal blows. What I am accusing you of is being as culpable as Stella, of being her partner-in-crime and of planning it all with her months ago. Then, this week, of impersonating Joshua to throw us all off the trail by making out he had survived the morning boat trip. Also, you identified when the pair of you had an opportunity to kill Martha – for you watched Martha leave via the snug door on Thursday evening to get to her room. You may as well have delivered the fatal blow yourself. Stella only knew where to wait for Martha because of the information you gave her. Furthermore, though I accept I don't think I'd be able to prove this in court, I believe you are also culpable of trying to kill me and possibly Ben by enticing us out to go swimming in the sea with you. We'd have never made it to 'Haslam's Faithful' and you knew it. Yet you still enticed us and would have happily kept leading us further and further out when we were asking, pleading more likely, to turn back. No doubt, all the while, leading us into dangerous currents and then sounding all brave when describing your unsuccessful rescue attempts to the coastguards as you alone sat on the beach following the double tragedy of two further swimming deaths by inexperienced swimmers on holiday."

"Balderdash and puppycock," retorted Nicholas. "I've had enough of this – I'm leaving."

"Please don't," said Alba softly.

"Why on earth would I want to stay?" challenged Nicholas.

"Well, to begin with to explain, if you aren't involved, why it was your swimming trunks drying, draped over Stella's bedroom window on Thursday lunchtime."

"Pardon?" said Nicholas.

"You see," continued Alba, "Joshua had been on a morning boat trip, not swimming. Yet, someone known to Stella was drying off a pair of men's trunks that lunchtime, something Cecilia observed whilst around the hotel herself on Thursday and commented upon as she and I discussed how idyllic this hotel is. Tongue-in-cheek, she said it was far from idyllic when people hang their swimming trunks to dry from the windows at the front of the hotel."

"What are you gibbering about?" said Nicholas.

"Or perhaps you would like to explain why Joshua, who was quite happily tucking into one of Alan's perfectly cooked steaks on Wednesday evening, was suddenly professing that anything would be suitable for lunch in the room on Thursday, upon his return from the wildlife watching boat trip, so long as it was vegetarian. Whilst boat trips might do funny things to Gerry's tummy, I doubt they turn people vegetarian."

"Oh, this is all nonsense," retaliated Nicholas.

As he spoke, however, Jed Peters stood up and moved to block the doorway into reception. A stern looking Cornishman was promptly joined by the bulky frame of Daniel Jones. Daniel spoke as he moved into position:

"Only four bedroom windows overlook the front of the hotel," he said sharply, as his investigator's mind picked up what Alba had deduced, "I'm in one of them and I'd struggle to walk down to the cove, let alone swim whilst down there and then get back up here. Gerry is in the room next to me with his boys – my word, can they talk about football a lot very early in the morning!"

"And he can't swim," contributed Alba, secretly thrilled this was no longer her 'show' and that others were seeing through the fog that had been placed around them all, all week. "I've seen the fear in Gerry's eyes as he saw Ben out in the sea with me yesterday morning."

"Mr and Mrs Constance are in the next room," continued Daniel. "Mr Constance has just said, before it was relevant, he can't swim and

I doubt his wife would have let him dry his trunks in the window if it annoyed her so much. Meaning, the only window they could have been drying from was Stella and Joshua's."

"Exactly," said Alba. "If they were trousers drying or a skirt, it wouldn't have lodged in my brain when Cecilia commented upon it. Yet no one staying in rooms at the front of the hotel can swim – nor could Joshua according to what Stella told me. Yet someone who could swim – and was a vegetarian – was having lunch with Stella Thursday lunchtime."

"Oh, this is a joke," said an angry Nicholas. "This is all so tenuous it's laughable." Then, to Jed and Daniel, he said, "will you two thugs move out of my way?"

The two men at the door remained unmoving and Nicholas realised that if 'flight' was being denied him, for Alan and Robyn had by now gone and stood covering the exit via the snug door, he would have to fight. Nicholas returned to where he had been sitting, picked up his coffee mug and threw it at Alba – yelling as he did so:

"This is all madness. The woman over there," he said, referring to Cecilia, "is probably as blind as a bat and didn't know what she was looking at in the hotel windows – a shadow, a reflection, a seagull, who cares. You can't keep me here based on that."

As Alba took her brand new but now coffee-stained 'Weird Fish' hooded top off, Emily spoke:

"I suspect any half-decent optician will be able to show Cecilia has more than adequate eyesight. I might add, Cecilia was more than able to watch Stella come and try and kill me last night in the darkness."

"Sorry, why would anyone want to kill you?" challenged Nicholas.

"Because of what I had seen."

"Which was what? Though I have no doubt you're about to tell me," answered Nicholas sarcastically.

"It was your face I observed as we all stood around looking at Martha's body. If I may say, you have fine facial features and I can see why Stella is infatuated with you. Yet, it was the look on your face, which was so mesmerising, so intriguing, which I had to paint. There we all were, standing around this poor woman's body, and whilst everyone else had looks of despair or sadness, yours was one of relief. It was such a strange emotion to show that I had to rush upstairs and paint what I had seen. In my haste, whilst I could remember the expression, I somehow forgot on whose face I had seen it."

"Emily's mistake, if you like," continued Alba, "was to show it to Stella and myself once she had completed it. Stella immediately realised the danger it placed you, Nicholas, and her in, were Emily to remember who had shown that look of relief. Had Emily remembered, it would have tied you to Martha."

"What's Martha got to do with all this?" asked Annabel.

Before Alba could explain, a movement of the heavy metal door handle on the snug door alerted everyone that someone was entering the hotel. As Alan and Robyn moved aside, an unknown man entered the dining area of 'The Jupiter Hotel'.

"I've been sitting in the car park waiting but no one has come out," said Jack. "A Miss Alba White has booked a taxi with 'Three Diamonds Taxi Services' and she hasn't appeared. Any of you know a Miss White? Cor, that hotel drive caught me out again. It's so steep, isn't it? And I was only here Thursday lunchtime dropping a Miss Peacock off." Then, spotting Nicholas amongst those gathered, Jack added:

"Oh, hello again – survived your swim, I see. We were amazed how far out you swam – all the way out to that little boat. Very impressive."

CHAPTER 26

With the turn of a card

Once the police had left, everyone else, including Jack, reconvened in the bar. Alba pressed on him some money for the fare but, when Alba started to explain why she had booked him, he went and deposited it in the Royal National Lifeboat Institute collection jar on the counter.

"So, that's where my missing room key was," said Emily to everyone. She was commenting on the fact that, during their search of Stella the police had easily found the bulky key fob and room key for Emily's room.

"She must have taken it when she and I came to look at the painting in your room, perhaps when she was in tears slumped over the table in your room – fake tears, as we now know," added Alba.

Then Annabel voiced what was still puzzling her:

"I understand Martha was cheating on our walks. I'm sort of impressed actually as I didn't really think she had it in her to be so devious; she was always such a timid creature when we worked together. However, I am curious, err, sorry, what is your name?" she asked the gentleman from the Truro taxi firm.

"Jack."

"Right, Jack. I am curious, Jack, why you and Martha remained at that cove further along the coast, where you picked Martha up, for so long; long enough to watch Nicholas Goodwill swim all the way out to the boat Stella was in."

"Silly, really," answered Jack. "Miss Peacock was having a cigarette as I pulled into the little parking area. Well, I fancied a break and a smoke myself and she seemed in no hurry to get anywhere – in fact she said the slower I could get her to the hotel the better – so we sat and had a smoke, chatted and watched this guy turn up in his car, strip down to his black trunks and head straight out into the water. Then I couldn't find my car key as it had slipped out of my pocket into the long grass on the bank we were sitting on. As a result, we were able to watch this guy swim much further out than we thought it was safe to do so but he made it to, as I say, this little boat. The person on it seemed to be expecting him as she was waving. Anyway, car key finally located, I brought the lady here as she requested." He paused before adding.

"You're sure this cake is complimentary-on-the-house?"

"Yes, and the tea" confirmed Alan.

"Blooming lovely. Shame about Miss Peacock," reflected Jack simply as he reached for a second hefty slice of Victoria sponge.

"But how did you know to contact Jack?" asked Annabel of Alba.

"When we were searching her room on Saturday morning – you, me and Cliff – I saw the little business card for the taxi firm Jack works for. Knowing that Martha had come here by taxi, unbeknown to you, Annabel, I pocketed the card to keep Martha's secret, secret. Had I known Martha was already dead I wouldn't have taken anything from her room but I thought I was doing her a favour. The little card, with Martha's personal note on the back saying he was a nice bloke, stayed in my jeans pocket until I was playing a game of cribbage with Cecilia."

Alba, seeing the sponge cake rapidly vanish before her eyes, deftly helped herself to a piece and a fork, before continuing her explanation:

"You see, being observed swimming out to a boat was a risk Nicholas had to take. If whoever saw him, never saw him again it didn't matter but, you see," she said as she tapped her fork against her plate as she resisted the temptation to start it, "tragically for Martha, Annabel had booked herself and Martha into the very hotel where Nicholas was about to take on the role of Joshua Mallory for a few hours."

Alba succumbed and enjoyed a mouthful of sponge before continuing once more:

"Martha told me herself, as she opened up to me about how she was cheating on her walking companion, how, upon her arrival here by taxi she'd passed a couple heading out of the hotel – Stella and Nicholas, though Nicholas was pretending to be Joshua at that stage. As she saw them, Martha said to me that she had said 'hello again' to the man. But why would she say 'hello *again*' – she'd never met Joshua Mallory before. That told me the 'Joshua' she had just spoken to was not actually Joshua. Those two simple words – *hello again* – unfortunately were Martha's death sentence. Stella waited upstairs on Friday evening, the supposedly worried wife, in fact waiting for Martha to retire to her bedroom; for neither Nicholas nor Stella could afford Martha suddenly realising the Joshua she'd seen wasn't the Joshua who was missing but in fact was Nicholas. As Martha made her way up the metal exterior staircase, probably not looking up to keep the rain out of her eyes, she never saw Stella waiting, nor the metal wheel brace or the metal bucket that sits on the top step brought down on her head.

"So, Stella killed her husband because she, Stella, was in love with Nicholas Goodwill," said Lizzie, "but then had to kill Martha because Martha had seen Nicholas swim out to take Joshua's place on the boat. Oh, my."

"And would have killed Emily," added Cecilia, "because Emily had seen the look of relief on Nicholas's face as he gazed down upon Martha's dead body."

"Relieved she now couldn't identify him and also, I guess, relieved because we were all talking about it being a tragic accident rather than suspicious," continued Annabel. "Poor Martha."

"Yes, and had I not spent a night away, painting the Godrevy lighthouse on the north coast," added Emily, "Stella or Nicholas may have come for me that night. Thankfully, Alba had pieced things together by the time I got back and she and Cecilia were incredibly brave and stayed with me all night until Stella came."

"And Nicholas might have been trying to lead you and my Ben out to your own deaths because?" queried Gerry.

"Because Stella would have told him I'd seen the picture Emily had painted and was worried I might recognise Nicholas within the picture and Ben because maybe he did turn round in the ticket queue on St. Michael's Mount and seen but not realised, the person in Joshua's clothing had a different face to the person he undoubtedly saw over breakfast that morning."

With that, everyone fell silent as they went over everything in their own heads.

*

In time, Gerry, remembering his two boys were still upstairs, spoke:

"Alba, if this is now all over – "

"It is," she softly answered.

"Well, then," Gerry continued, "would you come down to the cove with us shortly? I owe Gregory and Ben bacon sandwiches on the beach after all this."

"Leave that to me," said Alan. "Smoked or unsmoked?"

"On the house," chipped in Cliff.

"Gosh, thanks. Unsmoked, please. But plenty of ketchup for all of us," answered Gerry.

Alan turned to Alba and the pair of them exchanged a brief knowing smile.

"Actually," chipped in Daniel as he placed down his now empty cake plate, "if you're frying some bacon, any chance of slipping a couple of extra rashers into the pan and making up a sandwich for me? Nice cake by the way."

"Anyone else?" offered up Alan, sensing what was coming.

Three further hands went up, including Jack's, who was rather taken with this delightful, somewhat remote, Cornish hotel. He was already planning on asking the manager whether he could leave some of his firm's business cards on the reception desk or the bar counter, perhaps next to the RNLI jar.

As Alan opened the door from the bar back into reception, he almost collided with a man coming the other way. A man in his early thirties, who had a leather overnight bag slung over his right shoulder and had the look of someone who had enjoyed his journey on the sleeper train far more than he had expected. The man spoke as he stepped into the bar:

"Good morning. I'm looking for – "

His words, however, were cut short as Alba ran across the room and threw her arms around him.

"You're here. You've made it. I mean, wow, I can't believe it – you're really here. How's your grandfather – he is OK, isn't he?"

Alba took a step back to look at Andrew Chapman which, in turn, allowed Andrew to look properly at Alba. On the train he had played out in his mind how he would surprise Alba with his arrival by quietly walking up to her from behind and gently tapping her on the shoulder and how, in return, he would be greeted with the enchanting scent of her Lancôme Poême perfume as she turned. The reality proved to be very very different.

"He's much better thank you. But what the blazes has happened to you? You stink of coffee, don't look as if you slept at all last night and you're covered in bruising around one shoulder. What on earth has been going on?"

"I'll tell you in a moment. Leave your bag with Lizzie over there.

Come on, I'm taking you somewhere – it's just so thrilling you're here."

As Lizzie stood up and willingly took Andrew's bag, Alba turned to Gerry and spoke:

"Of course I'll come down – we'll come down – to the cove with you and the boys. Go on, get Gregory and Ben down. The five of us can build a sandcastle together."

"A sand-fort," corrected Gerry, "if my boys are in charge."

"Yes, of course, a sand-fort. Plus, I might be able to retrieve my rucksack, trousers, travel rug and flask from yesterday, whilst I'm down there," added Alba, suddenly remembering all that she had left down at the cove.

"Really, what on earth has been going on?" said Andrew as Alba pulled him out of the bar towards the hotel's front doors which he had only come through a few minutes previously – doors held open by a pair of silent wooden mice.

"Oh, I bumped into an old school friend…"

Yet Alba's further words to Andrew were lost to everyone else as the two of them stepped out into a glorious Cornish morning.

Epilogue

Two weeks later, as Alba sat at her dressing table in the bedroom of her own little cottage in the village on the Surrey-Sussex border where she lived – at the far end of which Hillstone Hall, home of the 7th Lord Hartfield, Edward Chapman, and his grandson and heir, Andrew, stood – she held the morning's post. At her feet, in a little wicker waste bin, and now forgotten about, lay a torn up wedding invitation; an invitation Alba had received many years ago from a Miss Stella Winterman.

Alba re-read the morning's post once again.

'Strange', she thought to herself, 'how both bits of post had come on the same day'.

The first item was a postcard. The picture was of Salisbury Cathedral and on the back three different handwritings were present:

Thanks for building so many sand-forts with us and for coming with us to St. Ives. Come and see us soon, Love Gregory.

Under that sentence, there followed:

We miss you, Aunty Alba. Thank Lord Andrew again for buying us a football. Thank you for showing me the banana trick and how you can slice it before someone peels it. Gregory is still cross with me that it

EPILOGUE

splashed milk all over his West Ham shirt when he opened it above his breakfast bowl. But I laughed.

Gerry's contribution followed – on a more serious note:

Her appeal failed. However, she says she would like to come home upon her release if that's what I want. She says a Reverend has been travelling up to see her and talking with him has helped. She wants us to start again. I'll let you know what I decide. Best wishes, Gerry.

Alba placed the postcard in her jewellery box. As she did so, she glanced at a little plastic soldier lying on his side in one of the square compartments previously assigned two rings; a piece of purple plastic now as treasured by her as the two rings were. The rings, however, were now consigned to the box's draw underneath.

*

The second item of post had been a letter from Mrs Cecilia Constance. Alba read it again:

Dearest Alba,
   Just wanted to let you know that since you left, I have spoken with Jed. He cried; we both did in fact, as you said we would. He was not cross with me though and that is such a blessing. He said it was fine to involve Geoffrey.
   Geoffrey has spoken at length with Jed and has come up with many good ideas. Jed is now hoping, if he is found to be the true heir of Trelyn, Trelyn can be sold and with (just a part of) the proceeds, he can buy his (half-) brother and sister out and keep the cottage. He said he wouldn't know what to do with a house such as Trelyn and that his father's fruit bushes were as important to him as all the gardens at Trelyn.

My dear Geoffrey is drafting letters to the relevant parties and is optimistic. I will write again soon and tell you how it develops.

Next time you come to Cornwall, as well as staying at 'The Jupiter' you must come and stay with us for a night or two at 'The Grey House' – the building work might be finished by then.

Geoffrey sends his love.
Cecilia.

Acknowledgements

There was a real Corporal Detz who served with the French Foreign Legion. In September 1903, as part of a half-company of the 22nd (Mounted) Foreign Regiment, under Captain Vauchez, he saw action at El Moungar. Corporal Detz, one of the few survivors, was awarded the *Médaille Militaire*. El Moungar, then in the Morocco-Algerian borderland, is now in modern-day western Algeria.

As I read about him and the history of France's Foreign Legion, I reflected on why he may have enlisted and what any descendants a hundred years on, would make of him and the life of a colonial soldier at the beginning of the twentieth century. As my story for 'Sandcastles by The Jupiter Hotel' came together, I realised I had an opportunity to explore – well, to at least touch on – those thoughts as a backdrop to this Alba White mystery. I thus created some fictitious descendants for him – Gerry, Gregory and Ben Detz.

I trust any living descendants of the real Corporal Detz will not be offended by what I have done. Any historical inaccuracies are entirely my own.

For anyone wishing to learn about the French Foreign Legion, I would suggest one begins with Martin Windrow's book (published by Phoenix (2011)):

'Our Friends Beneath the Sands: The Foreign Legion in France's Colonial Conquests 1870-1935'

It is excellent.

*

At one stage in my story, I refer to 'Matt'. At the time this Alba White mystery was set – the spring of 2003 – 'Matt' was The Daily Telegraph newspaper's front page cartoonist. He still is. The daily offerings of Matthew Pritchett, are consistently brilliant. Who doesn't smile at the morning 'Matt'?

*

The two wooden doorstops, with their beautifully carved wooden mice, undoubtedly would have been made by 'Robert Thompson's Craftsmen Limited'. 'Mouseman' furniture is of the highest quality and their workshops and showroom, in Kilburn, North Yorkshire, are well worth a visit. How two of their wooden doorstops ended up at a fictitious Cornish hotel one can only speculate.

See: www.robertthompsons.co.uk

*

Much to Gregory and Ben Detz's disappointment, at the end of the 2002/3 football league season (for this Alba White mystery is set in the spring of 2003), West Ham United, despite getting 42 points, were relegated from the Premier League. West Bromwich Albion and Sunderland AFC were also relegated.

*

ACKNOWLEDGEMENTS

I would like to thank my brother-in-law, Nigel Head, for the original cover design that he created for this book and which forms the basis of the cover design which we now have.

I would like to thank Sybil Coombes for being an excellent English teacher. Any remaining mistakes within the text are entirely my own.

Finally, I would like to thank the team at Troubador Publishing Ltd. They have guided me through the post-writing stage expertly once again and are a pleasure to work with. Here is to working together again on the third book in the Alba White series –

Sunday Falling

Also by the same author:

One Thousand Moons

In between jobs and living alone in a quiet village on the Surrey and Sussex border, thirty-year-old Alba White is drifting through life. At the other end of the village, Hillstone Hall is in a precarious position. Edward Chapman, the 7th Lord Hartfield, is in a financial hole and literally selling the family silver to keep the place afloat.

Then, when during a charity cricket match, one of his own elderly garden volunteers, still mourning the loss of his brother, who flew with the RAF in the war, is murdered, things take a further turn for the worse until an arrest is made. Yet Alba, who found the dying man and whose blood stained her beautiful white dress, is not convinced the police have arrested the right person. Suddenly she has direction but will she discover the truth in time?